P9-BZI-126

Crusader

~ BOOK SIX OF ~
THE WAYFARER REDEMPTION

Sara Douglass

TOR *fantasy*

A TOM DOHERTY ASSOCIATES BOOK
NEW YORK

CRUSADER

Copyright © 1999 by Sara Douglass Enterprises Pty Ltd.

Originally published in 1999 by *Voyager,* an imprint of HarperCollins*Publishers,* Australia

Map design by Miguel Roces

A Tor Book
Published by Tom Doherty Associates, LLC
175 Fifth Avenue
New York, NY 10010

www.tor.com

Tor® is a registered trademark of Tom Doherty Associates, LLC.

ISBN-13: 978-0-765-34280-5
ISBN-10: 0-765-34280-4

First Edition: August 2006
First Mass Market Edition: February 2007

Printed in the United States of America

0 9 8 7 6 5 4 3 2 1

PRAISE FOR SARA DOUGLASS

"A stunning tour de force with a full complement of action, mysticism, mystery, and magic, . . . Sara Douglass is a powerful voice in high fantasy that readers can equate to the likes of Robert Jordan, Marion Zimmer Bradley, and Anne McCaffrey."
—*Romantic Times BookReviews* (4¹/₂ stars) on *Enchanter*

"Treachery, spectacular magic, near and actual madness in major and minor characters, and lots of action."
—*Booklist* on *Pilgrim*

"A superior adventure fantasy right to the last."
—*Booklist* on *Starman*

"Epic storytelling on par with Terry Goodkind and Robert Jordan." —*Library Journal* on *The Wayfarer Redemption*

"Douglass smoothly fills in some backstory about the Sun-Soar dynasty. . . . Fans of this ambitious epic fantasy should be eager to find out what happens in book five."
—*Publishers Weekly* on *Sinner*

"Douglass is an assured and gifted storyteller."
—Terry Dowling in *The Weekend Australian*

✑ Acknowledgments ✑

I would like to acknowledge my debt to my editors Claire Eddy at Tor and Stephanie Smith at HarperCollins*Publishers* Australia for their work on the Wayfarer Redemption—the books have benefited enormously from their wisdom and efforts. I would also like to thank my agents Lyn Tranter (in Australia) and Jim Frenkel (in the USA) for their efforts in promoting the Wayfarer Redemption—both agents took on a huge risk with an unknown author, and I owe them a great deal.

✄— Contents —✄

And did those feet in ancient time
Walk upon England's mountains green?
And was the holy Lamb of God
On England's pleasant pastures seen?
And did the Countenance Divine
Shine forth upon our clouded hills?
And was Jerusalem builded here
Among these dark Satanic Mills?
Bring me my bow of burning gold!
Bring me my arrows of desire!
Bring me my spear! O clouds, unfold!
Bring me my chariot of fire!
I will not cease from mental fight,
Nor shall my sword sleep in my hand
Till we have built Jerusalem
In England's green and pleasant land.

—William Blake, *Jerusalem*

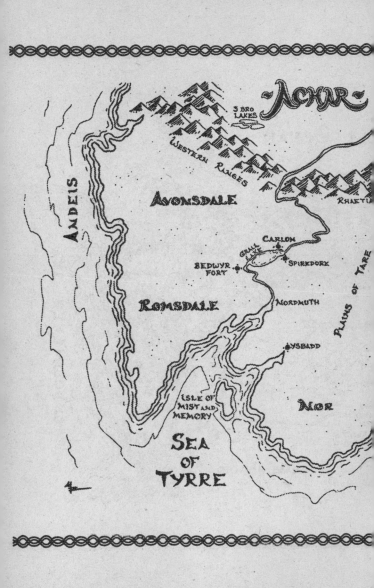

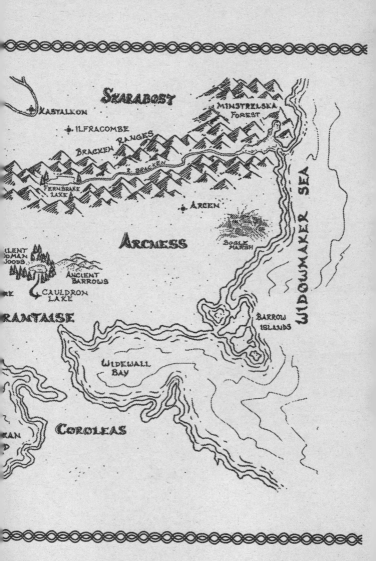

PROLOGUE

An Evil Released

"What can we do?" Fischer said uselessly, but needing the comfort of an endlessly repeated question. "What can we do? Bloody *what*, you ask?"

"Easy, mate." Henry Fielding laid a hand on Fischer's tense forearm.

Fischer shifted his arm away then turned his head towards the far, windowless wall. He was in his seventies, a white-haired, emaciated old man, his face deeply lined with the forty-year struggle against the evil that had savaged— *pervaded, consumed, destroyed*—his world.

When it had begun he'd been a man in his prime: copper-haired, bright-eyed, lithe and energetic, determined to fight and destroy the invading beings.

"Demons" was a strange, horrid word that Fischer had only now learned to use, but which he still found completely distasteful.

"Demons" did not fit a world that was based almost entirely on scientific theory. On logical explanation. On provable fact. On the complete belief in technology that was far more acceptable and comfortable than religious beliefs. "Evil" did not exist. Only scientific fact existed. Only the vagaries of nature and as-yet-to-be-controlled-and-predicted geographical events existed. Only the selfish and arrogant nature of human society existed. Only petty crime by social misfits and corporate crime by the socially successful existed.

Evil had no place in this most rational and explainable of worlds.

Until it dropped out of the sky over New York one blithe and fair Sunday morning.

That was what took us three decades to come to terms with,

Fischer thought. The idea that we'd been invaded, not by pastel-coloured and elegantly-elongated extraterrestrials with great dark eyes in shiny Spielberg-like metal-pocked spaceships, but by pure, and utterly hungrily angry, Evil.

And thus for three decades pure Evil in the shape of the TimeKeeper Demons ran amok. Countries were laid waste, save for the moaning, shuffling crazed populations that roamed their dusty surfaces. Cities were abandoned, jungles stripped of foliage, oceans dried and ravaged. Within a year the human population of earth had gone from billions to a few pitiful ten thousand huddled in bunkers, waiting out the demonic hours, and wondering how they could strike back.

The ten thousand were those left sane, of course. There were still countless millions left roaming above ground, their minds completely unhinged, utterly demonised, noisily breeding—and entirely successfully—countless millions of genetically insane babies. Those infants that survived their first five years uneaten (or only partially eaten), grew into even worse monsters than their parents.

Fischer shuddered. The insane (and by now there were billions of them) were still out there, haunting the as yet unreclaimed surface of the planet.

He and his companions might have managed to trap and dismember Qeteb, but the other five Demons continued to howl their destructive way about the planet.

They had trapped and dismembered Qeteb, but not destroyed him.

This was the problem Fischer and his companions now faced. What to do? *What to do?*

"The other Demons will break through the barriers within the month," said Katrina Fielding, Henry's wife. She'd been the one to suggest the idea that the Demons could be trapped by reflecting their own malevolence back at them.

Fischer glanced at her. She was young, in her early forties, a mere child when the Demons had first dropped in.

She'd lived virtually her entire life underground, and it showed. Katrina's shoulders and spine were stunted, her eyes dull, her skin pallid and flaky. She'd never been able to have children. And after the initial years underground only a scattering of babies, mostly physically or mentally disabled, had been born to the few women who came to term.

We're dying, Fischer thought. *Our entire race. The Demons will get us in the end, even if it may take them a generation or two longer than those they cornered above ground. If the Demons don't leave soon then* no-one *will be left who can breed!*

No-one sane, that is. The insane hordes above ground multiplied themselves with no effort, and certainly no thought, at all.

The idea terrified Fischer. "Whatever we do," he said, "we've got to get rid both of Qeteb's damned death-defying life parts, *and* the other five Demons as well."

"There is only the one solution," Henry said. "Devereaux's proposal."

Devereaux's proposal frightened Fischer almost as much as the idea that the sane component of the human race would soon die out, leaving earth populated by the maniacal human hybrids (God knows with *what* they had interbred upstairs!). But a decision had to be made, and soon.

Why, why, why, Fischer thought, is there no government left to make this decision for us? Why couldn't we leave it to a bunch of anonymously corrupted politicians to foul up so we can be left with the comfort of blaming someone else?

But there were no nations, no governments, no presidents, no prime ministers, no goddamn potentates left to shoulder the responsibility. There was only Fischer and his committee.

And Devereaux. Polite, charming, helpful Devereaux, who had advised that they just load Qeteb's life parts on separate spaceships (how convenient that the people inhabiting the bunkers when the Demons had initially arrived tended to be the military and space types) and flee into space.

"Drop them off somewhere else," Devereaux had said only the day before yesterday. "Or at the least, just keep going. The other Demons are bound to follow."

"What if Devereaux finds a place to leave them?" said Jane Havers, the only other woman present. "Or just crashes into some distant planet or moon. What then?"

"We pray that whoever inhabits that moon or planet can

deal with the Demons better than we have," Katrina said. "At least it won't be in our solar system, or galaxy."

Fischer dropped his face in a hand and rubbed his forehead. Cancer was eating away in his belly, and he knew he would be dead within weeks. Best to take the decision now, before he was dead, and while there were still women within their community with viable wombs.

Somehow the human race had to continue.

"Send for Devereaux," he said.

Eight days later the spaceships blasted out of the earth's atmosphere, their crews hopeful that at least they were giving their fellows back home a chance.

What they didn't realise was that when they'd blasted out of their underground bunkers, they'd left a corridor of dust and rock down which the maniacally hungry were already swarming.

Fischer didn't have time to die of cancer, after all.

1

The Wasteland

No longer did the ancient speckled blue eagle soar through the bright skies of Tencendor. Now Hawkchilds had inhabited the seething, scalding thermals that rose above a devastated wasteland. They rode high into the broiling, sterile skies seeking that which would help their master.

The Enemy Reborn has hidden himself. Find his hiding place, find his bolthole.

Find him for me!

Qeteb had been tricked. The StarSon had not died in the Maze at all. The Hunt had been a farce. Somewhere the true StarSon was hiding, laughing at him.

Find him! Find him!

And when the Hawkchilds found him, Qeteb did not want to go through the bother of another hunt through the Maze. All he wanted to do was to reach out with his mailed fists and choke the living breath out of the damned, *damned* Enemy Reborn's body!

The fact that he had been tricked was almost as bad as the realisation that Qeteb's plans for total domination of this world could not be realised until the Enemy had been defeated once and for all.

All Qeteb wanted to do was ravage, but what he had to do was stamp the Enemy into oblivion, obliteration and whatever other non-existent future Qeteb could think of as fast and as completely as he possibly could.

Find him! Find him!

And so the Hawkchilds soared, and while they did not find the Enemy Reborn's bolthole on their first pass over the wasteland, they did find many interesting things.

It helped immeasurably that all external inessentials, like

forests and foliage and homes and lives, had been blasted from the surface of the wasteland, for that meant *secret* things lay open to curious eyes.

Secret things that had been forgotten for many years, things that should have been remembered and seen to before the Enemy Reborn had hidden himself in his bolthole.

"Silly boy. Silly boy," whispered the Hawkchilds as they soared and drifted. "We remember you wandering listless and hopeless in the worlds before the final leap into Tencendor. Now your forgetfulness will crucify you . . ."

And so they whispered and giggled and drifted and made good note of all they saw.

Far to the south a lone Hawkchild spied something sitting in the dust that had once been a rippling ocean of forest.

It was but a speck that the circling Hawkchild spotted from the corner of his eye, but the speck was somehow . . . interesting.

The hands at the tips of his leathery wings flexed, then grasped into tight claws, and the Hawkchild slid through the air towards the ash-covered ground.

He stood there a long while, his head cocked curiously to one side, his bright eyes slowly blinking and regarding the object.

It was plain, and obviously completely useless, but there was something of power about it and the Hawkchild knew it should be further investigated.

The bird-like creature stalked the few paces between himself and the object, paused, then carefully turned it over with one of his taloned feet.

The object flipped over and hit the ground with a dull thud, sending a fine cloud of wood ash drifting away in the bitter, northerly breeze.

The Hawkchild jumped back, hissing. For an instant, just for an instant, he thought he'd heard the whispering of a many-branched forest.

A whispering? No, an angry crackling, more like.

The Hawkchild backed away two more paces, spreading his wings for flight.

But he stopped in that heartbeat before he should have lifted into the air. The whispering had gone now—*had it ever existed save in the dark spaces of his mind?*—and the object looked innocuous, safe . . . save . . . save for that irritating sense of power emanating from it.

This object was a thing of magic. A fairly sorry object, granted, but mayhap his master might find it amusing.

The Hawkchild hopped forward, flapped his wings so he rose in the air a short distance, and grasped the object between his talons.

A heartbeat later he was gone, rising into a thermal that would carry him south-west into the throbbing, blackened heart of the wasteland.

Qeteb laughed, and the wasteland cringed.

"He thinks himself safe in whatever hideaway he has built for himself," he whispered (and yet that whisper sounded as a roar in the mind of all who could hear him). "And when I find it . . . when I find its secret . . ."

The Midday Demon strode stiff-legged about the interior of the Dark Tower, his arms flung back, his metalled wings rasping across the flagged flooring of the mausoleum.

He screamed, then bellowed, then roared with laughter again.

It felt so good to be whole once more! Nevermore would he allow himself to be trapped.

Qeteb jerked to a halt, and his eyes, hidden beneath his black-visored helmet, fell on the woman standing in the gloom under one of the columned arches.

She was rather more beautiful than not, with luminous dark hair, a sinuous body beneath her stained and rust-splotched robe, and wings that had been combed into a feathered neatness trailing invitingly from her back.

Qeteb wondered how loudly she would scream if he steadied her with one fist on her shoulder, and tore a wing out with the other fist.

She said she was his mother, but Qeteb found he did not like to hear what she said. He was complete within himself, a oneness that needed no other, and he had certainly never been entrapped in *her* vile womb. She had never provided *him* with life!

But she had provided him his flesh, and for that Qeteb spared her the agony of sudden de-wingment.

For the moment.

There was a movement from another side and Qeteb almost smiled. There, the soulless body of a woman, waiting for him. He lusted, for he found her very soullessness inviting and reached for her, but was distracted by the voice of Sheol from beyond the doorway.

"Great Father. One of the Hawkchilds has returned with—"

"With the gateway to the StarSon's den?" Qeteb demanded.

"No," Sheol said, and stepped inside. Behind her walked a Hawkchild, carrying something in its hands.

"Great Father!" the Hawkchild said, and dropped to one knee before Qeteb. "See what I have discovered for you!"

He placed the object on the ground before Qeteb, and the Midday Demon looked down.

It was a wooden bowl, carved from a single block of warm, red wood.

Qeteb instinctively loathed it, and just as instinctively knew that it would bring him great fortune.

Beyond the mausoleum the Maze swarmed with creatures dark of visage and of mind; the vast majority of demented creatures within the wasteland had found their way to the land's black heart. They climbed and capered and whispered through every corridor and conundrum of the Maze, a writhing army of maddened animals and peoples, waiting only for Qeteb, waiting for the word for them to act.

Out there waited a hunting, for the hunt in the Maze had

proven disappointing in the extreme. The man, the false Star-Son, had offered his breast to the point of the sword without a whimper (indeed, with a smile and with words of love), and now the hopes and dreams of the maddened horde lay in drifts and shards along the hardened corridors of the Maze.

There was a hunt, *somewhere*. There was a victim, *somewhere*. There was a sacrifice, waiting, *somewhere*, and the whispering, maniacal horde knew it.

They lived for the Hunt, and for the Hunt alone.

There was one creature crawling through the Maze who was not at all insane, although some may have doubted the lucidness of the twisting formulations of his mind.

WolfStar, still covered in Caelum's blood, still with the horror of that plunging sword imprinted on his mind, crawling towards what he hoped might be a salvation, but which he thought would probably be a death.

Creatures swarmed around and over him, and although a few gave him a cursory glance, or a peck, or a grinding with dulled teeth, none paid him any sustained attention.

After all, he looked like just one more of their company.

2

The Detritus of an Epic

A rather tumbledown, grey-walled hovel sat in the centre of the clearing. Flowerbeds surrounded the hut, but they were overgrown with mouldy-stemmed weeds and thistles. A picket fence surrounded the hovel and its gardens; most of the pickets were snapped off. The once-white paint had faded and peeled from the pickets that remained whole, so that the fence resembled nothing so much as the sad mouth of a senile gape-brained man.

Ur's enchanted nursery had fallen into unhappy days.

Two women sat on a garden seat set in a small paved area.

Several of the paving stones had crumbled, and dust crept across the uneven court.

The Mother wrapped Her fingers around a cup of tea and tried not to sigh again. She was tired—the effort of closing off the trails to the Sacred Groves against any incursions by the Demons had been exhausting—but more worrying was Her overwhelming feeling of malaise. The Mother did not feel well. In truth, She felt profoundly ill.

Tencendor had been wasted by Qeteb, the Earth Tree was gone (surviving only in embryonic form in the seedling She had given Faraday), and the Mother could feel the life force ebbing from Her.

But not before—*oh gods, not before!*—that life could be restored elsewhere!

"Is it gone?" a cracked voice beside Her asked, and the Mother jumped.

"What? Oh, no, thank you, I still have a half cup left." And yet almost everything else had gone, hadn't it? Everything . . .

Ur grumbled incoherently into her cup, and the Mother looked at her. The hood of Ur's red cloak was lying over her angular shoulders, revealing the woman's bald skull. The skin over Ur's face was deeply wrinkled, but it stretched tight and angry over the bones of her skull.

Ur had lost her forest. For over fifteen thousand years Ur had tended her nursery hidden deep within the trees of the Sacred Groves. As each female Avar Bane had died, so her soul had come here to be transplanted out as a seedling in a tiny terracotta pot. Forty-two thousand Banes had transformed in this manner, and Ur had known them all—their names, their histories, their likes and loves and disappointments. And, having cradled them, Ur had then handed them over to Faraday to be replanted as the great Minstrelsea Forest.

Which, after only forty-two years of life, Qeteb had then turned to matchsticks.

Matchsticks! Ur rolled the word over and over in her mind, using it as both curse and promise of revenge.

Matchsticks.

Ur's beloved had been reviled, murdered, and utterly destroyed by the excrement of the universe.

Her lips tightened away from her teeth—incongruously white and square—and Ur silently snarled at her ravaged garden. Revenge . . .

"It is not good to think such thoughts," the Mother said, and laid Her hand on Ur's gaunt thigh.

Ur closed her lips into a thin hard line, and she did not speak.

The Mother fought again to repress a sigh and looked instead out to the forest beyond Ur's decaying garden.

Everything was fading. The forests of the Sacred Groves, even the Horned Ones themselves. The Mother had not realised how closely tied to Tencendor the Groves were—as was the health of all who resided in them. Tencendor had been wasted, and if DragonStar could not right the wrong of Qeteb and his companion Demons, and finish what the Enemy had begun so many aeons before, then eventually the Groves would die.

As would Herself, and all the Horned Ones, and even perhaps Ur.

The Mother shot another glance at the ancient nursery-keeper. And perhaps not. Ur appeared to be keeping lively enough on her diet of unremitting need for revenge.

"But We are safe enough for the while," the Mother whispered. "Safe enough for the while."

3

A Son Lost, A Friend Gained

Sanctuary should have been crowded. Over the past weeks hundreds of thousands of people, as well millions of sundry insects, animals and birds, had swarmed across the silver tracery bridge, along the roadway meandering through the fields of wildflowers and grasses and into the valley mouth. Yet despite the influx of such numbers, Sanctuary continued to remain a place of delightful spaces and untrodden paths, of thermals that seemingly rose into infinite heights, and Mazes of corridors in its palaces that appeared perpetually unexplored.

Sanctuary had absorbed the populations of Tencendor without a murmur, and without a single bulge. It had absorbed and embraced them, offering them peace and comfort and endless pleasantness.

And yet for many, Sanctuary felt more like a prison. The endless peace and comfort and pleasantness had begun to slide into endless irritation and odious boredom which found temporary release in occasional physical conflict (an ill-tempered slap to a face, a harder than needed smack to a child's legs) and more frequent spiteful words.

For others, it was more personal aggravations that made them feel like prisoners in a vast, amiable gaol.

StarDrifter, wandering the corridors and wondering what more he could do to ease Zenith into the love she tried to deny.

Zenith herself, wondering when it was that she would be able to think of StarDrifter's embrace with longing instead of revulsion.

DareWing, dying, yet still driven by such a need for revenge that he hauled himself from tree to tree and from glade to glade, seeking that which might ease his frustration.

Azhure, weeping for the children she had lost.

Isfrael, seething with resentment at the loss of his inheritance.

Faraday, her eyes dry but her heart burning, wondering if she would have the courage to accept a love she feared might once more end in her destruction.

Katie, clinging to Faraday's skirts, grinning silently and secretly, and wondering if Faraday would ever be able to accept the sacrifice.

Again.

Sanctuary was a brooding, sad place for something so apparently beauteous and peaceful.

Sanctuary was proving unbearable for yet one more man.

Axis had spent his life controlling the world that battered at his doorstep. As BattleAxe he had theoretically been subordinate to the Brother-Leader of the Seneschal, but in reality had largely controlled his own destiny as he had the destinies of his command. As a newly-discovered Enchanter he had found he had much to learn, but had gloried in that learning and the added power it gave him (as in the woman it brought him). As StarMan, Axis had held the fate of an entire land and all its peoples in his hand, and he had held it well, plunging the Rainbow Sceptre into Gorgrael's chest and reclaiming the land for the Icarii and Avar.

Yet in the past year Axis had learned that he'd only been a pawn in some Grand Plan of this ancient race known as the Enemy, and an even tinier pawn of the Star Dance itself which had manipulated not only the Enemy, but every creature on Tencendor.

And for what? To breed the battleground and the champion to best the most ancient of enemies; festering evil in the shape of the TimeKeeper Demons.

"We have *all* been for nothing," Axis whispered to himself, "save to provide the Star Dance with the implements for whatever final act it has planned."

And what part would *he* play in that plan?

"And damn you to every pit of every damned AfterLife," Axis murmured, "for making of me a mere pawn where once I had been a god!"

Then he laughed, for it was impossible not to so laugh at his own frustrated sense of importance. Axis consciously relaxed his shoulders, and looked about him.

It was a fine, warm day in Sanctuary—as were all days— and he was walking down the road from Sanctuary towards the bridge (at last! to have escaped the confinement of unlimited safety!). To either side of him waved pastel flowers, wafting gentle scent in the soft breeze. The plain between the mountains that cradled Sanctuary and the bridge that led from the sunken Keep apparently stretched into infinity on either side of the road, and Axis wondered what would happen if he set off to his left or right. Would the magic of Sanctuary eventually return him to the spot from which he had commenced, even though he walked in a deliberately straight line? Would he be *allowed* to escape the glorious inaction of Sanctuary?

"I wonder if I might ever manage to—" Axis began in a musing tone, then halted, stunned.

A moment previously he had been a hundred paces from the bridge, he could have sworn it! Yet now here he was, one booted foot resting on the silvery surface of the bridge's roadway.

"Welcome, Axis SunSoar, StarMan," the bridge said. "May I assist you?"

Axis grinned. The bridge sounded as enthusiastic as an exhausted whore on her way home after a laborious night's work entertaining her clientele. His grin broadened at the thought. The bridge *had* borne a heavy load of bodies recently, after all.

And every one of them to be questioned as to the trueness of their intentions.

"Well," he said, and leaned his crossed arms on the handrail so he could peer into the clouded depths of the chasm below the bridge. "I admit I grow lonesome for some witty conversation, bridge, and I remembered the pleasant nights I spent whiling away the sleepless hours with your sister."

And was she still alive, Axis suddenly wondered, in the maelstrom that had consumed Tencendor?

"She has ever had a more companionable time than I," grumbled the bridge. "Here I sat, spanning the depths between your world and Sanctuary, desperate for company yet hoping I would never find it."

Axis nodded in understanding. Company would have meant—*did* mean—that complete disaster threatened the world above.

"And, yes," the bridge added softly, "my sister still lives. The disaster is not yet complete, Axis SunSoar."

Axis shifted uncomfortably. This bridge was far more adept at reading unspoken thoughts than her sister. "And when the disaster is complete? What then?"

"What then? Victory, my friend. Utter victory."

Axis straightened, biting down his anger. "Disaster is utter victory? How can that be?"

An aura of absolute disinterest emanated from the bridge. "I am not the one who can show you that answer, Axis."

"Then who? *Who?*"

There was no answer, save for a flash of blinding light and a sudden rattle of hooves.

Axis swore softly and raised a hand to shield his eyes against the rectangle of burning light that had appeared at the other end of the bridge. A large shape shifted within the light, blurred, then shifted again, resolving itself into a horse and rider.

The light flared, then faded.

The bridge screamed . . .

. . . and then convulsed.

Axis fell to his feet, sliding towards the centre of the bridge as he did so. He lay for an instant, badly winded by the impact.

He was given no time for recovery. The bridge lurched and then buckled, heaving under him, and Axis repeatedly fell over in his scrambling attempts to get to his feet.

The bridge screamed again, and Axis was raked with the emotions of death.

The bridge was dying.

Axis grabbed at one of the handrail supports, but it melted under his fingers leaving them coated with a sticky residue.

One of his legs fell through a large hole that abruptly appeared in the bridge . . . she was dissolving!

With a desperate heave Axis lunged towards the safety of the roadway, but the bridge was literally falling apart, still screaming, and her death throes tilted Axis further towards her centre, further away from the safety of the ground.

Another section of bridge fell away, and Axis stared down into the chasm, and certain death.

The bridge whimpered, and vanished.

Axis fell . . .

. . . and was jerked to a halt by a hand in the collar of his tunic.

The odour of a horse hot with sweat enveloped him, and Axis felt himself bump against the shoulder of the plunging animal. He grabbed automatically, finding the Sanctuary of a horse's mane with his left hand, and the wiry strength of a man's forearm with his right.

"Keep still!" a man's voice barked. Axis turned his eyes up, and looked into the face of his hated son, Drago.

Except this man was not Drago. Axis instinctively felt it the instant he lay eyes on his face, and he knew it for sure once the man had deposited him on the road to Sanctuary.

This was a man who had *once* been Drago.

Axis bent over, resting his hands on his knees, and drew in great breaths, trying to recover his equilibrium at the twin shock of the bridge's death and the appearance of . . . of . . .

Axis looked up, although he did not straighten. "What happened?" he said, not asking what he truly wanted to know.

The man slid off the horse, and Axis spared the animal a brief glance.

Gods! That was Belaguez!

Utterly shocked, Axis finally stood up straight, staring at the horse.

"I do not understand why the bridge died," the man said, and Axis slid his eyes back to him. He was lean but strong, with Axis' own height and musculature and with coppery-coloured hair drawn back into a tail in the nape of his neck.

The way I used to wear it as BattleAxe, Axis thought involuntarily.

The man was naked, save for a snowy linen cloth bound about his hips, and the most beautiful—and most patently enchanted—sword that Axis had ever seen. Its hilt was in the shape of a lily, and Axis could see the glimpse of a mirrored blade as it disappeared into a jewelled scabbard. The scabbard hung from an equally heavily jewelled belt, balanced by a similarly jewelled purse at the man's other hip.

Axis slid his eyes to the man's face.

Plain, ordinary, deeply lined, somewhat tired . . . and utterly extraordinary. Alive and hungry with magic. Serene and quiet with tranquillity.

Dark violet eyes regarded him with humour, understanding, and . . .

"Love?" Axis said. "I do not deserve that, surely."

His voice was very hard and bitter.

"It is yours to accept or not," DragonStar said, "as you wish."

Axis stared at his son, hating himself for hating what he saw. "What have you done with Caelum?"

DragonStar paused before he replied, but his voice was steady. "Caelum is dead."

Axis' only visible reaction was a tightening of his face and a terrible hardening of his eyes. "You led him to his death!"

"Caelum went willingly," DragonStar replied, his voice very gentle. "As he had to."

Axis stared, unable to tear his eyes from DragonStar's face, although he longed desperately to look somewhere, anywhere, else. "I—" he began, then stopped, unable to bear the hatred in his voice, and unable to understand to whom, or what, he wanted to direct that hatred.

There was a movement behind him, and then Azhure was at his side, as she had been for so many years.

And as she had so many times previously, she saved him from this battle.

Azhure touched Axis' arm fleetingly, yet managing to impart infinite comfort with that briefest of caresses, then she stepped straight past her husband to DragonStar.

She paused, then spoke. "Did Caelum see you like this? As . . . as you were meant to be?"

DragonStar nodded, and Azhure's entire body jerked slightly.

Then she leaned forward and hugged her son.

He pulled her in tight against him, drawing as much love from her as she drew comfort from him.

Axis stared, not understanding, and not particularly wanting to.

Eventually Azhure pulled back and turned slightly so she could hold out a hand to her husband. Her eyes and cheeks were wet, but there was sadness in her face as well, and she continued to hold DragonStar tightly with her other hand.

"Axis? I—"

"What is this, Azhure?" His voice was harsh. "Caelum is dead. Dead! And—"

"Caelum knew he was going to die," Azhure said. "He accepted it."

Axis closed his mouth into a cold, hard line.

"And he accepted," Azhure said, "as we should have done earlier, that Drago . . ." she glanced back at her son, "that DragonStar was born to be the true StarSon."

Axis opened his mouth to say *No!* but found he could not voice the word. The man standing before him was clearly not the sullen Drago who'd moped about Sigholt for so many years, and he was just as clearly a man who wielded such great power that he . . . he . . . just might be . . .

Axis turned his head to one side, and was surprised to feel the wetness of tears on his own cheeks as the breeze brushed his face. "Oh gods," he said, and sank down on the ground.

"Will you meet with your father in our apartment a little later?" Azhure asked DragonStar hurriedly. "For the time being, I think it would be best if he and I had some time alone . . ."

DragonStar nodded.

"Thank you," Azhure murmured, then bent down to her husband. DragonStar vaulted back onto Belaguez's back and rode down the trail into Sanctuary.

DragonStar chose to ride unnoticed into Sanctuary; no-one noted his entry, and thus no-one disturbed him in the three hours before Azhure sought him out.

"Your father waits for you," she said, giving DragonStar directions to their apartment. She looked him over— DragonStar had discarded his linen hip-wrap for a pair of fawn breeches, brown boots and a white shirt, but he still wore the sword and jewelled purse at his belt.

"And?" DragonStar asked.

Azhure nodded very slightly. "And he is prepared to accept."

DragonStar laughed softly. "Prepared to, but has not yet."

"It is a start."

"Aye, it is that. Azhure . . . why have you accepted so easily? Even I denied it for long months."

"Perhaps because I fought to keep you to a viable birthing age when you fought so hard to abort yourself. I have a mother's belief in her offspring."

DragonStar paled, both at her words and at the hardness in her voice. He began to say something, but Azhure stopped him with a hand on his chest.

"I had no right to speak thus to you, DragonStar. I have no right to speak harshly to *any* of my children. I was too absorbed in my magic and in Axis to be a good mother to any but Caelum."

"Azhure—"

Azhure well understood why he would not call her "mother".

"—it is never too late to be a friend to your children. I think that you and I will always be better friends than parent and child."

Azhure smiled, and lowered her eyes a little.

"But," DragonStar continued softly, relentlessly, "I think that Zenith needs you as a friend far more than I. There are many things that can be saved from this disaster, Azhure, and I do hope that Zenith will be among them."

Azhure's eyes jerked back to DragonStar's face. "And I haven't even seen her since I came to Sanctuary!"

"I did not know that," DragonStar said, "but I am not surprised by it."

And then he turned and walked out the door without another word, leaving his mother staring at his back and with a hand to her mouth in horrified mortification.

Axis was waiting for DragonStar in a small and somewhat un-adorned chamber, so plain that DragonStar thought it almost out of character for Sanctuary. Perhaps Axis had spent hours here when he'd first arrived, throwing out all the comforts and fripperies and creating an environment austere enough for any retired war captain to feel at home in.

Axis had never been happy or content away from war, DragonStar thought, and wondered for the first time how frus-trating life must have been for Axis once Gorgrael had been disposed of and Tencendorian life was relatively peaceful. No wonder he'd handed over power to Caelum: the endless Coun-cils spent debating the finer details of trading negotiations must have bored his father witless.

Had it been any more challenging being a god? DragonStar wondered.

Axis was seated at a wooden table, or, rather, he was lean-ing back in a plain wooden chair, his legs crossed and resting on the tabletop, his arms folded across his chest.

On the table surface before him sat a jug of beer, two mugs, and a cloth-wrapped parcel. At the end of the table directly down from Axis sat an empty, waiting chair.

DragonStar paused in the doorway, nodded as an acknow-ledgment of Axis' presence, then strolled across to the table, pulled out the chair and sat down. "So tell me, Axis, how am I being greeted? As a drinking companion? Comrade-in-arms?" He paused very slightly. "Long-lost son?"

Another, slightly longer pause, and the ghost of a grin about his lips. "If the prodigal son, then should I expect poi-son in the beer? A knife thrown from a darkened corner by a faithful lieutenant?"

Axis stared at DragonStar for a heartbeat or two, his face expressionless, then he leaned forward, poured out the two mugs of beer, and slid one down the table. "There is no poison in the beer, nor knife waiting in the corner."

"Ah." DragonStar caught the mug just before it slid off the

edge of the table, and raised it to his mouth, swallowing a mouthful of the beer. "Then I am not here as long-lost son."

"*I* am here only because both Azhure and Caelum asked it of me."

DragonStar's face lost its humorous edge. "I have no reason to stay here, Axis," he snapped. "I could just take that," he nodded at the parcel, "and leave. *I* have no use for faded stars!"

To his absolute surprise, Axis burst into laughter. "And nothing could have convinced me more of your fathering than that speech, Drago! Ah, sorry, I should call you by your birth name, should I not?"

"I should always have been called by my birth name," DragonStar said. "As was my right."

"My, my," Axis said softly, "you have my humour and you have my pride." His voice tightened. "I have also heard it rumoured about this fabulous crystal place they call Sanctuary that you have Faraday as well."

With a jolt of surprise DragonStar realised that, if nothing else, Axis *was* treating him as an equal. This was man to man, and it was not about Caelum or who was or who was not Star-Son, but about the passing over of the baton of legend.

And Axis didn't want to let it go.

DragonStar took a deep breath. Axis had never felt threatened by fumble-fingered Caelum, but he now felt intimidated by DragonStar's surety of grip. The baton was slipping away from Axis' grasp . . . *had* slipped.

What if DragonStar had always been the point and the meaning of the high adventure of Axis' battle with Borneheld and Gorgrael? What if Axis had only ever been the pawn, and DragonStar the true champion?

If Axis had *not* been the true champion, then nothing would demonstrate this more in his eyes than the fact that Faraday had gravitated to DragonStar. Faraday's preferences in love would demonstrate who was the pawn, and who the king.

"Faraday chooses to walk alone," DragonStar said, and, just as Axis visibly relaxed, continued, "although I have let her know well enough that I would enjoy her warmth and company by my side."

Axis paused in the act of drinking some beer, stared coldly at DragonStar over the rim of his mug, then set it back on the table.

"Caelum is dead," he said. "I have lost my son and I am in mourning. Forgive me if I do not fawn at your feet." He stared at DragonStar. *You sent my beloved son to his death, and now you say you want to take the woman who was my lover.*

DragonStar half-grimaced, then turned it into a small smile. "I do not think you want another son, do you, Axis? But it would be better for you and I, and for Azhure, and for every one of the living creatures left in Sanctuary, if we could be friends."

Axis dropped his eyes, and turned his half-empty mug around slowly between his hands. Surprisingly, his overwhelming emotion was one of relief. DragonStar had just presented them both with the perfect solution. Axis knew he could never think of this man across the table as his son—too much love had been denied, and too much hatred had been passed between them for it ever to be possible for them to embrace as father and son. But "friend"? Axis suddenly realised how much he had missed having a friend . . . how much he had missing relying on and loving Belial.

Axis knew he would be catastrophically jealous if a son proved more powerful than he, but, strangely, he knew he could accept it if a friend was.

An aeon seemed to pass as Axis thought. A friend. DragonStar a *friend?*

Something dark and horrid shifted within Axis—jealousy, resentment, bitterness—and then shifted again, and, stunningly, slid into oblivion.

He needed a friend. Badly. The thought brought such profound relief that Axis realised he had tears in his eyes.

He blinked them away and raised his gaze back to DragonStar. "How did you realise how much I needed a friend?"

A corner of DragonStar's mouth twitched. "I have learned a

great deal of wisdom since I demanded of you that you set Caelum aside and make me StarSon instead."

Axis almost smiled, and then felt amazement that he *could* smile at this memory. "You were a precocious shitty bastard of an infant."

"Well . . . technically 'bastard' I was not, but everything else you say is true enough. Axis, whatever else has happened between us, and whatever else I have said to you and thought about you and hated you for, I do thank you for setting me on the path of adversity, for without it I would have been another Gorgrael, or another Qeteb. Do you remember what you told me in Sigholt, that first time you set eyes on me?"

"I said that I would not welcome you into the House of Stars until you had learned both humility and compassion." Axis paused, considering DragonStar carefully. "And sitting across from me now I can see a man whose face is lined, not with hate and bitterness as once it was, but with humility and compassion.

"DragonStar—" Axis shook his head slightly, "how strange it seems to call you that—I think the time has finally arrived to welcome you into the House of Stars."

DragonStar paused before replying, allowing himself time to cope with the emotion flowing through him. How many hours had he spent lost in useless bitterness as a youth and man, longing for this moment, yet refusing to admit the longing?

"I would be honoured if you would accept me in, Axis," DragonStar said, "but as your friend before anything else." Caelum had already welcomed DragonStar into the family House. The fact that Axis now wished to do the same meant that the final bridge between DragonStar and his birth family would finally be repaired.

Tencendor could not be rebuilt without it.

Axis stood, and as he did so the door to the chamber opened and Azhure walked in.

DragonStar rose, staring at her. He wondered if it was her womanly instinct that allowed her to walk into the chamber at precisely the right moment, or just her attentive ear at the keyhole. She had changed from the ordinary day gown she'd been wearing when she'd fetched him to this chamber, and now wore a robe of purest black that was relieved only by a pattern of silvery stars about its hem. Her raven hair tumbled down her back to be lost in the folds of her skirt, and her blue eyes danced with love and, possibly, even a little of her lost magic.

DragonStar stared, then collected himself and half-bowed in her direction, acknowledging her as mother, woman and witch.

Axis smiled and held out his hand to Azhure, then held out his other hand for DragonStar. "It seems, my beloved," he said to Azhure, "that we have a new companion for our faded constellation."

She laughed, then embraced them both. "I welcome us *all* back into the House of Stars," she said.

4

WolfStar

WolfStar rolled over on his back and screamed. Agony knifed through his belly, then ran down his legs in rivulets of liquid horror. He jerked his knees to his chest and hugged them, now gasping for breath, and trying to ride out the successive waves of pain that coursed through him.

Raspu's poison, he supposed, or Mot's, or Barzula's, pumped into him during successive rapes.

"Ahhh," he groaned, and rolled over, weeping with the pain and the loss and the overwhelming humiliation. Humiliation, not so much from the demonic rapes he'd been forced to endure, although that was part of it, but from the realisation that *everything* he'd done, and *everything* he'd thought himself master of during the past few thousand years had been a lie.

He'd been a tool and a pawn as much as had the sweatiest and stupidest peasant and now he'd been disposed of as easily.

The Maze—well taught by the Star Dance—was the hardest and cruellest master of all.

WolfStar—Enchanter-Talon, feared by every Icarii in existence.

WolfStar—crazed murderer, loathed by scores of generations of Icarii.

WolfStar—Dark Man, Dear Man, friend and ally of Gorgrael the Destroyer.

WolfStar—lover and ultimate destroyer of Niah.

WolfStar—manipulator of the entire world and all who lived within it.

WolfStar—utter, utter Fool.

A rat ran over his right foot, scratching deeply into his flesh as it went, but WolfStar paid it no heed. Over the past hours (days? weeks? he did not know) countless creatures had scrambled over him, trampled him, urinated on him, nibbled, bit and tasted him, and yet none had done him the kindness of killing him.

All WolfStar wanted was to die . . . to escape the utter humiliation his existence had become. But no thing or one would grant him death in this world of death made incarnate—this damned, cursed Maze. Bleakness swarmed constantly over him, and madness probed intermittently at his mind: the hours when the Demons raged drove him to the brink of insanity, but never *(oh please, stars, let the horror tip me over!)*, never beyond into the oblivion of total insanity.

Why? Why couldn't he become one of these mindless creatures that swarmed incoherently and incontinently through the Maze? All WolfStar wanted was to become mindless, because then he would feel no pain.

WolfStar's fingers scrabbled over his chest, feeling again the clotting blood of Caelum. He gagged, sickened by the feel, as also by the damned persistence of the blood.

He couldn't wipe it off, it wouldn't go away. It wouldn't even dry to a scab that he could *scrape* off.

WolfStar was marked by Caelum's blood, and he wondered if that was what protected him.

What had happened to the boy? Why had he walked onto the point of Qeteb's blade?

WolfStar had turned the horrific moments of Caelum's death over and over in his mind, and yet he still could not understand them. What had gone so wrong? Why hadn't Caelum fought back?

Or, at the least, why hadn't he made an effort to escape?

WolfStar could crawl no more. He propped himself up against a wall, holding his belly with one hand, dragging air into his lungs.

Suddenly Caelum walked about the corner and came directly towards him.

He had a beatific smile on his face.

"Caelum StarSon!" Qeteb screamed, and stood in his stirrups and raised his sword.

Caelum, now directly before WolfStar, turned and stared at the horror approaching, stared at the rearing, plunging creature above him, and at the Demon screaming on its back.

"Oh, how I love you," he said.

"No!" Qeteb shrieked, driven beyond the realms of anger, not only by Caelum's words, but also by the serene expression on his face.

The Demon drove down his sword.

WolfStar could not believe it. As the sword plunged downwards, Caelum held out his hand and seized the blade.

It made not a whit of difference.

The sword sliced through Caelum's hand and plunged into his chest, driving Caelum back against WolfStar, who grunted with shock.

Qeteb leaned his entire weight down on the sword, twisting it as deep as he could go, feeling bone and muscle and cartilage tear and rip, seeing the bright blood bubble from the StarSon's mouth.

What had the boy been doing, wandering through the Maze with a beatific smile on his face while all the Demons of Hell rode at his heels?

"There had been magic worked there," WolfStar whispered, inching his way further down whatever dead-end of the Maze he'd chosen this time. "An enchantment . . . Caelum was caught in enchantment . . . but whose? Whose?"

Suddenly WolfStar was angry, and it chased away all his bleakness and humiliation. Someone—not the Demons—had worked an enchantment on Caelum . . . *Who had control of enchantment in this Star Danceless world?*

And if someone did have control of enchantment, how could WolfStar work that to his own will?

"Who are you?" he whispered, now dragging himself along with one hand while the other held his ruined belly in vaguely one piece. "Who are you?"

He repeated the sentence, over and over, making of it a mantra. He repeated it for hour after hour, dragging himself through the Maze, ignoring the countless creatures—once-animal and once-human or Icarii—that flowed about and over him. He continued to repeat it through the Demonic hour of dusk that probed at his mind, and he continued to repeat it through the night until it almost drove him mad.

At dawn, as the light broke over the Maze, WolfStar realised something.

He was not mad. And he was not dead. Neither madness nor Demon had touched him, or even taken any interest in him. He had survived, for whatever reason and for whatever purpose.

And he had to have a purpose, because without a purpose he was nothing but a pawn.

A glow of light filtered down through the stone walls of the Maze, lighting the flagstones before him.

A million symbols flowed over and through the stone. The Maze, taunting him.

"Damn you! Damn you!" WolfStar whispered, furious that the Star Dance and the Maze had manipulated him for so many millennia. From the heights of power, the glory days of thinking that all Tencendor danced to *his* manipulations, WolfStar had fallen to being nothing but a useless puppet crawling through the stone corridors of the Maze.

A Talon-Enchanter with no more power than an ant.

"No!"

No, he could not bear that. There was power out there somewhere—he could *feel* it!—and that meant there was power available for the taking.

And he would take it. *No-one would laugh at WolfStar!*

"Who are you?" he whispered over and over as he crawled hand-over-hand across the rough stone. "Who are you?"

As crazed birds tumbled through the sky above his head, so plans and intrigues tumbled through WolfStar's mind.

There was power out there, and he would find a way to control it.

"Who are you? Who are you?"

WolfStar crawled for hours, lost in his own thoughts, his anger giving him strength when he should have collapsed, until eventually he thought he heard something whisper. He raised his head, and stared.

Then he laughed, knowing hope for the first time in many days.

Ten paces ahead rose the gateway into the wasteland.

5

Of Sundry Enemies

"This land is not enough," Sheol whispered. "We need the entire world and all its souls to feed from. When can we take it *all*?"

She was lying sprawled across the floor of the mausoleum,

writhing in an agony of need and desire. Her last feeding hour had been good, but not good enough.

There were other souls out there, and she wanted them.

She bared her teeth, and snarled.

Qeteb leaned down and grabbed her by the hair, hauling her to her feet. Sheol screamed, and then roared, her shape flowing from humanoid to dog and back to humanoid again.

StarLaughter, sitting with her back against one of the black columns, turned her face aside in a disgust she did not even bother to disguise. Nothing had gone well for her since her son had attained his full potential.

Qeteb laughed, and dropped Sheol.

The female Demon crawled a few paces away and then rose to her feet, smoothing down the pastel-coloured gown she'd chosen to assume and rearranging her facial features in an expression that came close to obeisance.

"Great Father," she said, and dipped her head.

Qeteb grunted. For the moment he was prepared to put up with Sheol's impatience—had she not fought through a hundred thousand years to resurrect him?—but he wasn't sure if his current good nature would last much longer than dusk this evening.

There was going to be an irritating delay before they could consume the souls of the entire planet, and Qeteb did not like to be made to wait for anything, let alone total domination.

"For the moment we are confined to this wasteland," he said. "We must be, until we have finally disposed of the . . . StarSon."

The Enemy Reborn.

It had rattled all of the Demons more than they were prepared to admit out loud each to the other. The damned, damned Enemy Reborn.

They thought they had been chasing the shadows cast by the fleet of the *Ark,* but instead the shadow had been chasing them.

"Once the StarSon is dead—once and for all—then the eating will be beyond compare," Raspu whispered. He was standing with Mot and Barzula behind the stone tomb that sat in the centre of the mausoleum. The three Demons were leaning with their elbows on the stone's flat surface and their chins resting in their hands, staring at Qeteb as he paced to and fro.

Behind them, almost lost in the gloom of the columned recesses of the mausoleum, lay the Niah-woman, limbs akimbo, blank-eyed head propped up at an uncomfortable yet unheeded angle against a cold marble wall. Her white skin was blemished with small lesions. Qeteb had amused himself well with her. His new body had needs to be sated, and her soulless one was useful only for the services it could provide—but his black metal armour had not provided the kindest of caresses.

No-one among them cared, least of all Qeteb. As far as he was concerned, the Niah-body needed to last only as long as it could provide a new flesh and blood form for Rox's lost soul. Qeteb was more than irritated with Rox's foolhardy attempt to brave the bridge at Sigholt, and had considered leaving him to float disembodied for eternity . . . but this was a land and a time of resurrection, and Rox would be more useful in bodily form than useless spirit.

They would need to meet the StarSon united. This time, Qeteb would let nothing stand in the way of a total victory over the Enemy.

"What do you mean?" StarLaughter said, moving forward. "I thought you rammed your sword through the StarSon in the Maze. What's this hold-up?"

Qeteb's impatience for power was nothing compared to StarLaughter's.

Qeteb turned slowly to look at the woman. He would have liked to destroy her, but at the moment he was loath to kill anything that might provide information, or might prove useful. If there was anything Qeteb had learned over the past hundred thousand years of imprisonment, it was a modicum of prudence.

"He was a false StarSon only," he said, allowing his voice to flow through his closed visor like honeyed chocolate.

It had its effect. StarLaughter visibly relaxed.

"A decoy," Qeteb continued. "The false StarSon bought the true StarSon time . . . for what I am not yet sure."

"Time," Sheol said, "to build a hidey-hole for the majority of souls of this land. He even took the insects with him!"

A soul was a soul was a soul, and each soul fed the Demons as much as the next one. The millions of insects that Drago's witches had squirreled away into Sanctuary had cost the Demons as dearly as the vast numbers of people who'd managed to escape the final ravagement.

Qeteb nodded slowly, letting his gaze drift away from Star-Laughter and around the mausoleum. This dark place was all very well, but Qeteb had had enough of confinement. Soon would be the time to go exploring.

"We will find his hiding place," the Midday Demon said, "and we will destroy it. We will feed on all it has to offer. And then we—I—will meet this StarSon, and teach him that which he refuses to learn."

Underneath his visor Qeteb's lips stretched in a humourless smile. The StarSon might be the Enemy Reborn, but he had been reborn with all the Enemy's mistakes tucked into whatever magic he thought he commanded. But *he, Qeteb, had spent his millennia of confinement learning ... and learning from the Enemy's errors. The Enemy Reborn, this uselessly tinselled StarSon, was bred to make the same mistakes as his forebears ... but this time Qeteb was ready, and this time the Enemy Reborn's mistakes would kill him.*

Qeteb felt a sensual thrill course through his being. He had waited a hundred thousand years for rebirth, while the Enemy had waited a hundred thousand years for death.

This time he would triumph. Qeteb knew it for truth.

"And what of that?" Barzula said, indicating the wooden bowl that lay at the foot of the tomb. "It is magic ... but what kind? And is it dangerous?"

Qeteb walked over and picked up the bowl, stroking the wood. "StarLaughter?"

She sighed, and joined him. She rested her hand on the wood. "It is of Avar craftsmanship. Pointless beauty."

"I disagree," Qeteb said, and brushed her hand aside. "But then, I do not blame you for it, for you are merely woman, and a mortal who has survived on the back of my brothers' and sister's power and their tolerance."

StarLaughter's entire body went rigid, and her eyes hard.

Qeteb either did not notice or did not care. "This bowl has a secret," he said. "A very big and probably very important secret."

His hand tightened about the bowl, and a tiny crack ran halfway along the rim.

"I do not like objects that are secretive!" Qeteb said, and his hand tightened fractionally more.

The crack widened.

"Ah!" Qeteb loosened his grip. He hefted the bowl lightly, and then in a smooth action threw the bowl spinning into the darkness of the domed ceiling.

It disappeared.

"The one thing I like about secrets," Qeteb observed, his visored face once more looking at StarLaughter, "is that they keep indefinitely. The bowl is mine, and eventually its secret will be mine."

StarLaughter held the Demon's stare, difficult as that was with no observable eyes to be found behind the latticed metalwork of the visor. "Your brothers and sister," she said evenly, "promised me power in return for all my aid."

To one side Sheol sniggered.

"Your *aid*," Qeteb said. "How amusing that you think you provided—"

"I provided you with life!" StarLaughter yelled, balling her fists at her side and taking a step closer to Qeteb.

Barzula and Mot glanced at each other, then back to StarLaughter, and then they smiled slowly.

You did not provide me with life!

The thought boomed about the mausoleum, and although no spoken word sounded, all heard Qeteb's words.

"You are my *son*!" StarLaughter screamed, unthinking anger giving her voice unusual strength. "I provided you with life, I bore you through adversity, I gave birth to you while I drifted among the stars. I loved and nurtured you through three thousand—"

"You provided the scrap of flesh which I *chose* to inhabit!" Qeteb stepped forward, and StarLaughter finally had the sense to retreat slightly. "My existence needs no 'mother'. You were merely the cow that delivered the meat for my needs. You are the one who should be grateful . . . and yet you have the stupidity to demand it of *me*! I do not *know*," he continued, growling now, and stepping forward once more, "why you still live or why your mind is still your own."

StarLaughter paled, although her eyes remained bright with fury. "Because no-one else in this gloomy tower knows their way around this land and its secrets like I do!" she said. "You deserve another hundred thousand years trapped in some Enemy's gaol if now you destroy the one Tencendorian remaining at your side, and with a reasonably intact mind!"

"You would be better crawling mad at my feet!"

"You wouldn't *dare*!" StarLaughter countered, squaring her shoulders in defiance.

Qeteb stared at her, then raised a fist and struck StarLaughter across her face so hard he flung her sprawling several paces away across the floor.

"Bitch-sow," he said, his voice tight with frustration. "One day I *will* dare, and I will leave just enough of your mind intact to know *exactly* what I will do to you."

StarLaughter raised herself on an elbow and stared at him. Her left cheek was livid, blood running freely down her chin and neck. "If there is one being in existence you should never alienate," she whispered, "it is your mother."

Qeteb took one heavy step towards her. He laughed, whispery and harsh. "When I inhabited this flesh, StarLaughter, I also gained its memories. Do you want to know what I can remember of your son, StarLaughter? Do you? I remember that he despised you—"

"No! My son adored—"

"—he regarded you with contempt, as he knew all the Icarii in Talon Spike felt nothing but contempt towards you—"

"No!"

"You silly, vacuous woman. You thought you were the most powerful Icarii in the land, didn't you? You thought that all power could be yours, didn't you? And yet you were nothing but an embarrassment to the Icarii nation, someone to be greeted with silent sneers at every entrance into a room, and with laughter at your departure. The Icarii loathed you, your husband was revolted by you, and your son could not wait to escape your body. He hated you, StarLaughter. He was sickened by you, and he escaped into death rather than spend an eternity amid the stars with you."

StarLaughter remained silent, rigid with shock. She stared at Qeteb.

Qeteb laughed again. "Queen of Heaven?" he said. "Never!" Then he spat a glob of phlegm through his metal visor into her face.

She gasped, recoiling.

"That was from your son, bitch, not from me."

And Qeteb turned and strode away.

StarLaughter lay on the cold, cold floor of the mausoleum.

Lies! Lies! He spoke lies! Her son had adored her, loved her.

From the moment he had come to awareness in her womb, her son had been the only one who had understood her power, and who had understood that she was destined for greatness and was justified in choosing whatever path she had to in order to grasp her destiny.

Qeteb spoke lies!

Didn't he?

StarLaughter lay on the floor of the mausoleum and hated. More, she lusted for revenge. Qeteb could not speak such lies and blacken her son's memory—

Gods! Was her son trapped under that mountain of metal and odious flesh, screaming for her to get him out?

—and think that she would do nothing about it.

StarLaughter bared her teeth, and made a small sound deep in her throat that was half curse, half growl.

Her hands clawed on the floor, her nails scratching at its surface.

She lay there and hated, and she lay there and lusted for revenge.

StarLaughter was very, very good at nourishing both hatred

and revenge. She had had many thousands of years of practice at both.

I nurtured my son, she thought, *her entire body rigid with the intensity of her animosity. I nurtured him and kept him and held and loved him through such extremes of pain and despair that you—a Demon—cannot imagine. I offered him my breast, and he took it.*

I loved him, and yet you stole him from me, Qeteb, and then sullied his memory with lies.

"My son hated me?" StarLaughter whispered, her hands still clawing slowly at the floor. "He didn't hate me, he adored me . . . *every Icarii adored me!* No-one laughed at me. *No-one!*"

She lifted her head slightly and stared at Qeteb, now on the far side of the mausoleum whispering with his fellow nightmares.

You are the simpleton, Qeteb, if you think you can deny both my son and myself our destinies.

At StarLaughter's thought, Qeteb turned slowly and regarded her.

StarLaughter did not move, nor drop her eyes, nor even disguise the hatred and resentment in them.

After a moment Qeteb turned his back to her again.

Now you have one more enemy, StarLaughter thought, and began to mop at the blood on her face and neck with a corner of her much-bloodied robe.

Her son hadn't hated her . . . had he?

StarLaughter paused in her attempts to clean her face, and her entire face trembled as doubt overran her mind.

Had he?

6

The Enchanted Song Book

"Tell us of Caelum," Axis said, as they sat down. "And tell us of yourself. We have heard only garbled snippets, and we would know the truth."

Where to start? DragonStar thought. "You realise," he finally said, "the depth of manipulation that has bound our family?"

Axis nodded. "I thought my task had been to defeat Gorgrael and unite Tencendor, but in reality, my task, as Azhure's, was to create the circumstances that would create the StarSon."

DragonStar's mouth quirked. "Yes. Even WolfStar had been manipulated in order that Azhure be created and Axis be trained, so that you might the better perform your task in creating . . ."

"You," Azhure said very softly. She did not look at either her husband or her son.

"The manipulation," DragonStar said, "extends beyond our family. It involves this entire land and its peoples, and stretches beyond that . . . back to the world of the Enemy. We are but the result of tens and tens of thousands of years of manipulation. Even longer, perhaps."

"By what?" Axis demanded. "By who?"

"By the Star Dance," DragonStar said. "Or whatever it represents."

"The Star Dance!" Axis said, and he spoke the words as a curse, as a hated thing. "The time was when I loved that beyond anything, save Azhure."

"It may be," DragonStar said, "that the Star Dance has been leading to this point, to us, for millions of years. Chasing the Demons through time and space, and being chased by them."

"*We* are the ultimate of millions of years of . . . manipulation?" Azhure said, and then laughed merrily, shaking out her hair. "Could the Star Dance have not made us less flawed? An Axis less arrogant and cruel? A DragonStar less resentful and ambitious? And I? I less determined to know my own power, and more willing to tend to my own family."

"Who knows," DragonStar said. "Our flaws may yet save us." And he smiled, as if he had made a joke to himself. "Ah, but you asked of Caelum and of myself. We both grew up amid lies—not of your doing, or even of ours, but lies bound about us by the Star Dance, via the Maze. These lies dictated our action, driving me into such overweening ambition I could contemplate the murder of Caelum, and making Caelum . . ."

"A weak ruler," Azhure finished for him, "and a murderer also, perhaps?"

Ye gods, DragonStar thought weakly, what should I say to *that?* Yes, mother. Caelum murdered our sister and your daughter. Do you *want* me to say that out loud, Azhure?

"Perhaps," he answered, and Azhure nodded and turned aside her head for a second time.

"A murderer?" Axis said. "What do you mean?"

"He means," Azhure said, "that we all have the blood of others on our hands, beloved."

And Axis nodded, accepting what she said without truly understanding what she spoke of.

"Caelum's true role was as a false StarSon," DragonStar said. "A decoy. I needed time to grow, to learn, and to allow Qeteb the confidence to destroy Tencendor . . . which he would not have done if he'd known the StarSon still lived."

Briefly, DragonStar told his parents of the hidden Acharite magic that could be touched only with the passage through death.

Axis stared at Azhure, his eyes excited, then looked back at DragonStar. "But that means that I, too, can use the Acharite power!"

DragonStar shook his head. "I'm sorry, Axis, but—"

"I've been to death's gate, even though the haggard old crone wouldn't let me through. *Why* can't I use my Acharite blood?"

"Because of your overpowering use of the Star Dance." DragonStar paused, feeling his father's frustration. "And you have been a Star God. Your Icarii-bred magic has killed whatever potential Acharite magic you had. When you proclaimed yourself StarMan, you also literally killed your Acharite magic in favour of the Star Dance. I'm sorry, Axis."

Axis subsided, bitterly disappointed. For a moment, just a moment, he'd thought . . .

Axis shook his head, putting his disappointment aside. "What else do you have to tell us?"

DragonStar hesitated, still sympathising with Axis. Then he continued, telling them of Urbeth, the original Enchantress and mother of races, and Azhure gasped and fingered the now-dulled Circle of Stars on her finger. He told them everything he could of the time he'd spent with the Demons, and what had happened to him once he'd returned to Tencendor. He told them of the manner of Caelum's death.

And, finally, he told them of the Infinite Field of Flowers, and what awaited Tencendor once—if—the Demons had been destroyed.

Axis and Azhure listened in silence, their faces growing more and more pallid, their eyes progressively rounder, as DragonStar spoke.

"And Caelum," Azhure said as DragonStar finally finished. "Caelum?"

"Is in the Field of Flowers," DragonStar said. "Be sure of that."

"Can we see him? You said that Zared and Theod saw the Field of Flowers. Can we—"

"No," DragonStar said. "Wait, let me explain. You cannot see it yet, but if all goes well, then, well, we will all experience the Field of Flowers. But I cannot take you from Sanctuary into the field. We need to go from Tencendor itself. There is only one gateway."

"But Spiredore," Azhure said. "Draw your door of light, take us into Spiredore, and thence into—"

"Azhure," DragonStar said, and leaned across the table to

take her hand. "Qeteb has risen, and the Demons now control the wasteland that once was Tencendor. I do not know if Spiredore is safe any more. It probably is, but 'probably' is not good enough to needlessly risk your lives. I will go first, and then one or two of the other five who have been through death and can resist the Demons, for a while at least. Wait. Please."

Azhure nodded, and dropped her eyes. They fell on the cloth-wrapped parcel that still sat on the table.

"Caelum asked us to give this to you," Azhure said, "if he . . . if he died."

She pushed the parcel across the table towards DragonStar. The Enchanted Song Book. DragonStar slowly unwrapped it.

"We deciphered the melodies, and then the dances," Axis said. "They were . . . unusual."

"They are the key to the destruction of the Demons," DragonStar said.

Axis stared at his son, remembering the dawn when Caelum had tried one of the dances atop Star Finger. "DragonStar . . . DragonStar, be careful with them. Caelum—"

"Caelum was not the StarSon—" DragonStar began, but Axis interrupted angrily.

"You have inherited all the damn SunSoar arrogance in its full blindness!" he said. "*Listen* to me, damn you!"

DragonStar dropped his eyes. "I am sorry, Axis. What happened?"

Slowly Axis described the dance's affect on Caelum. "It was as if he was *consumed* by hatred and violence. The dance did that to him . . . it infused him with whatever malevolence it had been made from."

"Qeteb was originally trapped by mirrors that reflected his own malevolence back on him," DragonStar said slowly. "He would never let that happen to him again. The dances, the melodies the book contain," his fingers tapped the cover thoughtfully, "will have the same action as the mirrors originally did."

"Maybe," Axis said, "and maybe not."

7

A Wander Through,
and Into, Sanctuary

$\int$araday, Zenith and StarDrifter were wandering slowly along one of the paths Sanctuary had provided for the comfort, pleasure and exercise of all who sheltered within its confines. It was, StarDrifter thought—and with a distinct, but not entirely successful, effort to avoid couching the thought in unpleasant overtones—just like it was on the Island of Mist and Memory. Me, Zenith . . . and Faraday's constant presence between us. Even her physical presence, for Faraday literally separated Zenith and StarDrifter as they walked abreast down the wide path.

Not even Sanctuary works in my favour, StarDrifter thought, for if the path were just the slightest bit narrower, then mayhap Faraday would have to walk behind Zenith and myself, and I could have the contentment of the odd fleeting touch as my elbow brushed the fabric of Zenith's lavender gown.

And mayhap not, for StarDrifter was sure if the path were narrow, he would be the one left to wander lost behind whilst Faraday and Zenith linked arms—as they had now—and chatted happily without him.

Aye, he thought, this *is* just like the Island of Mist and Memory, for Zenith feels more comfortable with me when someone else is present. It is as if she only feels at ease relating to me through someone else.

She only laughs freely when there is someone else present to protect the space between her and I.

She only smiles at me when someone else is there to act as a filter for her joy.

She only tilts eyes of love in my direction when there is someone else her glance can bounce off first.

StarDrifter was not feeling happy about the situation at all, but there was nothing he could, or wanted, to do. Zenith had to take her own time in learning to accept her love for him, or there would be no future time for the two of them at all.

The shared strolls through Sanctuary's soft daytime were bad, but there was nothing as bad as the long velvet nights adrift in his lonely bed knowing that Zenith had been born to share it, but knowing also she refused to do so . . . because . . .

. . . because she found his touch repulsive! StarDrifter shivered in utter panic. How could he *ever* shift from grandfather to lover in her mind?

"StarDrifter?" Zenith said, and StarDrifter jumped.

"Hmmm?"

"Look, we approach Sanctuary's answer to the Avarinheim. I wonder which Avar Clan we will encounter first? The JeppelSand Clan were here yesterday . . ."

StarDrifter truly didn't care, but he tried his best to summon an outward semblance of interest. They were within a hundred paces of a dark forest, and yet StarDrifter knew that on entering that forested darkness, they would find only space and light and music, just like the original Avarinheim.

And no doubt some Clan that both Faraday and Zenith would insist on sitting down with and sharing some in-depth conversation about the preparation of malfari bread, or some such.

Women! Didn't they understand that there were other pleasures to pursue?

But now Faraday was pulling back a little.

"I don't know," she said, and both StarDrifter and Zenith halted and regarded her.

"Faraday," Zenith said, and reached out her hand to hold one of Faraday's. "Isfrael is generally deep within the forest, and even if he isn't, he is hardly likely to linger about and disturb our morning."

Faraday did not answer, staring at the forest and chewing her lip. She loved chatting to the Avar, and they just as obviously enjoyed her visits, but the occasional meeting with Isfrael, even the glimmer of his hostile eyes behind the shadowy overhang of a branch, tended to send chills trampling up and down her spine.

"Perhaps you and StarDrifter should go on," she said, and StarDrifter's entire countenance brightened.

"Perhaps that's best!" he said, and took Zenith's hand to lead her away. "Zenith, Faraday obviously doesn't want to—"

"Faraday! Zenith! StarDrifter!"

They all turned and looked back down the path.

Azhure was walking quickly—and yet with such lithe grace that StarDrifter's breath caught slightly in his throat—towards them.

She smiled with exquisite loveliness as she reached them, and now StarDrifter's breath caught completely, not so much for Azhure's beauty, as alluring as it was, but for the resemblance to Zenith's smile on her face.

"Faraday," Azhure said softly. "Drago . . . DragonStar has returned."

Faraday's face paled completely, and her green eyes widened. She let go of Zenith's hand, and looked past Azhure towards the distant palace complex. An expression akin to panic flooded her face.

"Go to him," Azhure said softly. "Axis and I have talked to him, and now, perchance it is your time."

Faraday's eyes focused back on Azhure. "You talked . . . ?"

"Faraday, go to him."

Faraday looked once more at the distant palace. She and Azhure had talked at length in the days that Drago (why did Azhure call him DragonStar?) had remained above in Tencendor. At first, Faraday had wanted to talk Azhure into accepting her son back into her love, but had found it not necessary. Azhure had been won over the instant Drago had looked at her with unhindered love in that dank basement chamber in Star Finger. Instead, Faraday had found herself being lectured by Azhure on accepting her own love for Drago.

She and the Mother must somehow be in cohorts, Faraday had thought at the time.

But she had listened to Azhure, nevertheless, as she had listened to the Mother.

"I must get Katie," Faraday said. "She's with Leagh and Gwendylyr in—"

"No," Azhure said. "Katie can wait."

"I—"

"Go," Azhure said, and took Faraday's hand and pulled her very slightly down the path. "Go."

Faraday nodded, and went.

Isfrael watched his mother walk down the path with cold eyes, and even colder thoughts.

The Avar tolerated—nay, welcomed—his presence among them, but Isfrael was ever aware that they regarded him as *one* of them, not as one *above* them.

That place they now reserved for Faraday. Their Tree Friend was once more among them. *She* had returned in the hour of direst danger, and led them to safety.

Better his mother had stayed in legend, Isfrael thought, as he had thought a thousand times since he'd entered this pitiful underground dungeon they called "Sanctuary".

Better . . . better if she returned to legend.

Aye, far better.

Isfrael turned his back and walked into darkness.

Faraday smoothed the white linen of her gown nervously, tweaking out a fold that had become caught under the Mother's rainbow sash still wound about her waist.

For a moment she rested her hand on the faint outline of the twisted arrow and sapling that rested in the folds of the sash.

Then she raised her eyes and looked at the closed door before her. Here Azhure said Drago was waiting.

Here, the chamber he had taken as his own. Right next door to Axis and Azhure's chamber, which Faraday could not help wonder was a deliberate action on his part.

Choose between us, Faraday. My father, or me.

Which door, Faraday?

There was nothing in Faraday's mind of Demons, or how to restore Tencendor to its glory, or even of Katie. All Faraday could think of was what she should say to this man.

How she could gracefully tell him that, after all her hesitation, all her fright and denial, all her determination not to lay open her body and soul to the betrayal it had suffered with Axis and Gorgrael, she was prepared to do it all over again if it meant loving, and being loved.

The Mother had been right. Her life would be nothing if she refused to dare to love.

Faraday glanced at Axis' door several paces away.

There was no question of the choice, and maybe Drago knew that, but it would have amused him to have presented her with the mirage of alternatives.

No, Faraday's major problem now was how to back down with her pride intact from the position she'd dug herself into.

Having denied the man, and her love for him, for months, how could she now turn around and say she'd been wrong?

What superior smile would wrap his face? What triumph?

"None, Faraday," said a soft voice behind her, and she whipped about.

Drago . . . *no!* DragonStar (and now she could see why Azhure had used that name) was leaning against the wall several paces behind her.

Faraday's entire existence stilled, save for the painful thudding of her heart.

And save for the painful sensation of her desire crawling out of the very pit of her soul, through her stomach and up her throat to offer itself to this man.

Tears filled her eyes. He was glorious. Somehow, somewhere, in the week or more since she'd last seen him, he'd been re-transformed. Transformed into his true self, the self that Azhure and Axis had tried to hide, the self that the power of the Enemy had been successful in returning.

DragonStar was not handsome, nor even physically imposing. The tired lined face and the violet eyes were the same—and yet radically different. Both face and eyes were transfused with such depth of understanding (Faraday did not think she could call it "power"), and such heights of compassion that she thought she might choke on her emotion.

DragonStar half-smiled, acknowledging her reaction, straightened, hesitated, then brushed past her and opened the door to his chamber. "You wanted to speak to me?"

Faraday's temper flashed.

"Is that *all* you have to say?" She turned and followed him into the room. "What *happened* to you? And Caelum? And Qeteb? And Tencendor? None of us have heard—"

DragonStar laid a hand on her mouth. "Hush, Faraday. First, there are other things that must be said between us."

She didn't want to. She wanted to hide in the safety of hearing what had happened above. She wanted to tell him about her encounter with Isfrael. She wanted him to know that the Earth Tree had gone, but that was all right, because in her belt she had—

He slid an arm about her waist and pulled her gently against him. "I missed you."

"Who are you?" she whispered, somehow terrified of this being that Drago had transformed into.

"The same man," he said, his eyes travelling slowly over her face, "but deeper."

"Harder?"

He shook his head. "Softer." His arm tightened fractionally.

"Qeteb—"

"Qeteb can wait. Faraday, talk to me."

She took a huge breath and closed her eyes momentarily. What had the Mother said? *Until you learn to dare, you will never live. Take that risk, Faraday . . . take that risk.*

"I will not betray you, Faraday," DragonStar whispered, and she realised he was now very, very close. So close that his warmth burnt through the layers of linen between them. "Trust me, trust me . . ." His voice drifted off and she opened her eyes.

I will never betray you, she heard him whisper in her mind, *not for another woman, not for riches or glory, and not for this land.*

"I do not require your blood," he said aloud now, although still in a whisper, "Tencendor does not require your blood."

And still she had not spoken.

Faraday . . .

How hateful, she thought, that I have found it so difficult to accept his love.

Faraday.

How hateful that I have found it so hard to accept the Sanctuary of his heart.

Faraday.

How hard that I have found it so seductive to allow myself to remain the perpetual victim rather than allowing myself to live.

Faraday.

She shifted slightly in his arms, exploring the feel of his body against hers.

DragonStar, she whispered back into his mind. And then she smiled, and laughed a little, and relaxed against him, and then laughed a little more at the smile on his face.

"I have loved you forever," she said, and those were the easiest words she had ever said in her many existences.

8

The Ploughed Field

DragonStar's witches sat in a circle on their straight-backed wooden chairs, their hands folded in their laps, eyes downcast.

Faraday was dressed again in her white linen gown, the Mother's rainbow sash about her narrow waist holding the entwined arrow and sapling against the womb of her warmth. Her small feet, clad in elegant red leather slippers, were crossed beneath her chair. Her newly-combed chestnut hair tumbled in a restrained but joyous manner down her back, save for the single thick strand which had somehow wound itself over one shoulder and curved against one breast.

She had a tiny and almost secretive smile on her face. The past few hours had been sweeter than any Faraday had ever experienced previously. All fear had left her, all sense of betrayal had gone. All that was left was the warmth and memory of DragonStar as she had left him in the bed.

Leagh sat similarly clad and shod, although her distended belly allowed no encumbrance of sash or belt. Her face was as happy and content as Faraday's, and glowing and relaxed after her days of rest and good food within Sanctuary. Her thumbs surreptitiously pressed against her belly, feeling the tiny movements of her and Zared's child safe within.

An infinite field of flowers, Faraday had told her. She was growing an infinite field of flowers within her belly.

A tiny tear slipped down Leagh's face, but it was the result of joy, not sadness.

The third female witch, Gwendylyr, sat slightly less gladsome than Faraday and Leagh. Her lover and husband still throve, as did Leagh's lover and husband, Zared, but Gwendylyr and Theod shared the sadness of having witnessed the death of their twin sons. Tomas and Cedrian had passed into the Field of Flowers from the Western Ranges and, while Gwendylyr knew they lived and played among the flowers and paused in awestruck delight atop magical cliffs that thundered down into foamy seas, she still missed them deeply. She always would, however long she had to live in this existence before she walked for the final time through the gateway (never opened) into the Field.

Even if she and Theod conceived and raised other children, nothing would replace the lost laughter of their twin sons.

She slowly raised a hand and pushed it through her black hair, lifting a heavy wave off her forehead and pushing it further back over the crown of her head. Like Faraday and Leagh, she wore it loose, falling down her back in sliding, silken curls.

The fourth in the circle was Master Jannymire Goldman. He had no luxurious hair to tumble down his back, nor sinuous form to (barely) conceal within heavy folds of white linen. Nevertheless, his attire—a short tunic of a white linen identical to the material of the women's robes, and feet in red leather sandals—gave him a sameness with the other three.

The serenity in his warm-cheeked face and bushy grey eyebrows gave him an aura of astuteness that few people, witch or wizard or Enchanter, ever attained.

Goldman had discovered mystery and strange philosophies when DragonStar had hefted him through the gateway into the Field of Flowers, and now every hour Goldman found something new to explore, some strange thought that would lead him to even stranger pastures. He spent great lengths in every day seeking out those who would consent to spend even a few moments with him talking of these spiritual puzzlements and intellectual intrigues. Already he had a reputation within Sanctuary of being a man who might one day make the extravagances of the spirit knowable to all and the riddles of the unknown as accessible as a plate of bread and cheese.

Goldman sighed happily and closed his eyes, letting the power of his soul overwhelm his flesh. He was at home.

The fifth of DragonStar's witches was not sitting in a chair at all, nor was his place part of the circle. DareWing FullHeart lay on his back in the centre of the circle, making himself its focus. His chest rose and fell with great bubbling breaths, his body afire with fever.

DareWing was dying: a second death, which made it all the more painful, debilitating and spiritually draining.

They sat, or lay, under a great crystal dome in a secluded part of Sanctuary. The crystal dome rested on seventy crystal columns that rose the height of two men from the terracotta-tiled floor. Beyond the columns stretched a great plain of newly-ploughed earth.

Nothing else was visible.

Drago's witches waited, each consumed with their own thoughts, or with their dying.

He strode across the ploughed fields, his naked feet barely sinking into the soft earth.

His body was similarly naked, save for the white linen wrap about his hips, and the lily sword and jewelled purse that hung from his begemmed belt.

The skin of his body glistened slightly with sweat.

DragonStar, the Enemy Reborn.

Behind him walked the Star Stallion, relaxed and sinuous in every movement, his head nodding and dipping with each stride, the stars sprinkling over the naked earth as they fell from his mane and tail. From his withers, fixed by magic or perhaps merely by wish, hung the Wolven and the quiver of blue-feathered arrows.

Behind the horse, but slightly to one side of him, trailed the Alaunt. They loped in single file, each with head raised just enough that they could keep their golden eyes fixed on the man in front of them.

Their jaws hung very slightly open; enough that the glint of teeth and tongue spun through.

Behind them all trundled the blue-feathered lizard, occasionally snapping at imaginary gnats.

The crystal dome appeared on the horizon, but DragonStar did not increase the rate of his stride, nor change the expression of his face. He was at peace with himself, even though his mind was consumed with the image of millions of stars and galaxies tumbling through the universe, chased by a great dark cloud with the stinging tail of a scorpion raised threateningly behind it.

Thus had Evil subverted every good ever created.

Thus had the Star Dance been chased by the TimeKeeper Demons since the creation of the universe itself.

Now was the time to end it.

Now. Here. In this time. With this man, this Crusader. And then . . . then . . .

. . . *how many aeons had the Star Dance waited? How many worlds, solar systems, galaxies torn apart had it watched?*

. . . then could the Garden be created anew. And this time, without the scorpion's tail sting of temptation.

Only the Infinite Field of Flowers gently waving into eternity.

Faraday turned her head slightly, and she seemed to smile, even though her facial muscles did not move.

There, she could smell him.

And then he was behind her, and she could sense the sway of his body and its warmth, and her lips parted, and she shifted very slightly on the chair in remembrance.

He put his hand on her shoulder, and she relaxed back into his love. He bent swiftly down, and kissed her full on her mouth.

Leagh, Gwendylyr and Goldman lifted their faces and smiled with pure joy.

"DragonStar!" Leagh said.

He nodded, embracing each one with the warmth of his gaze, then looked at DareWing.

The birdman had turned his head in DragonStar's direction and opened his eyes. They were red, and horribly consumed with the weight of his sickness.

And yet, somehow, they were still glad.

DragonStar slipped past Faraday and entered the circle. He paused, then squatted down by DareWing's side. "I need you alive," he said.

"Good," croaked DareWing.

DragonStar grinned, then leaned down his hand and rested it on the skin of DareWing's chest.

"Do you feel like an adventure?" he said.

"For you," DareWing said, "I would fetch the coals that feed the flames in the firepits of the AfterLife."

DragonStar's hand rose to cup DareWing's face. "From you," he murmured, "I require far more. A flower a day from the field that surrounds you."

Both men smiled with love, and then DragonStar rose, and addressed the four witches in the circle.

"Yet the field that surrounds this dome," he said, "is a field of bare earth. It has been turned over and ribbed and ridged, but it lies barren. What does it represent?"

"Us," said Goldman, who delighted in such philosophical dabblings. "We have been ploughed, and the seeds laid within us, but we have yet to flower."

"Aye," DragonStar said.

"Perhaps we cannot," Gwendylyr said, "until DareWing is healed."

DragonStar nodded, but did not say anything.

"*We* must heal DareWing," Faraday said, her voice quiet and introspective. "Not DragonStar. *We* must."

Again DragonStar nodded.

"And I must heal myself," DareWing said.

"Stretch your wings," DragonStar said. "All of you."

And he stepped back out of the circle.

An expression of mild panic crossed Leagh's face, and one hand tightened briefly over her belly. "How do we do this?"

"We all have Acharite magic within us," Faraday said, "now freed, as we have all come through death."

DragonStar had now walked very quietly out of the dome, and was wandering through the ploughed field. The Alaunt had settled down into a restful, watchful pack to one side of the dome, while the Star Stallion rested his weight on one hip and dozed, ignoring the lizard who lay stretched out behind him idly swatting at the stallion's twitching tail.

A tiny star fell from the stallion's mane and fizzled momentarily in the damp earth.

"How strange," Faraday continued, her voice still very quiet, "that we have the use of Acharite magic, and that DragonStar has placed us within a field of ploughed earth, and has emphasised these things to us."

Of the others, only DareWing had enough memories of the old Achar to truly understand what Faraday alluded to.

"You speak of the old god of Achar," he said, then paused to cough violently. "Artor the Ploughman."

"Artor was evil!" Leagh and Gwendylyr both said together.

"Yes," Faraday said, "but perhaps we should not disregard the influence Artor would have had on the literal physical realm of Achar, as also the influence that that would have had on our power."

She paused, trying to sort out her thoughts. "Of the five of us, it is DareWing who is sick. He has a mixture of blood, Icarii and Acharite . . . and maybe the Artor influence that—possibly—exists in all of us has sickened him nigh unto death."

"I thought DragonStar said it was ground fever," Gwendylyr said, frowning.

"Ground fever is the outward face of the sickness," Goldman said, catching Faraday's train of thought, "but the stain on DareWing's spirit is the Artorite stain. It would affect him far more than any of us."

"And is that why this field has not yet flowered?" Leagh said. "And why DareWing cannot get better? We must expel the remaining influence of Artor?"

"Yes!" Faraday said, and the others all smiled, for the explanation felt good to them. "Yes. We must reject the rib and ridge of the ploughed earth."

"How?" said Gwendylyr, ever concerned with the practical. There was a silence.

"We must ask ourselves a question," Goldman said. "What is it that remains within us of Artor the Plough God?"

Another silence.

"Faraday," DareWing said, his voice now nearly a death whisper, "of all of us here, you have been the only one who has been thoroughly taught in the ways of Artor the Ploughman. I only fought against it, and Goldman . . ."

"Was but a boy of twelve when Azhure ran Artor into his grave," Goldman said. "Faraday, what can you tell us?"

Faraday sat in silence for a while, remembering her childhood lessons in the Way of the Plough, and her allegiance to, and love for, Artor the Ploughman. The months, months that, in all, amounted to years, she'd spent studying the Book of Field and Furrow. How blind I was, she thought.

But the faith of the Plough was so comforting. Why?

"We loathed and feared the landscape," she eventually said, "and Artor gave us a face and a name for that fear. Untamed landscape, mountain, forest and marsh, was the haunt of evil creatures—the Forbidden—who were undoubtedly planning to swarm over all that was good and beautiful . . . all over *us*."

DareWing's mouth curled in a bitter smile, and he turned his head aside.

"Having defined our fear—the wild landscape and all that lived within it—we felt comforted, and so we took to the forests with our axes, and to the mountains with our armies, and to the marshes with our engineers, and we pushed back the wild landscape as far as we could. We tamed the earth and made it our slave."

"We enslaved it with the plough," Gwendylyr said.

"Yes," Faraday said, "with the plough, and the neat square fields, and the straight and tightly-controlled furrow."

"'Furrow wide, furrow deep'," Goldman said. "I remember my father saying that constantly."

"Must we make amends?" Gwendylyr asked.

Faraday looked to DareWing. "Must we?"

"No," he eventually said. "Not as such. The earth does not require 'amends'."

"It merely requires us to let go our hatred and our fear," Goldman said.

"But I don't hate and fear the landscape!" Leagh said.

"There is still something deep within each of us," Faraday said, "that corrupts us. It is the legacy of a thousand generations of unthinking worship of Artor. We must let that corruption go."

"How?" Leagh said. She looked about at the other witches in the circle, then down at DareWing. He looked worse than she'd ever seen him, and Leagh realised that they must correct whatever was wrong very shortly.

Faraday smiled. "I think I know," she said, and in the ploughed field DragonStar raised his head and smiled also.

"We still fear some aspect of the landscape," Faraday said. "All of us. We must confront the fear, and let it go."

"But—" Gwendylyr began.

"We all fear some aspect of the landscape," Faraday said again, and looked at Gwendylyr steadily. "All of us."

"I know what *I* fear," DareWing said, but Faraday would not let him finish, either.

She stopped him with a gentle hand, leaving her chair to

kneel beside him. "DareWing, I think I know what you fear, and I think I know how strong that fear is."

Faraday grinned, but sadly. "No wonder you have ground fever." Then she raised her head and looked at the other three, keeping her hand on DareWing's shoulder. "We must confront our fears first, and then, stronger, be ready to support DareWing. Goldman?"

"What? Oh . . . I, ah . . ." Goldman lapsed into silence, his eyes unfocused, then his mouth thinned and his hands clenched on his knees.

"I *loathe* dead ends," he said, and Faraday nodded. Goldman was ever the aggressive, determinedly successful businessman.

"There is nothing worse," Goldman said, and his eyes were now flinty and hard, "than walking through the countryside and finding yourself in some dead end gully, and having to retrace your steps to find another way forward. It's so *time wasting!*"

"Non-productive," Leagh said, understanding a little more the process they must all endure.

"Yes!" Goldman said, and he stood and paced about the dome. "Dead ends are so frustrating! So pointless!"

Faraday watched him carefully. It seemed almost as if hate consumed Goldman, and she realised that somewhere here was a deeper lesson they must all learn.

"So pointless," Goldman said again, and then he vanished.

Goldman found himself standing before the infuriatingly calm—and very high and very steep—rock wall of the canyon, and he raged.

He had walked hours to get to this point, put in effort and time that could have been spent more profitably elsewhere.

He had walked and walked down this canyon, thinking it would lead him to a better life, more money, and even, perhaps, a profounder understanding of life itself, and all it had presented him with was a dead end, a rock wall, a point past which Goldman could not walk.

He raged. Was it possible to demolish the dead end? Perhaps a force of several hundred men armed with pickaxes and shovels could clear it in a week or so. Perhaps a smaller force of men armed with fire powder could destroy it in less time. Something had to be done to force this rock wall to give way to Goldman's needs and ambitions and . . .

. . . and Goldman quailed at the force of his rage. Why did he think such things? Why was he so angry?

He was railing at a stand of rock, for the Field's sake!

Goldman stared at the rock wall and wondered how best to combat his inner frustration and anger.

You have walked to this rock wall, he thought, and thus there must needs be a purpose to this dead end. What is it?

He sat down cross-legged on the ground and stared at the rock.

"What do you have to teach me?" he asked, and instantly all his frustration and hate fell away and he felt a great joy fill him.

The rock absorbed the joy . . . and then it leaned forward and began to speak to Goldman in a very earnest manner.

Goldman dusted off his tunic, and smiled at the four faces staring at him.

"Your turn," he said to Gwendylyr.

She was in the garden, almost incandescent with fury.

How long had she tended that hedge? How many hours had she pruned and clipped? How many days had she spent carefully digging in the soil about its roots to add light and air and fertiliser?

And the hedge was so necessary! Its (once) neatly-clipped length had tidily divided field from garden (and what a neat garden, with its carefully measured garden beds and precise rows of stakes), providing the line that everyone needed between order and disorder.

But now disorder had invaded the garden.

Disorder in the form of a rigorous ivy. It had taken over the hedge, weaving and creeping its way through the hedge's dark interior spaces before bursting triumphantly through to wave long, gleeful tendrils into the bright summer air down the length of the hedge.

The hedge was ruined! It was doubtless dying! How could it support the parasitic ivy and still manage to keep—

Gwendylyr realised suddenly that she was very, very afraid. There was no dividing line between order and disorder, was there? It was all a lie. Disorder would win every time. It could never be kept at bay.

Gwendylyr backed slowly away, terrified that one of those tendrils would reach out and snatch at her at any moment. Where could she hide? Was there anywhere to hide? Perhaps the cellar . . . surely the dark would keep the ivy at bay . . . the dark would be safe . . . safe . . .

Gwendylyr stopped, appalled. She would hide herself in the dark the rest of her life to avoid disorder?

Was that a life at all?

She swallowed, stepped forward, raised an arm, and took one of the waving tendrils gently in her hand.

"Very pleased to make your acquaintance," she said.

"Likewise, I am sure," said the ivy, and the sun exploded and showered both hedge and ivy and Gwendylyr in freedom.

"Leagh?" said Gwendylyr.

"No! No!" Leagh screamed, and grabbed at her belly.

It was completely flat. Barren.

As barren as the landscape about her. She ran, more than half-doubled over her empty belly, through a plain of hot red pebbles. A dry wind blew in her face, whipping her hair about her eyes.

The sky was dull and grey, full of leaden dreams.

"No, no," she whispered. She was trapped in a land that

had stolen her child to feed its own hopelessness. Both sky and ground were sterile, and both had trapped her.

"No." Leagh sank to the ground, gasping in pain at the heat of the pebbles, and then ignoring the burns to curl up in a ball.

Nothing was left. Best to just give up. Best to die.

Nothing worth living for.

She cried, her breath jerking up through her chest and throat in great gouts of misery. She wanted to die. Why couldn't she die? Wasn't there anyone about who could help her to die? Why couldn't someone just put a knife to her (hopelessly barren) belly and slide it in? The pain would be nothing compared to this . . . this horror that surrounded her.

This desert. This barrenness.

Leagh cried harder, and grabbed at a handful of pebbles, loathing them with an intensity she had never felt for anything or anyone before. She threw them viciously away from her, then grabbed at another handful, throwing them away as well.

When she grabbed at her third handful she stopped, aghast at her actions.

Why blame the land for her misfortunes? If she had lost the child she carried, then how could she blame this desert?

A cool breeze blew across and lifted the hair from her face.

A tiny rock squirrel inched across her hand, its tiny velvety nose investigating her palm for food.

Leagh smiled, and then laughed as she felt a welcome heaviness in her belly. She rested her hand over her stomach and felt the thudding of her child's heart, then . . .

. . . then she gasped in wonder and scrabbled her other hand deep in among the pebbles about her.

A heartbeat thudded out from the belly of the earth as well, and it matched—

beat for beat

—that of her child's.

"What are you telling me?" she whispered, and then cried with utter rapture as the pebbles explained it to her.

Leagh raised her head and stared at the others. A hand rested on her belly, and a strange, powerful light shone from her eyes.

"Faraday," she said.

Faraday knew what it was she would confront, but her prior knowledge did not comfort her at all within the reality of her vision.

She was trapped, as she had always been trapped (time after time after time). She had trusted—the trees this time—and they had turned their backs on her and left her to this.

A thicket of thorns.

Bands of thornbush enveloped her, pressing into the white flesh of arm and breast and belly and creeping between her legs and binding her to their own cruel purpose.

Thorns studded her throat and cheek so that whenever she breathed, blood spurted and the thorns dug deeper.

Must I always bleed, she thought, and must I always suffer the despair of entrapment?

"It's a bitch of a job," muttered a thorn close to her ear, "but someone's got to do it."

Yes, yes, Faraday thought, someone has got to do it. She had been so sure that she'd not succumb to the temptation of sacrifice any more, but here she was, embracing it again.

Someone would surely have to die if Tencendor was to be saved, and Faraday supposed she'd have to do it all over again.

Painfully.

Trapped, trapped by the land. Trapped by its need to live at her expense.

The thorns twisted and roped, and Faraday screamed.

It seemed the right thing to do, somehow.

"You have a choice," said the thorns. "You can succumb and the pain will end . . . reasonably fast. Or you can fight and tear yourself apart in the effort to free yourself. Which will it be?"

"I . . . I . . ."

"Quick! The decision cannot take forever, you know!"

"I . . ."

"Quick! Quick! Time is running out!"

Faraday panicked. She opened her mouth to scream—and then stopped, very suddenly calm.

"You choose for me," she said. "I trust you to choose for me."

"Good girl," said the land, approvingly, and Faraday found herself rising slowly through a lake of emerald water, rising, rising towards the surface.

She broke through the surface and shook the water from her hair, and laughed.

"DareWing," she said, and her hand gripped his shoulder more strongly. "We will be here for you."

DareWing spiralled through the air, more determined than at any time in his life.

The ground was not going to get him.

He was an Icarii! A birdman! The ground held nothing for him, nothing.

Then why did he feel the tug on his wings so painfully? Why did the weight of his body seemingly grow with each breath so that now he found it almost impossible to stay aloft?

The ground called him: "Walk on me, be my lover, bind yourself to me."

No!

"Bind yourself forever."

No!

DareWing made a supreme effort, his shoulders and breast and belly aching with the effort of staying within the thermal.

But now he was spiralling downwards, not up.

The speed of his fall increased, and DareWing screamed curses at the ground. He would never allow himself to be ground bound! He was a creature of the air, of the sky, of the stars!

The ground rushed towards him, and DareWing screamed in fear rather than anger. Not fear at death or even pain, but fear that he would be ground bound, that he would never fly again, never soar, never again be the proud Icarii warrior . . .

He hit the ground with a force that should have killed him outright, but the worst injury DareWing felt was a bruised shoulder and thigh. He scrambled to his feet, and almost overbalanced.

He kept to his feet only with a sustained effort. Why was his balance so out? Why was everything so heavy?

DareWing halted, horrified.

His wings had become a burden. For the first time in his long life, DareWing realised that his wings were a burden. They hung like great stone weights from his back, and he could barely move them, let alone will them to lift him into the sky.

"No! Damn you! Give me my grace back! My balance! Give me back—"

My Icarii pride, he thought, and halted, amazed. *Have I always been so arrogant?*

So contemptuous of the ground?

So blind?

"What do you want of me?" he whispered. "How can I redeem myself?"

"Relinquish your arrogance," the ground replied, "for that is what made the unwinged resent you in ages past."

Relinquish my wings? DareWing thought, and anger surged through him. *No birdman relinquishes his wings!*

The ground was silent, and DareWing hung his head in shame.

His wings hung heavy behind him. A burden, not of weight, but of arrogance.

DareWing turned his head slightly so he could regard them. His wings were creations of majesty and beauty, feathered in glossy black, powerful, graceful, the physical manifestation of the Icarii "otherness", the means by which the Icarii believed they were the creatures of the stars.

The Star Dance loved the Icarii for their beauty, and for their ability to fly.

"Wrong," said the ground. "The Star Dance has tolerated your beauty and your flight skills, but it has loved you for other reasons."

"Really?"

"Your inner beauty, which thrives despite your arrogance—"

DareWing winced, and hung his head.

"—as well your courage to dare. You and your people are composed of jewel lights, DareWing. Don't hide them behind your arrogance."

DareWing nodded. Courage, he thought, is not required for what I do now. It is boundless humility.

And so DareWing turned his shoulders, and lifted his arms, and he took hold of one of his wings. He took a deep breath, flexing the powerful flight muscles of chest and shoulder.

Then he tore the wing out.

He screamed, and doubled over, sobbing in agony, still gripping the wing. Blood poured down his back, obscuring the brief glint of bone.

DareWing dug his teeth into his lips, fighting to remain conscious, then he threw the wing aside.

It landed some two paces away, a useless appendage of flesh and feather.

Waves of blackness threatened to consume DareWing, but he fought against them. He took hold of his remaining wing, his hands slipping in the blood from his back, then he steadied himself, his eyes wild, his chest heaving in frantic breaths, and he tore it free.

It fell useless to the ground, and DareWing managed one final scream before the agony tipped him into oblivion.

Faraday knelt by DareWing's side, and her hand tightened its grip on his shoulder. His eyes were wide, staring but unseeing, and his body jerked and jittered as if caught in some crazed, sickened dance.

"Faraday . . ." Leagh said, her voice tight, and she shifted on her chair.

"He will come through this shortly," Faraday said. She paused, and her jaw tightened as if she shared DareWing's pain. "He must."

"Nevertheless," Leagh said, "he needs all of our aid."

She, as Gwendylyr and Goldman, rose from their chairs, circled slowly, then knelt with Faraday. Gwendylyr placed her hand on DareWing's other shoulder, while Leagh and Goldman each took one of the birdman's hands. "We love you," Leagh whispered.

We love you, whispered her voice through DareWing's tortured existence.

All of us, said a different voice, and DareWing realised it was the land itself.

"Really?" he said.

"Really?" DareWing whispered, and his eyes opened and stared into the four faces above him.

"I have relinquished my wings," he said, and smiled.

Faraday returned his smile. "Is that so? Then how is it that they still sprout from your back?"

DareWing jerked in surprise, and rolled so he could see them for himself. "Oh," he said, with such an expression of amazement on his face that his companions laughed.

"DareWing," Goldman said. "Did you realise your ground fever has broken?"

"I am well," DareWing said. "I am well."

And then Leagh gasped, and all looked about. Flowers were spreading over the entire field of bare, ploughed earth, covering the ridges and furrows so completely that no one could see where the plough had been.

"Artor is truly dead," Faraday said, "and we are finally free."

9

Of Predestination and Confrontation

They stood before the seven-sided, white-walled tower and hated.

"It stinks of the Enemy," Sheol said. "Badly."

Qeteb did not speak. He sat his black beast and regarded the tower thoughtfully.

Finally he turned his head slightly to where StarLaughter half-sat, half-crouched on the ground. "Tell me of its nature," he said.

StarLaughter hissed.

Something frightful reached out from Qeteb and sunk deep talons into StarLaughter's mind, and she screamed, writhing amid the dirt.

"*Spiredore!* Its name is Spiredore!"

"You are such a fount of information," Qeteb said. "Mother dear."

The other Demons giggled.

StarLaughter quieted, but her eyes never left Qeteb's form.

She had been a fool to allow this Demon to steal her son! Could she yet save her boy? Was there something to be done that might mean—

"Your son died thousands of years ago," Qeteb said. "Nothing can bring him back. Resign yourself to a worthless and unwanted motherhood, StarLaughter."

Her eyes glinted.

Qeteb took no notice. "Tell me about this tower."

StarLaughter thought about remaining silent, but her lust for revenge had imbued her with a strong sense of self-preservation. She knew Qeteb was now only looking for the merest hint of an excuse to kill her.

Qeteb shifted slightly, and StarLaughter spoke. "Only a very few Icarii have ever been able to use the tower. Its secret was closely guarded."

Sheol muttered irritably, but Qeteb sat his mount silently, waiting.

"Nevertheless . . ." StarLaughter smiled, remembering how powerful she had once been, and how great her destiny was bound to be, "I have eyes with which to observe, and a mind with which to think—"

Mot sniggered.

"—and I believe that the tower will take a person—maybe any who ask it—wherever they wish to go. Even its name points to its actions. It is a spire and it is a door."

Qeteb sat, staring at the Icarii woman, knowing she spoke the truth. A useful piece of Enemy magic, then, he thought, and pondered its implications. Could *he* use it? Perhaps. Was it a trap? Possibly . . . possibly . . .

Could he risk the trap?

He turned his head and regarded the other Demons. He could send one of them . . .

No. Rox was gone—for the moment—and Qeteb did not want to risk the others. Qeteb's eyes flickered over Niah, but she was an impossible choice. Niah had no soul with which to form the question, let alone a desire strong enough to make Spiredore act.

Who else?

Ah, of course! The Midday Demon lifted a mailed hand and beckoned.

A dark shape spiralled down from the sky and alighted before the Demons. It was StarGrace SunSoar.

"Great Father," she said, and bowed before him.

"StarGrace," Qeteb said. "I have a task for you."

StarLaughter looked at StarGrace, looked at Qeteb, and wondered. Would the Hawkchilds join her in exacting a revenge upon Qeteb *(he had stolen her son!)*, or would they remain blind to the Demon's duplicity, and continue to obey him?

StarGrace did not even look at StarLaughter, and bowed her

head as Qeteb spoke to her. Once he had finished, she moved quickly to do his bidding.

And still she did not look at StarLaughter.

StarLaughter's mouth thinned. She was alone, then.

Faraday blinked, and they were standing under a crystal dome in the midst of a field of flowers.

She blinked again, and she was standing with her four companions in an apple orchard in Sanctuary. A movement caught her eyes. It was DareWing, fully healed, stretching his glossy wings in the sun.

He smiled at her, but Faraday noted that the expression in his eyes had changed. No doubt, she thought, the expression in all of their eyes had changed.

"My witches," said a warm, humorous voice, and Faraday's smile widened.

DragonStar rejoined the group from the shade of an apple tree. He regarded them all carefully, and gave each a small nod and a smile, but otherwise made no remark on their final evolution.

What will he do? thought Faraday, and then the next thought sprang almost immediately into her mind. *What will he do with us?*

"Faraday?" said a small voice, and Faraday turned quickly.

Katie ran out from behind the same tree DragonStar had been sheltering under, and Faraday held out her arms and embraced her.

"She will stay with us for the time being," DragonStar said. "But when we venture back into the wasteland it would be safer if she stayed here in Sanctuary."

Thank all stars and gods in existence he isn't going to expose her to danger, Faraday thought, and planted a kiss on the girl's shiny brown curls.

"When do we go back to the wasteland?" DareWing asked, his voice thick with an emotion that Faraday only belatedly realised was the need for revenge.

"We will all need to go back," DragonStar said, "but you and I will return first, DareWing. No, wait, let me speak before you all bombard me with questions. Will you sit? This orchard is secluded enough for us to talk without interruption."

They settled themselves in a circle, Katie resting with her head on Faraday's lap.

As Faraday looked up from Katie, she caught Leagh looking at the girl with an odd expression on her face.

The instant Leagh realised Faraday had seen it she wiped her face clear of any interest in the girl. Katie had her own destiny, as did Leagh's child, and she could do nothing to change either.

Faraday wanted to ask Leagh why she'd looked so at Katie, but before she could speak DragonStar began to talk.

"Tencendor can be reborn," he said, "but it must first be cleared of all its corruption."

"The Demons?" Gwendylyr said. There was a tendril of black hair hanging un-neat across her forehead, and Gwendylyr lifted a hand as if to pat it back into place, but her hand hesitated, then dropped. Gwendylyr left the strand to its own devices.

"Yes," DragonStar said, "but also of all the crazed animals and . . . and . . ."

And the maniacal people crawling about, he almost said, but could not. But even with the thought unspoken, DragonStar could see the knowledge in everyone's eyes anyway.

"Which first?" Goldman said.

DragonStar hesitated, and ran the tip of his tongue over his lips. "Ideally, the Demons first," he eventually said, "but we, you five as well as I, need to be stronger before we can attempt their destruction."

Katie lifted her head at the latter words and stared briefly at DragonStar, then she dropped her face back into Faraday's lap. Her shoulders shuddered slightly.

No-one noticed her reaction, save Faraday, who assumed Katie had shivered with the gentle breeze blowing through the orchard. She pulled a section of her skirt around Katie, far more concerned at DragonStar's words.

Faraday and the other four had shared concerned glances. "Talk to us," Faraday said. "What do you mean?"

DragonStar took a deep breath. "I am StarSon, and Qeteb will be my battle," he said. "But the other Demons—"

"Ah," Goldman said, understanding, "as you will be responsible for Qeteb's destruction, so will each of us be responsible for one of the other Demons."

"Yes. It is preordained. Five of them, five of you."

"But, how can each of us contend with one of the Demons!" Leagh said. Her face was almost panicked, and she'd placed both her hands protectively over her belly. "I can't—"

"Right here and now," DragonStar said, his tone and eyes gentle as he regarded Leagh, "you can't. No, I agree. We need experience and perhaps even some more knowledge before we can dare the Demons. But eventually each of us will have our task to do, and for each of us that task will be a particular Demon."

"But there are only four Demons left," Gwendylyr said, "not counting Qeteb. Sigholt's bridge destroyed Rox—"

"Evil cannot be destroyed," Katie whispered into Faraday's lap, "it can only be transformed."

No-one heard her.

"—so surely that means only four of us need to confront a Demon. Leagh must wait it out in Sanctuary. We can't risk her."

DragonStar looked Gwendylyr steadily in the eyes, and then shifted his gaze to Leagh. "We will all be needed in the wasteland," he said. "Leagh as much as anyone else. Her pregnancy cannot excuse her. And as for Rox, well . . . all I know is what I *feel*. The balance will be restored."

"How?" asked Goldman.

DragonStar lowered his eyes, remembering his long disquiet about Niah, but not knowing *why* he was so disquieted. "Niah," he said. "Niah will become the fifth Demon."

Everyone stilled, dismayed at the thought, and yet instinctively feeling the truth of it.

Niah would become the fifth Demon . . . and yet . . . yet all felt that peculiar, edgy dissatisfaction that DragonStar did.

There was something *else* about Niah. Something else they should all know and understand.

StarGrace entered Spiredore, and hungered. She had been a SunSoar Enchanter once, and heir to the throne, if StarLaughter's child had not survived.

And he hadn't really, had he?

So, theoretically, she—StarGrace—should now be Talon.

If only WolfStar hadn't embarked on his murderous ambition.

WolfStar, WolfStar, WolfStar!

StarGrace ran the name in a litany of hate through her head. WolfStar! When would Qeteb throw them at WolfStar?

Ah! She calmed herself, remembering the instructions Qeteb gave her. There would be time enough for WolfStar.

StarGrace cocked her bird-like head to one side and regarded the interior of the tower. This was the first time she'd ever been inside. During her lifetime in this land only Icarii Enchanter-Talons had been allowed to know Spiredore's secrets.

Above her the tower seemingly rose into infinity in a misfit collection of stairways and crazily-canted balconies. Nothing made sense—no stairways linked to balconies, and no balcony gave way to any room.

There was, apparently, nowhere to go.

Except that Qeteb *had* given her a destination, hadn't he?

"Spiredore," StarGrace said in chirp-like tones that she thought might please the tower, "take me to Tencendor's lost peoples."

And she folded her black wings neatly at her back, and set her clawed feet to the first steps of the stairway that led upwards from the floor of the tower.

"You said that you and I must return first, DragonStar?" DareWing asked.

"Yes," DragonStar said. "For two reasons. One, I need to know if Spiredore is still useful."

"Is it our only link with the Field of Flowers?" Leagh said. She was still trying to come to terms with her spurt of fear at the idea that she'd be needed to battle one of the Demons. Her? What of her child? In what danger would she place it?

"We can only approach the Field through the wasteland that was Tencendor," DragonStar affirmed. "And unless I can find another route, or unless we want to climb the stairs through the Keep, Spiredore is our best way to reach the wasteland. But I don't want to risk everyone in the finding out whether the Demons have penetrated Spiredore yet—"

"Would they manage to enter Sanctuary?" Faraday asked. Gods, if they managed *that* . . . !

"No. They might find out where Sanctuary is, but they will not be able to break through its protective enchantments."

And yet . . . DragonStar's mind was consumed with the impression he'd had when he'd originally seen Sanctuary; it had looked just like one of the worlds the Demons had dragged him through in their leaps through space towards Tencendor.

What if there was a flaw? What if the Demons could find their way in?

Stars! Where would the peoples go then?

DragonStar gave himself a mental shake to get rid of the negative thoughts. The Enemy had built this place, and they'd damn well *meant* it as a Sanctuary against the Demons. They knew what they were doing, didn't they?

"Are you sure?" Faraday asked, and DragonStar sent her a reassuring smile.

"Of course. Now, I want to take DareWing with me," DragonStar turned to the birdman and managed a considerably more genuine smile, "not only for the company, but because there is something I need to show him. Something he, as we, will need in our battle to reclaim the wasteland."

"And that is . . ." DareWing said.

"Your army," DragonStar said, and then laughed at the hungry expression that filled DareWing's face.

10

A Busy Day in Spiredore

ake me to the lost peoples of Tencendor, StarGrace had asked, and Spiredore did. StarGrace walked up a series of stairways, across a myriad of balconies, and eventually Spiredore grew merciful on her aching legs and simmering temper, and led her to a short tunnel of blue mist.

At the end of the tunnel StarGrace could see the milling forms of a score of people, and she laughed.

"Maybe Qeteb will allow me my revenge on WolfStar for this service," she cried, and stepped into the blue-misted tunnel to see just where this new StarSon had hidden the millions of souls the Demons so hungered for.

When she'd almost reached the end of the tunnel, Star-Grace halted and stared, her eyes draining of all their triumph.

Then she snarled. This damned tower had thought to amuse itself at her expense!

Spiredore had indeed led her to the lost peoples of Tencendor . . . but not the *hidden* peoples. Beyond the end of the tunnel StarGrace could discern a cave, and in that cave huddled and whispered and scampered a score of crazed humans. They had torn off (or eaten) their clothes, and now were naked, clothed only in sores and abrasions. Their maddened eyes shifted constantly, and they scratched at themselves and at the others who shifted past them.

"Sssssss!" StarGrace almost fell over in her haste to get back inside Spiredore. Stars alone knew where that cave was, and she didn't want to waste time flying back to Spiredore (and a waiting and impatient Qeteb) to start all over again.

She relaxed slightly as her feet clicked onto the boards of a stairway again, and she halted, and spoke with some aspersion.

"Spiredore, take me to the place where StarSon has hidden the peoples of Tencendor."

And she set her feet to the stairs before her.

"My army?" DareWing said as he and DragonStar walked along the road towards the place where the silvery bridge had once spanned the chasm. DragonStar had left the Star Stallion, the Alaunt and the lizard in Sanctuary, saying he wanted only to risk what was necessary, but he carried the Wolven and its quiver of arrows over his back.

"Who do you think?" DragonStar said.

DareWing frowned, and then a thought so extraordinary occurred to him that he halted, and grabbed DragonStar's shoulder. "But they're *dead*!"

"So were you," DragonStar said, his eyes crinkling with humour.

"The Strike Force," DareWing breathed, his eyes unfocused, his mind remembering the thrill of the hunt through the thermals.

DragonStar nodded.

DareWing refocused his gaze on DragonStar's face. "No wonder you wanted to bring me back as one of your five."

"The Strike Leader. Yes."

DareWing breathed in deeply, filled with such joy he could hardly believe it. The Strike Force!

"But first we must negotiate Spiredore," DragonStar said, "and find out if its stairways are still safe."

They walked the remaining distance to the chasm in silence, and it was only once they were there that DareWing came out of his reverie enough to ask how they were going to get across. "Didn't you use the bridge to cross into Spiredore?"

"Not exactly," DragonStar said. "I used it as a focus for my own enchantment. I don't actually *need* the bridge to cross, but I do need something to focus on in order to return us—" he hesitated slightly over that word, and DareWing glanced sharply at him, "—to this point. But a bridge we do not actually need."

DragonStar reached behind him and drew an arrow out of his quiver. In one powerful movement, he thrust it into the ground before them.

Its blue feathers and its shaft quivered slightly with the residual force of DragonStar's action, then it stood still.

"And so," DragonStar said, unsheathing his sword and drawing the doorway of light, "now Spiredore."

StarGrace climbed higher and higher through the crazy world of Spiredore, her temper increasing with every step.

Where was this tower leading her? She'd climb to the sun before she ever reached a destination!

Suddenly she halted, and her entire body stilled.

There was something *else* in the tower. StarGrace didn't know in what other manner to describe the feeling, only that in the space betwixt one heartbeat and another something else had stepped into Spiredore.

Qeteb? One of the other Demons?

No. This presence had a different feel about it.

There! Above her! StarGrace crouched under an overhang of a balcony and peered upwards.

DragonStar paused in their passage through Spiredore. "It is not as safe as it once was," he said. "We must be careful."

She narrowed her eyes, searching the gloom above, then paused. Two men, one Icarii, one not, walking down a stairwell.

StarGrace almost panicked, for they were coming directly towards her, but just before they turned the curve of stairs that would have brought them face to face, the two men turned into a balcony, and vanished down a tunnel of blue mist.

StarGrace waited a few minutes until she was sure they were gone, then she resumed her climb.

Within two turns of her stairwell, Spiredore presented Star-Grace with another blue-misted tunnel.

They emerged onto a plain blasted with an icy northerly wind. Wind-driven snow stung at their faces and eyes before it hit the ground and disappeared into the numerous cracks and chasms that wove their demented way across the flat, barren surface.

"Where are we?" DareWing gasped, wrapping both arms and wings about himself in a vain attempt at protection against the wind and snow.

DragonStar looked about, as uncomfortable as was Dare-Wing. "Somewhere in the northern Avonsdale Plains, I think. See? Those must be the southern Western Ranges. Or maybe even a bit further west towards the Andeis coast . . . I'm not too sure."

Frankly, DareWing didn't give a damn about their precise location, and wished he hadn't asked. "How will you get us to the Field of Flowers?"

DragonStar turned to look at DareWing. "Oh, *I* am not. I think you should."

"Me? How am I going to do it?"

"Look within yourself, DareWing. You have been in the Field before. You have been through the gate. This time you must open it for yourself."

DareWing tightened his arms, wondering if he would freeze solid in four breaths or five. "Why couldn't you have told me this while we were still in Sanctuary? I could have thought about it before. I could have had it all worked out before we got into this—"

"DareWing. Do it!"

DareWing almost cursed before he realised he'd have to open his mouth and expose himself to more of the freezing air in order to do so. He contented himself with a hard glare in DragonStar's direction, then he concentrated on the problem at hand.

This was the first time since DragonStar had transformed him that he'd been well enough to even contemplate exploring the newly-resurrected Acharite power within himself.

Let alone use it to propel both of them into the Field of Flowers.

"Think," DragonStar whispered underneath the howling wind. "Think . . . what do you remember most about the Field?"

DareWing frowned. Flowers. He remembered flowers. Then he almost smiled, for he remembered the feel of the sun on his back, and the peace of the Field, and then he did smile, for those were things he'd enjoy feeling right now.

Instantly he was overwhelmed with the scent of the billions upon billions of flowers that existed within the Field, and then they were there.

DareWing leaned back his head and laughed.

StarGrace smirked. She stood at the edge of the blue-misted tunnel, still safe within Spiredore's power. Beyond her lay a chasm, and beyond the chasm a road wended its way through a plain dotted liberally with flowering shrubs. Far away rose a line of blue and purple mountains, cradling the entrance of a valley. With her powerful sight, StarGrace could see the shapes of Icarii spiralling above the valley entrance.

The hidden souls had been found.

Her smiled widened momentarily, then she stepped back into Spiredore.

"See," said DragonStar, and from the infinite sky above them floated down DareWing's warriors.

The Strike Force, and yet not.

That these warriors were Icarii was easy enough to see, for together with their human bodies they had the wings and the chiselled facial features of the Icarii.

And yet they had been changed. Every one of them had wings of a different colour—purple wings, another bronze, yet another gold, until all the shades of the rainbow had been represented—and each warrior had jewel-coloured eyes that matched the particular shade of his or her wings.

But it was their bodies that were the most amazing. Every one of them was diaphanous, almost completely translucent. They glowed with a silvery hue, and as they floated down by the score the outlines of individual bodies were lost in the collective rainbow-coloured shimmer of wings and flashing eyes.

DareWing had never seen anything so beautiful, nor so deadly. Each warrior's eyes shone brilliant with determination, with anger, with the need for the fight.

"Your Strike Force," said DragonStar, awed himself. "My vanguard."

"What do you want us to do?" DareWing said. His eyes had not left the milling hue before him.

"I want you to fight for me," said DragonStar softly, and a great cry went up from the massed warriors.

Qeteb leaned over the saddle of his beast and laughed. "It was that easy?"

StarGrace inclined her head.

"That tower will lead us straight to the huddled masses?"

StarGrace waved a hand about languidly. "Almost instantly."

"There *must* be a trap somewhere," Sheol muttered. "It can't be this straightforward!"

"The tower is a simple thing," StarGrace said. "It does as it is bid."

Qeteb sat and thought. It *was* too easy, but he wasn't sure where the difficulty would be: in their use of Spiredore, or in their attempts to reach the crowd of souls awaiting their appetites across the chasm.

"There is something else," StarGrace said, and Qeteb jerked out of his reverie.

"Yes?"

StarGrace told them of the two men she'd seen pass briefly through the tower.

Qeteb stared at her, then grinned. "We have them," he whispered, and the whisper reached into every corner of the land. "Not this hour, or even this day, but we will eventually have them."

He laughed, and then waved his fellow Demons through the door into Spiredore. As they entered, Qeteb turned and thrust his fist towards StarLaughter.

"Stay here, bitch," he said, "because if you are not here when I return, I will hunt you down and stake your naked body out on the wasteland for the dogs and boars to couple with."

"Stay here," DragonStar said, "until I need you."

DareWing raised one black eyebrow.

"Something is not right with Spiredore," DragonStar continued, "and I would rather not risk you. You will be safe enough—more than safe!—within the Field of Flowers."

"When will you call me?"

DragonStar shrugged. "When the time is right, my friend. What else can I say?"

"Be careful," DareWing said, and DragonStar nodded, letting his eyes drift over the shifting throng of silvery bodies before him, before giving DareWing a perfunctory smile.

Then he turned to one side, drew the glowing doorway, and stepped through into Spiredore.

DareWing stared at the spot where he'd vanished, then furrowed his brow thoughtfully. Surely he would be able to move back into the wasteland in the same manner he'd moved into the Field? To imagine the environment, the sensations, the smells? Then, of course, he'd be able to transfer back here whenever the need arose.

In the meantime, his band of glinting warriors could be what they'd trained for in their previous lifetimes: a Strike Force.

"Let me prepare the way for you, StarSon," DareWing whispered.

DragonStar knew the instant he stepped into Spiredore that he'd transferred into crisis.

When he and DareWing had come through previously,

DragonStar had felt a wrongness within the tower, but it had been nothing compared to this.

And he knew precisely what it was, for he had felt this before.

Qeteb.

DragonStar felt both terror and perfect stillness at the same time. Terror, because that was what Qeteb dealt in and what his entire fabric of being was, and again terror because DragonStar knew that currently he was no match for Qeteb—not for a one on one confrontation. He needed further thought, a knowledge of Katie's Enchanted Song Book, and far more experience before he could possibly confront Qeteb.

Qeteb was too malevolent for him right now.

And DragonStar felt a perfect stillness because he was almost relieved to at least *know* that the Demons could use Spiredore. He could not be trapped now that he knew.

Unless they trapped him right now.

DragonStar knew he should transfer immediately into Sanctuary, but he edged closer to the balustrade of his balcony and peered over.

Far below him a mass of black wound its way upward. As he watched, the leading figure stopped, and raised up his black metalled head.

StarSon!

DragonStar felt the power of a frightful malevolence (*hate, envy, despair, pestilence*) surge towards him.

"Spiredore," he snapped, without any thought, "take that power and vent it elsewhere!"

And far to the north a group of icebergs exploded as Spiredore redirected the power.

Clever, StarSon, Qeteb whispered towards him. *But how pitiful that you needed Spiredore to deal with that for you. Are you so weak?*

DragonStar backed away from the balcony.

Are you so weak, StarSon?

He backed against a wall, and listened to the taunts flow upwards.

Are you weak that you need others to protect you, StarSon?

DragonStar drew his sword—

Pitiful little StarSon. A chorus of laughter and howls echoed up the stairwell.

Pitiful little StarSon.

—and drew the doorway of light, hating the relief that flowed through his body as he stepped through.

DragonStar stopped by the blue-feathered arrow that he'd earlier stuck in the edge of the chasm, letting his shoulders slump in relief—and a feeling that he thought might be self-disgust. Had he been afraid?

He sheathed his sword, then flexed his hand, trying to work out some of his tension.

He needed to get back into Sanctuary, think about—

"StarSon! How nice to see you again so soon!" A mocking laugh followed the words.

DragonStar whipped about and stared across the chasm. Six black beasts, gruesome in their constantly shifting, fluid forms, stood on the other side. Behind them stretched one of Spiredore's blue-misted tunnels.

On the backs of the beasts were the Demons, as well the woman that DragonStar supposed was Niah reborn.

Qeteb—it could be no-one else—had edged his beast slightly forward. He was a vile creature, black metal armour encasing his entire form, and even plating his wings.

He was massive, at least half as tall again as the tallest man, and with a thickness of figure to match.

"Why not step across, Qeteb?" DragonStar called. "I am here. Reach me if you can."

Qeteb's laughter floated across the chasm. "You know as well as I that I cannot broach the enchantments that protect this—what do you call it?—ah yes, this Sanctuary."

DragonStar allowed a wave of relief to wash over him.

"But do not rejoice too soon," Qeteb continued, "for I surely see that all I need is a key, and I have all the time in creation in which to find it. Wait for me, DragonStar, and I will join you."

Again he laughed, a sound of genuine amusement rather

than forced maliciousness, and DragonStar tore his gaze away from the hypnotic figure of Qeteb and looked at Niah.

Again he had the strongest feeling that there was something so infinitely dangerous about her that, of all those in the group across the chasm, including Qeteb, she would prove the most formidable foe.

But then one of the black beasts shifted and snorted, and the spell was broken. DragonStar gave Qeteb one last stare, then turned his back and walked as slowly and as nonchalantly as he could into Sanctuary.

"Well?" said Sheol.

"He is still weak," Qeteb said, "and we must not give him the time to grow more powerful."

"How?" said Barzula.

Qeteb let his eyes roam over the enchantments that protected Sanctuary.

"They have been made, and they can be unmade," he said. "And all I need do is find the key."

Neither the Demons nor DragonStar realised that there was another observer.

Isfrael, hidden within a small stand of trees just before the entrance to Sanctuary. His eyesight and hearing were as keen as those of all Avar, and he'd witnessed and heard the entire exchange.

He stood and watched thoughtfully as the Demons swung their black mounts about and returned into Spiredore.

They were evil, Isfrael knew, and he loathed them before anything else in his life, but Isfrael had a burning ambition and that was to regain his rightful place at the head of the Avar.

The Demons were vile, worse than vile, but maybe they could be used.

They could help him into what Isfrael coveted more than anything else: the Sacred Groves. In the Sacred Groves Isfrael could regain his standing. Faraday would be nothing if Isfrael controlled the Sacred Groves.

The Avar would come back to him then.

But if he wanted the Demons to aid him, then Isfrael would need something. Information, perhaps, to exchange. And information good enough to enable Isfrael to navigate safely the hazards of demonic negotiations.

What? What would the Demons want?

Souls. They wanted souls. It is what gave them power.

So what might deliver more souls into the hands of the Demons? Isfrael grinned to himself. Sanctuary would. The Demons needed the key to Sanctuary.

Now all he needed to do was find it himself.

Isfrael turned and walked into Sanctuary, turning thoughts over and over in his mind. The Demons could be used—but it would be more than dangerous. And was he ready to risk everyone in Sanctuary?

Yes! Yes! But only if he could manage to get the Avar out before the Demons gobbled up everyone else within this pastel prison.

Isfrael's steps slowed as he contemplated the Avar safe forever within the Sacred Groves: no axes, no damned Icarii arrogance, and no Faraday to destroy his power.

11

StarLaughter

StarLaughter was far too insane to be intimidated by Qeteb's threat.

She stood as Qeteb stepped into the tower, the door closing behind him, and then she slowly turned and stared across the bleak wasteland to the east.

A cold and heartless, soulless, loveless desert. A frigid wind blew dust balls red with sparks and flames over the crazily-cracked surface of the ground. No vegetation survived, save for the occasional malodorous and cancerous versions of small shrubs and isolated grain stalks: weeping, fleshy lumps grew down their stalks and stems. Creatures—of both animal and humanoid origins—crept about its surface, whispering and wailing, digging claws in themselves and in whoever approached, copulating with rocks, and eating dust.

But the violent, twisting landscape of StarLaughter's mind was far more desolate than this nightmare which stretched before her.

She stood, and she stared, and even the occasional crazed creature that paused to nibble at her ankles did not distract her.

StarLaughter was alone. That thought dominated her mind.

She was alone. The Demons had abandoned her. The Hawkchilds had abandoned her.

Even, if Qeteb was to be believed, her son had abandoned her.

No! No! She must not let herself think that!

StarLaughter shuddered, and she moaned, a small rope of dribble escaping her lips.

The Demons had stolen her son, and there was no-one left who could help her.

How many thousands of years had she quested, believing the Demons' lies when they said they would help her gain revenge for her and her son's deaths? How much power, aid and advice had she given the Demons, thinking they would help her? Thinking they believed her? *Thinking that they had loved her?*

"And all they did was betray me," she whispered.

And all the while laughing at her behind her back?

StarLaughter screamed, her body jerking in a fit of madness.

"They stole my son!" she finally managed to wail. "They stole my son!"

She collapsed onto the ground again, writhing and moaning in misery amid the dirt. She was so alone; no-one to help her, no-one to understand the depth of betrayal she had suffered, no-one who would understand the depth of maternal grief she felt, no-one who could help her rescue her son from Qeteb's metalled madnesses.

That her son still somehow existed within Qeteb Star-Laughter had no doubts.

All she had to do was rescue him . . . somehow.

But there was no-one to help her! No-one who could understand—

Suddenly StarLaughter stilled, her eyes crazed with hope, and her dribbling mouth opened in a circle of amazement that she hadn't thought of this before.

Yes . . . yes, there was one who could understand her, wasn't there! There *was* one who would help her!

StarLaughter giggled, the pure joy of hope (mad, mad hope) suffusing her being, and she clambered to her feet again.

WolfStar!

Gone from her mind were the thousands of years lusting for revenge against him.

Gone was her hatred of him.

Gone was any sane thought that WolfStar was highly unlikely to want to have anything to do with her.

Instead, StarLaughter's mind embraced memories warped by her madness into untruths.

WolfStar, years older than her, tenderly playing with her when she'd been a toddler.

WolfStar, desperately in love with her (although, sweet fool, he would never admit it to her), teaching her to fly when her wings had first emerged.

WolfStar, unable to keep his raging desire under control any longer, seducing her when she'd been but eleven.

StarLaughter trembled, and laughed softly. He'd never been able to deny his love for her!

He'd been so powerful, so commanding, and StarLaughter knew the entire Icarii race had envied her when she'd married him.

How lucky WolfStar had been! StarLaughter knew she'd been the perfect wife for him, her beauty and power complementing WolfStar's own attractions and abilities.

And *how* she had helped him! WolfStar's lust for the throne had been more than matched by StarLaughter's own desire for power. She had been the one to suggest the murder of Wolf-Star's father, StarKnight.

She had been the one to fire the arrow that sent StarKnight tumbling out of the sky.

And for the throne that she helped him take, WolfStar had loved her.

He'd adored her!

StarLaughter *knew* that even now adoration could not be very far beneath the surface of WolfStar's sneers and outward contempt.

No, WolfStar still loved her, and WolfStar would aid her in the rescue of their son.

After all, wasn't it his son who'd been stolen as well?

And hadn't he adored his son, and adored her for conceiving him?

StarLaughter's face softened into something resembling love as she stared blank-eyed into the wasted landscape. How wrong she'd been to seek revenge on WolfStar. She'd always adored him, she could understand that now, and it would take but a little effort on her part to make WolfStar understand that he still adored her.

"We are SunSoar lovers, you and I," she whispered, one hand clutching at the tattered blue robe above her breasts. "One being, one soul. Nothing can keep us apart. Nothing."

And on these twisted thoughts, StarLaughter built hope.

"I have to get away from Qeteb," StarLaughter said, at what seemed like hours later. "And then find WolfStar. Oh, how happy he will be to see me!"

She jerked her eyes around the land, seeking answers. Where could she go? Where would be safe from Qeteb?

"*I* know the nooks and crannies of this land better than any Demon," she whispered, and then she nodded slightly. Yes, she knew a place to hide. A place that felt right. A place that called her.

But it would take her a while to get there . . . unless . . .

She turned her head and regarded Spiredore thoughtfully.

12

The Key to Sanctuary

Faraday and Gwendylyr were wandering through an orchard of green apples and cotton trees laden with pale pink and blue flowers. With them walked Azhure and two of the Star Gods, Pors and Silton. They were chatting about DragonStar, and what had happened in something called the crystal dome, but the man who observed them did not care to listen as closely as he could have.

Isfrael had other things to think about, and other deeds to be done. He stood unobserved and watched the walkers for a short while, then he slipped silently away amid the thickness of the heavily-laden boughs of the cotton trees.

Their beauty and scent left him unmoved.

Isfrael had no qualms about what he was going to do. He did not think of it so much as a betrayal or a treachery, but as an inevitability. Sanctuary was bound to crumple before the power of the Demons at some stage or the other, and whether or not Isfrael speeded up the process was immaterial.

What was important was regaining his position at the head of the Avar, managing to exclude Faraday (didn't the Avar realise that the time of their precious Tree Friend was well and truly over?) once and for all, and managing to save the Avar from the inevitable destruction of Sanctuary.

Isfrael wanted the forests, he wanted his position as Mage-King back, and he wanted the Avar to be safe forever from the axes and arrogance of the other two humanoid races. There was only one place left in this existence where he could accomplish this.

The Sacred Groves.

There the Mother still dwelt, there the trees grew thick and magical, there the Horned Ones still walked in power.

There, Isfrael could regain his place.

And perhaps . . . perhaps Shra's soul had found its way there when she'd died.

"Hello," a gentle voice said behind him. "I often come here to think as well. It is a place of great beauty and contentment, is it not?"

Isfrael whipped about, only barely managing to suppress a snarl of irritation.

Leagh stood there, her distended belly making her virginal white linen gown look ridiculous, and her brown hair tumbling down about her shoulders and back as if she was trying to pretend to be a Bane (how dare she!). Her eyes, the only part of her that demonstrated some sense, revealed her trepidation.

She actually seemed to be waiting for a response, so Isfrael glanced about him. They were standing in a small glade, a waterfall and rock pool to one side, and wildflowers spreading in drifts through the short grasses of the open space.

"It's lovely," he said, and forced a smile.

Leagh relaxed a little, and she indicated a small pile of smooth-backed rocks beside the pool. "Will you sit with me a while? I have not had a chance to talk to you before."

That is because you are a plains dweller and have not been welcomed in my forests, thought Isfrael, but he sat anyway.

Leagh began to chat about innocuous pleasantries, and Isfrael replied in monosyllables whenever she paused for an answer. By the Horned Ones, she actually seemed to be enjoying herself in this pastelised version of the real, vibrant world! Isfrael would have got up and left—this woman was more than annoying—but some part of him wondered if she might have some information that could help him achieve his ends.

After all, wasn't she close to DragonStar? Might she not know something that had been kept hidden from everyone else?

Once he'd thought of that, Isfrael paid more attention to Leagh herself. He began to reply more pleasantly, leading the conversation himself, making the woman laugh with some of his tales of life in Minstrelsea.

And Isfrael reaped rewards for his pains. After a short while Isfrael realised that there was something profoundly unusual about Leagh. She was not just a "plains dweller"; she was far more. In fact, the way she moved, her smile, and the shift of her eyes made Isfrael realise that an intriguing power played beneath the surface of her outwardly pleasant demeanour.

Leagh was as powerful, if not more so, than any of the Avar Banes had been!

But how could this be so? The Acharites had no access to power, had they?

Very gradually, and as carefully as he could, Isfrael started to redirect the conversation. He cloaked himself in an aura of innocuousness—

Aren't the horns growing from my forehead cute? See the cloth of twigs that cloak my loins: isn't that the most naively rural thing you ever saw? See my discomfort regarding my mother, Faraday: doesn't that make you want to hug me and make it all better?

—and harvested the prize, for Leagh lost whatever initial caution she'd had, and talked and laughed freely with him.

Yes, she had power now. Woken by DragonStar, although every Acharite had the potential for such power within them.

"What do you mean?" said Isfrael, furrowing his brow in muddled puzzlement.

"Well," said Leagh, and she told him of the original Enchantress, Urbeth—

"Urbeth!" Isfrael said, truly shocked. "Urbeth?"

"Yes! Isn't it amazing? Well . . ." Leagh told him of Urbeth's three sons. One had founded the Icarii race.

"And fathered by a sparrow, Isfrael!" Leagh said, laughing. "Can you imagine the affront to the proud Icarii?"

Another son had founded the Charonite race.

"And the third?"

"Urbeth sent the eldest son from her home, because he denied his own magic and his own potential. This son was fathered by the man she loved the most. Isfrael, you will never guess who it was!"

Isfrael wondered if this agonising process would proceed faster if he twisted his hands about her throat and physically forced the words out.

But he smiled congenially, and forced a pleasant bewilderment across his face. "No, I cannot. Tell me."

"Noah did!"

"Noah?"

So then Leagh told Isfrael about the Enemy, and their battle many millennia ago against the Demons. Having trapped and dismembered Qeteb, they then sent his life parts across the universe in a fleet of craft. When the four craft crashed on Tencendor, creating the four Sacred Lakes, only one of the Enemy survived: Noah.

"And he met Urbeth, and fathered the eldest son. But this son denied his magic, and when he founded the Acharite race, they not only suppressed their magic, they relentlessly hunted down all other wielders of magic."

Isfrael kept his face bland, although internally he seethed with fury. The Acharites and their axes had hounded and slaughtered his people for over a thousand years.

"And so all Acharites can use their power?"

And as he said that, Isfrael suddenly realised why this information was so vitally important. Sanctuary was a construction of the Enemy, or of their remnant power within the land . . . and the magic of the Acharites was the magic of the Enemy. By the Sacred Groves . . . was this what he'd been seeking?

As he thought that, Leagh gave him the final element.

"No. Acharites cannot use their magic unless they can return through death."

"What do you mean?"

"We've all suppressed our power so assiduously that only death can free it. Faraday, myself, Gwendylyr, Goldman, and even DareWing, who has ancient Acharite blood in him, can use the power because we have been through death, and have been recreated."

Isfrael nodded, and said a few more polite words, but he was not ungrateful when Leagh sighed and said she'd return to her apartment for a nap. "And to see Zared, who mopes about unbearably in this place."

Leagh smiled apologetically. "He is a man who thrives on the *doing*, not on the *waiting*."

Isfrael nodded, and let the woman walk away.

Was this the information he could trade for his freedom to get to the Sacred Groves? Almost . . . almost . . . but how could the Demons use it?

And then Isfrael remembered the soulless automat that the Demons had with them, and he laughed triumphantly.

He had the key!

Now all he had to do was get out of Sanctuary.

13

Hidden Conversations

Sometimes the most insanely unhinged of people manage to assume the demeanour of the coldly logical, and so it was with StarLaughter. She had her purpose—as madly illogical as it might seem to anyone else—and purpose gave her the appearance of sanity.

She stared thoughtfully towards Spiredore, her now composed face wiped free of any remaining spittle. Then, making up her mind, StarLaughter walked confidently back to Spiredore, its white-walled towers still gleaming incongruously in the devastated landscape.

"Pray to every star in existence I have the time to do what I must," she muttered, and then tossed her head at a low-flying mind-maddened egret. She smiled at it; one could not be sure these days, among this horde of demented livestock, of which reported directly to the Demons and which just eddied about in chaotic dementia, and StarLaughter knew she had to be careful.

After all, wasn't almost everyone in this devastated world plotting against her?

A hand grasped her ankle, and StarLaughter shrieked and tried to jerk herself free.

The hand tightened, and StarLaughter gave in to an instant of uncontrolled panic.

Only for an instant, as she realised who held her.

"WolfStar," she cried, almost unable to grasp her good fortune. This was a sign from the Stars themselves!

WolfStar completely missed the momentary joy that swept across StarLaughter's face. His fingers tightened fractionally about her ankle. "I can feel your heartbeat thudding through your veins," he whispered. "Did I surprise you?"

She pulled herself free—she would allow no-one to bind her again, not even WolfStar—and stepped back. Her husband was a mess; his body was covered in bruises, abrasions and weeping scabs. Clotting blood besmeared his chest and belly, and streaked his face and hands. StarLaughter thought he should at least make the attempt to wipe it off.

Almost as if he'd read her mind, WolfStar absently wiped a hand across his chest, and flicked some of the blood away.

It made no difference.

"Why are you still here?" StarLaughter said. "I thought you might have made good your escape by now."

But she knew why he was still here, didn't she? Destiny had meant him to find her. One of her hands twitched, half-extended itself towards WolfStar, then dropped.

"Who is it?" he hissed, making an unsuccessful grab at the hem of her tattered gown.

"What?" Surely he recognised her!

"Who still controls the enchantment in this Star-forsaken land?" WolfStar said. *"Why is there still enchantment about?"*

StarLaughter chewed her lip, wondering if WolfStar's experiences had left him slightly deranged.

"Tell me!" WolfStar shouted, managing to grab her ankle again and pull her over.

She fell atop him, puzzlement replaced with anger, and drove her fist into his belly.

WolfStar cried out and let her go, curling up into a ball and sobbing with agony.

"You are a fool!" StarLaughter said, finally understanding what WolfStar was on about. She scrabbled back to her feet, making sure that this time she retreated to a non-grabbable distance. "You backed Caelum, didn't you? You thought he was the one to defeat Qeteb, didn't you? Ha! *He* was not the StarSon."

"What?" WolfStar said, rolling over and staring at her. "Who is?"

She smirked, revelling in the knowledge that WolfStar needed her. "Think I am going to tell you? I—"

"Who?"

Something howled far to the north, and StarLaughter looked toward Spiredore anxiously. "The Demons will be back soon," she said. "We must be gone by then."

WolfStar gave a harsh bark of laughter. "Have you fallen out with them, my beloved? Have they not given you what you wanted? Have—"

Exasperated, StarLaughter threw caution to the wind and stepped close, leaning down to grab WolfStar by the hair. She gave his head a wrench.

"Shut up! Do you want to live? Do you want to stop the Demons?"

"Are you trying to tell *me*," WolfStar whispered, "that their destruction is what *you* want?"

She stared flatly at him. "They betrayed me," she said.

"Goodness," he said. "How utterly surprising."

StarLaughter pursed her lips, but let his sarcasm pass. "If you come with me," she said, "I will tell you who the true StarSon is, who controls the enchantment left in this land, and I will tell you where he is."

And for all this, she thought, *you will love me and aid me.* StarLaughter's face softened at the thought, and she half-smiled.

WolfStar's only response was a raised eyebrow. The bitch was mad!

"You *bastard*," StarLaughter said. "Would you lie there until the Demons ride their beasts over you? Would you lie here until the north winds finally rob your desiccated flesh of its last drop of moisture? Would you lie here until—"

"It seems," he said, "that at the very least I must lie here until you purge yourself of every last stored curse of the last four thousand years."

She threw his head back until his skull cracked on the cold-baked earth. "You are worse than a fool, WolfStar." She took a deep breath, then leaned down and grabbed his hair again. "Praise every star that exists that the Demons have not yet thought to rob me of the scrap of power they condescended to give me."

And she began to haul WolfStar effortlessly towards Spiredore, WolfStar howling with rage and frustration and agony the entire way.

StarLaughter paused in the atrium of Spiredore and looked carefully about. Then she cocked her head and listened.

Nothing.

WolfStar still hung from her hand, very slowly unwinding himself from the defensive huddle he'd been forced to assume when she'd dragged him inside the tower.

What in curses' name was she doing?

StarLaughter ignored WolfStar's almost inaudible mutterings and groans, concentrating instead on the silence of the tower rising above her. Should she risk it?

Ah, but what choice did she have! None! And WolfStar even less.

"Spiredore," she said. "We would go to the northern Icescarp Alps." And StarLaughter placed her foot on the first of the steps, and walked upwards.

WolfStar screamed as she dragged him effortlessly after her and the edge of the first step dug into his ribs and then his hip.

Within a few steps StarLaughter increased her gait to a trot, giving Wolf-Star's head an impatient twist to shut him up.

Qeteb raged when he emerged from Spiredore to find Star-Laughter gone. Not because he was in any manner frightened of her, or even because he needed her, but because she had disobeyed him.

She had *flaunted* him, and no-one did that and lived to enjoy their small rebellion.

"Sense her!" he hissed to the other Demons, and they sent their senses scrying over the entire land.

Nothing.

Then Qeteb sent his far sight and his power raging over the land. Where? Where? Where?

But wherever it was, StarLaughter had managed to evade him.

How? She had no magic that could withstand his!

Where?

Furious, Qeteb sent firestorms tumbling about Tencendor. They ravaged from the Murkle Mountains to the Nordra, and from the Minaret Peaks to the cliffs of Widewall Bay. Sheets of ice fell from the sky, and impaled creatures as they scrambled to avoid the fireballs. Molten earth spurted in great gouts from the chasms that wound over Tencendor.

And even this did not flush forth StarLaughter, nor reveal her presence.

Qeteb slid down from his beast, strode over to Barzula, and hauled him from his mount to the ground.

He sent a furious armoured foot booting into the Demon's abdomen. *"Where is she?"*

"I do not know, Great Father!" Barzula screamed.

"Where is she?" Qeteb roared as he punched Sheol in her throat, sending her to the ground as well.

"I do not know, Great Father!"

"Why did you not kill her?" Qeteb bellowed.

All four Demons now huddled on the ground, their faces pressed into the dirt.

"We thought you might like to play with her," Sheol eventually whispered.

Qeteb fell silent, regarding his Demons.

"Get up," he said, and turned away, staring into the northern distance. StarLaughter had escaped very far away, and that probably meant north. But not only had she escaped, she had somehow managed to cloak herself from his power, and that Qeteb did not like at all.

She should not know how to do that . . . and if she had found the means to do so, it meant that there was still some secrets left in this land that Qeteb did not understand.

Secrets probably powered with the knowledge of the Enemy.

"It should not be so," the Midday Demon whispered to himself. "Haven't I ravaged this land completely?"

But even as he said it, Qeteb knew that his power was not yet absolute. The power of the Enemy continued to linger within the land—the Sanctuary was the perfect example of such power—and until the StarSon was dead, Qeteb could not destroy it completely.

He looked skywards, and beckoned. "My lovely," he said. "I would speak with you."

StarGrace spiralled down from the sky.

"I need you to hunt," said Qeteb.

Spiredore deposited StarLaughter and WolfStar in a world that was different to the one immediately about the Maze and Spiredore, but that was, nevertheless, substantially the same.

StarLaughter stood and stared, smiling and seemingly uncaring for the moment that WolfStar lay crumpled and semiconscious at her feet.

The trip through Spiredore (or, rather, the journey up its sharp-edged stairs) had not been kind to him.

StarLaughter let him be for the moment, allowing her eyes and senses to absorb the scenery. The Icescarp mountains had always been frigid and barren, picked clean by the icy winds that whistled over the northern Iskruel Ocean and through every blackened crevice of the ranges. But before Qeteb had wasted the land, the mountains had always seemed alive . . . almost as if warmth smouldered under their cold, hard skin, and all one had to do was find the way down through the crevices to reach it.

Then, of course, the Icarii had made their home in the mountains. Talon Spike had been the greatest mountain of all, and the Icarii had gradually tunnelled and chiselled away its interior to create living spaces in which to enjoy their exile from the southern lands.

When she and WolfStar had plotted and hungered their way through murder and into destruction, Talon Spike had been a place of refuge and haunting beauty. Most of it had been excavated even then . . . and StarLaughter had actually grown up inside the mountain rather than in the southern Minaret Peaks. Her mother, CoalStar, had preferred the views and the scent of the ocean winds amongst the Peaks.

StarLaughter knew many of Talon Spike's secrets, and although she'd known the mountain had crumpled when Qeteb sent his destruction rippling over the land, she hoped that the one secret she needed to hide from the Demon had remained safe and intact.

And so it had.

The cellars and basements of Talon Spike—StarLaughter was unaware that Axis and Azhure had renamed the mountain Star Finger—were places of great enchantment. StarLaughter did not know the details, but she did know that the basements of Talon Spike were protected by wards to deflect the power of enemies who sought those Icarii who sheltered within.

If the enchantments still existed, they would protect her—StarLaughter hoped—from the Demons' power. Oh, the Demons would surely hunt for her, but they would not do it themselves. The Demons were obsessed with the hunt for the StarSon, and so Qeteb would set the Hawkchilds to Star-Laughter's discovery.

And that suited StarLaughter's logically-maddened plan perfectly.

They'd emerged from Spiredore's blue tunnel at the northern foot of Talon Spike. Of the mountain, only the lower third remained: the top portions lay over nearby peaks and in valleys in great, black, jagged boulders. StarLaughter looked about the area where she stood; it was pebbly, slick with ice and crisscrossed with cracks and chasms, but it was navigable nevertheless. Here had once wound a great glacier, but that had exploded into billions of deadly ice shards during Qeteb's rape of the land, and the shards had dispersed over the entire Alps.

Now, the hidden tunnels into the mountain's basements were revealed.

StarLaughter grinned, and dragged WolfStar towards the entrance to a tunnel slightly to the east.

After three steps, WolfStar finally managed to wrench himself free with a mighty effort.

"You cold-souled *bitch*!" he cried, his breath frosting in the air. "What are you doing now?"

"Trying to save your life," she said, leaning down to grab him once again. "You'll thank me for it soon enough."

WolfStar laughed, hard and bitter. "And doubtless you also work to save Tencendor from the Demons."

"There are better things for us to save than the damned land." *Don't you hear our son screaming for us to save him? Don't you hear him, WolfStar?*

"You were ever the traitor, StarLaughter. That is the one thing you cannot betray."

She straightened, and stared at him. Her face was inscrutable. "We loved each other once."

"It was a lie. We never loved each other. We only used each other."

She refused to hear his words. "We can love each other again."

"Have you gone *mad*?" WolfStar rolled over a little, laughing at his unintentional joke, and managed to get to his feet.

"Good," StarLaughter said. "You can walk. Now I won't have to drag you."

"I can walk away from *you,* you treacherous whore," WolfStar whispered, and he gave a sudden, great lurch to the edge of a chasm.

"No!" StarLaughter screamed, and lunged for him, but it was too late.

"You'll never get your claws into my soul again," WolfStar said, and stepped off the edge.

StarLaughter dropped to her knees, her wings rising behind her. Surely she could haul him out!

But the gap was too narrow. WolfStar had fallen into a chasm less than two arm-spans wide, and while it was wide enough to gobble him up, it was not wide enough to give StarLaughter room to manoeuvre her wings in order to effect a rescue.

The chasm dropped to unknowable depths, black rock slicked with ice, and there was no sign of WolfStar save for a smear of blood on a rock some two paces down.

StarLaughter stared, and then laughed, sending it ringing down the chasm. "You might think to escape me, or think to fool me into believing you dead, WolfStar," she shouted, "but your efforts are wasted. Our love is destined!"

And then she lifted her head, and glanced at the sky. The laughter died from her face, and she got to her feet, slipping very slightly on the ice, and turned towards the tunnel entrance. WolfStar had escaped for the moment, but StarLaughter knew that Fate would ensure their paths crossed again.

After all, weren't they meant to enjoy a destiny together?

An instant's hesitation, then StarLaughter ran inside the tunnel, wondering if, at the least, she might find a cloak left over from the Icarii's residency.

The Hawkchilds soared in a great black cloud in the thermals that rose from the central plain of the wasteland. They had been set to the hunt, and they revelled in it.

Save . . . save for the object of the hunt. Like StarLaughter had once done, the Hawkchilds had given their allegiance to the Questors in return for power and an entry back into the world they'd been tipped from.

Like StarLaughter had once been driven, the Hawkchilds were driven by one necessity: revenge on WolfStar. If the Questors—the Demons—gave them power, well and good. The Hawkchilds were grateful and they would do the Demons' bidding.

So long as their bidding did not interfere with the great quest for revenge, and so long as they were not required to hunt one of their own.

And the Hawkchilds still regarded StarLaughter as one of their own: they had not learnt of the shift in her priorities, or of the deeper madnesses that had claimed her mind.

Nevertheless, they did as Qeteb ordered and rose on the thermals before separating in a dozen different directions. They would find StarLaughter, but for their own purposes, not Qeteb's.

StarLaughter walked through the corridors of the deep underground interior of Talon Spike. Some sections of the corridors had crumbled when the top of the mountain had exploded, and the rubble forced StarLaughter to sometimes scramble over it, and sometimes detour through alternative hallways.

This was not the Talon Spike she remembered.

In her time the Icarii had used Talon Spike mainly as a summer retreat, a pleasure palace. Consequently, the very fabric of the mountain had been consecrated to the pursuits of pleasure: seduction nests, silken spaces for sleeping, great soaring halls for singing and flight dances. Even the walls had been steeped in music and laughter.

Now all was grey and silent. StarLaughter realised that this was largely due to the cessation of the Star Dance—the Icarii had breathed life into the mountain almost exclusively through the enchantments they'd woven from the Star Dance—but she could also see that Talon Spike had been put to a more sober purpose over past times.

She passed chambers that were more ascetic than luxurious—and what Icarii ever enjoyed asceticism? She walked into some of the lower halls that were filled with stacks of books and parchments, rather than silken banners and musical instruments. She glanced through sleeping chambers that had beds designed for one (for *one*!) rather than two.

StarLaughter paused in the doorway of one chamber and shuddered. It looked almost as if . . . as if the mountain had

been used as a centre of learning and study rather than pleasure!

"Well, at least Qeteb did nothing but good here when he destroyed," she muttered, continuing on down the corridor.
"Learning! What had come over the Icarii!"

Despite the depressing degree of soberness and asceticism,
StarLaughter finally found what she'd been looking for in a
chamber only two levels above the basement: a chest of silken
wraps. She sighed with pleasure as she lifted out a scarlet robe
edged with beaten gold, and she hastily shed her tattered and
bloodstained blue robe and put on the scarlet one.

StarLaughter wasn't sure how her blue robe had got so be-
fouled, nor why she'd allowed herself to continue wearing it
for so long.

There was a mirror to one side and StarLaughter stood con-
tentedly and preened, smoothing the material over her body,
twisting this way and that in admiration.

How many birdmen had lusted after this body? WolfStar
certainly, and StarLaughter knew that many other birdmen
had wanted her as well. Had she ever indulged any of their
lustings? StarLaughter's brow creased. No. No, she hadn't . . .
had she? She'd always been true to WolfStar.

That's why Fate would bind them together again.

StarLaughter laughed, immersed in her beauty and the feel
of the robe. WolfStar would not be able to resist her!

After a few more admiring moments, StarLaughter continued on her way. The corridors and stairwells were clear this
deep in, and she had no trouble finding the basements.

They were dank and cold, but StarLaughter could feel the
power that remained here. It was a residual power, as if the
enchantments were fading after whatever they protected had
been removed, but it was enough, and StarLaughter knew that
Qeteb, or any of the other Demons, would not be able to spy
her out here.

"It is not a palace fit for *me*," she observed, but sank down
gracefully in the centre of the chamber, folding her legs underneath her and her wings against her back.

She faced the door, and waited.

And as she waited she allowed herself to further remember, and she laughed very softly, remembering the first time Wolf-Star and she had made love.

Many hours passed, and StarLaughter succumbed to her lethargy. She dozed, for how long she could not tell, but when she came to awareness again, she sensed she was no longer alone.

StarLaughter raised her head and stared toward the door.

A young Icarii birdwoman stood there. She had white wings and fair, translucent skin, but their beauty was absorbed and murdered by the black gown she wore. She had fine gold hair that curled about her forehead, violet eyes and a full and sensuous mouth, but her beauty was spoiled by the expression of sadness that she wore, almost as a cloak over her depressing robe.

"Hello, StarGrace," StarLaughter said. "I have been expecting you."

StarGrace nodded, but said nothing, and she walked further into the chamber.

She had a peculiar gait, almost as if she were walking on claws rather than feet.

StarLaughter tilted her head to one side and regarded Star-Grace. It was a positive sign that StarGrace appeared so: the Hawkchilds *could* transform themselves back into a semblance of their former selves, but generally it did not suit them.

Revenge always required a much darker mien.

But here was StarGrace in at least a semblance of her former self, although StarLaughter could see she'd left her feet taloned and the material of the robe shifted from feather to cloth with every movement of the eye. And since StarGrace had returned to her former appearance, that meant only one thing: StarGrace was willing to talk, and to talk on StarLaughter's terms.

"Qeteb sent you to hunt me down?" StarLaughter said.

"Yes." StarGrace's voice was husky, almost whispery.

"How did you find me?"

"I haunted these corridors, too. Remember?"

StarLaughter nodded. StarGrace was her niece, daughter of

CloudBurst, WolfStar's younger brother. StarGrace had spent many years in Talon Spike as well, and as a SunSoar, close to the Talon, she would have known about these basements.

"I knew this would be the only place you could hide," Star-Grace continued.

"And yet you did not tell this to Qeteb," StarLaughter said. She wanted to smile—now she knew she could manipulate the Hawkchilds!—but realised the folly of revealing her triumph too soon, and so kept her face impassive.

StarGrace had moved to within a pace of StarLaughter, and now she extended a hand—StarLaughter noted that it, too, was in the shape of a claw—to help StarLaughter rise.

"I wanted to hear what you had to say," StarGrace said, and StarLaughter nodded.

She brushed out her gown, and spoke. "I have become disenchanted with Qeteb and the Demons."

"Questors," corrected StarGrace.

"No," StarLaughter said firmly. "*Not* Questors. Demons." She shrugged. "Although, in truth, the semantics of the matter bothers me little. Demons or Questors, they aided us when no-one else would, and gave us succour and hope."

"This is true."

"They said they would return us to Tencendor so we could revenge ourselves on WolfStar."

"This is true."

"But have they done this?"

StarGrace was silent, regarding StarLaughter thoughtfully.

"We *are* back in Tencendor, true—but look what they have done to it!"

"I don't think that the ruin of Tencendor means much to our plans for—"

"And do they let us do what *we* need to do?" StarLaughter continued, putting as much emotion and conviction into her voice as she was able. "Why can't they let us go to hunt down WolfStar? Stars knows it is the only reason we continue to exist!"

StarGrace shifted from foot to foot *(claw to claw)*, and blinked. She cocked her head to one side, thinking.

"It was the only thing that kept us going through our frightful deaths and then through thousands of years drifting in space!" StarLaughter grabbed the front of StarGrace's robe and gave her a little shake. "We are nothing without a fulfilment for our revenge!"

StarGrace finally nodded. "What do you want?"

"Will you tell Qeteb that you could not find me?"

"What?" StarGrace cocked her head, then tipped it to the other side, regarding StarLaughter almost as a mouse she might like to gobble up. "Why?"

"So I can be left in peace to find WolfStar. Who else can do it? When I find him, we can then have our revenge!"

StarLaughter was not finding it easy to lie to StarGrace, but she needed to do it. The last thing she could tell the Hawkchilds was that she and WolfStar were destined to reunite in love! StarLaughter had no intention of handing WolfStar over to the Hawkchilds for a nasty death, but for the moment she could do with their sharp eyes, and so for the moment they would prove useful.

StarLaughter was forgetting even her desire to rescue her son in her new-found love for WolfStar. Ah! They had been such magnificent lovers once, and would be again!

StarGrace narrowed her eyes at the emotions roiling across StarLaughter's face, and StarLaughter only just managed to remember her need to convince the Hawkchilds of her need for a revenge on WolfStar.

She tried to look as guileless as possible . . . no easy task.

"You want time and space to find WolfStar?" StarGrace said. "He is in the Maze, surely."

"No!" StarLaughter said, her voice horribly shrill. "I looked! I did! He's gone."

She leaned forward, dropping her voice to a conspiratorial whisper. "The Demons let him escape. When they had him in their very parlour! Do you see what I mean? Why didn't they give him to us then? Obviously we can't trust the Demons to hunt WolfStar down for us. I must do it."

StarGrace thought, her face unreadable.

"Have I not lusted for revenge with you for the past countless thousands of years? For the Stars' sakes, StarGrace, I want him dead as much as you do!"

"And so you want me to lie to the Demons."

"Yes. What *do* we owe them? Nothing. They used us and drained us. Now we are on our own. You and me and the other children. On our own."

"I do not like to have to lie to Qeteb."

StarLaughter could hear the uncertainty in StarGrace's voice.

"My dear," she said gently, and gathered the girl into her arms, "*will* you protect me? I need the space and the peace in which to find him so that we may all revenge ourselves on him. Will you grant me that?"

"And when you do find him?" StarGrace pulled back, but reluctantly, and StarLaughter knew it. "I and my companions would not like to be cheated of our revenge as well."

"When I find him, I shall call. StarGrace, will you tell Qeteb you could not find me?"

StarGrace was silent a long moment, then she gave a quick jerk of her head in assent. "Find him, and, finding him, do not fail *us*."

StarLaughter nodded. "I will not fail you, StarGrace, nor any of the others whom WolfStar murdered."

Then she smiled, and leaned forward and kissed StarGrace on the cheek.

The Hawkchild pulled back in astonishment. A hug was one thing, but a kiss?

"Do you not remember what it was like to be loved, Star-Grace?"

"I remember that love did not save me from a vile death."

And then StarGrace was gone, and StarLaughter had the time and space she needed. She sat down again, folding the material of her robe carefully to display her form to best advantage, and thought. The Hawkchilds would now work to her purpose, providing her, not only with a degree of protection from Qeteb (damn him for all time!) but also with hundreds of eyes to seek out WolfStar.

StarLaughter frowned slightly, chewing her lip. Who else

could help bring her and WolfStar back together again? Ah! DragonStar! WolfStar would doubtless worm his way into DragonStar's camp sooner or later, and StarLaughter would need to gain DragonStar's trust in order to get WolfStar back.

So . . . how to enlist DragonStar's trust and aid? StarLaughter thoughtfully cupped one of her breasts in her hand. Her body had tempted DragonStar once and no doubt could again . . . no! She needed to keep herself pure for WolfStar. She must use guile rather than seduction.

Ah! StarLaughter giggled. She had the perfect idea! Not only would it appeal to DragonStar's desire to wrest Tencendor back from the Demons, and gain her WolfStar, it might also cause the Demons enough trouble that she and WolfStar would be able to rescue their son as well.

She sighed, happy, contented, and as dreamy as a thirteen-year-old girl in love for the first time.

14

Envy

DragonStar sat in a great circular stone hall. It was flagged and walled with cream-coloured stone shot through with gold. Rose and sapphire glass windows rose to dizzying heights, their columns supporting a hammerbeam ceiling of golden wood. DragonStar had wanted somewhere quiet to sit, and Sanctuary had, as was its wont, provided him with this.

As with most things within and of Sanctuary, the peaceful beauty of the hall left DragonStar feeling uncomfortable. This perturbed him, not only because he was disturbed at the appearance of Sanctuary—it reminded him too much of the worlds the Demons had dragged him through—but because of the deep river of disquiet that ran through the peoples sheltering in Sanctuary. Stars! If they were bored and fractious here, then how would they cope with the eternal peacefulness of the Infinite Field of Flowers? Ah! DragonStar forcibly turned his mind away from his worries. No doubt his disquiet was caused by seeing Qeteb not only in Spiredore but at the gates of Sanctuary itself.

And by the unsettling sight of Niah.

"What is it about you, Niah," DragonStar whispered. "What?"

He sighed, and looked down. He sat cross-legged on the floor, the Enchanted Song Book in his lap. The blue-feathered lizard was curled up at his back, and DragonStar leaned back against him comfortably.

Every so often the lizard snored, and whenever he did, a shaft of light glinted from one of his claws.

DragonStar paid no attention. More than anything else, he wanted to get out and *do* things, but he knew—as he'd told his witches—that he needed experience as well as a thorough knowledge of the Enchanted Song Book before he could do anything against the Demons.

He opened the leather cover and slowly thumbed through the pages. The Book contained Songs, music and dance that symbolised the enchantments needed to defeat the Demons. They would mirror the Demons' own malevolences back to them and destroy them.

"And wipe them from the face of this land and of the universe for ever and ever," DragonStar whispered.

He thought about what Axis had told him. Caelum had tried one of these dances atop Star Finger, but had been consumed almost entirely by the hatred and malevolence the song contained.

DragonStar's fingers traced over a line of music: he could feel the emotion this particular song contained—envy. He ran his tongue over his top lip, stared at the form and melody of the song, then swiftly converted it to numbers and then symbols in his mind.

He felt sick with apprehension. Should he try it? See what happened . . . Could he control the Song more than Caelum?

At his back the lizard stirred and sat up.

"Well, my beauty," DragonStar said. "What do you think I should do?"

The lizard yawned, then flexed one of his foreclaws.

"So," DragonStar said, "we try it."

What other choice did he have?

He rose to his feet and put the Book down. As the lizard had just done, DragonStar flexed a hand, then rose and traced the symbol in the air before him.

The lizard traced it with light.

And Envy filled the Hall.

A wizened old man stood before DragonStar and the lizard. He was twisted and humpbacked, his limbs stumpy, his hands contorted with arthritis.

He was naked, and his skin was sallow and slick with the sheen of sweat.

Lumps and moles covered his face; his eyes were like narrow slits that saw everything, noting them all down to be examined in the privacy of disenchanted silence.

He smiled, revealing crooked, yellowing teeth, and horrid thoughts consumed DragonStar's mind.

Caelum had enjoyed it all. He'd had forty years of love, forty years of respect, forty years of lording it over the peoples of Tencendor. So he'd died horribly—so what? Now he dwelt in the Field of Flowers, no doubt enjoying the adulation of everyone else who lived there.

And what was Drago, poor Drago to do. Why! destroy the Demons of course, while Caelum continued to enjoy himself. He'd had only a few minutes of pain, while Drago had forty years behind him, and more ahead.

DragonStar felt such consuming envy ripple through him that he literally growled. He felt his own back hunch over, and his hands twist into claws. Caelum was nothing but a spoilt bastard who'd had everything handed to him on a golden platter, while he, *he,* had to do all the hard work.

The misshapen figure of Envy capered about before him, clapping its hands, and howling with merriment. "Why don't you visit the Field of Flowers and destroy him forever," he whispered. "You can do it, you know. You have the power."

The lizard growled, and backed away a few paces.

DragonStar whipped about, raising his hand as if to strike the creature—*what had that lizard ever done but enjoy a free ride? He'd spent aeons as an unfettered spirit in the Sacred Grove, and then the Minstrelsea forest, and had then simply attached himself to DragonStar's cause with no hard work involved at all*—and then halted the instant before his hand flashed down in a cruel blow.

What was happening?

DragonStar struggled to control the envy, and the other emotions envy bred—hate and cruelty and a cloying, horrid self-justification—but he couldn't . . . he couldn't . . .

The old man capered about him in circles, clapping his hands. "Enjoy it!" he cried. "Give in to it! Why bother with such inconveniences as regard for others? Enjoy it! It's the easiest way!"

And DragonStar could *feel* how easy it would be. All he'd have to do was give in and let the envy consume him, and all would be well, all would be well, and he could finally relax and bathe in the emotions that he'd nurtured for so many years as a resentful man locked inside the hate of Sigholt and the SunSoar family.

A small hand slipped into one of his, and DragonStar jerked. It was Katie, her eyes frightened, her mouth trembling.

DragonStar saw that she was terrified.

Envy howled with rage.

"The cats!" Katie whispered. "The cats!"

The cats? DragonStar stared at her. Why was *she* helping him . . . or was she helping him at all? Why, Faraday cherished this little girl in a way that she did not cherish him, DragonStar could see that now. Faraday gave this weak little girl all the love and attention that she never gave him.

DragonStar growled again, and jerked his hand from Katie's.

Envy laughed.

And something small and furry wound its way about DragonStar's legs.

He jerked his eyes down. It was a white and marmalade cat, and its body shook with the strength of its purrs.

DragonStar lifted his hand to strike the thing—

—and remembered. He remembered that the cats had given him nothing but unconditional love when he'd been rejected by everyone and everything else in Sigholt. He remembered that they'd left their food to comfort him; they'd been content in his company, and they had revelled in his friendship.

They had asked for nothing in return.

They had not envied him his strength, or his speech, or even his name.

They had just loved him.

DragonStar lifted his eyes to Envy. "I pity you," he said, and Envy screamed.

"Let me offer you my friendship," DragonStar said, and extended his hand, palm upwards.

Envy stared, whimpered, and suddenly disappeared.

DragonStar shuddered, and leaned down, hands on knees, trying to regain his equilibrium.

The lizard had scuttled across the room, and now was hunched down on the floor with his claws firmly tucked underneath his body. He wanted nothing more to do with enchantments from that Book.

The white and marmalade cat was curled up behind him, watching DragonStar carefully.

"I cannot use this Book," DragonStar eventually whispered.

"Use it you must," Katie said, "or all who have sacrificed themselves before you, and who will sacrifice themselves in the future for you, will have done so in vain."

DragonStar straightened and stared at the girl. "The Book contains nothing but foulness."

Katie stared at him.

"Dammit! What is its secret? How do I use it!"

She continued to stare silently at him.

"You have most to lose, damn you—so *tell me its secret!*"

"I cannot," Katie said, her voice sad. "You must learn it for yourself."

DragonStar fought an overwhelming urge to throw the Book across the room, then he forced himself to relax, slowly rotating his neck and shoulders, and finally offered Katie his hand.

"I am sorry."

She smiled and slipped her hand into his. "You should already have learned one lesson," she said. "What was it?"

DragonStar almost grated his teeth, then chose to think it carefully through. "Envy consumed me," he finally said, "and I could not control it."

"And what broke the spell that Envy had thrown over you?"

"The cat," Drago whispered. "Unconditional love."

Katie nodded, and kissed his hand.

Faraday found them sitting on a pillowed bench seat in a window. The view beyond the glass panes was breathtaking: gardens and ponds stretched over several leagues to where the enclosing blue-cliff walls of Sanctuary rose.

"It's so beautiful," Faraday said as she sat on the other side of Katie.

DragonStar turned his head from the window and smiled at her over the girl's head. It is cloying, he wanted to say, but he could not explain his emotions, so he merely nodded.

"What have you two been doing?" Faraday said, sensing the remaining tension.

DragonStar sighed, and indicated the Enchanted Song Book lying on the end of the seat. "I have been playing about with that."

"And does it tell you what you need to know?"

"Yes," said Katie, and DragonStar shot her a mildly irritated glance.

"It tells me many things," DragonStar said, "and all of them uncomfortable."

Faraday looked between DragonStar and Katie, her face growing more puzzled. She slid her arms about the girl and drew her back into her body, an instinctively protective gesture.

"Can you . . . we . . . fight against the Demons with what the Book tells you?" Faraday said.

DragonStar shifted even more uncomfortably. "The Book is filled with the Demons' hatred and horror," he said. "I know I should use it . . . mirror it back to destroy the Demons—"

Faraday felt Katie tremble in her arms, and she glanced down, worried.

"—but it feels so repulsive . . . so . . ."

"Whatever it takes to destroy the Demons will surely be taxing," Faraday said.

DragonStar finally raised his face and looked her full in the eyes. "I am very much afraid," he said, "that if I use that Book I will turn into a Demon myself. I do not think I will be able to stop myself."

15

The Secrets of the Book

DragonStar tucked the Book under one arm and considered the lizard carefully.

"You stay here for the moment," he said. "I will be back for you."

The lizard dropped its head, its emerald and scarlet crest deflating mournfully, and turned away.

Faraday's mouth quirked. "It is just as well he does not speak."

"He does not have to."

"Will you take the hounds, and the horse?"

DragonStar hesitated.

"DragonStar, please, take them."

He nodded.

"And be careful in Spiredore."

"I will be *more* than careful. I will use only its power to transfer myself into the Field of Flowers. I will not enter the tower itself."

Faraday stared at him, knowing his words were useless

bravado. Even if they only used the power of Spiredore to transfer from one location to the next, DragonStar, as any of them, would be vulnerable in that instant they stepped through the doorway.

For in that instant, if they were unwary, or unlucky, or damned by Fate itself, Qeteb could snatch at them.

They could only hope that he didn't spend his entire time wandering the stairwells of Spiredore.

"Not he," DragonStar said softly. "But he might have any one of his Demons patrolling. Faraday . . . I *will* be careful."

She leaned forward and hugged him, longing for that time when their fight against the Demons was truly over and she and he could find the time to indulge, and relax into, their love. "I hope Caelum can help."

"And if not he, then there is one other I can turn to," DragonStar said, but he was gone before Faraday could ask who this "other" was.

She sighed, and sat back on the window bench with Katie. "I am so glad you are safe here," she said, stroking the girl's head. "I could not bear it if you were exposed to danger again."

Katie smiled, and looked away.

DareWing felt a savage glee as he wheeled his Strike Force through the skies above the Field of Flowers.

They were superb.

Death had altered them, but only to give them a greater purpose, and a more lethal desire.

DareWing flew among them, almost lost in the swirl of jewel-bright wings and eyes and the haunting shadows and shapes of their silvery liquid bodies. The members of the Strike Force had lost none of their ability, or their tight discipline.

They wanted to hunt, to fight back, to *strike*.

And why not? thought DareWing. Stay here, DragonStar had said, until I need you, but DareWing was impatient with the waiting. *When* was DragonStar returning? In the waste-land there was corruption to be cleared, and DareWing and the Strike Force were doing no good sweeping colourfully through the skies here.

He alighted within the Field, letting his wings relax and trail luxuriously through the poppies and lilies, and looked up to the molten colour swirling above him.

"Come with me," he whispered, and then DareWing closed his eyes, and thought of the icy drifts of the northern Icebear Coast, the feel of the cold-edged wind sliding through his feathers, the cry of the seagull, the roar of the icebear . . .

. . . and they were there, the Strike Force wheeling above him, and crying with wordless voices.

DareWing smiled, and lifted into the air.

DragonStar passed through into the Field of Flowers without incident, and with a considerable amount of relief. Even Belaguez relaxed beneath him as he felt the spring of the flow-ered field beneath his hooves, and the Alaunt bayed with joy, and bounded among the flowers, snapping at butterflies.

And with every snap of jaw, the butterflies soared drifting into the air a handspan above the hounds, and DragonStar smiled.

He kneed Belaguez forward, letting his body fully relax for the first time in hours, and drank in the beauty about him. The scent, the gently waving flower heads . . .

. . . the crash and roar of surf in the distance.

DragonStar halted Belaguez for a moment. He could vaguely discern the smell of salt underlying the scent of the flowers. He let his eyes scan the horizon, stopping at a spot that was hazier than the rest. A coastline.

DragonStar urged Belaguez forward.

He found Caelum sitting at the very edge of a cliff that plunged down hundreds of paces into a foam of rocks and sea spray.

RiverStar sat with him, her arm linked into his, their heads close together as they murmured to each other.

"Caelum? RiverStar?" DragonStar lifted a leg over Belaguez's withers and slid to the ground. The Star Stallion snorted, then wandered away a few paces to nose among the flowers.

Caelum and RiverStar turned slightly, and smiled at DragonStar.

DragonStar stared, taken not only with their beauty, but at the peacefulness that they radiated.

Neither had been particularly peaceful in life.

Caelum's smile broadened a little, almost as if he could read DragonStar's thoughts. "Welcome, brother," he said. "Will you join us?"

RiverStar said no words, but she stood in one graceful, fluid movement, and took DragonStar's hand. She pulled slightly, encouraging him to sit with Caelum and herself, but DragonStar baulked.

In life RiverStar had loathed him, goaded him, and taken every opportunity to make his life miserable.

Who was this caring, lovely-spirited woman now standing before him?

RiverStar lifted her free hand and laid it against DragonStar's cheek.

"In life," she said, "I was hateful, jealous, and spiteful. But once I passed the gate into the Field of Flowers I entered a state of . . . of . . ."

Her brow creased slightly, as if her mind could not quite find the word to describe her state of existence.

"We entered," Caelum said, "a state of contentedness. Contentedness not only with our environment, but with ourselves."

DragonStar nodded slowly, realising the difference in his brother and sister. They were deeply at peace with themselves, because they were contented—a spiritual state rather than an emotional one.

And suddenly *he* was content as a huge weight lifted off his shoulders. DragonStar's mind had been worrying at the fact that so many people appeared bored and irritated with the peace of Sanctuary, and he'd worried about how they'd cope with the eternal peace of the Field of Flowers.

Now he understood. When people passed into the Field of Flowers they underwent a spiritual transformation.

And they became content.

Caelum nodded as he understood DragonStar's realisation. "There are only a few who do not undergo this transformation," he said. "Those who know that they must return to Tencendor, and those who know they have work unfinished remain impervious to the contentedness of the Field."

"The Strike Force," DragonStar said. "They remain vengeful."

"Aye," Caelum said. "But come, sit down. We are gladdened to see you again."

DragonStar smiled, and sat down beside Caelum. RiverStar let go his hand, and stepped back, saying that she would leave them to talk.

"There are flowers I have not yet seen," she said, her smile so sweet and gentle it made DragonStar's breath catch in his throat, "and walks yet to be explored. I will see you again, DragonStar, in the days when we will *all* live in peace in the Field."

She bent quickly, kissed DragonStar's cheek, and then she was gone, fading into the weaving, waving lilies.

For a long while Caelum and DragonStar said nothing, relaxing in each other's company and the scent of the flowers. Behind them, the Alaunt settled down in haphazard groups, stretching out in the sun or grooming each other with long, liquid tongues and gentle nips.

"You have the Enchanted Song Book," Caelum said finally, glancing at what DragonStar had under his arm.

DragonStar looked down the cliff, fighting a wave of dizziness. He missed so much of his Icarii heritage: the ability to fly, to dance, to sing, and, at the moment, the easy ability to withstand the lure of appalling heights.

"Aye," he eventually said. "I have the Enchanted Song Book. Caelum . . ."

"I tried it, you know."

"I know. Axis told me."

Caelum turned his eyes from the rolling ocean and looked back at his brother. "You have spoken to our father?"

"Yes."

"And?"

"And we are friends, if not father and son."

Caelum nodded, and let his eyes drift back to the sea. "I wish I had been able to be his friend."

Something in Caelum's voice made tears jerk to Dragon-Star's eyes. Only a few hours ago he'd been consumed with a fierce and hateful envy for Caelum, and yet here Caelum was expressing, if not envy, then regret, at something DragonStar enjoyed and not he.

"Did father tell you what happened when I tried one of the Songs?"

"You felled a Hawkchild, but were so consumed with hate and rage that you almost . . ."

"Almost became a Demon myself."

DragonStar could not help the cold shudder ripple through him. Gods, what *was* it the Book contained?

"And when you danced before Qeteb?" he said.

Caelum laughed, low and cynical. "I would have done more damage if I'd offered him a flower."

Something danced at the very edge of DragonStar's consciousness, but his mind could not catch hold of the thought.

"And what did happen when you met Qeteb in the Maze?" he asked, so softly his voice could hardly be heard above the roar of the surf.

Caelum took a very long time to answer. "I made him laugh," he finally said. "I made the entire world laugh."

DragonStar lifted a hand and placed it on Caelum's shoulder, and the two brothers sat there for a long time, only love, the scent of the flowers, and the bellow of the ocean between them.

DareWing had brought the Strike Force to the northern coast for a particular reason: here the Demons' influence was likely to be least. Although the demonic hours would affect none of them, DareWing wanted to keep the Strike Force as safe as was possible for as long as possible. The Icebear Coast would also have the least concentration of crazed animals. What

DareWing wanted more than anything else was to find a small pack of something that the Strike Force could whet their teeth on. And then a larger pack of something, and one day Dare-Wing wanted to launch the Strike Force at the entire mass of lunacy that milled about the Maze.

First, they would start with the mountains themselves.

"See here?" Caelum said, thumbing through the Book, "this one is of fear, and this one of despair."

DragonStar studied the Song of Despair, absently converting it to symbol in his mind. "This book is full of everything the Demons have ever projected," he said, "and I must be the one to let these 'emotions' consume me so I may project them back at the Demons."

"Is that so?" Caelum said, and his voice sounded more than mildly puzzled. Again DragonStar had the feeling that something of immense importance hovered at the very edges of his mind.

"Well, I suppose it must be you," Caelum continued, "for you are the true StarSon and the wielder of Acharite magic, without which no one can use this Book."

DragonStar closed the Song Book and put it to one side. "Caelum, what happened when Qeteb caught up with you?"

Caelum frowned, then his brow cleared. "I cannot remember," he said, and laughed with relief. "I remember only that the Dance of Death was such an abysmal failure the Demons ridiculed me. Then I remember fleeing through the Maze, and then something happened . . . I . . . I fell over, and despaired, thinking that this must have been how RiverStar felt when I killed her. I begged her forgiveness, and then suddenly I was in the Field of Flowers, and I knew no more of Qeteb."

"Ah," DragonStar said.

They sat in silence for another while longer, and then DragonStar stirred. "Where is DareWing? He should be here somewhere with the Strike Force."

"Oh, he grew impatient," Caelum said, "and thought to save Tencendor all by himself."

"What!"

"He took the Strike Force," Caelum said, "and went back into the wasteland. Contentedness is not yet their lot."

"Gods!" DragonStar wondered what he should do: go rescue DareWing from a situation he might well be able to control on his own, or go see the one person who might truly tell him the secret of the book?

Finally DragonStar got to his feet and whistled Belaguez over, tucked the Enchanted Song Book under his arm and leapt on the stallion's bare back. Best to make sure about DareWing first.

The Alaunt jumped up, milling about the horse's legs.

"Come back," Caelum said, wistfully, and DragonStar nodded, and drew the doorway of light with his sword.

DareWing wheeled above the ruins of Star Finger, the ghostly apparitions of his force dipping and swaying about him. He was lost in his memories of his early years spent in and about the mountain. Now it was broken and destroyed, and would never prove a safe haven for the Icarii race again.

Nothing in Tencendor would, come to that.

"Strike Leader."

A soft voice above his right wing snapped DareWing out of his reverie.

"What is it?"

There was a silence, and DareWing regretted his sharp tone. "I am sorry. What do you need to tell me, MirrorWing?"

MirrorWing—or the being that had once been MirrorWing—pointed to a canyon below.

"I think someone down there is trying to attract our attention."

DareWing looked down, and could not stop his exclamation of surprise.

WolfStar thought they'd never see him. Curses! What was wrong with their star-damned eyes?

But then, what were they to start with? The creatures were Icarii-shaped, but their bodies were indistinct, almost transparent.

And their wings . . . WolfStar knew that Enchanters would have committed murder to understand the spells that made these wings glow with such incandescent colour.

WolfStar waved an arm slowly, trying to get them to hurry up. Stars, but every movement was agony! He'd only fallen some twenty or thirty paces—bouncing from rock wall to rock wall—down the chasm before he'd tumbled onto a rock ledge that sloped backwards under an overhang. By the time StarLaughter had sent her merriment—*her mad, mad merriment*—chasing down the chasm after him, he'd been hidden from view.

And from there WolfStar had painfully, drop by drop, handhold by handhold, clambered to the bottom of the chasm, and then hauled himself along its rock-littered floor until he'd emerged into what passed for sunlight in this northern devastation.

And there he'd lain, thinking over StarLaughter's words: Caelum not the StarSon? Well, it made sense. The idiot had been useless against Qeteb. Wolf-Star's mouth curled in a small smile. The true StarSon was still out there somewhere, still controlling power. And WolfStar knew there was not a man alive he could not manipulate and eventually control. He *would* regain power again, but first he needed to know who the true StarSon was.

"Who?" he whispered. "Who?" That bitch StarLaughter had distracted him before he could force an answer from her . . .

He looked up again at the soft sound of wings. Perhaps a score of the Icarii-creatures were now only some fifty paces above him, and dropping fast.

With them was a more conventional Icarii birdman—at least he had a solid enough body, although he was incongruously dressed in a white linen tunic and sandals.

"Well," WolfStar said, as the group landed about him, "at least you do not seem demon-mad, even if the majority of you look a trifle vitreous. What has happened? Has the loss of the Star Dance bled you of your solidness?"

"Loss of life," said one, a female by the lightness of her voice, "has made us less fleshy than what we were wont to be."

"Who are you?" said WolfStar, wondering if he was going to spend the rest of his life asking: *Who?*

"Who are *you*?" said the one flesh-solid Icarii among them.

WolfStar rolled slightly so he could stare the birdman in the face. "I am WolfStar SunSoar and I demand you take me to the StarSon."

The birdman laughed, and, raising his eyes to a spot somewhere behind WolfStar, said, "I think he comes to greet you, renegade."

And WolfStar rolled over, groaning, and stared to the east.

A man and a white horse had emerged from a canyon, and the horse's mane and tail dripped with stars.

"Gods," WolfStar whispered as he finally recognised the man's face.

"Well met, WolfStar," DragonStar said, and grinned. "I should have known that you would somehow survive the Demons' attentions."

WolfStar could barely manage to keep his face bland as the man dismounted from his horse and walked towards him. *Drago? The StarSon? And, ye gods, feel the power that radiated from him!*

"And I should have known," WolfStar responded softly, "that you'd always find a way to realise your ambition, Drago."

"DragonStar," he corrected, and squatted by WolfStar's side, running a gentle hand over the Enchanter's body. "You are hurt. Badly."

"I have been out and about," WolfStar said, "while others donned pretty clothes." He flicked his eyes over DareWing and the members of the Strike Force that had gathered around.

DragonStar's face tightened, but he did not respond to WolfStar's taunt. "Whose blood is this?"

"Caelum's."

DragonStar rocked back on his heels in surprise. "*Caelum's?* You were there when Qeteb—"

"Killed him? Yes. The fool boy, he walked straight onto the tip of the Demon's sword. Had you enchanted him into stupidity, Drago? Or was it a natural fault . . . Caelum ever had a sackful of those."

DragonStar reached out and buried his fingers in Wolf-Star's hair, and the birdman winced in pain. Was everyone going to haul him about Tencendor by the roots of his hair?

"Caelum died a hero's death!" DragonStar said.

"How can you be sure of that?" WolfStar snapped. "Were you watching?"

"What happened?"

WolfStar chose not to respond.

DragonStar gave the Enchanter's head a wrench. *"What happened?"*

WolfStar growled, and grabbed at DragonStar's hand with both of his own.

DragonStar's grip did not loosen, and WolfStar could not pry him free.

"What happened?" DragonStar gave WolfStar's head such a twist that all present could hear the bones in the birdman's neck crack.

"Caelum walked into the portion of the Maze where I lay," WolfStar ground out, hate and resentment for DragonStar filling every nuance of his voice, "as if he were walking into a picnic ground. He had a stupid, vacant smile on his face."

He was already walking through the Field of Flowers, thought DragonStar, and the smile he had on his face must have been beauteous, not stupid. "And then?"

"Then Qeteb rode his black nightmare up behind Caelum, and Caelum turned."

"And?"

"And Qeteb ran his sword through Caelum—Gods! The

boy reached out and grabbed the blade as it sliced into him!"

DragonStar stared at WolfStar. There was something else . . . something that WolfStar was not deliberately holding back but thought so unimportant as not worth the relation.

"And what else?" DragonStar said, his tone compelling.

WolfStar sighed and rolled his eyes dramatically. "Caelum said something to the Demon that drove him crazy."

"What?"

"He said, 'Oh, how I do love you'."

DragonStar still stared at WolfStar, but his eyes were far, far away. Caelum must have turned in the Field of Flowers and seen RiverStar. He had spoken to her, not Qeteb.

But what he'd said had driven the Demon . . . "crazy"?

DragonStar refocussed his eyes on WolfStar. "I apologise for what I am about to do to you," he said, "but methinks you have used it on many a soul before now."

And DragonStar forced the memory of Caelum's death up from WolfStar's subconscious into the full light of consciousness.

Caelum, turning, smiling, holding out his hand. "Oh, how I do love you."

And Qeteb going crazy with . . . what? Hate?

Or . . . fear?

"For thousands of years you have roamed about doing nothing but mischief in the name of ultimate good," DragonStar said, "but finally I think you may have done this land a service. Come on, stand up."

DragonStar got to his feet, and—once again—WolfStar found himself being hauled upwards by his hair.

He shouted with rage and squirmed about, but DragonStar's grip did not loosen.

DragonStar turned to DareWing. He was annoyed with the birdman for leaving the Field of Flowers, but for the moment that annoyance could wait. "None of the Demons are about, and I think this place safe enough for the time being. Watch Belaguez and the Alaunt for me, will you? I think I know just the place for WolfStar . . . if it can bear the shock."

And, so saying, DragonStar unsheathed the lily sword, drew his rectangle of light, and stepped through Spiredore as quickly as he could into Sanctuary, dragging WolfStar with him.

16

Fischer

DragonStar moved briskly through Spiredore—gods alone knew how dangerous it was getting now—while dragging WolfStar behind him. The birdman was muttering something incoherently about StarLaughter and the tower and his hair, but DragonStar paid him no heed.

His mind was full of jumbled thoughts and images, and they were all to do with Caelum's smiling, love-filled face, and the mystery of the Enchanted Song Book, which, somewhat unbelievably, for he had not been aware of it for some time, DragonStar still clutched under his free arm.

Suddenly they were tumbling through the doorway of light onto the approach to Sanctuary, and DragonStar briefly wondered how he'd managed it with his hands full of the Song Book and WolfStar.

"Where are we?" WolfStar gasped, rubbing his head as DragonStar finally let him go.

"Somewhere I imagine you thought you'd never see," DragonStar said. "Somewhere safe. Sanctuary."

"What?"

DragonStar did not answer. An Icarii birdwoman was spiralling above them in the sky, and DragonStar beckoned her down.

"This is WolfStar SunSoar," he said, and the birdwoman paled. "He is injured. Can you arrange that he be taken where his injuries can be healed? But, ware! Do not trust him."

She shook her head violently.

"I ask also that Axis and Azhure supervise his care," DragonStar said.

The birdwoman nodded soberly and rose back in the air. DragonStar waited impatiently—refusing to respond to any of WolfStar's taunts or answer any of his questions—until he could see Axis and a group of four or five men draw near with a stretcher. He nodded to the group and smiled to his father, then he stepped back into Spiredore without further ado, the Song Book still in his grasp.

DragonStar had someone he needed to talk to.

Someone who could confirm what DragonStar had finally realised was probably the true purpose of the Enchanted Song Book.

The bridge at Sigholt was in mourning. Her sister was gone— a necessary precaution—but the bridge still missed her.

She was immensely grateful when she felt DragonStar's feet upon her back.

"StarSon! You have come home!"

"Only briefly, bridge. I admit myself glad you still stand."

"I can resist the Demons a while longer, StarSon."

He nodded, looking about. Sigholt was still standing, but it looked wan, as if its life was draining away.

"None of us will last for much longer," the bridge said, sadly.

DragonStar's attention re-sharpened on the bridge. "None of you? What about Spiredore?"

"She also will die," the bridge said. "The Enemy's heritage has passed into you, StarSon, and none of us have much purpose left."

Spiredore would die? But what would that mean? He'd be trapped either in Sanctuary, or in the wasteland.

And either would be fatal, both to him and to his witches, and, eventually, to Tencendor.

"Do you feel strong enough for a last request, bridge?"

"A conversation?" she said hopefully.

DragonStar smiled, but it was sad. "Yes . . . but not with

you, bridge. I would like to speak to the trap you harbour within you."

"That effort will kill me," she said, and DragonStar felt tears spring to his eyes.

"I know," he said.

The bridge hesitated. "I will do it for you. StarSon?"

"Yes?"

"Win for us."

"I will," he whispered. "Bridge . . . bridge, know that you go with the love of many."

She did not speak, but he could feel her emotion shuddering through her, and he stepped onto the roadway that led into HoldHard Pass.

"Goodbye," she said . . . and transformed.

Not into her arachnoid form, but into the shape of an archway constructed of pale, unmortared blocks of stone.

Goodbye bridge . . .

The archway formed over the moat between the road and Sigholt, its lip touching the ground several paces away from DragonStar.

A man walked out of the arch.

He was white-haired and emaciated, and his entire form trembled as he walked. His face was deeply lined, his eyes faded and tired.

"Who are you?" he said, stopping a pace before DragonStar.

"My name is DragonStar SunSoar," he said, "and I am the result of your mistakes."

The old man cackled with laughter. "DragonStar? What kind of a name is *that*?"

He peered about him. "Where are we? Topside again?"

DragonStar wondered if the old man still thought he was on his home world. "What is your name?"

"Me? Oh, my name is Fischer. Where *am* I?"

DragonStar stared at him. He'd talked to the bridge about the moment when this man—a vastly younger version, apparently—had appeared and taunted Rox and the other Demons. Then the man had been full of confidence and knowledge. Now?

Ah, but that man was only a phantasm of the trap. The bridge had sent him the original. No wonder the effort had killed her.

"You are in the remains of a land called Tencendor," DragonStar said, "where the craft from your world crashed tens of thousands of years ago."

Fischer looked sharply at him. "Ah, and the Demons have followed?"

"Look about you."

"Aye," Fischer said, and grimaced. "Aye, they followed. Have you summoned me to blame me?"

"No. I need to ask you a question."

"Ah! I'd rather that you blamed me! I am sick of questions . . . what to do? When to do it? How? How? How? It took us forty years of questions before we came anywhere close to a single answer, and even then we only patched up the problem, we did not solve it. What is your question?"

"You reflected the Demon's hatred back at him, thus trapping him."

"Yes. Is that your question?"

"No. It trapped him, and it dismembered him, but it did not kill him. Why not?"

Fischer looked at the man carefully. He was pretty enough, and had a strange charismatic appeal, but Fischer did not know if he would be strong enough to do what was necessary. If he was merely *told,* then he would never get the strength. If he discovered it for himself, then he just might have a hope.

"I cannot answer the question," Fischer said, "but I have a piece of advice. Evil cannot be destroyed, it merely festers."

"Why can't you answer the question?"

"I cannot teach you what is right or wrong. In this battle the answers must come from your spirit. You must learn what will work against the Demons." Fischer looked at him steadily. "You must learn from our mistakes."

DragonStar stared, and then relaxed. "Thank you, Fischer."

Fischer grinned, and nodded his head. "My pleasure, m'boy. Finish it for us, I beg you. Our world was destroyed. I hope yours will be reborn."

DragonStar started to say something, but jerked in surprise as a stone fell from the archway and thudded into the ground behind Fischer.

Fischer likewise jumped, then scurried back under the arch as another, and then another, stone fell.

"Finish it this time," he whispered, and then the entire arch caved in, and the last DragonStar saw of Fischer was the man's arms raised in a hopeless attempt to protect himself against the falling masonry.

There was a rumble, and the archway collapsed into the moat.

Finish it for us.

DragonStar stood there a long time, staring into the moat and the pile of rubble he could dimly see in its depths.

Then he pulled the Song Book out from under his arm and leafed slowly through it.

The Enchanted Song Book did not tell him how to destroy the Demons at all. It was literally a list of the Enemy's previous mistakes.

What the Enchanted Song Book told him was what *not* to do.

DragonStar hesitated, then, with a quick twist of his wrist, tossed the Song Book into the moat.

It flared briefly as it fell, its pages rippling and cracking in the wind of its passing, then it vanished.

DragonStar smiled sadly, then let it fade. He did not have much time, and he had much strength to gain before he could put this knowledge to use.

17

Escape from Sanctuary

Isfrael was impatient to make his deal with the Demons. Then he would escape with the Avar to the Sacred Groves, and leave the Acharites and Icarii to their fate.

But he had one small problem. Getting out of Sanctuary.

DragonStar could do it, wielding Enemy Acharite magic to do so, but Isfrael could not. This place was crafted of Enemy enchantment, and only those of Acharite blood—*and* who had reawoken into their powers—could use it. Isfrael had Acharite blood aplenty from his parents, Axis and Faraday, but he'd not been through the process of death that was needed to be able to make use of the power, and Isfrael had no intention of dying for his ambitions.

No, there had to be *some* other way to get out.

He sat under a great spreading whalebone tree in the heart of the forest that Sanctuary had created in order to make the Avar feel at home. Isfrael did not appreciate Sanctuary's efforts at all. The entire forest seemed false: it did not sing, and it did not vibrate with power.

And the Avar watched him out of the corner of their eyes . . . almost as if they were keeping an eye on him, by the Horned Ones, rather than waiting for his will!

Although the Avar people tolerated Isfrael among them, the Avar Banes avoided him completely, and that made Isfrael more furious than anything else. He knew the Banes talked with Faraday, although they took pains to do so in private.

The Banes—perhaps all Avar—are keeping secrets from me, thought Isfrael, and the wild blond curls on his forehead tightened into even crisper, angrier knots, and his horns twinkled, as if they sharpened themselves on his thoughts.

His fingers dug into the soft earth at his side.

How could he get out of here?

Isfrael remembered how DragonStar drew the doorway of light to move to and from Sanctuary—through Spiredore, Isfrael thought—and he lusted for a doorway for himself.

He almost laughed. DragonStar was hardly likely to give him the doorway, was he? And Isfrael did not like his chances of trying to wrest it off the man: he'd likely set his pet lizard (another of Minstrelsea's creatures that had betrayed Isfrael) or one of his hounds to his destruction.

There *had* to be some other way.

And then Isfrael stilled as memory came to his aid.

Faraday had used the doorway to evacuate the Avar from the forests into Sanctuary!

The same doorway, or a different one?

Isfrael could hardly breathe for excitement. DragonStar and his "witches" (Isfrael would have laughed had he not been so preoccupied) had had only a relatively few days to evacuate all of Tencendor. If Faraday had been given a doorway with which to work, then had the others?

Probably . . . probably . . .

And of the others, Leagh was the most trusting . . . and the most vulnerable.

Isfrael smiled.

Zared laughed at something Theod had just said, but there was a hard edge to his merriment. Here he sat with Theod and Herme in this marbled palace in Sanctuary, drinking the finest of wines and nibbling on the most delectable of fruits, and yet above their heads Tencendor lay wasted with horror.

And Leagh, as also Gwendylyr, were going to have to go out there and do personal battle with the Demons in order to retrieve it.

Zared did not like it at all, and neither did Theod. Herme hardly said a word, feeling both guilty and relieved that his wife didn't have to face a Demon.

The three men sat with Leagh and Gwendylyr in a square chamber that opened out onto a balcony. Scents of wildflowers and grasses wafted in.

It should have been peaceful, but Zared was left itching with the need to *do* something. He and Theod had kept themselves as busy as they could, making sure the Acharites were settled, reconstituting what councils they could, trying to keep people busy, but it was a sham business.

All Zared wanted to do was get on a horse and lead an army somewhere . . . or, at the very least, be given the chance to build a permanent home for his people somewhere. He hated being trapped in this boring prettiness.

Gwendylyr leaned forward and threw her set of gaming sticks onto the ghemt board, then clapped her hands in delight. She was winning, and loving it.

Herme chuckled and reached for some more wine, while Theod rolled his eyes in mock despair at Zared, and conceded his squares on the board to his wife. "And with that, my love, you have won the entire board!"

Gwendylyr grinned, and gathered up everyone's gaming sticks. "Another game?"

"No!" the others chorused, holding up their hands in protest.

"I do not trust your witches skills," Herme said, with a grin to take away any implied criticism in his words.

"Well, perhaps we can play again this evening," Leagh said. "I think we need time to plan our strategies against you, Gwendylyr."

"As you wish." Gwendylyr was still smiling as she packed the sticks and board away. "It will but delay the humiliation."

"Gods!" Zared said. "Did she always get her way like this in your home, Theod?"

"Aye. It got so bad I used to actually enjoy going over the county accounts in the evening rather than spend time with Gwendylyr."

But Theod's tone was light, and his eyes dancing, and none of the others doubted his love for his wife.

Leagh sighed, and rose. "I must lie down for a while—I

must admit this futile tussle against Gwendylyr has exhausted me. Will you excuse me?"

Zared stood as well. "Let me come with you, Leagh."

She smiled, and put a hand on his chest. "No. Let me rest a while in peace, and then perhaps you and I can go for a walk in the orchards. I can amaze you with my ability to climb the highest fruit trees in search of the juiciest fruits."

Zared opened his mouth to protest, then realised she was making fun of him. He smiled, very gently and with utter love, and kissed her hand. "Rest well, my sweet."

Herme rose as well, his face drawn and tired, and offered to escort Leagh to her chamber.

She smiled, and took his arm.

After they'd left the room, Zared turned to the other two and finally let the worry shine unhindered from his eyes. "How will she manage in the wasteland against a Demon," he said, his voice desperate. *"How?"*

Leagh slept, and dreamed.

She wandered through the Field of Flowers, so content and relaxed she was half dreaming even amid her dream.

Her hand was on her belly, and she and her unborn child talked—not with words, but with thoughts and emotions and laughter. She loved her child, and her child her, and while neither could wait for the time when the child would be born, they were not impatient for it.

The child curled up, protected and loved, deep within Leagh's body, and that contented both of them.

Leagh walked, and let the scent of the lilies seep into her innermost being.

The unborn child screamed.

Leagh jerked out of her reverie, although not out of the dream; wild-eyed she stared about, almost tripping in her hasty attempts to circle and spot the danger.

Her hands clutched protectively over her belly, no protection at all against knife or spear or iron-studded and hard-wielded club.

The child screamed again, and Leagh panicked.

What was wrong?

She twisted about still more . . . and saw it.

Perhaps thirty paces distant stood a great black bull. Its eyes were red flames, its breath sulphurous smoke, its face a mask of hate.

Give it to me, it bellowed in her mind, *or I will gore that child out of your belly.*

One foreleg pawed the ground, and his haunches bunched.

Leagh screamed, and, turning, ran.

She felt the thunder of the bull's hooves through her own feet, and she could hear the horrendous wet panting of his breath.

Something hard and vicious dug into the small of her back and sent her sprawling.

Leagh's hands scrabbled in the bare earth—*the flowers had fled!*—and tried to get up, tried to get away—

A horn caught under her ribcage and flipped her over, and the bull thrust his sweaty, ghastly face into hers.

Saliva dribbled from his mouth, and drenched the neckline of her robe.

Give it to me, give it to me!

"What?" Leagh screamed. "What?"

The bull lifted one of its massive, splayed fore-hooves—it was the size of a plate!—and thudded it down on her belly.

Give it to me!

"What? What? Take it, anything, *oh gods no don't do that don't don't don't stop it stop it stop it . . .*"

The bull leant its entire weight on its hoof, and Leagh could feel her child screaming, trying to get away . . . its flesh tearing, its skull bursting, she could feel her belly bursting apart, she could feel the bull squirming his hoof right down through her ruined belly to her spine, *oh gods the pain the pain the pain . . .*

Leagh jerked out of her sleep, still screaming—

—and found she could not move. A man—she could smell him—had one heavy hand on her throat, *and the other one dug into her belly, its fingers probing, probing, oh god, don't don't . . .*

"Give it to me," a voice rasped, and Leagh finally opened her eyes and stared into the face of Isfrael.

So panicked she could hardly breathe, let alone think, Leagh tried to fight him off, but he was so strong, so strong, and the instant she started to squirm his fingers dug agonisingly into her belly, and she could feel her child squirm, and Leagh slid completely into panic. She screamed, then screamed again, then—

He lifted his hand from her belly and struck her face so hard she blacked out for a heartbeat or two.

"Give it to me," he roared. "Give it to me!"

"What?" she finally managed. The hand was back on her belly again, and he was leaning virtually his entire weight on it.

"The door!"

"The door?" And then she screamed again as his fingers dug even deeper (how was that possible?) into her flesh.

"The door of light! Where is it?"

The door of light? For a moment Leagh could not comprehend what he meant, and then she remembered.

The doorway of light that DragonStar had given each of his witches, save for DareWing who was too sick. She'd compressed it down into a cube, and put it where? Where? All Leagh wanted to do was give it to him, get him away from her, get him away from her baby.

"In the pocket of my robe, you vile bastard," she hissed, and instantly the pressure was gone from her throat and belly, and she rolled away from him and slid onto the floor.

She could hear Isfrael scrabbling about on the other side of the bed . . . then nothing.

"Is this it?" Leagh heard him say, and she hauled herself onto her knees.

He held the cube of light in his hand.

"Yes. It unfolds."

Isfrael fiddled with it, then found one of the lines of light and unfolded the door to the size of a small box.

He grinned, feral, malevolent. Then, in an abrupt movement, unfolded the doorway to its full size and stepped through.

Using every bit of strength left in her, Leagh struggled to her feet, threw herself across the bed, and grabbed hold of the door. Her breath wheezing in panic, desperate to do this before Isfrael did. *Gods!* Leagh could see him on the other side of the door, turning back and roaring as he saw her, moving back towards her, reaching, reaching!—she pulled the doorway down, and refolded it back into its cube with hands trembling so badly they were barely useable.

Then, rather than placing the folded door back in a pocket, or even in a drawer of the nearby chest, Leagh thrust it under the mattress, and then sat down hard, both hands clutching the edge of the bed with white-knuckled fear.

She opened her mouth, heaved in as much air as her lungs could take, and screamed: *"Zared! Zared! Zared!"*

The bitch had closed the door!

Isfrael fought to contain his fury. The doorway could have been an inestimable object of barter. Then, finally containing his rage, he turned around to survey the interior of Spiredore.

And a wondrous thought occurred to him. Spiredore would take him to the Sacred Groves! He wouldn't have to deal with the Demons at all!

Isfrael stood thinking. If Spiredore took him there, then that would mean that he couldn't return to get the Avar. They'd die in Sanctuary when the Demons finally managed to break through its defences (as they surely would once they realised the treasure they had in Niah).

But maybe, once he was in the Sacred Groves, either the Horned Ones, or the Mother, could help him evacuate the Avar.

And maybe the Avar deserved to burn amid the Demons' fury for the fact that they'd deserted him for Faraday.

"I will do what I can," Isfrael announced to Spiredore, "but

I will not do enough to endanger either myself or the Sacred Groves."

Having settled the matter in his own mind, Isfrael prepared to enter the Sacred Groves. He had been brought up with the rest of the SunSoar brood, and well knew Spiredore's secret.

"Take me to the Sacred Groves," he said, and set off up the nearest stairwell.

What Spiredore led Isfrael to was not quite what he'd expected. A blue-misted tunnel, surely, but it ended only in a drift of cold stars, not in the Sacred Groves.

"The *Bitch!*" he spat, and sent a string of cold, vile curses into an uncaring universe.

The Mother had closed off the approaches to the Sacred Groves—nothing else could have stopped Spiredore!

"The stupid, thoughtless Bitch!"

And Isfrael stormed back down the blue mist tunnel until he was back in Spiredore. He would have to trade with the Demons, after all.

No matter. He could best them any day.

"Take me to Qeteb," he said, and stepped upwards.

18

The Joy of the Hunt

"DareWing," DragonStar said when he returned to the foot of the Icescarp Alps, "I must get back to Sanctuary . . ." He told DareWing about Spiredore's eventual death.

"When that happens then I do not know of an effective way to move so quickly between Sanctuary and this wasteland."

"And what will you do once you get to Sanctuary?"

DragonStar looked about the landscape for a few moments, avoiding the question. What *would* he do?

"I am torn, DareWing," he eventually said, "between simply bringing you and the Strike Force back into Sanctuary with me, or leaving you here."

DareWing shook his head. "The Strike Force cannot easily go into Sanctuary. They . . . they . . ."

"They are too far beyond death to be able to tolerate its—" DragonStar hesitated, "—to tolerate its confines."

"You must bring the other witches out," DareWing said. "Out into the wasteland."

"Yes," DragonStar sighed. "I know that. We will do no good huddled in Sanctuary, but the thought of exposing them prematurely to the Demons . . . DareWing, I *must* go back and get them, but there is something you should know."

"Yes?"

"The Enchanted Song Book was not a book of solutions, my friend, but a sad list of errors. The Song Book told us what *not* to do."

"And so what is left?"

"Everything the Demons cannot stand," DragonStar said softly.

DareWing made to say something, shifting impatiently, but DragonStar laid a hand on his shoulder and quieted him.

"Listen to me. I am going back to Sanctuary, and I will come back with the girls and Goldman. DareWing, will you start to clear Tencendor while I am gone? The north must be crawling with corruption, and all of Tencendor must be cleansed before it can be reborn."

"And if I meet up with one of the Demons?"

DragonStar took his time in replying, his fingers gently tapping the book, his eyes unfocused.

He remembered what WolfStar had told him about Caelum's death, and he remembered what Fischer had said. Reflecting the Demons' malevolence back at them had not truly defeated them: it had only driven the evil underground for it to fester.

Evil cannot be destroyed—and certainly not by using evil against evil.

A word of love had driven Qeteb to distraction.

DragonStar's face softened, and he smiled.

"DareWing," he said, and put a hand on the other's shoulder, "let me tell you what I have learned this day . . ."

DareWing wheeled the Strike Force over the Alps. Dragon-Star had returned to Sanctuary with his assorted animals. Having heard what the StarSon had theorised, DareWing almost wished he *did* meet up with one of the Demons. Either DragonStar's theory was correct, in which case DareWing could deliver to the Demons an almighty shock, or he was incorrect, in which case it was better for DareWing to fail than DragonStar. DareWing could feel the probing of Sheol in his mind—it was mid-afternoon now, and Despair reigned over the wasteland—and he smiled . . .

He understood very well that although Sheol could not touch him, she could nevertheless *feel* him, as she could feel every one of the almost two thousand members of the Strike Force.

DareWing's smile widened, and he soared in the air, and he spoke to his command.

She hissed and crouched down on all fours about the fire she shared with the other Demons.

Qeteb stared curiously at her, one hand paused in the act of raising a half-burned, half-raw joint of flesh and bone (it was possibly cow, but it had transformed so much during its demented life that it was now impossible to determine its original species). "What is it?"

"They are back!"

"Who?" Qeteb threw away the half-eaten joint and stood up.

Sheol's form flowed into that of a misshapen cat, then a pig, then finally back into a vaguely humanoid form again. She got to her feet, brushing down her gown with something resembling disdain.

"Those who can resist us."

Qeteb grunted. "How many?"

"Many."

"Where?"

"To the north."

Qeteb thought, and then smiled behind his iron mask. "Go," he said to her, and Sheol gurgled with happiness, and her form shifted yet again into that of a winged serpent, and she lifted *(wriggled)* into the air and disappeared into the raging winds of dust.

DareWing soared his command into the sky above the eastern Icescarp Alps. His sharp eyes scoured the landscape below him, but there was nothing but the plunge of icy black cliff and the drift of frost.

Nothing lived here, apparently.

South? No, best to check the eastern regions before he sallied south, thus DareWing led his command—deadly jewel-bright silence—over the flat plains between the Icescarp Alps and the coast of the Widowmaker Sea, an area that had once been, before the wasteland encroached, the approaches to the unmapped northern tundra of the Avarinheim.

"The Demonic hordes have not travelled this far north," DareWing eventually said to the Icarii-wraith flying beside him. "We may have to—"

And he stopped, stunned. Behind him a low buzz of un-worded comment rose from the Strike Force. There *was* a pack of something moving south towards the wasteland, but it was not what DareWing and his Strike Force had thought to encounter.

"Stars in heaven," DareWing whispered. "Skraelings!"

"Skraelings!" DareWing said again, hardly able to believe what his eyes told him were there.

Skraelings?

Hadn't Azhure destroyed all Skraelings?

But no, she hadn't. Only the ones in Tencendor itself. The unmapped tundras in the extreme north had always had a breeding population of the creatures, and DareWing supposed that now the forests had gone, they would almost naturally drift south.

Evilly curious and perpetually hungry creatures that they were . . .

The grey wraiths were moving slowly through the snow, perhaps about a dozen of them, and concentrating so hard on their journey they had not yet noticed the Strike Force.

DareWing motioned one Wing after him, then very gradually began a downward spiral that would eventually bring him to the Skraelings' backs.

As he drifted lower, DareWing stifled another exclamation. A small rabbit was bounding through the snow before the Skraelings; one of its ears was missing, and its fur looked as though it was streaked with pus.

One of Qeteb's creatures, then.

The Skraelings are in league with Qeteb! And that thought did not surprise DareWing overmuch, either, for the Skraelings had ever sought someone to lead them in their perpetual quest for misery.

Well, this was one group that would never make it as far as the Maze.

Again DareWing motioned with his hand, and the Wing behind him lifted silvery bows from their back, and filled them with arrows fletched in feathers the same colour as their individual wings.

DareWing's hand dropped, and the arrows flew.

Most found their mark, although they did the wraiths little damage. The arrows flew straight through their grey insubstantiality, and the only wraith that dropped was one who'd turned at the sound of arrow flight and had been skewered through the eye.

"Aim for their eyes!" DareWing shouted, cursing himself that he'd not remembered this fundamental rule of the Skraeling hunt. "Aim for their eyes!"

But the hunt was harder now, for the Skraelings had dispersed, scattering over the snow and ice, blending in so perfectly with their surroundings that the Icarii found it difficult to distinguish them.

The rabbit, however, had turned to snarl and snap at the Strike Force members now wheeling overhead, and one of the Icarii sent an arrow thudding into its side.

It toppled over, screaming thinly.

The Wing had now dispersed to deal with the Skraelings individually, and DareWing hovered above the action, shouting advice and encouragement, but mostly staying out of the way. The Icarii needed no aid to do what they'd come back to do: exact revenge and clean the wasteland of the corruption that tainted it.

Much higher, so high they were but specks in the sky, the remainder of the Strike Force hovered, waiting, and hungering for the time when they, too, could loose their arrows.

Another Skraeling fell, then another, then three more in quick succession.

DareWing permitted himself a smile of quiet satisfaction. These might only be Skraelings rather than the Demonic hordes, but they were a start, they were a start . . .

Something frightful suddenly, stunningly, appeared in the sky to DareWing's south.

He did not see it at first, but rather, became aware of a change in the rabbit, still noisily involved in its dying on the bloodstained snow.

It was still screaming—but in triumph, not pain.

DareWing stared, and then the looming figure to the south caught his attention.

He looked up, and his breath caught in his throat.

A gigantic serpent wriggled its way through the sky towards them. It had wings, two pitiful feathered contraptions just behind its head, but was flying more through the sinuous undulations of its body than the motion of its wings.

It was grinning.

DareWing recognised Sheol instantly. Despair radiated out from her in waves, but underlying the despair was a far more sinister power. DareWing knew she would be difficult to deal with.

He breathed deeply, calming himself, then motioned the Wing back to join the rest of the Strike Force.

He stared an instant longer, then flew after them.

Sheol grinned even harder. The pretty flying things, no doubt toys of the StarSon, were afraid.

She redoubled her efforts to reach them.

The translucent, jewel-bright creatures massed above the first of the peaks of the Icescarp Alps, an undulating cloud of colour and silvery nothingness, but Sheol ignored them, concentrating instead on their leader, a dark-visaged and winged man dressed in a ridiculous white tunic and considerably more fleshy than his command.

"Greetings, fool," said Sheol pleasantly, as she wriggled near. "You must be one of the StarSon's acquaintances."

She'd moved very close now, and her form rippled and changed until she resembled a cross between a dragonfly and a fairy.

She was exquisitely beautiful, and exquisitely threatening.

DareWing felt flames spread along his wings.

He reflexively panicked, then regained his equilibrium. He could deal with this. He imagined himself plunging into the Iskruel Ocean until the frigid waters closed above his head . . .

The flames fizzled out, and DareWing soared a dozen paces further into the air.

"Very good," said the dragon-fairy. "I am impressed. Perhaps I shall just capture you for Qeteb to play with at his leisure."

DareWing's feathers fell out.

This time he found it harder to control his panic. He beat his de-feathered wings frantically, but without the means to caress the air they could not hold him aloft. DareWing tried to imagine new feathers sprouting along his wings, but he could not hold the image, and he fell through the air towards the ground.

DareWing closed his eyes, and prepared to embrace it. The ground would not harm him, for he did not fear it. He could exist without flight, he had already proved it . . .

The sound of a choir filled the air, and, distracted, Sheol let her magic waver.

Suddenly DareWing found himself soaring again, his

wings whole, and he grinned. "Sheol!" he cried. "Do you like the music?"

And he started to sing himself. It was no enchantment, and had no inherent magic, and no real meaning in its words. Its enchantment and power lay in the emotions it caused to well up in the breasts of both singers and listeners.

It was a song all Icarii sang when they celebrated a particularly blessed event—a marriage of a well-loved friend, or the birth of a child after a difficulty-fraught labour.

It was called Freedom Flight.

> *Feather drifting*
> *Skyway beckoning*
> *Freedom flight*
> *Never ending.*
>
> *Sun is burning*
> *Crest is rising*
> *Wings are arching*
> *Soul is soaring.*
>
> *Child seeded*
> *Hands uniting*
> *Friendship laughing*
> *Love triumphant.*
>
> *Feather drifting*
> *Skyway beckoning*
> *Freedom light*
> *Never ending.*

Sheol's eyes widened. "Think that will hurt me?"

DareWing grinned yet more, and waved at the choir behind him, floating in the thermals rising from the black peaks below.

Their singing doubled, if not in volume, then in intensity.

Many among the Icarii were crying with the strength of their emotion—with the strength of their joy.

Sheol hissed, and wriggled back a little. "You cannot hurt me with that!"

"No?" whispered DareWing. "No? What would happen, Sheol, if I could make you sing a verse? Hmm? Would you like to try? Now, come on. You have heard enough to know the words, surely. Come, sing with me . . . *Feather drifting, Skyway beckoning . . .*"

DareWing flew towards her with a hand outstretched. "Come . . . *Freedom flight, Never ending.*"

She snarled, and wriggled further away. "Think that pitiful song will destroy me?"

No, maybe not, DareWing thought, but it is a step in the right direction. And then hope did consume him, and he knew beyond any doubt that DragonStar would find the way to defeat these Demons.

"Get you gone, Sheol," DareWing snapped, "for you are not welcome here in these wastes."

She stared, not knowing what to do, wondering if somehow this entire episode was meant to be a preamble to one of the preordained challenges, and, if so, what she should do about it. Then, fortuitously, Qeteb touched her mind.

Come back! Come back! We have a visitor.

"Fool!" Sheol shot at DareWing as a form of goodbye, then she flowed her form back into that of the winged serpent, and retreated back south.

19

The Apple

Spiredore deposited Isfrael in the Demons' den. It surprised him. Somehow Isfrael had expected something truly horrific: a seething atmosphere of flames and acidic smoke filled with the screams of the tormented and the stink of the damned.

A chamber furnished with rocks and chasms, and with blood-rusted spikes to embrace welcome and unwelcome visitors alike.

Instead the Demons had constructed for themselves a boudoir of pleasantness. There was a circle of apple trees, stunted, true, but sweetly fruited nevertheless, and an inner circle of stumps each topped with a tasselled violet or scarlet cushion. Overhead spread a sky that was only mildly stained with grey-streaked clouds.

The only aspect that was truly unpleasant was the torn and half-eaten body of a dog that lay to one side (possibly the remains of a picnic) and, of course, the Demons themselves.

They each stood between and very slightly behind the apple trees. A silent, watchful semicircle. Four were clad in pastel robes of varying hues, their faces bland, their eyes glowing like gems.

Qeteb had not varied his dull black armour, and trailed his metalled wings on the ground behind him in a parody of the Icarii gesture of welcome.

When he stepped forward, as he did now, they gouged great wounds into the earth.

"And you are . . . ?" he inquired. He stopped just under one of the apple trees. As Qeteb moved, Isfrael could see that behind him lay the form of the Niah-woman. She was arranged neatly, her legs straight, her arms at her side, her eyes gazing upwards without thought or warmth.

Isfrael walked forward until he stood just before the inner circle of stumps. Qeteb was directly across the clearing from him.

"My name is Isfrael," he said, "and I am Mage-King of the Avar, Lord of the Forests."

One of the other Demons, the female, smirked, and Qeteb make a quick gesture to stop her laughing.

"Lord of ashes only," Qeteb said, and took another step forward, "and Mage-King of nothing but a pack of huddled prisoners." His voice harshened. "What do you here?"

"I have come to deliver you the Sanctuary and all its fodder," Isfrael said. He relaxed slightly. This was going to be easier than he thought.

"Ah," Qeteb said, "a traitor."

"And how," said Sheol, "can we possibly trust a traitor?" She had sidled forward until she stood just at Qeteb's left shoulder.

"I can see that a new world beckons," Isfrael said, "and I merely want to carve out my own niche within it."

Qeteb laughed, but it was Barzula, Demon of Tempest, who spoke. "And now we have hit the heart of it, eh? You want something from us, and to obtain it you are prepared to sell us Sanctuary."

"I am prepared to sell you victory," Isfrael said softly.

"We do not need your help!" Qeteb said, but all the Demons shared the one thought.

Had DragonStar grown stronger than when they'd last spotted him? Sheol's news of what DareWing's bravado had done had been more than unsettling, and his disinclination to use any of the Enemy's Songs was . . . almost frightening.

He had made no mistakes, and the Demons did not like that at all.

"You need all the help you can get," Isfrael said. "Only fools refuse aid. I am prepared to sell you the *assurance* of victory."

"We do not need your—"

"You *are* a fool!" Isfrael shouted, and strode through the circle of stumps until he stood directly before Qeteb. "You've been trapped before, why can't it happen again? Why can't it go one step further?" He stabbed a finger into the centre of Qeteb's chest plate. "What if this land is to prove your grave, Qeteb, rather than your playground?"

Qeteb hissed. "I have learned and grown the stronger for my captivity!"

"And what if the Enemy has, too?" Isfrael countered, his voice quiet, his eyes steady. "What if the Enemy has, too?"

The Demons were silent, although Barzula, Raspu and Mot had crept forward until they'd joined Sheol just at or behind Qeteb's shoulders. *What if the Enemy had, too?*

"What do you want," said Qeteb.

"The Sacred Groves," Isfrael said, "and peace within them."

"The Sacred Groves?" Sheol said. "What are they?"

"The Sacred Groves are the most holy glades and forests of the Avar people—"

"We did not destroy them?" Qeteb said, his voice combining both anger and puzzlement.

Isfrael dared a slight sneer. "You know none of the secrets of this land, Qeteb, and there are many spaces still hidden you have not even dreamed of yet."

Behind his visor Qeteb smiled. He could play this idiot like a lute. So, there were other spaces still to be explored and hunted for fodder, were there? *And you, with your foolish bravado,* he thought, *are going to lead us to them all, like it or not.*

But he kept the angered puzzlement in his voice, and twitched his fists, to make it all the more convincing.

"Spaces?" he roared.

You metalled oaf, Isfrael thought, *the dullness of your armour has spread to your brain.* "I want the Sacred Groves," he said. "I want them in peace. You can have everything else."

"The Groves must be very special to you," Sheol said, and she made her voice wistful.

"They contain all that is holy and precious to the Avar peoples," Isfrael said. "The Horned Ones, the Mother—"

Sheol raised her eyebrows questioningly, and Isfrael was foolish and dull-brained enough himself to fall into the trap.

"The Mother is the personification of all nature," Isfrael said, and the Demons instantly hungered, "while the Horned Ones are the most powerful of our Banes, transformed over the centuries into forms close to that of the stag, our sacred animal."

And all this sounds like good eating, Qeteb mind-shared with his companion Demons. *I am sick of cockroaches and sheep.*

Imagine the power we would gain from such a meal! Sheol whispered among their minds.

"You want the Sacred Groves," Qeteb said, "but what are you prepared to give *us?*"

"The secrets of the Enemy," Isfrael said, and watched in satisfaction as those of the Demonic faces he could actually see stilled in amazement. "Did you know that you have among you," and he indicated the form of Niah still lying behind the trees, "a weapon so powerful that you could destroy the Star-Son with it?"

"Her?" Qeteb said, and this time he did not have to feign the puzzlement. *"Her?"*

"Promise me," Isfrael said. "Promise me the Groves."

"Of course," said Qeteb. "Of course. You have them. In peace, forever and ever. Amen."

"I need assurance," Isfrael said. "I need proof of your goodwill."

Qeteb laughed, low and uncomfortable. "And you shall have it." He leaned backwards, brushing aside Sheol and Raspu, and plucked an apple from one of the trees.

"Take this apple and eat of it," Qeteb said, "and you will know my sincerity."

Isfrael stared at the fruit. "An *apple?*"

"Assuredly. Eat of it, and you shall eat of knowledge. You will know if I lie or not."

"And the Sacred Groves will be yours," whispered Mot.

"Forever," whispered Sheol.

"And ever and ever," echoed Barzula.

Isfrael took the apple and weighed it in his hand. It felt warm, heavy, inviting.

He could see himself wandering the paths of the Sacred Groves, safe, contented . . . powerful.

He did not know that in the instant he'd taken the apple the Demons could penetrate the inner spaces of his mind.

Although they could not see details, they could see that he did indeed have a powerful secret regarding the Niah-woman, but they could also understand that there were other secrets in there . . . other amusements . . .

Isfrael was still caught in his vision. *The Mother walked by his side, not a god at all but a companion. She was asking his advice, and listening gratefully to his answers.*

Qeteb saw a glimpse of what Isfrael wanted, perhaps more

than anything else, and the vision altered slightly for the Mage-King . . .

And Shra walked by his other side. She had transformed as did all female Banes when they died, and now she awaited him in the Sacred Groves. She waited for him . . .

Isfrael lifted his hand and took a bite of the apple—

The Demons screamed with silent triumph.

—and realisation that the Demons *did* speak the truth flooded his being. They would help him to the Sacred Groves, and there they would leave him in peace, and all for the price of a piece of information that they would surely have figured out sooner or later for themselves.

Peace, power, and all for the tiniest of prices. Isfrael could hardly comprehend his good fortune.

Qeteb grinned, malevolent with exultation behind his mask. The apple always did the trick.

"Let me tell you about the Niah-woman," Isfrael whispered. "She is a treasure you can hardly comprehend. It all has to do with Acharites and death . . ."

And Isfrael talked, the words tumbling out and falling over themselves. All Acharites carried the seeds of Enemy magic within themselves. Only those who'd come back through death could use it. Niah, if only she could speak and think, was a weapon that could breach the walls of Sanctuary, and perhaps could be thrown at the StarSon himself.

"Was that worth the Sacred Groves?" Isfrael finished. "Was it?"

"Oh, assuredly," Qeteb said, and his voice quivered with triumph.

The StarSon was his!

"I can't get to the Groves by myself," Isfrael said, desperate now that the Demons had their information to receive his payment. "I need your power to breach the defences that the Mother has placed around them."

"But how can we—" Qeteb started.

"All I need is *power*," Isfrael said. "Surely you must be more powerful than the Mother? Just create that small rent for me, and I will pass through, and then I can seal the fissure from the other side."

Qeteb glanced at his companions, and they all remembered the strange bowl that one of the Hawkchilds had found. It was of great magic, and StarLaughter—and curses that she had not yet been found!—had said it was of Avar magic.

Without a spoken word, but with mutual agreement, Qeteb lifted a hand and gestured at the sky.

A round-shaped object spun down, and Qeteb caught it in a hand.

"Tell me about this bowl," he said to Isfrael.

Isfrael's face brightened with excitement. "That is my mother's bowl!"

"And its significance is . . ." Qeteb said patiently.

"It does many things, but one of its main purposes was to allow my mother to travel to and from the Sacred Groves."

"Do you know how to use it?"

Isfrael stared at the bowl, then raised his eyes to Qeteb's mask. "Yes. I can use it, but I will need your power added to the power of the bowl so that I can propel myself into the Groves. And . . . one more thing."

I do hope your flesh is going to be sweet enough for all the trouble you are causing me, Qeteb thought, but he answered pleasantly enough. "Yes?"

"I take the bowl with me," Isfrael said. *And then I shall be safe for all time!* he thought.

"But of course," Qeteb said. "I would not dream of keeping it."

And even his visor seemed to smile reassuringly.

Isfrael relaxed with complete relief. "My people are in Sanctuary—" he began.

"No," said Qeteb. "No. They were not part of your original bargain."

"But—"

"No!"

Isfrael subsided. The Avar *had* abandoned him after all. And even then he had tried to save them. He'd done his best.

He had. He really had. Now he should concentrate on saving what was left.

"Very well," he said, and reached out for the bowl.

Isfrael may not have been told of the exact way in which Faraday had used the bowl to reach the Sacred Groves, but he was Mage-King of the Avar, instructed and expert in all of their secret arts. He knew the bowl for what it was: a conduit, a means of entering the Groves either when all other means were closed or, as in Faraday's case, by a person who normally would not have the power or the knowledge to access the secret paths.

The Mother had forgotten the bowl when She'd closed the paths. She'd forgotten that She'd left the back door open.

And here it was, Isfrael thought, in the hands of the Demons. The silly Bitch, She needed him there to guide Her. Why, if he hadn't come along, the Demons would have accessed the Groves for themselves! The Mother was fortunate indeed that he was here to save Her and all who still dwelt within the Groves.

Isfrael placed the bowl on the ground. "I need water."

Instantly Sheol was at his side, solicitously offering him a pewter pitcher filled with clear, sweet water.

She poured it into the bowl, and as it swirled about, the water changed to a deep emerald colour.

Isfrael's chest constricted with excitement, and he had to fight to calm himself. He opened his right hand, and hesitated.

Qeteb, deep inside Isfrael's unwitting mind, instantly leaned out his own hand, one finger extended.

Isfrael stared at the mailed hand, then took a grasp of it—

It was deathly cold, as if it had been entombed for centuries within one of the great bergs that drifted in the Iskmel Ocean.

—and used one of the sharpened overlapping joints above a knuckle to slice a small way into his thumb.

Blood welled, and Isfrael let Qctcb's hand go.

He had not noticed the intensity of its cold, or the intensity of the coldness that now coiled deep inside his mind.

A trace, that the Demons could use later, at their leisure.

Isfrael stood over the bowl murmuring prayers and invocations to the Mother, then he let a single drop of blood fall into the bowl of water.

Blood swarmed over the entire surface of the emerald water.

Isfrael bent down, picked up the bowl, then straightened. He closed his eyes, tilted his head back slightly, and prepared to enter the groves.

"Do it now!" he whispered. "Use your power to propel me *now*!"

And the Demons did. They sniggered and they capered, they dribbled and they scampered, and they concentrated their entire power on the man and the bowl before them.

After all, they had promised.

Isfrael screamed, and then emerald light consumed him. He found himself caught up in a whirlpool of the light, and he almost panicked, until he realised that he was being propelled towards the Sacred Groves with such power that he was being forced through the barriers the Mother had erected.

It hurt. Dreadfully.

But he could feel himself being forced through.

Isfrael clung even tighter to the bowl, concentrating as hard as he could on the image of the Groves . . . and suddenly he could feel the firmness of a forest floor beneath his feet, and he could smell the pungent odour of the trees, and then the emerald light resolved into the form of a thousand trees.

He was in the Sacred Groves. Finally.

Isfrael stood triumphantly. He had done it! He was safe! He turned slightly, and he saw a silver-backed Horned One walking towards him. The Horned One's stag head was trembling, and his liquid dark eyes were filled with anger.

Anger . . . and panic.

"What have you done!" the silver-pelt hissed. "What have you done?"

And he knocked the bowl from Isfrael's hands. "What is this abomination you introduce into the Groves?"

Qeteb stood in the centre of the apple grove, Faraday's bowl in his hands.

"I do hope he liked the imitation I sent with him," he said, and all the Demons howled with laughter.

20

Qeteb's Mansion of Dreams

What DragonStar found in Sanctuary appalled him. Leagh, lying bruised and tearful on her bed, with Zenith at her side, Zared at her other, and StarDrifter, Axis, Azhure, Goldman and Gwendylyr all hovering about, whispering uselessly.

Faraday stood to one side by a window, calm but clearly upset. Katie clung to her skirts, looking resigned.

"What happened?" DragonStar said, striding into the chamber. He'd known the instant that he'd stepped back into Sanctuary that something was wrong. The air smelt vaguely tainted, as if corrupted with the tang of a rotten apple that someone had thrown to one side and then forgotten.

Leagh half raised herself, ignoring Zenith's and Zared's protests. "Isfrael forced me to give him the doorway that you gave to each of us," she said. "And he stepped through it into Spiredore."

DragonStar sat down by Leagh's side as Zenith stood to give him room. She stepped back and stood with StarDrifter.

"He hurt you," DragonStar said.

Leagh attempted to smile, but it did not work very well. "I will be well enough," she said. "A few bruises, both to body and soul."

DragonStar glanced at Faraday, exchanging unspoken concerns with her, then he gently rested a hand on Leagh's abdomen.

"Faraday said the child was well," Leagh said.

"Aye," DragonStar said, and smiled for Leagh. "The child is well." Physically, yes, but spiritually frightened and lost and feeling so insecure that DragonStar wondered if it might try to fight its way free of the womb. If born now it would never survive.

"I saved the doorway," Leagh said, and her voice cracked with tears. "I did not allow him to take—"

"Hush," DragonStar said, and lifted his hand to caress Leagh's cheek. "Hush. There is no guilt or blame in what happened. None that *you* should bear. Faraday," he lifted his eyes, "where do you think Isfrael went? What do you think was his purpose? Helpful . . . or foul?"

Faraday took a deep breath, and her shoulders trembled. Katie clung a little closer. "I cannot think but that it was foul."

DragonStar waited, his gaze steady.

"He hates me," Faraday continued, her voice a little steadier, "for many reasons, but most recently and perhaps most powerfully for disinheriting him, as he understands it, from his position as Mage-King. I think that he may have had some plan to regain that power and position."

"How?"

Faraday shrugged her shoulders helplessly. "I don't know. We have all discussed this, and none of us know."

"Where could he have gone from Spiredore?"

Axis answered, stepping forward and giving Leagh a reassuring smile before he looked at his son. "We all thought the Sacred Groves, but Faraday has told us that the Mother closed off the paths to the Groves before Qeteb was finally resurrected."

"And Spiredore would not have been strong enough to breach Her barriers," Azhure put in. She linked an arm through Axis', and they shared a small smile.

Always the love for themselves, DragonStar thought, and not so much for others. But the thought caused him no resentment, and he wondered if he and Faraday would ever have the time and the peace to indulge in the same luxury of love. How much time had they shared over the past days since he'd arrived in Sanctuary? A few hours snatched here and there, and no more.

"Is there anywhere he could have gone where he could have avoided the Demons?" DragonStar asked. His frustration was clearly evident in his voice.

Silence.

"We cannot think of anywhere," Faraday said eventually. Her voice was breaking.

He went to *the Demons!* The same thought exploded through all their minds.

"Gods!" DragonStar whispered, and rubbed his forehead. "Why? Why?"

"Our son," Axis said, and looked at Faraday, "our son has betrayed us."

DragonStar had to struggle to repress bitter laughter. *You always have to have a son to betray you, don't you, Axis?* But he managed to banish the thought almost as soon as it surfaced.

Damn it! He had to think! *Why would Isfrael have gone to the Demons?*

"And how did he think he was going to survive?" he muttered.

Again, silence, and again it was Faraday who eventually broke it. "He would have gone to bargain with them," she said, "but with what, and for what, I do not know."

DragonStar lifted his eyes to hers. "We are going to have to find out," he said.

This was difficult, and extremely dangerous, but DragonStar had no choice. He had to know what Isfrael was about to do.

Or what he had already done. Stars alone knew if they were going to be able to stop Isfrael, or if the situation had gone too far to remedy the damage.

They were in a small room: DragonStar, Faraday, Gwendylyr and Goldman, and Axis and Azhure. Axis and Azhure could not help with power, but DragonStar somehow wanted them there, not only for the knowledge and experience they shared, but also because their presence comforted him.

And DragonStar was gladdened beyond measure by that sense of comfort.

They all sat in a small circle of chairs, close-touching, save for Faraday who knelt within the circle before DragonStar, her hands on his lap.

"Faraday," DragonStar said, "of all of us present, you are the one with the closest bond to Isfrael."

"And that not very close at all," she said, sadly.

DragonStar smiled for her, letting love and tenderness wash over his face. "You held him within your body for many months, and you bear a mother's love for him. You *have* a bond, and you also have power."

She nodded. DragonStar had explained what they must do. Follow Isfrael through the door with their minds and their power. Follow the memory of where he went, and what he did. See.

The entire procedure was horrendously risky. They were all exposing themselves to attack by the Demons, for their mind power would provide a direct link back to their bodies which remained in this room.

Faraday looked at DragonStar, and, in turn, DragonStar looked at Axis.

Axis gave a slight nod, his face stiff with tension and fear. *If the Demons follow our minds back into Sanctuary,* Dragon-Star had told him, *and seize control of our bodies, then kill us. It will be your—and Sanctuary's—only hope.*

Axis had spent many long years longing for the chance to kill DragonStar. Now? No, he did not think he could do it. Not even with a Demon leering at him with DragonStar's eyes.

And Faraday! *How could he kill Faraday?*

Axis looked at Azhure, and her eyes were steady. Axis took a deep breath. "We are ready," he said.

DragonStar checked Gwendylyr and Goldman. They sat to either side of him, their hands on his shoulders.

They nodded, their faces as tense as Axis'.

DragonStar closed his eyes, and Faraday, Gwendylyr and Goldman followed suit. Axis and Azhure were the only ones who stayed alert, and their eyes they kept watchful.

Seek, DragonStar said to Faraday with his mind voice, and she sought.

She remembered the feel of Isfrael within her body, the thud of his infant heart against the walls of her womb, the *feel* of him, of his body, his spirit, his soul. She concentrated so hard that eventually she could feel the sensations again, feel the weight of him within her, feel the love that they'd shared during that time.

And she sent her senses scrying through space and time, searching out the recent memories of her son.

In Leagh's chamber. Faraday knew he'd been in Leagh's chamber, so she started there.

Where was Isfrael's memory? Where? Where?

There! A shadow slipped across her mind, and Faraday concentrated as hard as she could. She was distantly aware of DragonStar's, Gwendylyr's and Goldman's minds accompanying hers, but they were familiar and loved and safe, and she paid them no heed.

All she thought of was Isfrael.

There he was, his hands on Leagh, his hate rippling across his face. The door, in his hands, stretching so he could step through it . . . Leagh, desperately fighting her way upright and across the bed so she could close the door before Isfrael could take it with him—

Quick! DragonStar's mind spoke. *Quick, we must go through the door before Leagh closes it!*

And there was a surge of power from the other three, and Faraday felt herself being propelled through the doorway even as Leagh closed it down about . . . them. Yes, Faraday allowed herself a moment of relief. The other three had come through with her. They were with her. They would protect her.

Back in the room Axis and Azhure stared at the four forms before them. They were still there, but slumped and almost lifeless.

"They've gone through the door," Azhure said very softly. "Stars help them now."

Axis' hand slipped down to the sword at his side, then lifted back to his lap again.

*They were fleeing with Isfrael through Spiredore—Gods!
DragonStar's mind said, this memory is so cold!* First to the
dead end of the blue-misted tunnel when Isfrael had thought
to enter the Sacred Groves direct . . .

*The Sacred Groves! thought Faraday. He wants to go to the
Sacred Groves!*

. . . and then into the circle of apple trees.

*They saw with his eyes the circle of stumps, and then they
saw with his eyes the Niah-woman, and felt his joy that she was
there.*

And then they saw the Demons.

"Hello," said Qeteb. "So glad you dropped in."

And all four felt fingers of iron close about their minds.

Axis and Azhure jumped, and Axis swore briefly, softly.

The bodies of DragonStar and the other three slumped
completely, losing all muscle tone and all colour.

Axis would have thought them dead save that their chests
continued to rise and fall; slowly, reluctantly, almost imperceptibly.

"What do we do?" Azhure said.

"Wait," said Axis.

His hand closed about the hilt of his sword.

They found themselves in a mansion of many rooms: they
stood in a central atrium, with numerous doors and corridors
darting off at odd angles.

DragonStar felt Gwendylyr panic, and he steadied her.

She looked at him with frightened eyes, although her panic
had eased. "I can feel you," she said.

DragonStar nodded, trying to think out what had happened.
But whatever *had* happened, it had gone badly. Qeteb had
pulled them into a different existence or dimension. Were their
bodies still back in the room with Axis and Azhure? He
glanced at his own body, tapping his hands together gently.

They felt insubstantial, and when DragonStar looked at Faraday, he saw that there was no depth behind her eyes.

"I have created for you a semblance of your forms," a voice echoed about them, and all four looked about, instinctively bunching together.

"An apparition only," the voice continued, and Goldman jerked up a hand to point down one of the corridors.

At the far end was an old, hunchbacked man dressed entirely in black. He had long strands of silver hair brushed over a balding scalp, and his face was cadaverous.

"And yet," the man whispered, "were I to plunge this dagger—" he lifted a hand, and it held a gleaming, jagged edged knife in it, "—into any of your hearts, your true body would spurt blood and die."

Before any of them could react, the horrible, wizened old man scuttled with the speed of an attacking spider down the corridor, the dagger raised high above his head.

Both Gwendylyr and Faraday gasped in horror, and DragonStar thrust them behind him. "Goldman," he began, "get the girls away from—"

The old man vanished, and they were left with the sound of their own harsh breathing and the sad comfort of their fear.

"How do we get out of here?" Goldman said eventually. He turned slightly to look DragonStar in the face, and DragonStar was surprised by how quickly Goldman had managed to compose himself.

"We *find* a way," DragonStar said.

"But don't you want to know what Isfrael was doing here?" the old man's voice said again. This time it came from high above them, and their heads jerked up.

There was a balcony running around the top third of the atrium, and the man was hanging by one hand from its railing, dangling into the space above their heads.

He still held the dagger threateningly in the other hand, and he swung to and fro, his legs bent, as if deciding which one to drop on first.

"Isfrael knows who will win," the man said, "and has acted

accordingly. I find I quite like the fellow. Especially after he gave me the secret to your eventual destruction."

He let go, and dropped.

He fell directly towards Gwendylyr.

DragonStar grabbed at her arm, but Gwendylyr held her ground, staring as if totally unperturbed by the curled black shape hurtling towards her.

It hissed, and vanished the instant before it hit her, and only when it had gone did Gwendylyr allow herself to flinch.

Faraday took her hand, and pulled her close, but she spoke to DragonStar. "Do you think he is telling us the truth?"

Watch . . . a voice echoed through their minds, and the air rippled before them, and they saw Isfrael standing in the circle of stumps, talking to Qeteb. They could hear no words, but they saw him gesture emphatically towards Niah.

"Niah," whispered DragonStar. *"What is it about Niah?"*

They saw the Demons gather about Qeteb . . . and then they saw Qeteb produce the wooden bowl.

Faraday gave a low cry, her free hand clasped to her mouth, her eyes wide with horror.

"Can he get to the Sacred Groves using that bowl?" DragonStar hissed at her, and Faraday nodded.

"With the Demons' power behind him, yes!"

And then the vision gave truth to her words, for they saw Isfrael use the bowl, and then vanish.

The vision faded, but as it did so, there was a clunk on the floor before them, and there was the bowl.

Brimming with clotted blood.

The blood that will run through the Sacred Groves, whispered the voice in their minds.

Faraday let Gwendylyr go and lunged for the bowl, but it vanished the instant before she could grab it.

"DragonStar!" she said, standing up and turning about.

"We need to get out of here," he said, and reached for their hands. "Get back to our—"

No.

The atrium and the doors and corridors rippled, and then

vanished, and in the instant before they, too, vanished, DragonStar shouted: "It is an illusion! There is nothing to fear!"

There is everything to fear, fool.

Each felt the comfort of the others' hands evaporate, and the four found themselves standing in individual corridors.

Each twisted around, trying to see from which direction the danger would come down the bland, pastel-walled hallways.

DragonStar stared, and then half-smiled. Two could play at this game. He closed his eyes, concentrated, and in the next moment two insubstantial hounds appeared at his side.

Sicarius and FortHeart.

"I have lost my comrades," DragonStar said. "Hunt."

The hounds scented the air, and then they bounded down the corridor, DragonStar close behind them, the lily sword in his hand.

He fought down his apprehension. Why hadn't he found the time to tell the other three of what he'd learned about the Book?

But he had not had the time, and DragonStar knew he would have to find them before the Demons either killed them, or took control of their minds.

Faraday turned about, and found herself face to face with two Demons.

At least, that's what she supposed they were, although they had taken the form of a broom and a rake.

Both were enormous, twice the size of any broom or rake Faraday had ever seen. Their handles were constructed of rough, splintery wood, three times the thickness of her wrist, and while the rake had teeth made from razor-like bear claws, the broom had bristles of nails.

Each had elongated eyes towards the top of their handles, and each had tiny, clawed hands protruding out just beneath their eyes.

"We've come to help you tend the field," one of them whispered in a sing-song voice. "We've come to do our very, very best!"

They rushed towards her.

Faraday fought down her fear, and did not flinch. She reacted with pure instinct, as she had when confronted with the rat when trying to help the people of Carlon.

"Have you ever smelt the scent of the Field?" she asked pleasantly, and cast towards them every memory she could dredge up of the overwhelming fragrance of the billions of flowers.

The rake and broom screamed, and then crumpled.

"Bitch!" one of them said, and then vanished with its companion.

Faraday blinked her eyes, and then turned slightly to see Axis and Azhure leaning over her.

She twisted back to DragonStar's form, and grasped his hands tighter.

"Come back!" she said. "Come back!"

DragonStar and his hounds found Gwendylyr in tears, hunched over the still forms of her twin boys.

"They are *not* what they appear to be," he said, and, as he spoke, the boys rose, their faces taking on the likenesses of long-snouted dogs.

Sicarius and FortHeart snarled, stiff-legged.

DragonStar stared at the boys, perturbed more by the Demons' ability to see inside their minds than by the apparitions they chose to weave about them.

How had they known about Gwendylyr's boys?

The two demonic dogs grinned, and their entire bodies waggled and writhed, as if highly amused.

Then they quieted, and their fleshy lips drew back from their teeth. They snarled back at Sicarius and FortHeart, and the two hounds sidled forward a pace or two, stiff-legged.

"No!" DragonStar commanded, and the Alaunt stopped. FortHeart flicked her eyes his way, and in that instant the two Demons attacked.

Gwendylyr screamed, and DragonStar seized her by the

shoulder and hauled her away from the twisting, snarling pack of savagery before her. She stumbled, almost fell, just saved herself, and shrank against a wall, her arms hugged tight about her, her face pale and wide-eyed as she stared at the dog fight.

DragonStar stepped close to the four dogs and tried to seize either Sicarius' or FortHeart's ruff to drag them back. Gods! He hadn't wanted the two Alaunt to get involved in a one on one fight with the Demons! Apparition and illusion this all might be, but DragonStar did not doubt it when Qeteb said that any fatal wound delivered to any apparition would also deliver a fatal wound to the reality.

All DragonStar received for his efforts was a savage bite to his left hand.

In the chamber in Sanctuary, Axis, Azhure and Faraday stared in alarm at the deep wound that suddenly, unexplainably, appeared on DragonStar's hand. Faraday seized a cloth from a nearby table, and wrapped it tightly about Dragon-Star's limp hand, staunching the flow of blood.

"What is happening?" Azhure said, aiding Faraday to tie up the bandage.

"I do not know," Faraday answered, her voice tight and hard with frustration.

The pack was a writhing, twisting and largely indistinguishable mass of heat and teeth and ferocity. Blood and sweat and pieces of fur scattered about as the four creatures within the pack wriggled and wormed, each trying to get the death grip on the throat of their opponent.

DragonStar hesitated on the outer, not knowing what he should do. Curse his stupidity for bringing the hounds into this nightmare—

A cascade of ice-cold water appeared from nowhere, drenching the dogs and soaking through DragonStar's shirt and breeches.

"It is easy to see that none of *you* have had to deal with a dog fight in the streets of Carlon," said a calm voice, and there was Goldman, standing to one side with his arms folded and a satisfied look on his face.

DragonStar nodded at him, relieved not only that Goldman was well and had managed to find them, but that he'd had the presence of mind (and enchantment) to do what was necessary.

The dogs had separated, Sicarius and FortHeart standing just in front of DragonStar, the two Demons several paces away. All were wounded: Sicarius carried several deep gashes on his flanks, while one of FortHeart's ears hung almost completely severed and she limped badly on two of her legs.

The two Demons, also badly gashed, healed themselves simply by flowing back into their humanoid forms complete with pastel-coloured gowns and smug faces.

It was Sheol and Mot.

Behind DragonStar, Goldman moved to stand with Gwendylyr. DragonStar glanced at his two Alaunt. They were panting heavily, and were in obvious pain.

"We have you trapped," Sheol said in a conversational enough tone, "in our mansion of dreams. How do you think you will get out, DragonStar?"

DragonStar held her gaze easily. "By wishing you love," he said.

Sheol flinched, and Mot instinctively took a step back, but before anyone could say and do anything else, the hunchbacked, wizened old man appeared behind the other two Demons, cackling with laughter.

He still held the knife in his hand, but he was laughing so hard it hung useless at his side.

"Love! Love!" the old man cried. "You wish me love, DragonStar? Is that how you think to defeat me? By *redeeming* me? You utter fool! Ah, bah!" And the man suddenly raised his arm and slashed the knife through the air.

Goldman, Gwendylyr and the two hounds disappeared. "It is time you and I talked, my Enemy," Qeteb said, and assumed his true form. "There are some things I ought to explain."

The forms of Goldman and Gwendylyr gasped and twitched, then their eyes flew open.

"What's happening?" Faraday cried, seizing Goldman by the hands.

"Qeteb has DragonStar," Goldman said, and looked at Axis.

Axis stared at him, then switched his gaze to the still limp and insensible form of DragonStar.

21

Legal Niceties

"**D**o you recognise the place?" Qeteb said, and waved a hand about. "I thought you might feel more at home here."

But for the moment DragonStar could not take his eyes from Qeteb. The Demon had assumed a form that was a reflection of DragonStar himself, save that his body was better muscled, his face less lined, and his mouth far more sensual.

DragonStar wondered why he'd assumed so close a likeness, and then thought that perhaps Qeteb wanted to remind him of the close blood relationship between the body the Demon inhabited—WolfStar's son—and DragonStar, who was WolfStar's grandson.

Qeteb had dressed himself elegantly in shades of grey and ivory, his hair neatly combed, his hands folded innocently before him.

He wore no weapons.

Qeteb stood waiting, his handsome face wearing an air of exaggerated patience, and so DragonStar looked about.

They were standing in the kitchens of Sigholt. The tables were spread with the implements of cooking—bowls, foodstuffs and sundry knives and spoons—and the ranges glowed comfortingly against the far wall.

Four cats lay curled up in front of the ranges: all bald, and all with horns protruding from their skulls.

Qeteb grinned. "Would you like to cook for me?"

DragonStar walked about the table before him, running his finger lightly over its surface. "You know a great deal about me," he said.

"I have had a great deal of spare time in recent millennia to learn a great deal," Qeteb said, and clapped his hands together once, sharply.

Instantly the cooking ingredients and implements before DragonStar transformed. A meal appeared before him—roast meats, pastries, mounds of steaming and well-buttered vegetables. The table was laid with heavy silver and cut crystal, and ruby wine glowed in pitchers and the tall-stemmed glasses.

The table was laid for two.

Qeteb picked up one of the glasses and sipped. "Ah, yes. Tasty. Dry but full-bodied. Won't you have some?"

DragonStar did not reply, moving so that the table remained between him and Qeteb at all times.

Qeteb smiled again, all congeniality and consideration. "Please, sit. It was so convenient for you and your . . . ah, what do you call them? your "witches", to drop in like that. I apologise for the indulgence of the mansion. I couldn't resist playing a little."

DragonStar made no reply.

"Ah, please, do sit," Qeteb said. "We've both had a few hard days recently, and surely a good meal and a long chat will relax us."

DragonStar did not move.

Qeteb noisily pulled out a chair and seated himself, lifting a snowy napkin and making a great show of placing it on his lap. "Please . . . sit."

DragonStar did not move.

"Sit!" Qeteb said, a hardness now underlying his voice, and DragonStar found himself bodily lifted up and placed in the chair opposite Qeteb.

A napkin gracefully unfolded and slid itself solicitously over DragonStar's lap.

Trying to take back the initiative—if ever he'd had it since

Qeteb had trapped him within this illusion—DragonStar picked up a glass of wine and sipped.

It was, as Qeteb had said, rather good.

"What do you want?" DragonStar asked.

"Ah," Qeteb said, and began to pile food on his plate, "I thought it might be a good idea for you and I to have a bit of a chat. You see . . ." Qeteb paused as his hand hesitated between a plate full of roast pigeon haunches and one laden with grilled swan tongues. His hand eventually dipped towards the swan tongues. ". . . I was thinking that you and I might actually be at cross purposes, you see."

"Cross purposes?" DragonStar contented himself with sliding some cheese and slices of fruit onto his plate.

"Yes. Oh, these tongues are delicious! Try some, do!"

DragonStar ignored the invitation, wondering where in the world Qeteb had dragged this particular persona from, and why he thought it useful in the first place.

"You don't think it charming?" Qeteb said, assuming an expression of the most utter surprise. "It doesn't relax you?"

For the first time DragonStar laughed, genuinely amused. "Stop toying with me."

Qeteb grinned, also apparently a gesture of genuine cheerfulness rather than malevolent sarcasm.

"You and I," he said, waving a piece of roast pig, "come from much the same place. Disinherited, betrayed, thrown to the stars in the most despicable of ways—"

"I've heard all this before," DragonStar said.

"Ah, but from my dear travelling companions, who—"

"Your companion Demons."

"—often have the most unfortunate turn of phrase. And their manners! Frightful at times, I'm sure you'll agree!"

By the range, the four cats hunched into sorry bundles of the most abject misery.

It was a pity, DragonStar thought, that the entire thing was such an obvious farce.

Qeteb grinned around a mouthful of meat, and DragonStar pulled himself up. The Demon could obviously read his mind at will . . . and he? DragonStar sent his power scrying out, probing Qeteb's mind.

All he saw was a grassy riverbank under the midday sun, willow trees gently swaying and dipping, young men and women lying languidly about in hammocks, adjusting their cream linens, and sipping cups of sweet tea.

"It didn't help you much, did it?" Qeteb whispered, and just for that instant DragonStar saw the malevolence and hatred seething beneath the urbane surface.

Then the instant was gone, and Qeteb was again the epitome of graciousness and solicitousness.

"As I was saying," Qeteb said, sipping his wine, "you and I may have found ourselves at some cross purposes here. Let me just summarise our situation. No, please, let me speak without interruption for a moment or two longer.

"Now, let me see. You have found yourself the final product of several hundred millennia of manipulation by a power that we can call the Star Dance. Now, myself and the Star Dance, or the intelligence it represents, have been . . . um, shall I say . . . at loggerheads for some time. Since the time of Creation, actually. And here you find yourself caught up in a struggle that is none of your doing, none of your concern. You find yourself bred for a purpose . . . but what if the purpose doesn't suit? What if it were better for you simply to shrug your shoulders and say, 'It doesn't concern me?' and walk away."

"You have destroyed the land that I love—"

"And yet which rejected you beyond anything you deserved. After all, you were merely trying to execute your duty in claiming the title of StarSon and in divesting Caelum of it."

A vision of his parents and sundry inhabitants of Sigholt standing around the boy-Drago in Sigholt's courtyard filled DragonStar's mind. They were simultaneously laughing derision and screaming hatred at him, pointing fingers, their bodies stiff with rejection, their faces implacable.

"That was a long time ago," DragonStar said quietly.

"Was it?" Qeteb whispered, and another vision filled DragonStar's mind.

Faraday, turning to Axis with love. "I only used DragonStar to make you jealous," she whispered. "You are the only man I have ever wanted."

"With you at my side I can reclaim my position as StarMan," Axis replied. "Tencendor will be mine again."

"We can dispose of DragonStar," Faraday whispered, and pulled Axis' face down to hers.

"That was a pathetic effort," DragonStar said, and the vision faded as Qeteb shrugged.

"I am offering you a choice, delightful boy," Qeteb said. "Leave me alone, leave Tencendor to me and mine. Enjoy your life elsewhere. There is no point in continuing a battle which is not only *not* your fight—"

"Your destruction and murder across Tencendor *make* it my fight," DragonStar said, but Qeteb continued on without acknowledging the interruption.

"—and which you cannot possibly win."

DragonStar smiled, and Qeteb paused before resuming. "Take you and yours—"

"What is left of them."

Qeteb took a deep breath, his eyes hardening and the veins on his neck standing out, "—and flee with them south. Coroleas, I believe the land is called. There you will be safe."

DragonStar shook his head. "No-one will be safe, Qeteb. You will suck Tencendor dry of every piece of love and beauty and spirit it possesses, and then you will absorb the other lands on this world, one by one, bit by bit. Nowhere will ever be safe from you."

"I am making you an offer, my dear chap. Do try not to refuse without giving it some thought."

"Why the offer at all, Qeteb? Surely you could just eat me as I sit here?"

An expression of pure delighted malevolence crossed the Demon's face. "But, my dear DragonStar! Don't I have *enough* to eat right now?"

His hand swept over the table, but DragonStar knew he meant something else.

"I will eat everything within this land," Qeteb hissed, leaning forward. *"Everything!"*

"It appears to me that you have already had your glut of all the land, Qeteb. What else do you have your hungry eye on?"

"The Sacred Groves." Qeteb sat back in satisfaction at the expression on DragonStar's face. "Won't the Mother make a good meal, don't you think, DragonStar? And after I've finished Her, well . . . there's the small matter of dessert."

He paused, and DragonStar waited, knowing what he would say.

"Sanctuary, and all that it hides."

"You can't get in."

"On the contrary, my delightful fellow," Qeteb said, "I can indeed. What do you think Isfrael traded for his freedom?"

Short freedom, DragonStar thought, if soon the Sacred Groves are spread over the Demons' dinner table. "The bowl," he said. "Isfrael gave you the bowl."

"No. Isfrael only showed us what the bowl was for, and even that was unintentional. He traded us something else . . . something that will enable me to eat Sanctuary as well, and then to destroy you."

Niah! DragonStar thought, desperately trying to work out what it was about her that was so dangerous, so frightening . . .

"No," DragonStar said. "You are afraid of me. That's why you bargain with me, and why you offer me and mine an escape route through to Coroleas."

Qeteb laughed. *"I* . . . afraid of *you*? No! I was merely toying with you for my own amusement! I will kill you, Dragon-Star. Have no doubt about it."

He sipped some more of his wine, and let his amusement suffuse his entire being. "Sheol has told me of what Dare-Wing did to her. Poor girl, she was slightly put out. Being somewhat tuneless herself, she resents all aspects of harmony."

DragonStar said nothing.

Qeteb drained his wine, and poured himself another glass. "Do drink up! Please! No? Well then, let me continue. As I see it, DragonStar, you think you have the key to my destruction. No, wait! Redemption would be a better word than destruction, wouldn't it?"

DragonStar fought to keep both his face and mind blank, but his thoughts were working far too furiously to be successful at either.

"You think," Qeteb said, "that you will use love to confound me, joy to confuse me, and forgiveness to emasculate me. Well," he leaned forward, his face red with fury, "*none* of those things will touch me! I am incapable of being touched by love or joy or forgiveness. They ceased many aeons ago to have any meaning for me!"

"And yet Caelum managed to—"

"Caelum infuriated me because he would not struggle against me. I found that . . . irritating. His love left me cold."

Ice spread over the table, covering wood and platter and glassware alike, and DragonStar had to jerk his hand away from his glass to save it from being similarly encased.

"Sheol may have been frightened by it," Qeteb continued, his voice now a vicious whip, "but your redemption will never, never, *never* touch me!"

"So why bring me here?" DragonStar said. "Why?"

"To explain the rules of this confrontation. The Star Dance and I have been jousting since the beginning of time. Now it has made you its final weapon. Your problem, DragonStar, is that you've only been around some forty years, and you have some catching up to do. Now," Qeteb leaned forward, "listen up.

"You think that you and I must meet in a final confrontation. Correct?"

DragonStar nodded slowly, his eyes not leaving Qeteb's face.

"Well, in that you're right. You also believe that before you and I meet, there must be individual confrontations between your five and my five companions. Right?

DragonStar nodded again, but even more cautiously.

Qeteb beamed, and sat back. "My dear chap, again you are perfectly correct! Well done!

"But," Qeteb's entire demeanour darkened, and became triumphantly malevolent, "although you instinctively know the broad outlines of the rules of the game, some of the subtle, legalistic niceties have entirely escaped your attention.

"Did you know, you starry-eyed piece of shit, did you have any *realisation*, that the confrontation between yours and mine *will decide the outcome between you and me?*"

DragonStar went cold. He desperately did not want to believe what Qeteb had said, but . . .

"You can feel the truth of the matter can't you?" Qeteb said. "Oh! You naive simpleton! You were so damned sure that because you think to represent the forces of righteousness and love and gods know what else, you think you will win!

"Wrong. Five of yours will meet five of mine. There can be no even score. If one of yours fails, you will be weakened, as I would be if one of mine failed. If two of yours fail, you would be seriously weakened, as I would. If *three* of yours fail, *you* will fail because the balance will have fallen in my favour. *Do you understand?*"

DragonStar stared, unable to speak.

Qeteb smiled slowly, and folded his arms across his chest. "You poor boy. You are upset. Well, I am prepared to be magnanimous. After all, me and mine have had far longer to think about it all, to prepare, than your sweet witches . . . and isn't one of them pregnant? The poor girl! She must be quaking in her dainty boots! Therefore I will allow your witches the choice of weapons and place—although you and I are more bound by the rules, of course."

There was a sweeping darkness, and a wind, and the faint cries of the Hunt through the Maze.

"You have lost Rox," said DragonStar. "Leagh doesn't have to—"

Qeteb snarled. "Know that Leagh *will* have to attend!"

The Demon leaned forward again, swarming over the tabletop like a deformed spider. "I've had enough of this pretence, DragonStar! I brought you here to make sure you know, beyond any doubt, that you will *die*, DragonStar. To make sure you know beyond any doubt that you will *fail*. To make sure that you know beyond any doubt that everything you love and treasure will be swallowed up to live eternity in the dark, writhing masses of my belly. There is no way that your five can triumph over my five. I *will* hunt you through the Maze, StarSon. And when I do the outcome will be inevitable!"

The four cats leapt screaming into the air, and DragonStar lifted his arms reflexively. As he did so, he felt Qeteb reach dark, clawed fingers into his mind.

DragonStar's body jerked and sat up.

"DragonStar?" Faraday said.

"No, you bitch," Qeteb whispered with DragonStar's voice. "Not your lover at all, but one who will nevertheless eventually love you anyway."

Faraday, as did everyone else in the room, jerked back in horror.

"DragonStar can do nothing against me," Qeteb continued, and he twisted DragonStar's features into a parody of a grin. "He will die, you will all die, and everything you love shall be utterly destroyed."

Axis' hand fiddled with his sword, and Qeteb saw, and laughed. "If you kill this body now, then you will still not touch me," he said. "Nothing can touch me."

DragonStar's hand jerked up and touched Faraday's face.

She scrambled back in horror.

"I can penetrate his mind at will," Qeteb said. "Take over his body at will. I *can* do it. Whose voice will issue forth at what time of the day? Whose orders will it mouth? Whose hands, Faraday, will caress your body?"

The Demon laughed, and DragonStar's body jerked in a violent fit. "I give you back DragonStar," the Demon said, "for he has some important information for you."

DragonStar's body gave one final jerk as Qeteb howled in laughter, and then it slumped back in its chair.

22

The Sacred Groves

Isfrael stared at the silver-haired Horned One. "I introduce no abomination into the grove!" he said. "I have every right to be here and—"

The silver-pelt stepped forward and slapped Isfrael's face so hard the Mage-King stumbled and almost fell.

Isfrael snarled, and swung back at the Horned One, but the creature was too fast for him, and kicked Isfrael squarely in the ribs.

The Mage-King fell to the ground, heaving in breaths in great gasps.

The Horned One kicked him again. "You gave the Demons the enchanted bowl!"

Isfrael rolled away and struggled to his hands and knees. "They already had it, you horned aberration! Faraday, your beloved Tree Friend, gave it to them! *I* brought it back! We are safe, and—"

"That," the Horned One said, pointing to the bowl where it had rolled several paces away, "is a copy. A fake. A *trick!*"

Isfrael stared at him, then shifted his eyes to the bowl. "No. It can't be."

He looked back at the Horned One and saw for the first time the tiredness in the creature's liquid black eyes, the slump of his shoulders, the sagging muscles. The creature was dying.

Isfrael narrowed his eyes. "What's happening here? Why are

you so ill?" He finally struggled upright and looked about him. The trees of the Sacred Grove were as touched by malaise as the Horned One: their leaves were blotched and mouldy, their bark was peeling away in great strips, their roots arched out of the earth as if trying to escape the disease within.

"The bowl is a fake," the Horned One said again, and lifted his hands in despair. "What are we to do?"

Two women walked slowly out of the tree line. One, the Mother, leaned on the other's shoulders for support.

Ur walked strong and determined, and her ancient face was lined with anger and resolution.

"My friend?" the Mother said to the Horned One.

"Isfrael has broken through the barriers You built to seal off the Sacred Groves," the Horned One said.

"Impossible," the Mother said. "No-one had the power to—"

"He sought the aid of the Demons to do so," the Horned One said. "*And* Isfrael left the enchanted bowl with the Demons. I'm afraid they now know the way along the paths."

The Mother's face crumpled, and She pressed a hand to Her mouth to suppress a moan.

"What does this mean?" Ur said.

"It means," the Mother answered in a tiny voice, "that the Demons will be able to access the Groves. They have the power and they have the vehicle."

"Then we will fight!" Ur said, and she half-raised a fist.

The Mother smiled, a small, desperate attempt. "What with, my dear? Everything about the Groves—the soil, the water, the air, the very *soul*—has been corrupted by the Demons' influence over Tencendor. We have nothing left to fight with. Nothing."

"I have my pots," Ur said, and her fist raised a little higher.

Isfrael gave a harsh bray of laughter, and turned away. Fools! He had managed to secrete himself with *fools!*

He sank down under a tree, ignoring the constant patter of dead leaves that fell about him. So . . . the Mother and Her impotent companions are sure the Demons will destroy the Groves? Isfrael thought about it . . . what *else* did he have that he could bargain for his life with?

23

Niah Reborn

"Well?" said Axis, his voice hard.

"Isfrael has betrayed us," DragonStar said. "He has given Qeteb some secret that will enable him to—"

"That is not what I asked."

DragonStar looked up. His parents, Faraday, Gwendylyr and Goldman were all standing about his chair, their faces carefully unreadable.

Only Faraday allowed the barest of emotions to glimmer forth: her eyes were pools of horror . . . a remembered horror.

"What did I say?" DragonStar said. "Why do you all look at me like that?"

"Who are you?" Goldman asked. "You look like Dragon-Star, and you sound like DragonStar, but who are you?"

DragonStar frowned. "What . . ."

"Qeteb spoke through your mouth," Faraday said softly. Her hands were clutched before her, twisting and writhing as if they, too, might be in the grip of some demonic possession. "He said . . . he said that he could take possession of your mind at will."

DragonStar closed his eyes and tipped his head back to rest against the back of the chair. *Gods, what had he done?* Let his confidence get the better of him! Let his arrogance lead them all into ruin!

And Qeteb could take possession of him at will?

"I cannot believe that," DragonStar said, opening his eyes and staring at the five gathered about him.

"He spoke to us," Faraday said. "DragonStar, it was *not* you."

DragonStar closed his eyes again. He remembered how

Qeteb had reached claws into his mind as he'd sat at that table, but he'd not known that he'd . . . he'd . . .

DragonStar was suddenly filled with such a repugnance he leaned forward and retched. Stars in heaven, was this how a woman felt when she'd been raped?

Faraday swayed forward, then hesitated, and it was Azhure who put her arm around DragonStar's shoulders.

"What we are afraid of," Azhure said, "is that we, or any who speak to you or take your orders, may not be aware that Qeteb speaks through you."

"We will always look at you and wonder," Faraday said.

DragonStar wiped his mouth, jerking his eyes to meet hers. "You cannot trust me?"

"How can we trust you?" Goldman said. "Is this you now, or a cunning persona of Qeteb?"

DragonStar stared, then rose unsteadily to his feet. "You have no choice. You *must* trust me."

"How 'no choice'?" Axis said. His hand had finally drawn the sword, but he kept the blade flat against his leg.

"Because if you choose *not* to trust me, then Qeteb automatically wins. But if you choose to ignore what he *says* he can do, then you have an even chance of coming through. Either I am who I say I am, or I have lost my wits and voice and body to Qeteb. Even chance."

There was a silence.

"Besides," DragonStar continued, his voice hard, "no-one has any idea if Qeteb can indeed take possession of my mind and voice at will. When he did so just then he had me at his mercy in his lair. Can he repeat that trick when I am on my own territory and in possession of my own body?

"Dammit, you have no choice but to hope and to trust! If you decide to abandon me now then you will automatically sign your own, and this land's, death warrants!"

Axis and Azhure looked at each other, and Faraday dropped her eyes. Only Goldman and Gwendylyr continued to regard DragonStar with a steady gaze.

"He's right," Goldman suddenly said. "We have no choice

but to trust DragonStar. If we do, then we may win and we may fail, but if we *don't*, then we guarantee our failure."

Gwendylyr nodded. "I agree."

She remembered how DragonStar had aided her when they'd all been trapped in Qeteb's illusion. Gwendylyr would not abandon him now.

Axis sighed, and sheathed his sword. He attempted a small smile. "I hate the odds, DragonStar. I loathe them. But you are right. None of us have a choice."

Azhure, her hand still on DragonStar's arm, nodded, and gave his arm a slight squeeze, but did not speak.

DragonStar looked at Faraday.

She stared at him, and gave a bright, utterly false smile.

She looked like a glass statue that would shatter at any moment.

"Of course I trust you, DragonStar," she said, and in that one, calamitous sentence, DragonStar knew he had lost her.

"Niah," DragonStar said. Only a moment had passed since Faraday had spoken, but in that moment a chasm had opened between them. "It has something to do with Niah."

"Isfrael went to Qeteb with some information about Niah," Goldman said. They'd all resumed their seats again, but the mood between them was stiff and uncomfortable. How long, DragonStar wondered, before any kind of trust can be rebuilt between us? Qeteb did well . . . very well indeed.

"There was *something* he told Qeteb about Niah," Goldman continued, his face creasing in thought, "that has made Qeteb so confident he thought he had the leisure to toy with Dragon-Star, and with us through DragonStar."

"Toy?" wondered DragonStar, and then furthered wondered when—or even if—he should tell his witches of the consequences if they failed against the Demons. No, he must tell them. But not yet . . . not yet.

"Something about Niah," he said, remembering Qeteb's

words, "that will enable Qeteb to 'eat' Sanctuary and destroy all of us. *What?* Azhure, can you help?"

Azhure shrugged helplessly. "Niah is much changed since I knew her. Death warped her soul so much that she has lost any—"

"Oh dear gods!" DragonStar leapt to his feet so abruptly that his chair fell over. *"Oh dear gods in heaven!"*

No-one could speak, all shocked by the look of horror on DragonStar's face.

DragonStar groped behind him for the chair, righted it, and sank down again. He was trembling so badly he had to grip the armrests with his hands in order to steady himself.

"Niah . . ." he cleared his throat and began again. "Niah is an Acharite reborn. She has access to the power of the Enemy."

There was a horrified silence.

Then Gwendylyr spoke, her voice surprisingly calm. "And thus, through her, so also does Qeteb have access to the power of the Enemy."

DragonStar nodded. "He can use her power to dismantle the enchantments and barriers that the Enemy erected to protect Sanctuary."

No-one spoke for a long time.

"And does that mean he can counter whatever you throw at him?" Axis said.

"I do not know," DragonStar whispered. "I do not know!"

No wonder Qeteb was so damned confident! Would his witches have any hope at all?

"But Niah has no soul," Gwendylyr said, trying desperately to find some shred of hope in the situation. "She is an automat only. She is—"

"She is a body ready to be filled with a soul," DragonStar said. "As was the child StarLaughter carried about with her. Niah is willing flesh imbued with the power needed to defeat Qeteb, but which Qeteb can now use to turn against us." DragonStar looked about at the others, meeting each of their eyes in turn. "I think none of us doubt but which soul Qeteb will use to fill her with purpose."

"Rox," Faraday eventually whispered. "He will fill her with Rox's soul."

"Are you saying," Azhure said, "that Sanctuary will fall?"

DragonStar nodded, his eyes sick with grief and self-recrimination. Curse him, he should have realised this earlier! He thanked the Stars that Axis hadn't killed him earlier when Qeteb had spoken through his mouth. If Axis *had* done so, then Qeteb could possibly have had the power of the Star-Son at his fingertips! *They had all come so close to complete annihilation!*

"And the Sacred Groves?" Faraday said, pulling Dragon-Star's thoughts back to the problem of Niah.

DragonStar nodded again. "They will go first, my beloved," and he paused as Faraday flinched, although whether at the thought of the Groves falling, or at the endearment, Dragon-Star did not know. "Qeteb will destroy them first."

"Why?" Azhure said.

"Because he wants to grow on the power of the Mother before he comes after us," DragonStar said. "He wants to feast on the Mother."

"No!" Faraday screamed, and threw herself at DragonStar.

A massive storm held the Icebear Coast trapped. The land had witnessed nothing like this since the days of Gorgrael, and even he hadn't had the power to generate this much fury. Sleet lashed down from the north in almost horizontal sheets, stinging into ice and snow with such force that shards of ice shot through the air like shrapnel.

DragonStar grabbed his cloak in the instant before the wind tore it away, and tried to shut his ears against the screaming of wind and ice about him. He was leaning against the lee side of an ice wall, but even here the storm threatened to pick him up and hurl him into some ice-needled eternity.

Nothing was sane in this world, nothing at all.

Not even him, if one believed the fearful eyes of Faraday.

From the chamber where DragonStar had realised the appalling significance of Niah, he had gone to check on Sicarius and FortHeart. They'd been in a different part of Sanctuary when he'd called them into Qeteb's illusion, and DragonStar eventually found them under a buiche-fruit tree, being tended by an Icarii Healer.

Sicarius was the lesser wounded of the two, and likely to make a full recovery. FortHeart had lost her ear, and one of her legs was swollen, but the Healer had said that she, too, would recover, if not to her former prettiness.

From there DragonStar had dared the uncertainties of Spiredore to come to this spot. Why? DragonStar tried to force his half-frozen face into a grin as he thought that one through. Why? Because somewhere on the Icebear Coast was the one person who just *might* be able to help.

Urbeth.

DragonStar had not seen nor heard from her since Qeteb had been resurrected, but he had no doubt that she had survived the wasting of Tencendor, and currently sat with her daughters, waiting out the time before DragonStar managed to best Qeteb and set Tencendor to rights.

"Well, my lady," DragonStar muttered through ice-hardened lips, "DragonStar doesn't have a hope of besting Qeteb if the Demon harvests both the power of the Mother *and* the power of the Enemy!"

He lifted his head slightly and stared into the white oblivion before him. "Urbeth!" he screamed. "Urbeth! Where are you!"

Nothing but the shrieking of the wind and the groaning of the ice.

"Urbeth, you hairy cow, answer me now!"

Nothing. DragonStar struggled to keep his footing. Everything was coated with a slick of ice: not only the ground, but his boots, his cloak, and even his hands glistened under a thin layer of the loathsome stuff.

"Urbeth!" he yelled, his voice thinner now. "Urbeth!"

Nothing.

DragonStar groaned and sank to his haunches, trying to tug

his cloak even more tightly about him. He couldn't stay here. . . . he must leave . . . Urbeth was gone . . .

His head sank downwards. He was so tired. Perhaps if he just closed his eyes a minute, rested a bit before he returned to Sanctuary. Some rest would be good.

His head dropped lower.

"Urbeth," he whispered, and slumped forward onto the ice.

He woke to the frightful smell of rotten fish. He jerked awake, his head pounding so badly he thought it might explode.

He opened his eyes.

He was in an ice cave, the floor of which was covered in decomposing fish.

DragonStar gagged, and struggled to his knees. He was covered in bits of rotting fish.

"Look to what this land has been brought," a voice said behind him, and DragonStar struggled to turn about amid the fish. He slipped over twice before he managed to turn completely around and gain his feet.

Three women stood there. All were tall and willowy, all dressed in pale grey robes, and each of them was standing with arms crossed so that her hands rested on her shoulders. Two had raven-black hair that cascaded down their backs and over their breasts, the other, the middle one, had iron-grey hair with streaks of silver through it.

"Urbeth," DragonStar said. "Your housckccping skills have slipped."

She snarled, but DragonStar did not flinch. "I need your help."

She arched an eyebrow at him. None of the three had stepped forward, nor relaxed their hands from their shoulders.

"Qeteb will win through to the power of the Enemy," he said. "Sanctuary will fall."

For the first time Urbeth's face registered shock.

"Worse," DragonStar continued, "Qeteb has access to the

Sacred Groves. If you have any love, or even a single regard, for the Mother, Urbeth, then aid her now."

And then, with hands still shaking from the cold, Dragon-Star drew the lily sword and created the doorway of light. Before Urbeth or either of her daughters could say anything, he was gone.

24

Zenith

Zenith checked Leagh before she retired herself. The woman was sleeping quietly, her skin slightly flushed but cool, her breathing calm and deep. Zenith nodded to Zared, sitting silent in a corner under the pool of light cast by a lamp, and then left the room, sighing as she closed the door.

Zenith was feeling excluded and forgotten—and feeling guilty that she felt that way in the first instance. Her brother DragonStar, her best friend Leagh, and even her parents (who had spent the greater portion of her life being distant and uninterested), were caught up in events of such great magnitude that all existence depended on the outcome. There were hurried comings and goings, hastily convened councils, newly-discovered magics and dark treacheries happening everywhere . . . but they were happening behind closed doors for all Zenith felt involved. She played no part in them—she might as well not exist for all the influence she could bring to bear on the current crisis.

Zenith was not a proud woman, nor one to seek attention or lust after her own role in whatever power play consumed the nation, but she *was* a SunSoar, a princess of the House of Stars, and she was not used to being brushed aside as if she was of no import at all.

"And yet what have I accomplished?" she asked herself as she walked the halls of Sanctuary towards her own apartment.

"I played a small part in enabling DragonStar to escape death at Caelum's hands, and then . . . nothing. I was forcibly seduced, then as forcibly excluded from my own body. I have ever reacted, not *acted*."

And then Zenith smiled at her own foolishness. What was she doing, thinking dark thoughts about being excluded from whatever secret councils were being held this night? What was she doing lusting after some dark and dangerous furtive role in bringing about Qeteb's downfall? All she wanted, if truth be told, was a quiet life away from the intricacies of high politics and enchantment: perhaps with a husband to love and care for her, and children to love.

Now Zenith hesitated again, pausing and resting a hand on one of the corridor walls.

She could have all that if she really wanted it, couldn't she? StarDrifter was never far away. He never demanded, he never even mentioned the fact that what he wanted most of all in life was to have her as his wife, but Zenith could almost *feel* the intensity of his thoughts: StarDrifter's hunger kept her awake at nights.

Guilt, guilt, guilt—that's what kept her awake at nights. There was no reason why she couldn't respond to StarDrifter save her own inhibitions and prudery. She loved him—Zenith had no problems admitting that to herself, nor even to StarDrifter—but whenever she thought of bedding with him, then the strength of her physical repulsion made her stomach turn over.

Would time ease her repulsion? Erode her prudery?

But how much time, and how long was StarDrifter prepared to give her?

Zenith lifted her chin, straightened her shoulders and walked forwards. *Why did she always feel so guilty?* What fault was within her that made her—

A birdwoman hurrying along the corridor interrupted Zenith's flow of thoughts, and she studied the woman, grateful for the interruption and the opportunity to think about something other than her own inadequacies.

The birdwoman, an Icarii Healer by the name of StarWalker,

was carrying a bowl of soiled cloths. The pungent aroma of ginnet—a herb used to stifle infection—rose from the cloths.

"Someone is ill?" Zenith asked, laying a hand on Star-Walker's arm to halt her.

"Yes," StarWalker said, watching Zenith carefully. The healer licked her lips, and her eyes slid away from Zenith's.

Zenith's eyes narrowed. "Who is ill?" she asked. "And why the ginnet? Is she—he?—so badly injured they need its strength?"

"The man *is* badly injured," StarWalker said. "Crippling wounds . . . inflicted by the Demons, I believe."

Zenith's interest was piqued. Who had been so badly hurt? And why was StarWalker being so reticent? The birdwoman's eyes were now sliding this way and that so desperately she looked as though she were about to have a seizure.

Dammit! Zenith thought. Is everyone resolved to keep me in the dark about every trifling detail?

"I really must go," StarWalker said. "If you will excuse me . . ."

Zenith's hand tightened on StarWalker's arm. "Where is the sick room?"

"Oh, it's too far for you to be troubling yourself—"

"I don't think so, StarWalker. *Where* is the sick room? I might as well make myself useful."

"Zenith," StarWalker said, finally looking her in the eye, "you do not want to go there."

"Why? Is the patient so infectious? And if so, then what are you doing wandering the corridors with a bowl full of infection in your hands?"

"Zenith," StarWalker was now leaning close, her eyes wide and full of an emotion that Zenith could not quite read. "Zenith . . . DragonStar found WolfStar within the wasteland. He brought him back—frightfully injured by the Demons. I . . . I did not want to tell you."

Zenith was so shocked she could not say anything for a moment. WolfStar . . . *here?* In Sanctuary? She had hardly thought of him since she'd come down to Sanctuary herself; somehow her mind had come to the unconscious conclusion that he'd been killed by the Demons and she need never worry about him again. But now . . .

"WolfStar?" she whispered.

"There is no need for you to be concerned," StarWalker said, laying the bowl on the ground and taking both of Zenith's hands in hers. "He is kept under close guard. He can't be a danger to you now."

Gods, Zenith thought weakly, does *everyone* know about his rape of me? Has everyone else been told that WolfStar is here, and is everyone wandering about thinking, Poor Zenith, we must keep this from her in case she shatters?

"Where is he?" Zenith said, looking StarWalker in the eye.

"I don't think I should—"

"Where is he?"

StarWalker hesitated, then spoke. "He's being kept in the underground chambers in the complex next to the apple and plum orchard."

Zenith nodded slowly; she knew it. StarWalker must be heading back to the series of herb storerooms that were situated on the second level of this building. If Zenith hadn't happened across StarWalker, nor pressed her for details, she would never have known about WolfStar.

"Thank you, StarWalker," she said, absently, disengaging herself from the woman's grip.

"He won't harm you," StarWalker said.

"I'm sure he won't," Zenith said, and abruptly turned and walked away.

She sat in her darkened room for many hours. Thinking. Remembering. Trying to decide on some course of action.

Zenith was stunned at her own reaction to the news that WolfStar had been found and then secreted within Sanctuary. She would have imagined she might have felt fear, or anger, or even repulsion.

But she felt none of these. All she felt was an overwhelming desire to see him.

Why? To gloat perhaps. To spit in his face? To finally lay

aside the memory of his repulsive rape and then misuse of her body as he encouraged Niah in her attempts to control it?

Zenith didn't know, and that was what distressed her most of all. She had thought anger and revenge would have been at the forefront of her mind . . . but all she found herself thinking of was the single glimpse she'd had of WolfStar at Fernbrake Lake. She'd been horrified by his condition—but she hadn't felt any anger or repulsion when she'd seen him, *had* she?

"No, no," she muttered, her hands twisting in her lap, "I was distracted by the sight of Niah, that's all. I would have been angered and repulsed if I hadn't been distracted by Niah."

Zenith rose and paced about the room. She badly wanted to talk to someone, but there was no-one left. Faraday, Gwendylyr and Leagh were each preoccupied with their own problems and their newly-discovered roles and powers, while Azhure, although she'd been closer and warmer to Zenith in the past few days than Zenith could remember in many years, was still not a confidante. Not for this, and certainly not where WolfStar was concerned. Azhure might superficially acknowledge WolfStar's failings (murder, manipulation, treachery, rape . . . the failings of any mere mortal) but he was nevertheless her father, and she had emotional ties with WolfStar that precluded any detached discussion of him.

Besides, Zenith could not get out of her mind the fact that Azhure had also encouraged the Niah-soul's attempt to take over Zenith's body.

StarDrifter? Could she go to StarDrifter? Zenith found herself standing before the door to the corridor. She trusted him more than any. She loved him. He would be understanding.

About WolfStar?

"Why am I feeling this way?" Zenith whispered. *"Why?"* She felt as though some mean-spirited giant had taken an enormous wooden spoon and stirred up her entrails. She was a mass of conflicting emotions, and yet she could not identify any of them.

And she did not know what to do, nor who to talk to. Was it just mention of WolfStar, or was it that combined with her feelings of disassociation and uselessness which had been growing for weeks now?

Zenith closed her eyes, gripped the door handle tightly, and made up her mind.

She *had* to talk to someone.

She turned the handle, opened the door, and walked into the corridor, vanishing into the gloom.

25

Into the Sacred Groves

"**I** am not sure it was such a good idea to goad the StarSon," Sheol said. "Nor tell him about the Sacred Groves. And most certainly it was *not* a good idea to let him know how vital the individual combats between us and his are!"

Sheol's mouth pouted in a show of petulance that Barzula, Mot and Raspu privately thought would bring her to a very, very bad end.

But Qeteb surprised them. He had retained the congenial, handsome facade he'd shown DragonStar, and now walked about their glade, tossing an apple from one hand to the other.

Qeteb was in an extremely good mood. Infinite power coupled with infinite destruction lay in his immediate future, and that made him a trifle mellower than usual. He took a bite out of the apple.

"DragonStar would have guessed the fate of the Sacred Groves soon enough," he said around the bits of creamy apple flesh that fell from his mouth. "And knowing precisely what rides on the individual combats will make him insecure, not more powerful. Sometimes knowledge undermines, not empowers."

His eyes slid to Niah, still lying waiting soullessly for whatever his pleasure might be next.

Qeteb's lips curled in a sly smile, and he spat out the remaining fragments of the apple, tossing the core away to a rabid weasel nosing amid a dungheap behind one of the fruit trees.

Qeteb's face flickered in distaste as the weasel snatched at the core. He thought that once he got the new order working nicely within this wasteland, he might do something about the more pungent aspects of his horde of maniacal admirers.

Then he bent down to Niah, and stroked her hair. Bitch. Her form did not appeal at all, but it was female and it was fertile, and that is all that Qeteb cared about. His hand slid down to her belly, and pressed down.

Her body nourished the foetal flesh that would eventually harbour Rox's soul. A shame that the new flesh took so long to grow. There were magics and enchantments that could be used to speed up the process, but even so it would be many weeks before Niah's body had fulfilled its purpose and Qeteb could dispose of it once and for all.

"Good little wife," he muttered, and patted her cheek. "Dear girl."

Weeks it might take, but in the meantime Niah was going to come in very, very useful.

Barzula appeared at his shoulder, and Qeteb looked up.

"What are you going to do?" Barzula asked. His voice was laden with suppressed excitement. His three companions and he had thought that Qeteb would act instantly to use Niah's latent powers, and now they grew impatient.

Best not to show it too much, though.

Qeteb stood up and straightened out the fine grey wool tunic he wore.

"We go to the Sacred Groves, and we *eat*," he said, and the other four Demons broke into howls of anticipation, holding hands and capering about in a circle.

"We need the power that we will obtain there," Qeteb continued, and then paused, his eyes fixing on some distant, unseen point as he thought of all the power he and his could feed on in the Sacred Groves.

The silence lengthened.

Qeteb visibly shook himself, then spoke again. "We need that extra power to—"

"Destroy Sanctuary?" Sheol said, letting her eagerness get the better of her sense.

Qeteb roared, and flung out a stiff arm, hitting Sheol in the cheekbone.

There was a distinct crack, and Sheol fell over, but she scrambled to her feet, letting neither Qeteb's anger nor her swelling face distract her from her hunger.

"What then?" she whispered. Her cheek quivered, and then rearranged itself back into a normal shape.

Qeteb stared at her, then spoke. "We restore Rox's soul to the scrap of flesh within that woman's belly—"

"But that won't do any good!" Mot said. He stepped forward, his skeletal arms wrapped about himself as if his over-abundant hunger would make him consume himself at any moment. "He can't be born yet, and—"

"Will no-one allow me to finish?" Qeteb bellowed, and the other Demons subsided, dropping their eyes and shuffling their feet.

It was a show of respect only. They were far too excited at the thought of the power that lay ahead to be too submissive.

"Have you learned *nothing* from all the worlds we have consumed? All the souls we have absorbed? Ah!"

Qeteb stalked away a few paces, then strode back, bent down and seized Niah by the hair, and hauled her to her feet.

Her face registered no pain, no offence.

Qeteb shook her so violently her arms and legs jiggled. "She is *soulless*. There is nothing there! If Rox inhabits the flesh within her flesh, then he can control her from her womb. He can control her *power*!"

"Why not simply give Rox *her* body to inhabit?" Sheol asked. Why bother with all this waiting for the foetus Qeteb had planted to reach a viable state?

Qeteb stared at Sheol, allowing rage to suffuse his face. Initially, he'd wanted to give Rox a new body of flesh to inhabit— Niah's flesh had been somewhat overused, after all. But now there was a very, very good reason he didn't want Rox to have permanent control of this woman's body: if she was so infused with the Enemy's power, then Qeteb wanted *none* of the other

Demons to control it for very long. That Rox would do so for some few short weeks or months did not trouble Qeteb—after all, he was sure he could keep Rox under control for that length of time. But Qeteb would not, *could* not, tolerate a permanent situation where Rox controlled the vast power of the Enemy.

It might put Qeteb himself under threat.

No, better to dispose of the Niah person once and for all the instant her purpose was served.

There was one further reason why Qeteb did not give Niah's soulless body to Rox, a reason that he did not even want to voice in his mind, let alone aloud to the other Demons: *there was something inside the Niah-woman that stopped him doing it.*

Qeteb could not understand it. There was no logical reason why he shouldn't have been able to suffuse the Niah-woman's body with Rox's soul, but *he could not do it.* All his exploratory probings had been repulsed. By what? By what?

He growled, and flexed his fists, and the four watching Demons took a simultaneous, co-ordinated step backwards.

"*Her* body is foul and corrupted," he said, "and I wish Rox to have flesh of this flesh," he slapped his thigh, "to use. I am honouring him thus."

The other four stared at him, then decided to accept his words.

"Once Rox is installed in the foetus and has control of the woman's body," Qeteb continued in a pleasant voice, as if none of the previous unpleasantness had occurred at all, "then we will destroy Sanctuary. We will *consume* everything within it—"

There were howls of laughter and hunger.

"—and then I will set you to hunting down each of Dragon-Star's helpers, pitiful that they are, and to slaughtering them as they cringe begging for mercy."

"And then DragonStar!" Mot cried, flinging his arms wide.

"Yes! Then DragonStar," Qeteb said, and raised his arms heavenward. "And once His Prettiness is disposed of, we can turn our attention to this entire world!"

"And then?" Sheol asked, sidling close to Qeteb and laying an arm about his waist.

"Then we can rest awhile, my dear," Qeteb said, and patted her cheek. "Before the next world."

Beyond the apple grove, the wasteland ran with corruption. There were now hundreds of thousands of beasts—both human and their livestock, and formerly wild creatures—that ran the wastes. They had bred in past weeks and the young that they dropped only days after the frenzied copulations that had created them grew at a maniacal rate—and grew into maniacal shapes. The breeding itself had been utterly indiscriminate—men-things with cow-things, rooster-things with bitch-things, bull seal-things with woman-things—and the results of these copulations were worse than horrific, more imaginative than the darkest nightmare, and far more aggressive than the most ill-trained and starved guard dog.

The wasteland crawled with corruption that could have been barely imagined by the most drug-crazed mind.

There was an eating ahead. Their master, Qeteb, had issued an invitation.

But first, Qeteb and his Demons must needs attend the Sacred Groves. Eating aplenty lay there, too, but the Demons were not about to share this meal with anyone. The power of the Mother, and of the Horned Ones, and of whatever other enchantment the Groves harboured was far too potent and far too glorious to share with the misconceived darkness that slavered in the dirt.

Qeteb stood in the centre of the apple grove and raised his hand above his head.

He twisted it in an abrupt motion, and the wooden bowl spun down out of the sky.

It wailed a little as it fell through the air, as if grieving.

Qeteb caught it in firm fingers, and squeezed the wooden flesh of the bowl until tiny cracks appeared.

"Careful!" Sheol muttered, shuffling from foot to foot.

Qeteb raised the bowl as if to strike her with it, then relaxed. "I have never been careful, my dear, only successful."

Sheol grinned. "May I be the one to—"

"We all must shed our blood for this," Qeteb said, "if we all want to go to the Groves."

He put the bowl on the ground and the five Demons grouped about it. Qeteb waved his hand, and the bowl brimmed with water; it was the colour of a murky day.

"Mother, you cow-bitch," Qeteb said in a voice that bordered on the pleasant, "we're coming to *eat* you!"

He lifted his hand to his mouth and bit down savagely on his thumb.

Blood spurted out, and Qeteb let it spatter into the bowl of water.

He looked up.

The other four lifted their own hands to their mouths, bit down, and then let their blood spatter into the bowl.

Large amounts of blood also dribbled down their clothes, and stained their chins.

One of them had bit too hard, and the severed tip of a thumb fell into the bowl with a splash.

The water in the bowl turned to blood.

Qeteb laughed—then he began to howl with mirth. He abruptly stopped, his chest heaving, his eyes bright. "It's time!" he cried, and he grabbed the hands of the two Demons next to him.

They all joined hands . . . and as they did their forms changed. They blurred and ran like candle wax placed too close to a fire, and each of them lifted a foot—now too metamorphosed into free-flowing form to be distinguishable as a foot—and placed it on the rim of the bowl.

A great wind howled through the apple grove, shaking the trees and knocking over several of the stumps the Demons used as seats.

It was laughter, the laughter of a world gone completely mad.

The Demons' forms flowed completely into a black-green liquid, and then they flowed completely into the bowl of water.

The laughter quieted, and a new grove, a sacred place, was invaded.

26

A Gloomy and Pain-Raddled Night

She did not know exactly why she had come here, but she thought it was because she needed to put an end to it. If she could do that, then perhaps she could move on with the rest of her life.

And maybe she could come to terms with StarDrifter.

"First things first," Zenith muttered as she lifted a hand, clenched and unclenched it to try and control its unwelcome trembling, then grasped the door handle before her.

It did not budge, and Zenith took that as a sign from the stars that she should not be here. She heaved a sigh of relief, let the handle go, and turned away.

"My Lady Zenith?" a polite voice inquired behind her.

Zenith's throat went suddenly, horribly dry, and she turned her head back to the door.

It was open now, and a birdman, one of the Lake Guard, stood there.

"My Lady?" he repeated, ever polite and deferential.

"I, ah, I wondered if I might, ah, see . . ."

"Yes?"

"I wondered if I might spend a few minutes with Wolf-Star."

There. The words were out. The action had been stated, even if the motives remained horrifyingly unclear.

"You want to see WolfStar? My Lord Axis has left very clear instructions that—"

"Surely they do not pertain to me?" Zenith said. "His daughter? Besides, I have heard that WolfStar is seriously ill, and I thought—" What could she say? Everyone knew she was no Healer! "—that I might sit with him for a while, perhaps while he sleeps, and give the Healers some respite."

The guardsman hesitated, and glanced at someone over his shoulder.

Then he looked back at Zenith, nodded, and opened the door wide. "Please enter, my Lady."

Zenith clenched her hands amid her skirts, and walked in, carefully folding her wings so that they touched neither door frame nor guard.

She entered a small chamber. There were several chairs and stools scattered about, a chest, a table, and a wooden crate packed with bottles of unguents and herbal potions.

In the far wall was a closed door.

WingRidge CurlClaw sat on one of the stools, leaning back against the wall, his arms folded, his eyes steady as they gazed at her.

"What do you here, Zenith? I would have thought that you would be the last person to offer her services to WolfStar."

Zenith smiled, bright and artificial. She spread her arms wide and waggled her fingers. "Look! No knives!"

WingRidge continued to gaze at her. He did not smile.

Zenith's own face lost its feigned humour, and she let her arms fall to her sides. "WingRidge . . . please."

"Why?" He had not unfolded his arms, and his eyes were keener than ever.

"To put an end to it," she said. "I need to put an end to it."

WingRidge continued to stare a heartbeat longer, then he nodded and stood up. He stepped forward and gave Zenith a brief but warm hug. "I understand. He is asleep at the moment, but sleeps only lightly. You can wake him or not, as it pleases you."

"Is there anyone else in there?" Zenith eyed the door nervously.

"A Healer. Do you want me to ask her to leave?"

Zenith ran the tip of her tongue over her lips, then she jerked her head in a nod.

WingRidge looked at her. "I will be out here if you need me."

Zenith nodded, unable to speak, her eyes full of unshed tears.

WingRidge opened the door, and motioned the Healer out.

It was cool and dim inside, and Zenith jumped when WingRidge clicked the door closed behind her.

Had it woken WolfStar?

No . . .

There was no movement, and only the sound of slow, deep breathing from a bed placed close to the far wall.

The room reeked with the stench of infection.

Gods, Zenith thought, how ill *is* he?

She took a step forward, and then another when the sound of the breathing did not alter, and then jerked her eyes about the room, orientating herself.

A fireplace in the wall to her left, the fire damped down to the glow of coals.

A table pushed against the same wall, laden with bowls, bandages and several bottles of soap and unguents.

A pressed metal lamp hanging from a hook in the ceiling, exuding only the faintest of glimmers through the holes punched in its metal sides.

It sent strange, wobbling, hunching shadows chasing each other about the room.

A stool sat by the foot of the bed, another sat against the otherwise bare wall on her right.

And there was the bed itself, clad in snowy linens, patch-work quilts flung over its foot railing.

A form lay sprawled across the bed.

It was pale naked in the dim light, save for a towel draped over its hips, and the odd patch of bandage. Its wings, a pale bronze in this light, falling over both edges of the bed and spilling over the floor.

Arms: one flung so that it extended stiff and rigid, the other curled over the sleeper's face.

WolfStar.

Zenith stood a very long time, terrified to even move should she wake him.

What she wanted was for WingRidge to miraculously re-alise that she wanted to leave *(now, now, now)* and open the door and pull her out before WolfStar could wake to his senses and realise she'd been here.

But the room remained still and silent, save for the sound of WolfStar's breathing and Zenith's thudding heart.

The fire crackled (traitor fire!) and WolfStar stirred.

Zenith gasped, and WolfStar's arm lifted from his face. "Who is there?"

Zenith opened her mouth, but could not speak. One hand she had clenched in the material of her robe over her breast; the other was lost somewhere among the folds of material about her thigh.

WolfStar opened his eyes, and blinked. "Niah?"

"No! No!"

WolfStar stirred further, and half-raised himself on an elbow. He groaned, and lowered his face as he fought the pain.

"No," he finally said, his voice low and riddled with the agony coursing through his body. "It is not Niah at all, is it? You are Zenith."

She did not speak.

"Why are you here?"

Still she did not speak.

WolfStar raised his face and stared at her. "Girl, if there is one thing that I know about you, it is that you do not lack courage. Why are you here?"

"I do not know."

His mouth twisted. "Come to crow delight at my downfall, perhaps?"

She shook her head.

"No? Then I cannot think what else. I can scarce think that you have come to pass pleasantries with me."

He paused, and looked her in the eye. "Not *you*."

He shifted slightly in the bed, and Zenith took a pace back.

"Oh, come now! I am hardly likely to harm you in this condition, Zenith. Sit down on that stool by the far wall, if you like, but sit down and let me talk to you."

WolfStar had never been one to miss a chance when he saw it . . . and he realised, the instant he knew who his visitor was, that Zenith represented the most magnificent of chances. Here was DragonStar's remaining sibling, obviously upset and frightened. Deep inside, somewhere so dark that not a glimmer of emotion reached the light of WolfStar's face, the Enchanter gloated. Zenith could be used, and she could be used to manipulate DragonStar. Niah had been a failure, but Zenith would be a victory. She would bring him power.

Triumph roared through WolfStar's being, but not a smile crossed his bland face, nor a sound passed his carefully pain-thinned lips. His mind raced, constructing the trap.

Zenith stared at him, then looked at the stool against the wall *(a safe, safe distance)* before finally sitting down on the stool at the foot of the bed.

WolfStar smiled, a careful expression that contained surprise, some satisfaction and a great deal of pain. He relaxed back against the pillow. "Has anyone told you what has happened to me?"

"No."

"The Demons raped me, Zenith. Each one took their pleasure—if that it can be called—many times."

Zenith froze. A tightness in her chest made her realise she'd also stopped breathing, and she jerked in a shallow breath.

"Surprised?" he said, and laughed hollowly. "Yes, you are. And no doubt pleased."

"Having experienced it myself," she said, her voice surprising her with its eagerness, "I would not wish it on anyone else."

"I thought I lay with Niah."

"She was there."

"But you were, too?"

She nodded, and then, to her horror, began to cry with great gulping breaths.

"Zenith . . . Zenith . . ." WolfStar stirred as if his injuries made him totally unable to comfort Zenith.

"I only had mind for Niah," he eventually said. "I thought that she would destroy you, and I thought only to enjoy her strength."

Zenith continued to sob, slightly louder now.

"But I was wrong. *You* had the strength to defeat *her,* and I have ever admired strength and—"

"Oh, shut up!" Zenith slammed a fist down on the bed.

"Tell me why you are here," he said quietly.

She turned her head away.

"Why did you come back to me, Zenith?"

She whipped her eyes back to him. "I came to see you so I could put some of my own demons to rest!"

"And have you?"

She shook her head.

WolfStar extended his hand. "Please, take my hand, Zenith."

She ignored him.

"Please . . . I think that you and I are alone in this night, and I think that you and I both need some comfort."

"Not from *you*!"

"Nevertheless," he said, "I am all that shares this gloomy and pain-raddled night with you. Take my hand."

And eventually, she stretched out her own hand and took his.

Later, when she had gone, WolfStar lay on the bed, and allowed himself to laugh.

27

Axis Resumes a Purpose

DragonStar looked at the group before him, and wondered at how he would tell them the worst of possible news. They had trusted him, and he had not been able to provide for them.

Now he had to tell them that, in all likelihood, the entire struggle had been in vain. That Sanctuary would fall. And if Sanctuary fell, then, in all likelihood, they would die.

"Well?" Axis said.

He stood belligerently before his son, hands on hips,

dressed in his habitual, comfortable black clothes, booted, armed, and prepared for war.

Azhure stood beside him, calmer, but DragonStar knew her well enough to know that Azhure's exterior calm was a face she'd cultivated over the years to provide an antidote to Axis' tendency for confrontation. Internally, she would be as angry, as frightened, and as unsure as everyone else in the room.

DragonStar glanced behind his parents. Many were here: the four witches still in Sanctuary—Faraday, with so many mental and emotional barriers in place she looked like a piece of fragile Corolean glass; Leagh looking wan and exhausted; Zared, Herme and Theod, almost as belligerently anxious as Axis; StarDrifter, looking distracted (and DragonStar wondered if it had anything to do with the fact that Zenith wasn't in her quarters and couldn't, for the moment, be found); FreeFall and EvenSong, looking as useless as DragonStar himself felt; several of the Avar Banes, and Sa'Domai, the Chief of the Ravensbund. Sa'Domai looked, by far, the most collected person in the room, and DragonStar supposed that anyone who spent much of their life dodging collapsing icebergs and battling the storms of the Icebear Coast might possibly find interstellar Demons a mild threat by comparison.

"I have no good news," DragonStar said, unable to keep the bitter twist from his mouth. He gestured helplessly. "I hope that Urbeth will do what she can to aid the Mother and the Sacred Groves, but I cannot rely on her being able to stop the Demons. If the Demons manage to feast on the power of the Sacred Groves, then—at the moment—I cannot think what might stop them."

"You are StarSon," Axis said flatly. "You have demanded that title since infancy. It is your *job* to know what is to be done!"

"And you went through your entire battle with Borneheld and Gorgrael with nary a single doubt, Axis?" DragonStar said. "*You* walked through the entire adventure gloriously confident and without putting a single foot wrong, without losing a single bloody life to your mistakes?"

Axis looked away.

"The icepack cracks and reforms," Sa'Domai said. "No-one ever knows where the cracks will appear next, but the icepack *always* reforms."

DragonStar took a deep breath, both grateful for Sa-Domai's philosophical interjection, and resentful at his calmness.

"I do not doubt that Sanctuary will fall," DragonStar said. "At the least, we have to plan for it."

"And what," FreeFall said, "*do* you plan to do about it?"

"If myself," DragonStar said, "or Faraday, Goldman, Leagh and Gwendylyr are trapped here, then we can do no good at all. We must return to the wasteland—"

"No!" Zared said, stepping forward and brushing past Axis. "Take Leagh back into the wasteland? Have you *seen* her, DragonStar? Have you *seen* how sick and exhausted she is? Have you—"

"We have no damn choice, Zared!" DragonStar said. "None. It will be up to myself and my five companions to battle the Demons, and we cannot do it here. I doubt that Spiredore will remain viable much longer. We must leave now."

And I must get my witches to the places where they will confront their respective Demons, DragonStar thought, and where they will prepare the "weapons" that Qeteb has so kindly allowed them to choose. We *must* leave now if they are to have enough time to prepare.

"And the rest of us?" Axis said as Zared turned away in disgust. "What happens to the rest of us? You and yours might be able to survive the wasteland and the Demons' influence, but none of us can. What happens if—when—Sanctuary falls? *Where do we go?*"

And the rest of the people and animals of Sanctuary. Where do they go now? Where, if nowhere is safe?

DragonStar spread his hands helplessly. "I do not know, Axis. I simply do not know—"

Axis stepped forward and stabbed his finger into DragonStar's chest. "If you walk out of here now and take your four damn witches as you call them, with you, then *I* am assuming command of Sanctuary! *I* will work to keep safe what remains of Tencendor! Run about the wasteland all you like, Dragon-Star, play whatever game you want to, *but I will assume responsibility for the saving of Tencendor's life!*"

There was a silence as DragonStar stared into his father's eyes. Then . . .

"Thank you," he said. "That would be a great weight off my mind."

Axis stared at DragonStar, then he burst into laughter: genuine, heartfelt laughter.

"Thank *you,*" he said, "for allowing me some purpose back into my life."

DragonStar nodded, smiling a little himself, then looked at Faraday. "When we leave," he said, "we will leave Katie behind."

"No!" Faraday said in a low, harsh voice. "You've said yourself that Sanctuary will fall. She will die if we leave her here!"

"I thank you for your vote of confidence," Axis said to one side, but Faraday ignored him.

"We take her with us! I can protect her! I will—"

"No," DragonStar said. His voice was very flat, very hard. "She must stay here."

Faraday stared at DragonStar, almost loathing him. Ever since she'd seen Qeteb speak out of his mouth, seen the Demon's malice shine from his eyes, she'd not been able to forget that voice asking her if she would ever know whose hands caressed her body, whose voice spoke to her of love, whose love reached out to her in the night . . . It had been enough to undermine the hard-found trust she had in DragonStar, and in herself. Would she ever know who it was? DragonStar, or Qeteb? Who was it now saying, "We must go forth into the wasteland?" DragonStar, or Qeteb?

Katie, and her desire to protect the girl at all costs, was all that was left for her. Illogically, even though she was not sure *who* was going to lead her back into the wasteland, and what might be waiting for them there, Faraday wanted to keep Katie with her. If only Katie was with her, then she would find some way to protect her, some way to keep her from harm. The vision she'd had many, many weeks ago of the armoured man—Qeteb—slicing open Katie's throat with a kitchen knife returned night after night to haunt her.

Faraday would let nothing harm Katie. *Nothing.*

"Faraday," Azhure said gently, putting her hands on Faraday's arm, "I will look after Katie as if she were my own."

"As if she were your own?" Faraday hissed. "You were never good at playing the caring mother, Azhure!"

"Faraday," DragonStar snapped, "that is enough!" He stepped forward and took Faraday's other arm, pulling her away from Azhure and the rest of the group.

"Faraday," DragonStar said in a low voice as he pulled her, stiff and resisting, over to a far corner of the chamber, "if you cannot trust me then we might as well lie down and offer our throats to Qeteb here and now."

She was silent.

"You have let me lay by you at nights," DragonStar said, his voice softer now, "and let me love you. You trusted me then. Trust me now."

She stared at him with hard eyes, and then tried to pull away from him.

He grabbed her before she could walk away, hanging on to her arm and speaking hard and low into her ear; she would not look at him.

"You will know in here," he tapped her breast with his other hand, "when it is DragonStar who speaks to you, and when— *if*—it is Qeteb. *You will know that!*"

Faradày finally turned her eyes to him. They were wide, stricken, and so frightened that DragonStar felt his chest constrict.

"I want more than anything in this world, or in the thousand worlds that surround and touch ours, to be able to trust you, DragonStar. Yet to think that by trusting you I will be laying down and offering my throat to yet another demonic lover terrifies me."

DragonStar felt his heart break. "Gods, I love you, Faraday," he whispered, his mouth almost touching her ear. "I will never harm you, I will *never* offer you to Qeteb to save Tencendor. Please, gods curse it, *please* believe me."

"I will try," she said, a tear finally escaping from an eye. "I will try, DragonStar."

She pulled away again, and this time DragonStar let her go.

He wondered if he would ever have her back.

Was there nothing that could be saved from this chaos?

"I wish you luck," DragonStar said, gripping Axis' hand and arm, "with your self-appointed task."

"As I wish you well with yours," Axis said.

They fell silent, each staring into the others' eyes, each wondering if this was the last they'd see each other, and if this was one of the last moments of hope that Tencendor would have.

Azhure stepped forward and briefly, but fiercely, hugged DragonStar, then she turned and embraced the other four who would leave with him.

Katie clung to Azhure's skirts, and Faraday embraced the girl so tightly she squeaked in protest. Azhure had to prise her loose from Faraday's grip.

"Let nothing happen to her!" Faraday said to Azhure, and Azhure touched Faraday's cheek with her fingers.

"I promise to do my best for her, Faraday. Will you accept that?"

Faraday hesitated, then nodded, her eyes brimming with tears. Azhure's best was better than virtually anyone else's. But even though Faraday knew she left Katie in the best of hands, she still hungered to be able to watch her herself.

"I love you," she whispered to the tiny girl.

"Love DragonStar instead," Katie said. "He needs it as much as I do."

Faraday's face closed over slightly, and she straightened and stood back, turning her face to look about her.

They were standing at the entrance to the valley of Sanctuary: Axis and Azhure, Zared and Theod, and DragonStar and his group. Behind DragonStar sidled Belaguez, anxious for war; the Alaunt, sitting, but very evidently impatient for action as well; and the blue-feathered lizard, irritably combing out some of the feathers on his off-hind leg. His emerald and scarlet crest was rising up and down so rapidly his plumage appeared blurred.

Zared was holding Leagh, as Theod held Gwendylyr; hard and angrily *(why did their wives have to go?),* desperately, knowing they would, in all likelihood, never see them again.

"We will meet again," Gwendylyr tried to reassure Theod, "in the Field of Flowers, if nowhere else."

"And if the Demons get into that, as well?" Theod said. "If they destroy the Field? If they destroy everything else, Gwendylyr, and if they control the power of the Enemy, then they will inevitably get into the Field."

Gwendylyr clung to Theod, burying her face in his chest, fearing the truth of his words, and totally unable to speak.

Theod met Zared's eyes over her head. They were as hard, as angry, as implacable as his own.

Of the entire group, only Goldman seemed at ease, bending down and ruffling the thick hair on FortHeart's head, and clucking to her as if she was a child.

The hound relaxed into his hand, seemingly grateful for the reassurance.

"What will you do?" Axis asked DragonStar.

DragonStar shrugged a little. "What I must. And you?"

Axis smiled slightly. "This place must have some other way out. I cannot believe the Enemy built Sanctuary without a back door."

A back door to where? To *what?* DragonStar wondered, but said nothing. He gripped Axis' hand and arm again, then let go.

"Goldman, girls . . . it is time we left." And he adjusted the Wolven where it hung over his shoulder, raised his sword, and drew the door of light.

"Come," DragonStar said, "let us dare Spiredore one last time."

28

Destruction

The Mother sat on the bench outside Ur's cottage and contemplated death.

Even the mere contemplation of Her utter annihilation seemed out of place, let alone the imminent reality of it.

The Mother *knew* She was about to die, but She simply couldn't quite come to grips with the concept. She represented the life and well-being of the land of Tencendor, and in the past, even though wars and destruction had rained above and through the land, nothing had come close to harming the land itself.

But now Tencendor lay wasted and barren. The Earth Tree and the forests were gone, the Lakes were dried up, all hope and love had been consumed and translated into the despicable.

All that was left was here, and the Mother knew that this, too, would shortly be gone.

She could hear the Demons hunting through the glades and forests of the Sacred Groves.

The noise was appalling. Trees screamed and tore themselves up by the roots in an attempt to get away from the Demons. The Horned Ones bellowed and roared . . .

. . . and fell, one by one, as the Demons ate them alive and absorbed their power.

The Mother winced every time another was consumed, for She could feel the teeth slice into Her own flesh as Demon fangs tore into the Horned One.

There was a whistling and a screaming in the air: the sound of Death approaching. The sky was being torn apart, the earth destroyed, and the Mother put Her hands over Her face and wept.

Isfrael crouched, one arm flung over his head.

He wept and bellowed at the same time as both fury and fright coursed through him.

Everything he had ever loved was being destroyed about him.

The corpse of a Horned One lay torn apart not five paces from him, and a Demon—Barzula, Isfrael thought—was tearing into it with the fangs and talons of a bear.

The Demon had, somewhat incongruously, chosen the body of a stag to go with the bear's teeth and claws . . . then again, Isfrael thought in some detached part of his mind, maybe the Demon had chosen deliberately.

Now the Sacred Groves were being sacrificed, but for what, Isfrael wasn't so sure. His own stupidity? No! He had done only what he'd thought best, and there was still a possible way out.

"Filth," Isfrael said, lowering the arm from his face, "I need to talk with you."

Barzula stopped and raised his blood-soaked head. "I *revel* in filth, fool. You flatter me by your ill-intentioned curse."

Isfrael half-rose, meaning to further speak, but something seized him about the neck from behind, and the Mage-King screamed in agony.

Claws sliced down to his spine, narrowly missing the throbbing arteries in either side of his neck.

"Then speak," a voice whispered behind him, and Isfrael whimpered through his pain, for he recognised the voice of Qeteb.

"There is much still I can tell you," Isfrael stammered. "Much information I can give you—"

"When I consume you," Qeteb said, not only tightening his grip about Isfrael's neck, but sinking the claws of his other hand—*Mother! What form had he assumed to inflict such agony?*—into the base of Isfrael's spine, holding him so high in the air that Isfrael's legs writhed a full pace above the ground, "when I consume you then I consume all your knowledge and memories. Think that I need to bargain with *you?*"

And he wriggled his claws in even deeper, and Isfrael felt such agony course through his body that he gibbered, begging for death.

"I hold here the trees in my hands," Qeteb said, "I hold here the Mage-King of the forests—"

His claws sunk deeper, deeper, and Isfrael screamed.

"—the life of the trees—"

Far away, tucked into the cellar of her cottage, Ur cackled with laughter. "Not yet, not yet," she whispered.

"—and the hope of the Avar," Qeteb finished. "All . . . all . . ." his claws started to tighten and clench within Isfrael's body, "at the tips of my fingers!"

And he clenched his claws as hard as he could, tearing Isfrael's neck and lower spine apart.

Beyond sound, Isfrael writhed about Qeteb's hands, his face twisting, his eyes bulging, and . . .

. . . and Qeteb's own eyes widened, and his mouth dropped open, for as Isfrael died, so indeed did the Mage-King's memories and knowledge pass into the Demon's own understanding. Most of them were trifling, concerned only with power and ambition (and these qualities Qeteb already had enough of to last him through the next few hundred worlds he chose to ravage), but there was *one* thing, one thing that made the Midday Demon caper about, howling and screaming with mirth, for this one memory would be enough to completely destroy the StarSon, even if the man's witches *did* manage to do well against the other five Demons. A memory that would aid Qeteb into a final victory.

A memory of Faraday and her role in the previous battle for supremacy within Tencendor.

The bait, the sacrifice, that which Gorgrael used in order to distract Axis away from his purpose to annihilate the Destroyer.

It hadn't worked, Axis was too single-minded, too selfish (not a flaw at all, under the circumstances) to be distracted.

Besides, he had truly loved Azhure, and was thus prepared to watch Faraday die.

But DragonStar was another matter. Here was a man much too warm, and far too caring, to let Faraday sacrifice herself again. He loved Faraday before any other, and he would sacrifice Tencendor, and himself, rather than let her die again so alone and terrified.

DragonStar was not the man his father was.

"I have you!" Qeteb roared through the entire universe. "I have you, you weak-hearted bastard!"

I have you, you weak-hearted bastard!

The words echoed through Spiredore, where DragonStar had just led his group.

I have you . . .

DragonStar's head jerked up, and he halted halfway down a stair.

I have you . . .

"Pay no attention," he muttered, but his voice was weak, and it trembled, and the other four with him shuddered.

I have you . . .

DragonStar pointed down the blue-misted tunnel that appeared at the end of the stairwell. "Here . . . we are here . . ."

He almost ran as he started down the tunnel, desperate to get away from Qeteb's mocking laughter.

I have you . . .

Qeteb shook Isfrael's corpse until it fell apart, and then the Demon's form metamorphosed, fluid and beautiful, changing into that of a gigantic black raven.

He cocked his head as if curious, his bright, beady eyes flitting about the clearing, then he carefully placed one of his claws on Isfrael's body, holding it firm, and dipped his beaked head and tore into the flesh.

With each morsel of flesh and sliver of bone that slipped

down his throat, Qeteb consumed yet more of the power of the trees and the earth.

By the time the Demon had devoured the entire bloody mess his feathers were iridescent with power, and the raven tipped back its head and cackled with happiness.

Nothing would stand in its way now.

Nothing.

Not even the Mother.

The raven snapped shut its beak and cocked its head, thinking. Its eyes blinked rapidly.

The Mother. Another meal sat waiting ahead! The raven burped, then flapped its wings and rose into the air. As it did so it crowed, calling to the other four Demons.

They lifted their snouts from the dead flesh they'd been consuming and looked to the black shadow circling in the air. Then, as one, they loped to the east, where waited the final meal.

Urbeth snarled, and paced restlessly in a circle through the snow. Behind her, shore-bound icebergs groaned and cracked. Her two daughters, as impatient but not as restless as their mother, sat to one side, their claws red from the dead (and sour, for it had been crazed) seal they'd eaten earlier.

All that was left was the abandoned rib cage lying at the very edge of the sea, red shards of flesh flapping in the wind.

Urbeth ignored both her daughters and her surroundings. Everything was wrong, wrong, wrong! It was not *her* task to save the Mother! Her role was only to wait in the snow, dispensing advice and tart wisdom, and keeping her eye on her children and their descendants.

Hadn't she done enough for this cursed land already?

All Urbeth wanted was to spend the rest of whatever and whichever eternity her residual powers allowed in jumping from icefloe to icefloe in the southern Iskruel Ocean, sinking her teeth into the spines of shrieking seals, and enjoying the odd, amusing discussion with whatever sentient being came within conversational range.

Instead, she'd been forced to hide the Ravensbundmen during Gorgrael's stupid grab for power, and ever since then she'd been obliged to step in and guide the footsteps of her irritatingly dense children.

And now DragonStar wanted her to save the Mother. What? Couldn't the Mother save herself?

"We'd better go," one of her daughters remarked. "The sky is falling apart."

Urbeth glanced upwards, but her daughter's comment was metaphorical only. If the Mother died, if the Demons consumed Her power, then the sky would indeed fall apart.

"*And* the icepack will melt," observed the other daughter, and at that Urbeth's temper cracked completely.

"Why can't the Mother mind Her own back?" she roared. "Why am I supposed to do *everything*?"

Her daughters slowly got to their feet, stretching backs and paws as they did so.

The Mother sat and watched the forest to the west. There were only a few score trees left, and even as She watched, many among them trembled and fell.

There was a darkness moving through them.

Worse was the darkness winging overhead. The Midday Demon, in the shape of a raven, its feathered and shadowed wingspan seemingly reaching from horizon to horizon.

There was no sun left, no beauty, no hope. Nothing but approaching despair, bleakness and destruction.

"I am the only thing left alive in the Groves," the Mother whispered.

And shortly even She would be gone.

The Mother fought an overwhelming urge to run. Run where? At Her back were nothing but shifting shadows and pools of darkness. The Sacred Groves had all but been consumed, and the only patch left was this island of cottage and garden, and the tumbling patch of forest before her.

The winged nightmare in the sky flapped slowly closer.

The Mother stood up, and smoothed out her gown.

"I'm sorry," She whispered, thinking of Faraday and the now-hopeless sapling secreted within her rainbow belt. "I'm sorry."

"You're the last person I thought to see submit to despondency," an aged but sharp voice said behind Her, and the Mother jumped.

Ur had emerged from the doorway of the cottage, holding a large terracotta pot and saucer in her arms. The saucer sat over the opening of the pot, hiding its contents.

"I . . . I thought you'd . . ." the Mother said.

"Been eaten?" Ur said. "Everyone always forgets me," she added, grumbling, and plonked herself down on the bench the Mother had just risen from.

The Mother looked between her and the approaching storm of Demons.

"I don't think we have much longer," She said.

Ur's mouth twisted in a ghastly parody of a smile, and she clutched the pot even tighter.

Her hands had tightened like claws.

The Demons screamed closer.

Urbeth, her two daughters a few paces behind her, leapt from icefloe to icefloe. Even in this stark portion of the world, far, far north from the Demons' central influence, disease and blight had left their mark.

Many of the icefloes had turned a sad grey from their previously sharp blue-white, and were rent with cracks and soggy, sad saucer-shaped depressions that threatened to give way whenever one of the icebears put an inadvertent paw on one.

Urbeth's head swung from left to right as she leaped and ran. How much longer would the Icebear Coast be safe? Not long, not long at all if the Mother was consumed.

Urbeth abruptly stopped, sinking back onto her haunches and swiping a furious paw at the sky and at all of creation.

"I've had *enough*!" she bellowed. *"Enough!"*

Her daughters grinned, and their jaws dripped in anticipation of the hunt.

Urbeth recommenced her run north across the ice. But even as she moved into her stride, a shadowy movement in the distance, over to the east caught her far-seeing eye.

A pack of Skraelings, shimmering south to join in the general slaughter and mayhem.

And for a second time Urbeth halted and sank back to her haunches. But this time she remained silent, her eyes fixed on the Skraelings, and then her eyes drifted north-east, and yet further north-east, until she had concentrated her entire being on the unmapped tundra that stretched into the infinite unknown.

The sorry breeding grounds of the Skraelings, to be sure, but what else did it harbour?

An escape?

DragonStar shivered, and wished he'd thought to cloak himself in something other than a simple linen shirt and breeches of only slightly heavier weave. He'd brought his witches, his Star Stallion, the lizard and his pack of nosing, roaming Alaunt to the one place he thought they could use as a base. Far enough north to escape the worst of the Demons' influence, and yet close enough to slowly begin to win back some of the wasteland, and rid it of its corruption.

Star Finger.

Here also waited DareWing and the ethereal Strike Force.

Somewhere.

"Where is he?" Faraday said.

She, as did Gwendylyr and Leagh, looked warm enough wrapped in scarlet cloaks, while Goldman was suffering as badly as DragonStar. Why do women always remember to be sensible, wondered DragonStar, and us men always forget?

"DareWing?" DragonStar said. "He must be hereabouts somewhere. I told him to stay . . ."

"Is it possible to get out of this wind?" Goldman asked, pleasantly enough, even though his face was turning blue and his arms were shaking as he attempted to wrap them about his chest.

DragonStar nodded. "Yes, of course."

They were standing on the remains of the glacier, just to the north of the shattered mountain, and DragonStar pointed to a shadowed opening amid a tumble of boulders about the skirts of the mountain. "That must be the entrance to the underground chambers of the mountain. DareWing must be there."

And that is where we found Katie, Faraday thought, unable to keep the girl out of her mind, but she said nothing, and contented herself with aiding Leagh as they stumbled over the rocks towards the entrance.

A figure waited for them just inside.

Qeteb circled down from the sky above the ruins of the Sacred Groves, his feathers and eyes positively glowing with anticipation.

Nothing would ever stop him now.

Below, two women sat on a wooden bench before a simple cottage. Around them spread a smoking wasteland. Every tree had been destroyed, every flower crushed, every hope decimated. The women were the only things left alive in the Groves—such as they were—and Qeteb had every expectation that they would not long stand between him and a total devastation and death for the Groves.

He lifted his wings back, slowing his descent, and stretched his raven claws out, preparing for a landing. Just behind him on the ground his four companion Demons were likewise slowing down, digging talons into the drifting dust and ashes, sliding haunches beneath them.

All four had taken the forms of dog-people: canine lower bodies, human torsos and heads . . . save for the wriggling pig snouts on two of the Demons.

In their excitement they had misjudged their appearance.

One of the women rose from the bench, wiping nervous hands down Her gown. She was patently ill, Her skin as grey and as ashen as the landscape about her, Her eyes dull, Her muscles trembling with fatigue as much as fear.

The other woman, ancient and gap-gummed, continued to sit, hunching her brittle-boned form over a terracotta pot.

What was she going to do with *that*? Qeteb wondered. Throw it at him?

He broke into derisive laughter, and Ur raised her head and regarded him with the bright eyes of hate.

One of her wrinkled, age-spotted hands patted the side of the pot, as if in reassurance.

Urbeth and her daughters had resumed their run. They continued to leap from icefloe to icefloe, but the grey of the ice (just occasionally blue-white, this far north) sometimes appeared to have streaks of ash in it, as if the bears strode over burned and ravaged ground.

Above them swirled wisps of emerald light.

DragonStar halted, stunned, as he recognised the person waiting just inside the entrance.

"My, my," Star Laughter said, leaning back against a rock and making full use of the situation to display her body. "Haven't you grown handsome since I last saw you?"

"What are you doing here?" DragonStar asked.

StarLaughter smiled. "Waiting, of course," she said. "DareWing said you'd be back."

Another form emerged out of the gloom behind her. It was the Strike Leader.

DragonStar switched sharp eyes to the birdman's face. DareWing? In league with StarLaughter?

StarLaughter's smile stretched, but she remained silent. Privately she was wallowing in self-satisfaction, knowing her plan to convince DragonStar of her trustworthiness was bound to succeed. He was so guileless, so malleable.

"We have found a haven in the bowels of this destruction," DareWing said. "And, I believe we have found a friend. Many of them."

DragonStar looked back to StarLaughter, completely unable to believe that she'd so easily (and conveniently) swapped allegiances.

"Oh, but you should trust me," she said softly. "I have grown tired of the Demons, and I admit a modicum of sorrow for what I've aided them to do. I wish to—"

"I find this somewhat hard to believe," DragonStar said.

"*You* did it," she said, and her face was entirely serious now. What better way to gain his trust than to pretend she'd travelled the same pathway to redemption he had? Fool! The weak were always prepared to believe others shared their weaknesses.

DragonStar stared at her.

"Come below, and talk," DareWing said, and disappeared into the gloom.

Faraday caught at DragonStar's arm. "It's a trap," she whispered.

StarLaughter's eyes slid momentarily to Faraday, hardening as they did so, then back to DragonStar's face.

"I can help you against the Demons," she said.

DragonStar stared at her, trying to discern the truth—or otherwise—in her words and her face. He didn't find it hard to believe that the Demons had abandoned StarLaughter, but on the other hand he found it difficult to believe they'd just let her go.

It wasn't in their nature to just "let someone go".

It was very, very easy to believe this was a trap. The Demons were using StarLaughter as an ambush. No doubt once they'd finished consuming the Sacred Groves they'd drop by here to finish him off.

She was bait . . . but such unbelievable bait that DragonStar started to think that this couldn't *possibly* be a trap. Surely the Demons wouldn't expect him to fall for this?

There was a movement at his side. Sicarius, sidling forward to sniff at StarLaughter's skirts.

He nosed about, then lost interest, sitting down to scratch at a spot just behind his right ear.

And then DareWing re-emerged from the gloom at Star-Laughter's back. With him he had several members of the Strike Force.

One of them stepped forward. "She is a cold-hearted bitch," the birdwoman said, "but she has given us the one thing we needed to make us believe in her."

"Yes?" DragonStar said after a moment, and then froze in horror as another form emerged from the gloom.

It was one of the Hawkchilds. StarGrace.

"She has brought us the Hawkchilds," DareWing said, "and a highway to the Demons' den."

Qeteb's form flowed back—horribly, for his flesh assumed many loathsome lumps and bumps in doing so—into his handsome, human form.

For the moment he had grown tired of the encasing black armour.

He advanced a step towards the Mother.

"You're a sorry looking cow for all the power and glory you are supposed to represent," he remarked.

Her expression—exhausted, resigned—did not alter, although one hand spasmed briefly within the folds of Her skirts. "I am what you have done to Me," She said. "I am the living representation of the land, and I—"

"Do not have much longer to live," said one of the other Demons, sidling closer. Its pig snout snuffled along the ground, as if it wanted to suck up the Mother's skirts, and perhaps Her with it.

The Mother's mouth trembled in a smile, or perhaps an expression of fear. "No. I do not think that I do."

"With you gone," Qeteb said, and he took a pace forward, "the entire land will be mine."

Both his hands dangled at his side, but his right one shifted and changed, reshaping itself into a gigantic fist some five or six times normal size.

It had hammerheads for fingertips.

"There is the small matter of some remaining resistance," Ur muttered from her bench. Her arms were now so tightly gripped about her pot they were completely white.

Qeteb leaned back his head and roared with laughter.

"DragonStar? His useless lieutenants? A Sanctuary full of ter-rified incompetents? There is *no* magic left I do not control; or will not, within days. There is *no* place anyone can hide. *And there is no soul that will not eventually be mine!*"

He was screaming by the end, spitting out words and saliva in a torrent of hatred.

Ur turned her head aside, hiding her expression from the Demons.

Qeteb's massive right hand suddenly shot out and seized the Mother's neck. "Stupid, stunted bitch," he seethed, and the muscles of his arm rippled up and down. "Your time is *done.*"

And his fist tightened.

DragonStar was leading his band down into the bowels of Star Finger when Faraday halted, put a hand on one of the corridor walls for support, and groaned.

She sagged, her moans becoming frightful, and DragonStar wrapped his arms about her.

"Faraday? Faraday? What's wrong?"

StarLaughter looked on, mildly curious. Was it the gloom this far down? Was she a girl who needed light to feed her good temper and optimism?

Faraday screamed.

The Mother began to writhe, although She was obviously making some effort to keep still and accept death.

Her hands half lifted, then dropped as She forced them down.

Her eyes She kept still on Qeteb's straining, reddened face, although panic and fear swam about in them.

Ur leaned forward, and grabbed the Mother's skirt.

Qeteb's fist tightened, and the Mother's eyes bulged in agony.

Faraday was convulsing, and DragonStar did not know what to do. Leagh and Gwendylyr hovered about, their hands patting helplessly, their faces frantic.

Everyone else stood about in a powerless circle.

DragonStar raised his head and stared at StarLaughter, his expression hard.

"It's not me," StarLaughter said, and shrugged her shoulders. "I don't know what ails her."

More than anything else it was her utter disinterest that convinced DragonStar. He glanced at StarGrace—she also shrugged—and then he looked back to Faraday.

Red weals had appeared about her throat, and her eyes were bulging and agonised.

"In my fist," Qeteb said, turning his face slightly to talk to the other Demons, "I hold the life of the land. Pitiful, isn't it?"

Blood now stained the neckline of the Mother's robe, running down in rivulets to blotch and dampen its bodice.

"Nothing can stop us now," Sheol said. She had rearranged her snout into a more elegant form.

"Except blindness," Ur said, and Qeteb growled.

"Will blindness save Her, now?" he said, and his fist abruptly tightened.

The Mother's neck broke with a snap.

Ur's face contorted, her hand clenched even tighter within the Mother's robe, and then she sagged, almost lifeless, and let go.

A scream tore through the air of the corridor, and DragonStar stared at Faraday, not understanding how she could have screamed so loudly and not opened her mouth.

He'd thought she'd been calming somewhat.

"Leagh!" Gwendylyr yelled, and DragonStar blinked and realised that it was not Faraday who had screamed at all.

Leagh had turned away, and was now rolling about on the floor of the corridor, as agonised as Faraday was, her arms wrapped about her belly, screaming and shrieking as if she was gripped by the final extremities of death.

StarLaughter turned away and rolled her eyes. Couldn't they manage a simple walk down a corridor without enduring some drama of epic proportions? Who *had* DragonStar gathered about him?

"Tch, tch," she muttered.

Qeteb's fist opened, and the corpse of the Mother dropped to the ground.

His fist shrank back to a more normal size.

Ur blinked, blinked again, and looked up, as if she had just woken from an afternoon slumber and was mildly disorientated by the encroaching scenes of death and destruction.

Qeteb stood, not two paces from her, a charming grin on his face.

The Mother's corpse lay huddled between them.

"Silly little woman," Qeteb said, pleasantly enough to Ur, "time to die."

He reached forward, both his fists now expanding.

Ur lifted her head, scented the air, and then roared.

Urbeth and her daughters bounded and leapt through the devastated landscape.

They grinned, for hunting lay ahead. The Mother was dead, and that was annoying, but the Hunt still went on, even if the earth screamed and died.

Qeteb flinched, and momentarily pulled back his fists, then he recollected himself. Silly woman, what was she doing, yelling like that?

He reached forward again. The Mother had been disgustingly easy. This one would be even—

Something sharp, heavy, and very, very painful hit him in the centre of his forehead.

He reeled back, blinking.

Ur sat back on her bench, replacing the heavy terracotta saucer on top of her pot.

None of the Demons had noticed that, as she'd struck Qeteb, her other hand had slipped something into the pot.

"Senile old nag!" Qeteb roared, shape-changing into a huge, nail-bristled boar.

He shook his tusks at Ur, his small, piggy eyes red and raging.

"Now that," Ur said, quite calmly considering the circumstances, "is a little *too* infantile. Why can't you meet me as a man?"

Qeteb's form flowed back into the fully armoured version of his being.

"Better?" he said, and Ur smiled happily.

"Oh, much," and from nowhere she produced a length of branch, tempered by the fires of the Demons' destruction, and began to belabour Qeteb about his helmeted head with it, all the while keeping her pot safely clutched under one arm.

The other four Demons circled in closer, but they nevertheless kept their distance, their eyes very carefully watching Qeteb.

Surely he should be able to handle this one, decrepit woman? Was he weak, then?

Ambitious plots began to hatch in each, individual Demonic head.

Was Qeteb . . . vulnerable?

Qeteb roared, lifted his hands and tried to catch the branch.

But Ur was in her element, dancing about on suddenly nimble feet, cackling and crowing, the branch weaving through the air to escape Qeteb's clutching hands and thunder repeatedly against his metal head.

Qeteb suddenly had enough. In the blink of an eye he transformed into a tiny weasel, and he scuttled under Ur's robe, biting at her ankles.

Her cackles stopped, although her capering continued even more frantically, and she lowered the branch and struck about her legs, trying to catch the darting, annoying animal.

Suddenly she shrieked, and toppled to the ground (all the while falling so that she protected the pot), her skirts stained with blood.

The weasel poked its inquisitive (bloodied) head from underneath her hem, then wriggled free.

Qeteb assumed his armoured form again, and raised one metalled foot.

"Your belly," he snarled, "is never going to be quite the same again."

And his foot smashed down.

"The Mother is gone," Faraday whispered, her fingers to her throat. "Dead."

DragonStar lowered his face into a hand. Urbeth hadn't helped, then.

A pace or two away Leagh lay quiet. She was conscious, although very wan and weak, and Goldman and Gwendylyr both crouched by her side, frightened for her.

Leagh's hands were still clutched tight about her belly.

Gods, DragonStar thought, looking about the group. How are we supposed to defeat these Demons and bring Tencendor back to life?

A step at a time, he answered himself. A step at a time.

"StarLaughter," DragonStar said, rising. "If you and Star-Grace have had such a change of heart, perhaps you can aid Faraday to walk to the chambers below."

StarLaughter hesitated, her face closed, then she motioned StarGrace forward, and they leaned down ungracious hands to help Faraday up.

StarGrace limped slightly, adjusting her feet from talons to flesh and then back again.

Qeteb's foot never found its mark. Even as it drove down on Ur's form, a white blur flew in from one side, and Qeteb found himself driven to the ground, and rolling desperately to avoid the weight of the *thing* that had attacked him.

His companion Demons were having their own problems with two other white beasts that had driven them fifteen or eighteen paces back with the strength of their attack.

Ur rose to her feet, her movements once again those of an arthritic old woman. She put the pot carefully to one side, and methodically dusted down her gown.

She completely ignored the sound of the battle going on about her.

Finally, robe and hair in order, Ur picked up the pot, settled it comfortably in her arm, and said: "I'm ready now."

As one the three icebears backed towards her, keeping their snarling heads weaving in the Demons' direction.

"A pretty trick," Qeteb said, "but one not guaranteed to serve you forever."

One of the icebear's forms changed, resolving itself into a tall, elegant woman, her hair grey and iced with silver.

"All magic is *not* dead," she whispered, "and even amid death, Qeteb, you must surely remember that resurrection is always possible."

The Midday Demon had endured enough. Drawing upon all of his strength, all his power, every trick he'd ever learned, he rolled back his head, his visor opening with a snap.

Black smoke issued from within, roiling about his head.

"A *very* pretty trick," Urbeth whispered, "but none of us, I fear, have the patience to wait about to see what it does."

She extended her arms, and the other two bears, as Ur, crowded close.

"You took your time, sister," Ur said, and Urbeth's face tightened.

Above Qeteb's head the black smoke formed itself into a snake's head.

"I have no time for a discussion of my faults now," Urbeth said, as she enveloped the four of them in a blinding snowstorm.

Qeteb's death leaped forward with the speed and accuracy of a striking viper, but it bit nothing save empty air.

The two women and the icebears had vanished.

29

Family Relations

StarDrifter found Zenith wandering down one of the more isolated corridors of their palace complex in Sanctuary, and wondered at the furtive—almost half guilty—look she gave as she recognised him and reluctantly stopped.

She carefully replaced her furtive expression with a warm and almost genuine smile.

But the hesitancy was still there. StarDrifter could see it crowding the depths of her beautiful eyes.

"Hello, Zenith," he said, and reached out to take some of the pile of linens from her arms. "Let me help you with these."

"But I thought . . . Axis would need you."

StarDrifter laughed. "Axis? Need me? Never! He has an army, the Lake Guard and thousands of willing winged men and women to aid him. He does not need me."

Since DragonStar's departure Axis had lost no time in searching out an—*any*—escape route from Sanctuary. The bridge couldn't have been the only way . . . could it?

"And has anyone had any luck?"

"Zenith, it's only been a few hours. And Sanctuary . . ." StarDrifter lapsed into silence as he fell into step beside Zenith. Sanctuary was massive. It apparently stretched into infinity. All the reports StarDrifter had ever heard from those Icarii who'd flown as far as they could was that it just stretched, and stretched . . . and stretched. There was no "end". There was no back wall let alone a back door with a helpful sign saying *Use In Case Of Emergency*.

"And Sanctuary hides its secrets well," StarDrifter finally finished, rather lamely. "As do you. What have you been up to? No-one has seen you for the past few days."

Where have you been? Who have you been with?

"I've been keeping myself busy," Zenith said, her tone as false as her words.

"Stop," StarDrifter said. He dropped his pile of linens on the floor, took the pile from Zenith's arms and threw them to one side, and grasped her hands in his.

She stiffened, and a look of mild panic entered her eyes. "You said you wouldn't," she said.

"Wouldn't *what*? Love you? I cannot help that, nor stop it. Zenith . . . what's going on?"

She looked away, her eyes desperately searching for something else she could legitimately look at.

In this barest of corridors there was nothing, and so Zenith reluctantly looked back into StarDrifter's face.

"Who have you been with?" he asked, very low. His hands tightened fractionally.

She briefly closed her eyes, took a deep breath, and answered with all the courage she had. "WolfStar."

"*What! What!*" StarDrifter let go her hands and stepped back in shock and utter anger. "Why WolfStar? *Why?*"

Zenith's eyes filled with tears, and she clasped her hands. "StarDrifter, I wanted to end it. I needed to see him, and come to terms with how I felt about him."

"And have you?" StarDrifter's face had gone completely white, but his eyes blazed with such rage that Zenith barely restrained herself from running away.

"I have found . . . I have found it easy to spend time with him," she whispered.

StarDrifter was so profoundly shocked that he was incapable of speech. She found it easy to spend time with *Wolf-Star* and not with him?

"It has been good to be able to talk things through with him."

"And you can't talk things through with me?" StarDrifter said.

Zenith flinched, and turned her head away.

"You don't feel comfortable with *me,* but you can sit and

chat comfortably with the man who raped and abused you?"

"He has changed—"

"Bah! WolfStar never *changes*! Zenith, what can you possibly find with him that you cannot find with me?"

Her eyes blurred with tears. "I do not regard him the same way as you," she finally managed.

StarDrifter's face and voice were rock hard. "And that is?"

"As a grandfather."

Nothing else she could have said would have shocked StarDrifter more. He stared, helpless, his mind unable to come to terms with what she'd just said.

"And have you," he whispered harshly, "managed to go to his bed, then, if you can't stomach mine?"

She stared at him, then she lifted a hand and struck him hard across his face.

Without a word, Zenith bent and collected the linens, then marched, straight-backed, down the corridor.

StarDrifter stared after her, his entire world collapsing within him.

The room was cool and dim, only a single lamp burning on a far wall.

Zenith silently placed the linens in a chest, then turned and sat on the stool by WolfStar's bed.

He stretched out a hand, and she took it without hesitation.

"What is wrong?" he said.

Zenith let her tears slide down her cheeks. *This* was all wrong. What she wanted was for StarDrifter to so take her hand, and for her to lean against him and sob out all her woes and let him make them all better.

StarDrifter was all she wanted, and yet here she was with WolfStar. Why? Why? *Why?*

Because, strangely, she felt comfortable with WolfStar in a way she never could with StarDrifter. StarDrifter was her loving, protective grandfather.

WolfStar was merely another man: one who caused her

complex and conflicting emotions, true, but he was just another man.

Although he was also technically her grandfather, Zenith found it impossible to perceive him as such.

Just a man. But a SunSoar. A man of her own blood, and a man she could possibly learn to trust.

She pulled back her hand, and WolfStar let her go.

"Has the Healer seen to your wounds today?" she asked, even though she knew the answer from talking to the guardsman on duty outside.

"Yes. I feel . . . better."

Indeed, WolfStar looked remarkably better. Whether it was the attention he was receiving from the Healers, or the undoubted benefit of breathing the untainted, undemonised air of Sanctuary, or simply his own remarkable recuperative powers, WolfStar was very definitely improving. His colour was good, his breathing unlaboured, his wounds scabbing and crusting over cleanly, and he could move about the bed without wincing with every minor effort.

Very soon, Zenith thought, he would be up and moving about the room.

She stiffened at the thought.

"I will not harm you again," WolfStar said, looking at her carefully.

Her mouth twisted. "But will I harm myself?" she said.

WolfStar struggled up onto one elbow. "Why should you?" he asked.

Zenith looked at him. His face and form were half-hidden with the shifting shadows cast by the lamp, but she could see the gleam of his eyes, the hard planes of his face, the rise and fall of his chest.

"StarDrifter and I," she said, in a matter-of-fact tone, "have been having some personal difficulties."

"Yes?"

Zenith stared at WolfStar suspiciously, trying to find the merest hint of sarcasm, or even triumph, in his voice. But it was not there. What she could see of his face was merely wearied by the effort of raising himself up to look at her.

Zenith shrugged, letting her eyes drift away. "We are Sun-Soar," she said. "And our blood calls each to the other."

She glanced back at WolfStar, but his face was unreadable, and he remained silent.

"But . . . but however much I love StarDrifter, and I *do*, and however much I *want* to be his lover, and that I desire as well, I cannot."

"No," WolfStar said, and his voice was low, thoughtful. "You could not, could you?"

Now it was Zenith's turn to remain silent.

"You are Azhure's daughter," WolfStar said, "and you could no more sleep with your own grandfather than you could thrust your own child into the fire."

And then he burst out laughing, apparently with genuine amusement. "Ah! I forgot. *That* you could do, and that you *did* do, very well, didn't you? Oh no, Zenith, do not go. I am laughing, but at my own stupidity and careless words than at you. Please, stay. Please."

Zenith sank back onto the stool, and let WolfStar take her hand again.

It was warm and dry and very soft and reassuring.

"I used the wrong words," he said, "but the meaning is true enough. StarDrifter is your beloved grandfather, and as much as I like to belittle the man, there are some things he does well—and being the warm, protective grandfather *is* one of those things. But now he wants to bed you. Poor Zenith. Your Acharite reserve must be at full war with your Icarii longings.

"And yet I," his voice lowered, and his hand slipped down to grasp lightly her wrist, "am a full-blooded Icarii man with no such reserves. A man who abused and wronged you, true, but one who has now been suitably punished, is suitably regretful . . . and who is of SunSoar blood."

"Shut up!"

His fingers tightened. "Hate yourself, Zenith. Not me. Not for speaking the truth."

WolfStar paused, and when he resumed his voice was hard with truth. "Why are you here? Why? Why come back?"

30

The Unexpected Heavens

As StarDrifter had said, Axis had more than enough help without begging assistance from anyone. Sanctuary was peopled with helpers, and while few as yet realised the imminent danger that faced Sanctuary, those that did were numerous enough, and eager enough, for what Axis needed.

There was the Lake Guard, twiddling their thumbs about now that DragonStar had no immediate need for them. There was Zared, and the vast army and loyalty he commanded. The Icarii numbered in their tens of thousands, and while Axis had only told FreeFall and EvenSong and their immediate aides about the demonic danger facing Sanctuary, they could command enough Icarii into the sky to blot out even Sanctuary's apparently limitless light.

"Just a few score will do," Axis had said, smiling.

Now he, Azhure, Zared and FreeFall stood about on one of the larger balconies of the main palace complex, Katie clutching Azhure's skirts as she had once clutched Faraday's. Katie had been very, very quiet in the past few hours, and while Azhure had worried about it, and tried to ask the girl what was wrong, Katie had only shaken her head and refused to speak.

The Mother's death had made her fully conscious of the terms of her own sacrifice.

A light, warm breeze blew over the balcony, tugging at coat and shirt-sleeves and wrapping the folds of Azhure's gown about her body. Zared, tired of the inaction, wandered listlessly about the balcony itself. It was tiled in a wondrous translucent turquoise, and it had salmon crystal columns supporting a balustrade of the same material.

"Not something I would have commissioned myself," he said dryly.

"It could be," Azhure said, one of her hands absently ruffling Katie's hair, "that the original Enemy had a more ostentatious taste in colour and vibrancy than their later children."

"And it could be," FreeFall said, walking to the balustrade and looking out over the orchards and fields spread out below them before turning back to the others, "that Sanctuary is merely storing all the colour and vibrancy that has been lost above. 'Tis no wonder, perhaps, that at times it appears a trifle gaudy."

Axis sighed, and restrained the urge to pace about restlessly. Where were the scouts he'd sent out hours ago? Was there *no* news?

"Storage for no reason," he said, folding his arms and tapping a foot impatiently, "if Sanctuary is about to collapse about us."

Axis' eyes flitted skywards as if he could see the cracks appearing in the sky already. He remembered how the wards covering the Star Gate had sickened and died, and he thought that much the same would eventually happen to the skies of Sanctuary.

I curse Isfrael, he thought, and then let his mouth twist wryly. He had spent the past forty years cursing the wrong son; he would have done better to raise Drago in love rather than hate.

But would *love* have tempered him into the man he is now?

"What are the other Star Gods doing?" Zared asked.

Azhure glanced at Axis, and then shrugged elegantly. "The events of the past few months have been, I think, rather too much for them."

"They can't cope?" Zared raised a disbelieving eyebrow. "What sort of gods are they, then?"

Axis gave a harsh laugh. "None of us are gods any more, Zared. For Adamon, and Xanon, as for the others, the shock was overwhelming. They lost contact with their mortality over the tens of thousands of years they revelled in their immortality. It is no wonder they find it difficult to adjust. For Azhure and myself," he lifted a hand, and briefly touched his wife's hair, "the shock was less, although still profound. Our mortality was still close, and . . ."

"And we have slipped the more easily back into its restrictions," Azhure finished for him. "The other once-gods now tend to keep to themselves, hating their uselessness."

"And now," Zared said, looking at Axis, "you have a use once more. Get us out of here, Axis!" Zared's voice rose, and he stepped three or four paces towards Axis. "Get us out of here! Leagh is up there somewhere," he gestured impotently towards the sky, "and I need to be with her."

"I will do what I can, Zared," Axis said quietly, and stepped close enough to place a hand on his brother's arm. "But we can do nothing—"

"Axis!" It was FreeFall, pointing to the sky.

Eight Lake Guardsmen and women were circling high above their heads, and one by one dropped lower towards the balcony.

WingRidge was the first to land. "StarMan," he said, and saluted.

Axis' heart gave a lurch at the title. It had been years— *years!*—since anyone had called him that . . . and to use such a tone of respect . . .

"Yes?" he said.

WingRidge waved an arm helplessly, and Axis felt despair wriggle its vicious way through his body. Nothing, then.

"Nothing," WingRidge said.

"Nothing?" Azhure said.

WingRidge sighed as the other members of the Lake Guard unit settled about him. "We overflew all of Sanctuary that we could," he said.

"But not all?" FreeFall queried.

"Then why are you back here?" Zared said.

WingRidge shot him an irritated glance. The groundwalkers always thought they knew *everything!*

"We are back because we have overflown all of Sanctuary that *anyone* possibly could even in an infinite number of years," WingRidge said, turning so that he talked exclusively to Axis. At least this man had some patience!

WingRidge paused, gathering his thoughts, and trying to find the phrases he needed to explain what was almost unexplainable.

"If there were only twelve people who needed Sanctuary," WingRidge finally said, his voice soft and reflective, "then Sanctuary would make itself big enough for twelve people. If twelve million needed Sanctuary, then it would make itself big enough for twelve million. We . . . we flew as far as we could . . . but we will never be able to reach Sanctuary's limits, Axis, because—"

"Because Sanctuary simply keeps expanding itself as you fly towards its current limits," Zared said. "It is merely being helpful, and expanding to fit the perceived need."

WingRidge blinked, reassessing his previous ill-tempered thoughts regarding the man. "Yes. As we flew outwards, we could see Sanctuary expanding itself in the distance. New vistas kept expanding themselves. Continuously. The faster we flew, the faster the vistas unfolded before us. There is no end to Sanctuary, and no back wall. It's too damn helpful and far too cursed accommodating!"

"Stars," Axis said weakly. He turned away and walked a few steps, trying to sort out his thoughts. Very well, so there was no physical back door, but surely there must be something else they could do, something they could find . . .

"Axis!" he heard Azhure cry in a panicked voice, and he whipped about.

Everyone on the balcony had scattered, most diving for whatever cover chairs or balustrade could offer.

Axis lifted his head, and, in the next instant, instinctively flung himself to one side.

Something very large and black was tumbling out of the sky.

"Well," said Urbeth, picking herself up off the gaudy turquoise-tiled floor of the balcony, "someone's taste is absolutely awful."

Behind her two other icebears were rolling into a sitting position, their faces scrunched up in scowls as they combed out bits of disarranged fur.

And behind the three bears sat a very disgruntled and immensely old woman, clutching a terracotta pot. She was mumbling something under her breath, and from what Axis could hear of it, he was rather relieved she wasn't saying it louder.

Old women weren't supposed to know such gutter oaths.

"Urbeth?" Azhure said weakly, rising to her feet. Katie rose with her, and for the first time in hours she was looking far more relaxed . . . almost cheerful. She stared at the pot the old woman was holding and, without further ado, let Azhure go and walked over to Ur, sinking down beside her.

Katie reached out a tentative hand and touched the pot, and her face broke into a sunny smile.

Ur stared at her, then relaxed and smiled herself. "What a pretty girlie," she said. "Do you know if there is anywhere about here that a grumpy old lady could get a cup of tea?"

Zared and FreeFall together with the members of the Lake Guard had retreated to the palace wall, and were watching the proceedings carefully. Hands rested on weapons, but as Axis and Azhure did not seem too perturbed, they did nothing else.

Besides, Zared was sure the two icebears still irritably combing out their fur looked surprisingly familiar. Somehow.

"Urbeth," Axis said, in a tone of voice that he was immensely relieved to hear was firm and strong. "What is going on? How did you get here? Who is that?" he said, pointing to Ur.

"Well," Urbeth said politely, "could you tell me where 'here' actually *is*?"

Axis glanced at Azhure. She shrugged, and so Axis turned back to Urbeth. "Sanctuary."

"Ah," Urbeth said, and paced about, looking this way and that over the balcony. "Useless, useless Sanctuary. What are *you* still doing here? Looking about at the view?"

"We've been seeking a way out," Axis said. "A back door, perhaps, as the front entrance is denied us. But . . ."

Urbeth heaved a great sigh and sat down. "Can *no-one* accomplish anything without my aid? Ah!"

She rolled her eyes.

"Can you help?" Azhure asked slowly.

Urbeth grinned, frightening and malicious. "That depends," she said.

"Depends on what?" Axis said.

"On how you feel about a renewed acquaintance with the Skraelings," Urbeth said.

31

StarLaughter's Astonishing Turnabout

"Talk," DragonStar said.

They were gathered in the lowest part of the basements of Star Finger. Here it was that Faraday had finally found the child whose cries had been haunting her dreams; here that Caelum and DragonStar had made their peace.

Now, it was slightly more crowded and far, far more uncomfortable.

StarLaughter and StarGrace had seated themselves in the centre of the chamber. StarLaughter's scarlet robe was again carefully arranged to display it and her body to their best advantage. StarGrace had hunkered down on her haunches, a beautiful, sad, gloomy, ugly girl-woman, whose dark gown alternated between material and feathers, and whose hands were always slightly blurred as they shapechanged from claws to plump innocent fingers and back again.

So long used to the visage of the hawk, StarGrace was finding her old form uncomfortable.

About them were grouped DragonStar and his five witches, plus two wings of the Strike Force. The ethereal bodies of the Strike Force members, their vivid plumage undulled even in this dank cellar, drifted this way and that, creating a silvery jewelled backdrop to the central drama.

The rest of the Strike Force lined the corridors outside the basement.

"Talk about what?" StarLaughter said, widening her eyes disingenuously.

DragonStar gestured impatiently, and walked away a step or two. Faraday and Gwendylyr sat slightly to one side, supporting Leagh between them. Leagh still looked exhausted, but her face was calm, and she wore a light smile. Goldman and DareWing stood just behind them.

"StarLaughter," DragonStar said, "you drifted for thousands of years with the Demons. Their revenge was your revenge. They were your friends."

"They were yours once, too."

"I do not trust you, StarLaughter."

She laughed, a pretty, light sound. "And for that I cannot blame you! I was as much to blame for your horrific handling by the Demons as they."

DragonStar's eyes shifted to StarGrace. *And what was she doing here?*

"The fact is," StarLaughter continued, "StarGrace and myself have become somewhat disenchanted with the Demons."

StarGrace shifted slightly, but said nothing.

"They promised us revenge—" StarLaughter hissed the word "revenge", "—and yet what have they done? Nothing! They had WolfStar within their grasp, and let him slip away. I, as StarGrace and all the other Hawkchilds, have come back to Tencendor for only one purpose: to kill WolfStar."

StarGrace suddenly spat, flinging her arms up as if they were wings.

Black material billowed out behind.

"We want him *dead*!" she said.

Gwendylyr caught Faraday's eyes, and raised her eyebrows in an expression of wondrous distaste. Faraday inclined her head slightly, but immediately returned her attention to DragonStar and StarLaughter. What *had* DragonStar told her about StarLaughter? Not a great deal, when she thought about it.

Faraday narrowed her eyes.

"What StarGrace is trying to say," StarLaughter said, rising in a sinuous movement, "is that while the Demons helped us as far as getting us back into Tencendor, they haven't done much else. Well, not much else apart from completely destroy the land."

"You must have known they were going to do that," DragonStar said.

StarLaughter shrugged dismissively. "That's as may be."

She walked slowly in a circle about DragonStar, moving ever closer with each step. She shifted the material of her scarlet and gold robe slightly, pulling it closer against the curves of her body. She did not take her eyes from his face.

"Now it appears that the Demons have wandered off on their own crusade," StarLaughter continued, "and forgotten entirely their promises to us. StarGrace and I admit some impatience."

She pouted, then tilted her face to one side and smiled at DragonStar. "We are tired of the Demons," she said, "and would rather concentrate on our own purpose. WolfStar."

DragonStar stared at her, then looked down to StarGrace. "And you? And the other Hawkchilds?"

"We are being used to hunt you," StarGrace said, and smiled. Unlike StarLaughter's, her expression was utterly feral and malicious. "But we would rather hunt *WolfStar!*"

"Thus, we," StarLaughter said, moving away a pace or two and airily waving a hand, "are prepared to do a deal. Help us find WolfStar and we will help you against the Demons. We all have a chance at succeeding if we work together."

"How?" DragonStar said. "How will you help?"

StarGrace laughed, low and husky, and answered for them both. "By not telling the Demons where you and yours are, DragonStar SunSoar. Qeteb will use the Hawkchilds in the effort to hunt you down. We will soar and we will swoop, but, oh dear me, we will never find!"

"Do we have a deal?" StarLaughter said. "Do we? You give us WolfStar, and we aid you against the Demons."

DragonStar stared at her, wondering what it was that she wasn't telling him. These were explanations that he could accept . . . on the surface. But there was something *else* going on hère that he could not yet discern, and that made him unsure.

He turned to look at his five witches. *Well?* he asked them.

DareWing, who had previously heard StarLaughter and StarGrace's deal, nodded. *Can we afford to refuse? We need every piece of aid offered us.*

Gwendylyr and Faraday again exchanged glances. *I don't like her,* Gwendylyr said in DragonStar's mind, *but does that mean we can't trust her? DragonStar, you know these two. You decide.*

DragonStar's mouth twitched in a very small grin—who could ever know StarLaughter and StarGrace? Their inner minds and emotions were the end product of three thousand years of twisted hate, and their inner writhings could not be tracked by any observer who had not travelled the same three-thousand-year road with them.

Faraday? he asked.

She shrugged. *Your decision.*

Thank you very much, he replied, but without any rancour. *Goldman?*

He grinned, including StarLaughter and StarGrace in his smile. Surprisingly, StarGrace returned it, although Star-Laughter looked surprised. *I'm with DareWing,* he said. *We have little choice. Besides, they are an adventure, and I for one relish the chance to explore them further.*

Just don't let them bed you, DragonStar said, grinning himself. *It's murder.*

Now Faraday did look at him sharply, the question all over her face, while Gwendylyr's mouth dropped open.

DragonStar ignored them, squatting down before Leagh. *Well?*

She smiled, a very gentle and sweet expression. *I think they are true . . . or, at least, true enough for us. If you think Wolf-Star's sacrifice worth the bargain, then agree. Trust them as much as you dare, DragonStar.*

DragonStar blinked, surprised more by Leagh's inner calm and happiness than by what she'd said—what had happened to her since she'd fallen screaming to the floor earlier?—then nodded, and rose again.

"I think we have a bargain," DragonStar said to the two birdwomen.

"Do you know where WolfStar is?" both asked in unison, both equally eagerly, and DragonStar narrowed his eyes.

StarLaughter and StarGrace had, at that moment, revealed completely different purposes: to him, if not to each other.

"Yes," he said. "WolfStar is in Sanctuary."

They ate from the remains of whatever dried food had been stored in the lower levels of Star Finger, and then DragonStar told his witches to lay down and rest.

"In the morning," he said, "we will begin."

Faraday curled up next to Leagh, pulling her cloak tight about them both, and DragonStar smiled cynically. He and Faraday were, it seemed, back to the coolness of their initial pilgrimage north to Gorkenfort and back to Carlon.

Goldman had cleared a space for him close to the fire that DareWing had built, but DragonStar shook his head.

"There is something else I need to do first," he said, and turned away.

He looked around. StarGrace had left an hour earlier saying that she needed to return to her sky patrol before Qeteb and the other Demons reappeared, but StarLaughter was curled up in a thick woollen cloak against a far wall.

DragonStar walked over, and gently shook her shoulder.

StarLaughter opened one eye and peered irritably at him. "Yes?"

"We need to talk," DragonStar said. "Now."

"Then talk," she murmured, closing her eye.

"Alone!" DragonStar said, and shook her harder.

Now StarLaughter opened both her eyes, and she grinned lasciviously. "So! I thought you would never ask!"

"Don't play games with *me*!" DragonStar snapped, and grasped her arm tightly, hauling her upwards.

"You're hurting!" StarLaughter said, and tried to wrench herself free.

But DragonStar was too strong. He pulled until she was on

her feet, then gave her a none-too-gentle shove towards the door. "Outside."

"Not all the way outside, I do hope," StarLaughter muttered, but DragonStar did not speak, contenting himself with an impatient shove in the small of her back.

As they left the room, Faraday opened her eyes and stared at the empty door.

"Whatever my companions think," DragonStar said as he pulled StarLaughter to a halt in a deserted part of the corridor several twists and turns away from the chamber, "I admit harbouring some doubts about the sincerity of your turnabout. Frankly, I find it astonishing."

StarLaughter's eyes darted about the corridor. It was deserted. The Strike Force were either at ground level to watch the sky, or were patrolling what was left of the complex, either to find if there was anything left that could prove serviceable to DragonStar or to search for any traps and surprises that StarLaughter and StarGrace may have planted.

She sighed theatrically. "You have discovered my secret."

"Oh, for the Stars' sakes, woman! Stop performing these dramatic roles! What is it you really want here? *You* were lying back in that chamber, although StarGrace was not. *What is going on?*"

StarLaughter stared down the corridor, her eyes unfocused, silent for the time being.

DragonStar was content enough to let her think, although he still wondered if she was assuming a facade she believed would aid her cause.

"The Demons tricked me," StarLaughter said eventually, quietly, still staring into infinity down the corridor, "and then they tired of me. They said they were going to restore my son to me, but all they did was make use of his—" her voice broke a little, "—dead flesh to create a haven for Qeteb's warmth and breath and movement and soul. Having tricked me, they then tired of me."

DragonStar hesitated, then placed a hand on her shoulder.

StarLaughter did not react. "I escaped, but only barely."

"And?" DragonStar prompted as StarLaughter hesitated.

"And I began to think," she said, "about myself and Wolf-Star."

StarLaughter shifted slightly, bringing herself closer to DragonStar's body.

"When we were husband and wife I loved him desperately, completely, with my entire being and purpose," she said after a moment's silence.

"And yet you plotted against him."

She half-smiled, lost in her deluded memories. "We were so mutually ambitious, DragonStar. We could not help ourselves. We became cold and hard and calculating, and somewhere along the way the love was lost. I planned his murder; he accomplished mine instead. WolfStar was ever quick on his feet."

"And now?" DragonStar said very softly. "And now?"

"And now I want him back," StarLaughter said, "as he must want me."

DragonStar drew back from her in complete shock. "You *what*? *He wants what?*"

"I want him back!" StarLaughter turned to DragonStar, her face alive with passion and purpose. "As he must want me! Who else can WolfStar ever love? Who else can I? We have made our mistakes, true, but—"

DragonStar laughed hollowly. "You're mad, StarLaughter. Mad! WolfStar will never—"

"Yes! Yes! He *must*!"

"Wait . . . have you told StarGrace this?"

"No. She would not understand. All she wants is his death."

"And the other Hawkchilds? They want the same?"

StarLaughter nodded.

"So let me see if I understand this completely," DragonStar said. "You have decided that, against all odds and expectations, your purpose in life is to love WolfStar again—"

"And he me!" she said. "We were born for each other, and we have spent the past several thousand years moving back towards each other!"

Gods, DragonStar thought. The woman is completely insane!

"Let me finish," he said. "You have decided you want to find WolfStar to throw yourself into his arms, while you have managed to convince the Hawkchilds that you remain committed to his death."

"They would accept no other arguments," StarLaughter said.

"True," DragonStar said, "but what will happen if the Hawkchilds realise that you are double-crossing them? Or if you get away with that, what will you do when you all happen on WolfStar? You want to love him, the Hawkchilds want to kill him. It's bound to be a mess, StarLaughter."

"Leave that to me," she said. "All that need concern you is that I and the Hawkchilds work on your behalf—"

"Until the Hawkchilds realise you're tricking them," DragonStar said a little dryly.

"And who will tell them, DragonStar. *Who?*" She sighed. "You do not need to concern yourself about me, or the Hawkchilds, or even WolfStar. Help us to find him, and then turn your back. You get what you want, and I will get what I want."

And the Hawkchilds, thought DragonStar. What *do* you plan to do when everyone finally meets up with WolfStar?

She pressed herself against him, burying her fists in the folds of his shirt, her face upturned to his, her eyes blazing. "WolfStar and I—what a team! We can best the Hawkchilds, and then . . . then . . ."

StarLaughter lapsed into silence, her mouth open, her eyes moist with emotion.

DragonStar stared into her face, and with a sudden shock realised that she was either completely mad, or absolutely, frighteningly sane.

And DragonStar did not know which he feared more.

"StarLaughter," he finally said. "I need something solid to convince me that I can trust you. For all I know, you are still in league with the Demons."

"What would convince you of my genuineness? The secret to the Demons' destruction?"

"That would help."

She sighed. "I thought you already knew that."

"You thought wrong."

She thought a moment before she spoke. "If there is one thing I have learned about the Demons during my sojourn with them—and Qeteb behaves as do the others—it is that they are one-dimensional only."

"One-dimensional?"

StarLaughter gave a small smile. "They are boring. Predictable. They are pure evil, true, but that is *all* they are. Completely one-dimensional. DragonStar, if you want to defeat them, then make them two-dimensional."

"I have no idea what you mean—"

She turned her face fully to his. "Give them a choice, DragonStar, and they will fall apart. Perhaps."

He was silent, thinking. Was this the weapon his witches could use against the Demons?

"Give them a fork in their straight and narrow roads, DragonStar, and you may be able to confuse them enough to choose the path leading to their doom rather than yours."

32

Revival

The Demons were angry beyond any anger that had ever filled them in previous millennia. And of all five, Qeteb was angry beyond compare.

Fury consumed him.

Rage ate his entire soul.

Revenge, destruction, the blight and devastation of all that still somehow survived: these were his only thoughts.

Now!

"They escaped me!" he bellowed across the land.

Well, so what if they had? They could escape nowhere he would not eventually find them.

If they were in Sanctuary? Then he would *consume* Sanctuary! He would shred it! Ravage it! Vomit forth its remains into the interstellar wastes to float lonely for eternity!

If they hid somewhere in a secret cave or dungeon?

Then it would not survive his might and power. What devastation he had wreaked on Tencendor to this point was but a foretaste of what he would eventually do.

Qeteb smiled. What he would eventually do with the power of the Enemy. He would turn the Enemy's own power back on them and laugh as they screamed.

Qeteb had never been this powerful in his entire existence, nor ever this potentially powerful. He could feel the power he'd eaten in the Sacred Groves ripple through him, making him stronger, more magical . . . more dangerous.

And soon he would revel in the power of the Enemy.

And after that, after that lay Sanctuary.

Qeteb's stomach gurgled with anticipation. So many souls, all waiting for him. Fattening themselves on the false hope of Sanctuary. He laughed.

And after Sanctuary, the entire planet.

And then Qeteb knew he could ravage at will through the universe. The Star Dance would quail and then fail.

"There is nothing that can stop me now," he whispered, and the whisper fled through the clouds and the thin air of the upper atmosphere and fled screaming through the universe.

There is nothing that can stop me now!

They had returned to the scene of Rox's death. Sigholt. Sheol, Raspu, Mot and Barzula stood in a semicircle before the moat where the bridge had once stood. As one they were silent, concentrating, pooling all their power and directing it where Qeteb wanted it.

Before them, supine and willing, lay the Niah-woman. Her arms were by her side, her eyes staring sightlessly into the low and heavy sky.

Her belly, still flat, nevertheless quivered and throbbed with the burgeoning life within.

Qeteb was leaping and screaming atop Sigholt's Keep, a black, maniacal figure, all spindly arms and legs and grinning face full of teeth.

Qeteb was calling Rox's spirit home.

Evil never died, and was never destroyed. It only festered, and Rox's spirit had been festering ever since the bridge's trap had killed him.

Lost, lonely, angry, revengeful, it had drifted among the stars where the bridge had flung it.

Now its master was calling it, singing to it *(screaming through a bloody, foaming mouth to it),* and Rox's spirit responded.

It crashed through the universe, wailing past galaxies, tearing apart planetary systems, destroying moons and asteroids alike.

Qeteb became a blur of mania atop Sigholt. He flung his arms and legs about with such violence his joints creaked and popped; his voice screeched and wailed through his throat; his teeth waxed and waned in his jaws—now long, razored fangs, now rickety, decayed grinders; his body parts grew to tremendous size and then exploded, reforming in the same instant into grotesque parodies of anatomy that wriggled and reached as if they had a life of their own.

The surface of Tencendor heaved and shuddered. Boils opened and exploded dirt and filth into the air. Chasms writhed across the plains, meeting and breeding and reproducing until the sound of their passing became a nightmarish roar.

Mountains jiggled and jumped, oceans wailed, caverns sobbed.

Qeteb laughed.

Deep in the bowels of Star Finger DragonStar put his hands to his ears and screamed. Every horror that Qeteb visited on the land was visited on his soul.

"DragonStar!" Leagh yelled, and threw herself against him.

"DragonStar!" And she grabbed at one of his hands, and held it tightly against her belly. "Believe!"

DragonStar's eyes widened, and he fell silent.

Rox exploded through the sky as the craft of the Enemy had once done.

Fire rained down, and ice sheets shattered the air.

Qeteb screamed in triumph, every part of him wriggling and writhing.

He was a master!

Blood showered down from the sky, and the four other Demons tipped back their heads and let it wash over their faces.

They were very, very happy.

Something black and horrible slowly spiralled down from the heavens.

It was a worm, wriggling and writhing in complete harmony with Qeteb, slick and moist, covered in the oils and juices of its reincarnation.

Rox's homecoming soul.

"Yes! Yes! Yes!" Qeteb screamed, stabbing one finger down towards Niah's still supine body. "There! In her womb! *There!*"

And the worm saw, and rejoiced.

It spiralled closer, slowly, slowly, slowly, and then suddenly it became a blur of movement, dropping *(squelching)* down to the ground before Niah, humping and wriggling, making frantic mewling sounds, desperate . . .

"Yes! Yes! There! *There!*"

And the worm saw, and went. It wriggled up to Niah's feet, and forced them apart.

It began the final journey up the valley of her legs, moving to its sweet haven between her thighs . . .

Qeteb roared with laughter. "*This* is what I will do to *you,* DragonStar!"

And the worm wriggled home, and disappeared.

Niah's belly roiled.

And DragonStar screamed, and retched, and Leagh pressed his hand even harder against her belly, and said, "Use me, DragonStar, use the flowers."

He wiped his mouth with the back of his hand, stared at her, and then felt what throbbed forth from her belly.

Life. Wonder reborn.

And DragonStar used it.

Niah's body convulsed, once, twice, a third time, and then it lay still. One of its hands twitched.

Qeteb flung himself into the air, tumbling down from Sigholt's tower like a deranged acrobat determined upon his own destruction.

He landed next to Niah, a jerking, black thing all arms and legs and grinning face, and he grabbed at her arm. "Wake up! Wake up!"

And Niah did.

She turned her exquisitely beautiful face to Qeteb and she smiled with a frightful malevolence.

Niah's body, controlled from within her womb by Rox's soul.

"This feels good," the Rox-Niah said, and it spoke with the voice of Rox, harsh from disuse and the fright and loneliness of his death. It raised itself up on an arm, and waggled its tongue experimentally. "Two bodies to control."

"The outer will be disposed of when you grow enough to wriggle your way free again," Qeteb said. His form flowed and reshaped itself into the handsome man clad in grey and ivory. "Now, how do you *feel*?"

The Rox-Niah—Roxiah—sat up and furrowed its brow thoughtfully. "Strange. Odd . . . as if . . ."

"As if you have access, perhaps, to a new and strange power?" Qeteb asked eagerly.

"Yes . . . yes, that's it. It feels," Roxiah twisted its features into an expression of hate and loathing, "familiar."

"Indeed, my sweet," Qeteb said, "for 'tis the power of the Enemy."

And Roxiah opened its mouth and roared, and all beasts left in Tencendor quavered and wailed.

Except those surrounding DragonStar.

Lifting his hand from Leagh's belly, calm and assured now, he stared into the ceiling of the basement chamber, as if he could see right through it to the sky above.

"Why not come and get *us,* Qeteb," he said, and grinned. "If you can find us!"

Qeteb screamed, and lurched to his feet. Roxiah rose as well, and the Demons, now a complete circle of six, capered and reeled about.

Why not come and get us, Qeteb. If you can find us!

"Fool! Fool!" Qeteb screeched. "I have better things to do before I come to eat *you!*"

DragonStar smiled, and kissed Leagh gently on her forehead.

"Good," he said. "It will be the sweeter for the waiting."

33

Urbeth's Plan

"The Skraelings?" Axis said. "What do you mean, 'the Skraelings'?"

Urbeth stood up, and suddenly she was an icebear no longer, but the tall woman of grey and silvered hair.

A circle of stars blazed from her left hand.

"The Enchantress," Azhure said, and dipped her head in reverence.

"Ah," Urbeth said, "no time for such polite niceties now. We have work to do." She walked over to the balustrade and looked at the scene before her. "Pretty, but ultimately destroyable. I can't think what the Enemy were thinking of."

"They were thinking," Axis said, "of a means to give us a respite."

"Mayhap so," Urbeth said, and turned back to face him. "But what now?"

"Well . . ."

"Ha! Haven't an idea, have you?"

Axis grinned, and folded his arms nonchalantly. "No. But I think that you do."

Urbeth waved a hand. "I have grown used to the fact that I must, apparently, save the day whenever everyone else gets themselves into a hopeless muddle. So, review the situation for me. You!"

She pointed at Zared. "What does this Sanctuary contain?"

Zared stared at Axis, and then looked back to Urbeth. "Ah . . ."

"Speak up, dammit! For all we know Qeteb might be chewing his way down through that make-believe sky right now!"

"Sanctuary contains all the Tencendorian peoples that were left sane after the Demons' initial push through into the land, and before Qeteb's final resurrection. All its peoples, and all its animals."

One of Urbeth's daughters—they had also assumed human form—moved forward to stand before Zared. "And by all its animals you mean . . . ?"

Zared lifted his hands, not quite knowing how to explain. "Everything that DragonStar's witches—"

"DragonStar's witches?" Urbeth asked sharply.

"His 'helpers', I suppose you could call them," Axis said. "Those who share the same source of power that he does. Acharite power—the power of the Enemy."

Urbeth smiled. "Ah. Good."

"Faraday and Leagh," Azhure put in, moving to stand and link arms with Axis, "DareWing, the Strike Leader, and Goldman the Master of the Guilds of Carlon. Lastly, there is Gwendylyr, Duchess of Aldeni."

"An eclectic bunch!" Urbeth said. "But I suppose DragonStar knew what he was doing. But you were saying, Zared, everything that DragonStar's witches . . . ?"

"Could pull into Tencendor before Qeteb's final resurrection," Zared said. "Deer, sheep, bloated creatures from Bogle Marsh—"

"Which Sanctuary has most genially recreated for them," FreeFall put in under his breath. All this discussion was making him impatient.

"Insects, birds . . . everything," Zared finished.

Urbeth shared a glance with her two daughters. What a clutter! And *they* were going to have to fix it!

She turned back to Axis. "And so you were . . . what was it . . . looking for a back door?"

"Yes."

"And what, pray tell," Urbeth said softly, walking up so close to Axis her face was only a handspan from his, "were you going to do then?"

He held her grey gaze, although it was not the easiest thing he'd had to do in his life.

"I don't know."

Urbeth returned his stare, then gave a soft laugh. "You 'don't know'. You were going to lead this entire zoo out this 'back door' . . . to what? Instant madness at the hands of the Demons? Were you going to lead them back into a wasted Tencendor, Axis? *What in stars names were you going to do?*"

"I was going to judge that circumstance when I encountered it!" Axis shouted.

Urbeth did not flinch.

"I suppose you have a better idea?" said Axis, no less hostile.

"Of course," she said, and smiled.

Axis was not to be placated by a smile. "Well?" he snapped.

"Behold," Urbeth said, and, turning to one side, she waved a hand through the air.

Instantly, the garish turquoise tiling of the balcony floor rose up in ridges and dips.

Everyone, save Urbeth, her daughters, and Ur, who still sat quietly, her arms about her pot, gasped in astonishment. Urbeth had created a relief map of Tencendor.

Urbeth moved so she could point out individual features. "Qeteb has wasted all this portion," she said, and with a sweep of her hand indicated the bulk of Tencendor. "Coroleas still lies safe, although it, too, will be consumed if Qeteb manages to best DragonStar. The Demons' influence extends some way out over both the Andeis and the Widowmaker Seas, perhaps a league's distance. The Corolean fishing industry has been badly affected, and the Emperor is not pleased."

Axis grunted. The diplomatic disasters of the situation did not concern him. "What else remains clear?"

Urbeth hesitated, glancing at her daughters. "The icefloes of the Iskruel Ocean are still navigable, although growing more unsound by the hour."

"If Coroleas is still free," Azhure said, "can we go there? Can *you* get us out of here, Urbeth? Into Coroleas?"

Urbeth did not answer immediately. "Coroleas is a possible destination, although not entirely desirable. The Emperor will be *entirely* displeased at the sudden influx of guests, two-, four- and eight-legged."

"He'll just have to put up with—" Axis began.

"But there is a better place for us to go," Urbeth said. "Here," and her finger moved. "The tundra to the extreme north-east of Tencendor."

"What!" Axis exploded. "But that's frozen! How can we survive there? And that territory is full of . . ." he trailed off, remembering what Urbeth had earlier said about the Skraelings.

"Skraelings," Urbeth said. "Yes. It is also very close to Tencendor, and the way south is relatively unrestricted now the forests have gone."

Behind her, Ur moaned, and hugged her pot tighter.

"But the biggest positive is the Skraelings," Urbeth finished.

"Why?" Axis said.

"Because I think we can come to some arrangement with them," Urbeth said, and Ur cackled with laughter.

"One that might not be entirely to their liking," she said, and then Urbeth and her daughters, and Katie also, who still sat with Ur, were laughing as if the entire future were clear of Demons and shadows alike.

34

WolfStar Feels Better

Urbeth said the tundra, and so the tundra, Axis supposed, it had to be. As for the Skraelings, Urbeth (and Ur, whom Axis privately thought was more than slightly senile) remained silent on that point, and said that it would be easier to show than explain.

Skraelings. Stars! Axis thought he had seen the last of them when Azhure and the eastern forests had destroyed Gorgrael's Skraeling army in Gorken Pass. But they'd all forgotten that the Skraelings came from the far north-eastern frozen tundra, and Axis supposed that a breeding population would have survived there even after the debacle of Gorken Pass.

Now they'd had forty-odd years to breed back to pre-Gorgrael numbers. Axis shuddered, remembering the nests that he and Azhure had discovered under the ruins of Hsingard. A breeding pair could lay hundreds of eggs per year. No doubt the northern tundra was now riddled with Skraelings.

And now they didn't even have the Alaunt, or the Wolven, let alone their magic.

What Axis wouldn't give for just one of Azhure's Moon-wildflowers drifting down from the night skies!

He shook himself out of his memories and his regrets. There was far too much to do without wasting time in fears, as warranted as they were.

Urbeth had told him that the populations of Sanctuary, in

escaping to the frozen tundra, would not need to survive very long before they would have a permanent shelter arranged.

"What kind of shelter?" Axis had asked, and Urbeth—back in her ursine form by this stage—had grinned and slouched off.

And what was "not very long"?

Axis sighed again, and turned back to his task.

Himself, Zared, Theod, Herme, WingRidge and Gustus, Zared's lieutenant, were deep within Sanctuary's main stores complex. Until an hour ago they had not known where this complex existed, but when Axis voiced a wish to see what stores Sanctuary contained, a corridor and a flight of stairs leading down into a series of massive stone-vaulted chambers appeared.

And these chambers were packed with stores. Food, clothing, blankets, medical supplies. All was here . . . except . . .

"What would be more than useful," Zared said to Axis as they began the tiring task of inventory (which, if truth be told, Axis had delegated to the Lake Guard, but someone had to supervise the procedure), "is a few hundred carts with which to transport them."

And precisely at that moment, FeatherGrip, a Lake Guardsman, shouted from twenty-odd paces away: "StarMan! There's a series of chambers here filled with carts!"

Axis glanced at Zared and Theod, grinned, and added, "Equipped with sleigh runners for their easier movement across the snow and ice would be nice."

"And they've got sleigh runners fitted over their wheels as well!" came FeatherGrip's voice.

"Anything else we need?" Axis said quietly. "I do not think that Sanctuary will deny us a single quilt, if we ask it."

"I'll make a list," Theod said, "once WingRidge can tell me the precise numbers we've got in Sanctuary."

"Don't forget to put millipede food down," Zared said, grinning. "As well as starling fodder, seal snacks, and Bogle Marsh creature dinners."

Theod rolled his eyes, and walked away.

Zared's grin faded. "How long do we have? The logistics of the situation, the help of Sanctuary notwithstanding, are beyond a nightmare."

Axis stared into the distance of the underground vaults. "I have no idea, Zared. It could be two hours, it could be two weeks."

Pray gods that it's the latter, Zared thought, for we would never save more than ten percent of the peoples and creatures in Sanctuary if we only have two hours.

Roxiah, still naked, and delighting in that nakedness, stood before Sigholt—legs apart, arms wide, head thrown back and eyes closed.

Inside its body, the Rox foetus was exploring the Enemy's power contained within Niah's flesh. So many thousands of years—so many tens of thousands of years!—had the Enemy denied them, and toyed with them, and made them scamper across half the universe, and now the Enemy's power was *theirs*!

Or mine alone, if I work this well, thought the infant Rox deep inside its developing brain cells, but, like most foetuses, it was patient, and was content that it should, for the moment, work its master's will.

And so it was doing: Roxiah was employing the Enemy's power to destroy Sigholt, stone by stone.

For thousands of years Sigholt had stood, a bastion of magic by its magical lake. It had laughed with its companion bridge, frowned at the mistakes of the Icarii and human alike who had lived within it, overseen the conception of Axis Star-Man atop its roof (ah! the day that StarDrifter had spiralled down from the skies to seduce Rivkah!), witnessed the birth of Caelum, and tended—as much as it was able—the growing SunSoar brood.

Now, Sigholt was dying.

Noisily.

Sigholt did not so much scream in its dying, as it wailed. Its wails crept up and down the scale, a dirge to mourn its own passing, as well a melancholy lullaby to croon Tencendor through its prolonged dying.

Sigholt's incessant wailing was annoying the Demons hugely.

Qeteb, as did Sheol, Raspu, Mot and Barzula, strode up and down behind Roxiah, screaming abuse at Sigholt, shaking fists and exposing various bits of their anatomy as their anger took them. As each stone tumbled down, and Sigholt's wailing continued, the Demons grew more irked, their curses more foul, their exposings more puerile.

Why couldn't the cursed thing just collapse!

Finally, after hours of wailing, Sigholt obliged them. It had resisted Roxiah's destruction to a point where it just gave up: it was too tired, it had seen too much in its long life, and resisting Roxiah's power was, in the end, futile.

Besides, Sigholt knew that something better awaited. The Field of Flowers.

So it decided to just collapse. Implode. Create a mess.

The roar of collapsing masonry enveloped the Demons an instant after the dust and shrapnel of Sigholt's self-destruction struck them.

In a heartbeat the Demons' curses turned to gut-wrenching coughing as they struggled as far away from the rubble as they could.

Behind them, the rubble sighed, and passed on.

Qeteb finally managed to get his breath, and spit out all the black grime that had found its way down into his throat and lungs, and pick out the shards of rock from his anatomy.

"Spiredore!" he said. "Spiredore is next! Destroy the means of movement for the StarSon and his ineffectual helpers and for those cowering ants in Sanctuary, and we have them!"

"And after Spiredore?" Sheol said, wiping her nose with the back of her hand.

Qeteb glanced at her distastefully. "Then? Then Sanctuary. We will be there by the morning."

Sheol smiled.

StarDrifter threw open the door to WolfStar's chamber—the single Lake Guardsman on duty outside had been no match for StarDrifter's fury—and confronted the Enchanter.

WolfStar was alone in his sick chamber, sitting on the edge

of his bed, holding his chest carefully with one arm as he coughed into a snowy cloth.

He looked at the cloth carefully—good, no blood—before he looked up.

"Well, well," he said softly. "If it isn't StarDrifter come to offer me his good wishes for my recovery—"

He got no further, for StarDrifter had crossed the room in five strides and hit WolfStar as hard as he could.

WolfStar fell back across the bed, but made no move to either rise or strike StarDrifter himself.

"Did that make you feel better?" he said, his tone still soft, although more than sarcastic. "If you like, I could recommend you for a place in the Strike Force . . . such aggression should not go unused."

"You piece of filth!" StarDrifter said, standing several paces away. His fists were clenched, although he held his arms rigid by his sides.

WolfStar raised an eyebrow. "What have I done now?"

Although StarDrifter had come to this chamber to accuse WolfStar of tampering with Zenith's already damaged soul, all he could think of were the past three thousand years in which WolfStar had manipulated and controlled, sending tens of thousands to their death along the way, and all the time justifying his every crime and sin as necessary for the achievement of the final end.

"What have you *done?*" StarDrifter whispered. "What have you done? Oh Stars! Don't get me started!"

"Zenith knows her own mind," WolfStar said, not in the mood for indirect conversations.

"Zenith knows her own mind?" StarDrifter began.

"Oh for the gods' sakes, man, stop repeating everything I say!"

StarDrifter stepped forward a pace. "Then let me say *this! Were you the one who helped save her when Niah—with your encouragement!—tried to destroy her? What of my efforts, and Faraday's, in pulling her through the shadow-lands until she could reclaim her own body?*"

"You meddlesome idiot. Perhaps it had been better that

Niah had succeeded, for then she wouldn't be in the Demons' grasp!"

"Oh no, don't think to justify your own failures by blaming either me or Zenith—"

"I wasn't blaming *Zenith*," WolfStar put in quietly. He rose slowly from his bed, one hand still gripping his ribs.

"—when it was *you* who has done so much damage. *You* who put Niah into the Demons' hands. *You* who—"

"Oh, shut up! What in Stars' sake did you come down here to say? Just say it and leave me in peace!"

"Keep your bloodstained hands off Zenith."

WolfStar gave a nasty smile. "I have hardly laid a single 'bloodstained' finger on Zenith, let alone an entire hand."

"Leave Zenith alone."

"Why? Do you think her yours?"

"Leave her alone."

WolfStar brushed past StarDrifter and poured himself a glass of wine from the jug on the table. "Would you like some wine, StarDrifter?"

"Leave Zenith alone!"

"Zenith is revolted by the idea of your bloodless hands touching her, and she is certainly unable to placidly contemplate the act of love with you, fool! Let Zenith make up her own mind about who she wants, and how she wants them."

"She loves me!"

WolfStar's mouth curled. "But she cannot stand your touch. A poor kind of love, wouldn't you say?"

StarDrifter stared, knowing he was coming off the worst in this exchange, but needing to not only let off some of his raging emotions, but also to *somehow* make this fiend realise that he should leave Zenith alone.

"You have raped and abused her," he said, making his voice as calm and as even as he could. "You have willingly conspired with another for the death of her spirit, her soul. Isn't there even a scrap of guilt in you?"

"No."

StarDrifter closed his eyes, refusing to believe he'd lost Zenith.

"Have you slept with her?"

WolfStar grinned. "Oh yes, but that was many months ago. Don't you remember? It was under the warmth of the moon—"

"I mean recently! Since you've been in Sanctuary!"

"No. I have held her hand." WolfStar shifted slightly, standing more erect, letting the light of the lamp play over his body. "But I think it is time to correct that. I am feeling so much better."

StarDrifter stared at him, then turned and stalked out of the room.

The door crashed shut behind him.

WolfStar's grin broadened, and he drained his glass of wine.

35

Dispersal

"We have almost no time," DragonStar said to his five witches grouped about him. They were alone in the basement chamber of Star Finger, save for the pack of Alaunt, the lizard among them, huddled in an indistinguishable pile of pale fur against a far wall. StarLaughter was wandering some of the still-intact apartment complexes on a higher level—no doubt searching for the right shade of colour to drive WolfStar mad with lust, DragonStar thought dryly—and the Strike Force were sheltering amid the tumbled rocks on the surface. They would all have to move. Soon. And very, very fast.

"And so—" Faraday began.

"And so you must listen to me, and listen well," DragonStar said, matching Faraday's stare.

She dropped her eyes.

"All of you must meet one of the Demons," DragonStar said. "This you know. But which ones? DareWing and Goldman, your task will be the easiest, for you will eventually work as a team rather than individually. You will meet Barzula and Mot; which of you meets which one, I care not."

"Why together, and where?" DareWing said.

DragonStar hesitated briefly before replying, again wondering how much he should tell his five.

"I thought it was happenchance that I created five of you," DragonStar said, "but now I realise it to be the Star Dance's design. There are five Demons, not counting Qeteb whom I must meet, and there are five of you.

"As there were five Sentinels."

The others looked among themselves, their faces reflecting varying degrees of shock. None of them had realised the connection.

"In this game I do not believe in coincidence," DragonStar said, watching them carefully, "and I will not ignore the signs posted along our torturous route. DareWing and Goldman, despite your different temperaments, you work well together, and you will make a team—"

"Ogden and Veremund," Faraday said softly. "Cauldron Lake."

"Yes—" DragonStar began, but was interrupted by Goldman.

"Are you trying to say that DareWing and I *are* Ogden and Veremund?"

"No. The Sentinels still exist, but are far distant, drifting among the stars. What you are is simply another aspect of the Enemy's plan that the Sentinels once represented."

"And I . . . I represent Yr," Faraday said, her eyes far distant.

DragonStar smiled at her, and she did not look away, or frown. "Yes. At Grail Lake."

Now she shuddered, and averted her eyes. "The Maze."

"I am sorry," DragonStar said. "But at least I will meet up with you there."

"You will meet Qeteb in the Maze?"

DragonStar nodded. "The final hunt *must* be conducted within the Maze."

"And which Demon must I meet?" Faraday asked.

"Sheol. Despair."

Faraday's eyes widened. She, who always despaired of her own future, must *confront* despair?

DragonStar held her eyes, and eventually Faraday nodded. "Very well, I will meet Sheol at Grail Lake." Mother, how would she manage this task!

And at the Maze, she would also be close to Qeteb, for Qeteb would surely gravitate there in order to meet DragonStar.

Close to Qeteb. Close enough to be snatched.

Faraday shuddered again, and lowered her face into her hands.

DragonStar pitied her, but could not comfort her now. Time was too short, too precious.

"And I?" Leagh asked.

"You," DragonStar smiled, a beautiful, loving gesture, "carry life within you. You *are* life, and so your place will be Fernbrake Lake, the Mother of all Life. You represent Jack, for you share the same strength and determination. At Fernbrake you will meet the Rox-Niah."

"Why?" Leagh's face showed no fear, no denial, only acceptance and courage.

"I cannot put my knowledge into words," DragonStar said. "I can only say that this is where, and this is the Demon, that you *must* meet."

She nodded.

"Gwendylyr," DragonStar said, and took her hand.

"There is not much left for me, is there?" she said, and her face was as determined as Leagh's. DragonStar thanked every star in existence for the strength and trust of these five.

He glanced at Faraday. Of them all, she was both the weakest and the strongest link.

"I represent Zeherah, and I will meet Raspu, Demon of Pestilence, at the Lake of Life," Gwendylyr said.

"Yes."

DragonStar looked down at his hands, hesitating before he told them of what was at stake, resting on their success. That he *had* to tell them, DragonStar had no doubt, but he also had no doubt of the frightful pressure the knowledge would place on every one of them.

"DragonStar?" Faraday said, concerned and frightened, because knowing him as well as she did she knew he was concealing something.

DragonStar raised his face. "There is more," he said quietly. "Whether or not you are successful will directly affect whether or not I can defeat Qeteb."

As his witches watched, their eyes riveted on DragonStar's face, he explained the "legal niceties" of their confrontations.

"Thus," he finished, "if three or more of you fail—"

"Then *you* must inevitably fail," Goldman said, "for the balance will have tipped irretrievably in Qeteb's favour."

DragonStar nodded, watching the pale faces before him, more concerned about how the knowledge would affect them than whether or not they could succeed.

"Then," Goldman said, "we will do our best for you."

"DragonStar," Leagh said. "How *do* we confront these Demons? They are so powerful . . . and we . . ."

DragonStar managed a smile for her, but included all five in his response. "Qeteb is so confident of his overall victory he has 'magnanimously' given us the choice of weapons and place—".

"I know nothing of weapons!" Leagh cried, sounding suddenly panicky, and DragonStar spoke quickly to reassure her.

"These confrontations will have no need of lances or pikes, Leagh. We will, I think, employ a little trickery, along with a touch of love, and we are going to employ some information that StarLaughter gave me in order to choose our 'weapons'."

"What do you mean?" Goldman said.

"Listen," DragonStar said, and he spoke low and intensely for a very long time.

Both the frigid night air and time itself had closed in about Spiredore. Demons ringed it, whispering and shrieking of death, but Spiredore was made of stronger stuff than Sigholt had been, and it caused the Demons even greater angst.

Here again Roxiah stood with its head thrown back and

arms and legs spread wide, bringing to bear all the power of the Enemy that it could upon the obstinate tower.

But Spiredore was holding out: grimly, painfully, and using every last bit of strength and resistance it had.

Spiredore had one more task to do, and it prayed and begged that it could do it soon.

DragonStar looked up as he finished, his face ashen. "We have almost no time!"

"What is happening," DareWing said.

"The Demons are laying siege to Spiredore, trying to destroy it . . . and you need to use its power to transport yourselves to—"

"Gods!" DareWing and Goldman rose as one, the women not far behind them.

"DragonStar," Faraday said, taking his arm. "Leagh . . . I am so concerned for her . . . she is not far away from birth, and—"

He stopped her words with a finger to her lip. "Leagh is a strong and determined woman—and weren't you, when you planted out Minstrelsea while carrying Isfrael? Faraday, I can watch over her."

Faraday nodded, accepting, although she did not like the situation, nor envy Leagh her aloneness with whatever she met at Ferabrake Lake.

No, DragonStar whispered in her mind. *Faraday, be still, and trust and believe in Leagh.*

Again she nodded, and, as did Gwendylyr, Leagh and Goldman, withdrew her folded doorway from a pocket in her robe.

"The Strike Force?" DareWing said.

"I will command them for the moment," DragonStar said. "They are mobile enough without Spiredore."

"And you?" Goldman asked. "How will you travel about once Spiredore is gone?"

DragonStar grinned. "I have my Star Stallion," he replied, "and he is as effective as Spiredore for travelling about Tencendor itself . . . and less vulnerable."

The worried look reappeared over his face. "Quick! Quick!"

Then DragonStar turned his head to one side and gave a piercing whistle.

The feathered lizard bounded out from the pack of Alaunt, grinning from ear to ear as if it had been summoned for a game of hide and chase.

Goldman and DareWing looked at him, and smiled.

"Share!" Qeteb whispered in Roxiah's ear. "Share the Enemy's power with me, and together we can tumble this tower to the ground!"

He rested a splayed, hammer-fingered hand on Roxiah's belly, and pressed.

Roxiah considered this request. It knew it was a good idea so far as demolishing Spiredore was concerned, but to share this new-found power with Qeteb? What if Qeteb did not want to give it back?

"Share!" Qeteb whispered, and dug his fingers in a little.

Roxiah trembled and, fearing for the life in its womb, shared.

Qeteb shuddered as the strange power thudded through him, then he leaned his head back and laughed.

"Spiredore! I have you!"

"Quick! Quick!" DragonStar almost pushed the other five towards the glowing doors. "Fast!"

DareWing and Goldman stepped through, the lizard bounding after them, and their doorway folded closed.

Then Gwendylyr stepped into her door, having given Leagh a fierce hug and a kiss goodbye.

Then Leagh picked up her skirts and stepped through her door, DragonStar watching and wishing her luck silently.

He turned to Faraday. "I wish you would trust me," he said.

She blinked back tears, then stepped forward and hugged

him. "I love you," she said, her head against his chest, "but I find it hard to forget the past. DragonStar, please, do not abandon me in the Maze!"

He tilted her chin up with a finger, then leaned down and kissed her.

"Go with my love, and my promise that I will *never* let Tencendor claim you as sacrifice again."

She trembled. "Katie . . ."

"I will watch over Katie, and you will surely see her again."

"Keep her safe," Faraday said, but at that DragonStar lifted his head and avoided her eyes.

"There must always be some pain, mustn't there," Faraday said, her voice bitter, and she drew back from DragonStar.

"Go," he said sadly. "Go."

And she was gone.

For a moment DragonStar stood, gazing into the emptiness where once had been friends and lovers and glowing doors.

Then he turned and walked out of the chamber, his footfalls echoing about the dank walls for a long time after he had gone.

Qeteb could not believe his good fortune. He'd entered Spiredore in order to wreak destruction within—and had encountered DragonStar's five witches!

They were not all together, moving around different portions of the complex, but Qeteb knew that if he could pull Spiredore down about their ears, and kill them all *now,* before even they met his companions, then DragonStar could do nothing against him.

Nothing. The matter could be settled here and now.

Qeteb smiled, pure evil, then closed his eyes and tilted his head back, combining his power with that of Roxiah still outside.

"Tumble down," he whispered, "tumble down, you masonried piece of shit . . ."

And matter shifted within the tower.

DareWing and Goldman, preparing to exit through the blue-misted tunnel that Spiredore had opened for them, both fell to their knees several paces away from the tunnel.

"Get up!" DareWing screamed, and physically lifted Goldman by an elbow.

The lizard made sure DareWing had a secure hold on Goldman, then he scrambled down the tunnel to safety.

The birdman's wings beat frantically, for they were never meant to carry the weight of another grown man, but DareWing managed to fly down the tunnel. He bounced off walls as his own wings threatened to fail him and Spiredore screamed in its death throes about him, but he eventually dragged Goldman to the other end.

They fell through blue mist into a forest of sharp and angry crystal.

Tumble down, you piece of Enemy excreta. Qeteb's power expanded, thriving on the chaos about him.

Faraday cried out, and clutched at a balcony railing. She fell to her knees so heavily she knocked the breath from her chest.

A movement far below caught her eye, and she saw Gwendylyr, crawling up some stairs on her hands and knees.

"Fast!" Faraday shouted down to her, and Gwendylyr nodded slightly and crawled towards the tunnel that was opening before her.

Spiredore opened a tunnel for Faraday as well, but both women cried out in horror because, just as the tunnels formed, they fell apart, shattered by Qeteb's death grip on Spiredore.

"Spiredore!" Faraday cried, finally managing to rise to her knees. "Do this for Azhure! Please! Be strong for Azhure!"

Azhure? The name rippled through the tower, and just for a moment Spiredore fought back, hard enough to give Qeteb pause, and long enough to reform both tunnels again.

Neither Faraday nor Gwendylyr wasted time. They literally clambered to their feet, picked up their skirts, and fled down the tunnels as fast as they could go.

Leagh was not so lucky.

Of them all, she was the one on the lowest stairs of the tower. Spiredore trembled violently when it lost concentration, will and power once Faraday and Gwendylyr had passed through, and Leagh was flung down a series of stairs until, horribly, horrifically, she rolled to the feet of Qeteb himself.

"Well, well," Qeteb said, "what a pretty lady."

Leagh rolled away as far as she could, but she was hurt and winded and terrified beyond measure, and she feared that she, and her baby, were dead.

Oh, DragonStar! I couldn't even reach Fernbrake Lake for you!

Qeteb reached down enlarging hands—

What was that strange smell? It seemed to be emanating from the woman . . . no! It was rising as a smoke from around her figure!

Qeteb's hands halted, and an expression of utter surprise came over his face.

It was the heady scent of a field of lilies.

"No," he whispered, and reached out for the woman again.

Leagh backed away on hands and buttocks, trying desperately to get out of his reach, yet knowing it was impossible.

Qeteb grinned, shunting the scent to one side—a field of flowers was not going to stop him!—and reached out hands that had turned into talons.

The woman was as good as dead. He could take one, at least—

Suddenly Qeteb screamed, for it felt as though fire had enveloped his feet.

He looked down. There was a ball of light enveloping his

lower legs, a light with no discernible form, but with what certainly felt like terrible teeth.

And it smelt. Horribly. Like crushed lilies.

Behind Leagh, Spiredore roused itself one last time, one last desperate time, and a tunnel of blue mist formed.

Get you gone, girl!

Leagh was still terrified by Qeteb, even though something had distracted him for the moment, but she managed— infinitely slowly—to turn her head and look behind her.

Whimpering, hardly able to believe that she would be able to make it, she turned over onto her hands and knees and scrambled as fast as her cumbersome figure would allow her towards the end of the tunnel.

Qeteb paid her no notice. He was directing all his power down to the light . . . more . . . more . . . now! that had the thing! Qeteb scampered about until he'd managed to get both legs free of the mass of white light. Just as he thought he'd succeeded, the light surged forward, concentrating its burning fury on Qeteb's left foot. Roaring, he drew his leg back, then kicked it forward, trying to finally dislodge the irritating piece of—

The ball of light flew off his foot . . . straight down the blue-misted tunnel.

As it flew through the air, it transformed, until it took the shape of a white lily.

A portion of railing fell from above and struck Qeteb on the head. He grunted, and thrown momentarily off-balance, he missed the chance to direct his power after the fleeing woman.

The tunnel wavered, and closed.

Qeteb went berserk.

By the time he'd finished, there was nothing left of Spiredore save a wisp of smoke and a pile of pitiable debris.

36

Pretty Brown Sal

They'd slipped through Qeteb's fingers for the moment, but he knew they had not slipped far.

Qeteb *knew* where the five had gone and, knowing, he could afford to wait. They would be going nowhere—and could accomplish nothing.

In the meantime he and his could grow stronger. Invincible. Sanctuary.

Once Sanctuary was gone—and those within it, as their power consumed—there was nothing that could stop the Demons. They were six again, they controlled the power of the Enemy, and DragonStar and the five would be crushed like delicate spring flowers within Qeteb's fist.

Qeteb had, for the moment, forgotten the virulence of that lily.

He laughed and strutted as he looked over the pile of debris that had once been Spiredore, his fists opening and closing with infinite patience as he moved, the mail of his armour creaking very slightly as his joints flexed.

Then Qeteb raised his head and gazed about. Behind him rose the Maze—the dark, glorious Maze, both his prison and his heaven—while to the north, west and south lay only the devastation of drifting ash and dead earth under the hopeless night sky.

And those eager to please.

There was one thing Qeteb could do to keep DragonStar's witches out of mischief until he could give them his full attention.

He began to whisper, and about him the air filled with howls and screams as the demonic gibbered their approval.

There was little peace in Sanctuary. Urbeth was here, and while Urbeth said she could help them escape, Urbeth remained completely silent on the "how's" and "wherefore's", and spent much of her time snapping and growling and making sarcastic comments about everyone's state of readiness.

Axis spent as much time snapping back at her. The entire land—all that had survived Qeteb's resurrection—was hidden here. Sanctuary throbbed with life, but it was life that lay only a moment away from total annihilation, and all that stood between them and that moment was Urbeth's damned reticent aid and Axis' need to get everyone and everything organised.

There may have been little peace, but what stunned Axis was the fact that there was utter calm. He'd always believed that peace and calm went hand in hand, but apparently not. Everyone within Sanctuary was now aware of the imminent danger, and everyone was aware that an escape was being planned—although not everyone was aware that, apparently, Urbeth meant to dump them (how? how? how?) in the frozen wastes of the northern tundra.

It was not only the Icarii, Acharites, Ravensbund and Avar who were aware of some of these things. The animal, bird and insect life also seemed apprised of not only the threat, but of the plans for escape. And of everyone, the exiled fauna of Tencendor seemed the calmest and the most organised.

Striding about Sanctuary supervising the loading of supplies that would continue through the night, Axis came across population after population of beetle, or millipede or butterfly, patiently clinging or clumping to baskets and panniers: none of the packhorses or mules seemed to mind carrying a load of insects or even birds. Axis stood open-mouthed with astonishment at the sight of one draughthorse standing, so covered with bats, that only his drooping head appeared from the shifting, squeaking (but not complaining) mass of grey and brown fur that had buried its myriad claws into his thick winter coat.

Several hundred carts were filled with dozing seals: cats,

dogs and poultry snuggled with no hint of squabbling or rancour between the seals' warm, gently heaving sides. Oxen, cows, mules and horses stood waiting yoked or collared to the carts, many with birds clinging to spines or manes. Elsewhere grouped herds of livestock or of wild creatures, each herd ignoring nearby animals even though under more normal circumstances they might be natural competitors or even enemies.

Ravensbundmen and women moved about among the animals, checking and adjusting the gear of those creatures yoked or collared to carts, murmuring and soothing any creature that appeared nervous and jittery. Axis had seen Urbeth talk to Sa'Domai earlier: undoubtedly the Ravensbundmen were the best adapted to working in the conditions that faced them, but they also appeared to be particularly suited to working and empathising with animals. Was it because they were hunters and used to the ways of wild creatures, Axis wondered, or simply because the Ravensbundmen were more than half-wild themselves?

Intermingling with everything and everybody were the fey creatures that had once populated the forests. Shifting shapes and colours, winking jewel-like eyes and horns, with strange, soft cries and gentle touches, the fey creatures slipped in and out of every pack and herd, spreading calm and even, Axis suspected, some sense of hope.

But, strangest of all the creatures that Axis saw, were the huddled creatures from Bogle Marsh. They were grouped so closely that Axis could not tell them apart. They simply formed one massive lump of grey, steaming flesh that extended some thirty paces into the air and spread some sixty or seventy paces wide.

The entire pile was gently humming to itself: some strange, marshland melody that rose and fell in gentle, if gigantic, undulations over the other creatures about them.

Axis could feel it vibrating up through his feet, and was strangely soothed by its touch.

"Axis?"

He turned. It was Zared, looking cross and tired.

"Urbeth," Zared said with more than a trace of aspersion, "has just had a new thought."

Axis repressed a smile. He did not think it had helped Zared's temper.

"She wants us," Zared continued, "to pack some four or five hundred large, shallow bowls, as well three hundred barrels of potent malmsbury wine."

Axis remained silent, although he let the question flood his face.

"I have no idea why!" Zared said, and gestured aside impatiently.

"Undoubtedly Urbeth has her reasons," Axis said gently. "Zared . . . Zared, I know there is little I can say to help you. I know how you must be feeling with Leagh—"

"Do you?" Zared said, his eyes hard. "Do you?"

"Aye," Axis said, "I do. Azhure and I fought apart much of our time, and I spent much of that time in agony wondering whether or not I would ever see her again. Do not blame me for the fact that currently I know she is safe."

Zared visibly forced himself to relax. "I'm sorry. But . . . none of us are 'safe', are we? Azhure perhaps stands in as much danger as does Leagh."

"As do you and I."

"Yes," Zared sighed. "As do you and I." He swept his eyes about the scene before him, letting them linger briefly on the pile of humming Bogle Marsh creatures. "As does every creature in this gods-forsaken place."

"I assume that Sanctuary has supplied the bowls and malmsbury?"

Zared sighed again, managing a rueful smile as he did so. "Oh, aye. The best quality malmsbury wine I have ever seen. I think you and I, brother, should broach a cask before morning."

Axis grinned. "I look forward to it. I doubt overmuch if Urbeth will notice a glass or two gone."

Once Zared had left, Axis continued his wander through the hordes slowly gathering for the exodus. He had a vague, very slightly uncomfortable feeling, almost as if he was looking for something, but not knowing what.

So he walked through the half twilight that, in Sanctuary, passed for night. As people approached him and asked questions, so Axis answered as best he could, but he did not seek out conversation. He knew that Azhure and StarDrifter awaited him back in their apartments—StarDrifter in particular had appeared anxious to discuss something with him—but Axis' need to find *something* drove him deeper into Sanctuary and the milling hordes of peoples and creatures awaiting escape.

How many millions had DragonStar made him responsible for?

Axis felt an immense burden of responsibility literally weigh down on his shoulders and he had to force them back to stand straight. Even with Urbeth's uncertain aid, could he pull this off?

And how did he feel about the Skraelings? Gods, he had *never* thought to have to face them again!

Then Axis stopped, stunned out of his thoughts.

What he'd been searching for so vaguely and uncertainly stood in front of him—as nervous and unsure as he was.

She was plain and brown and with the skittishness of the very young. She lifted her head and caught sight of Axis. She stilled.

Axis smiled, and held out a hand, moving very slowly towards her.

She did not move, although her black eyes rolled with her inner uncertainty.

Axis smiled, and touched her cheek.

She trembled, and he ran his hand down her neck.

A fine, brown, but very young mare of only three or four years.

Axis' smile broadened. "You're not quite Belaguez, but somehow I think you will do just as well."

Suddenly he relaxed. He had a task, impossible as it might seem, and now he had a mount, as insignificant as she might appear. Life was falling together neatly.

Axis tugged at the brown mare's forelock, and she lowered her head and gently butted him in the chest.

" 'Er name's Sal."

Axis looked over the mare's withers; a small, wizened man sat upon a bale of provisions on the other side almost hidden in the shadows of a pile of canvas-covered provisions rising behind him. His small body was hunched and rounded, his skin brown and splotched, his head covered only by several strands of drab hair, and his face so layered with wrinkles his bright brown eyes were all but hidden. His entire demeanour was generally plain and brown and drab, enlivened only by his mischievous eyes.

Apart from the incongruity of his eyes, there was something else about the man's appearance that made Axis stare. This old man, plain and drab as he was, had Icarii features.

And his cloaked, hunched form looked as though it hid wings within the shadows at his back.

But what Icarii aged, or was plain and drab, *for the gods' sakes?*

The man's mouth twisted wryly as he saw Axis' stare. "Yer recognise a fellow, don't you?"

And what Icarii affected such common, country speech?

Axis opened his mouth, hesitating before he spoke. "You are Icarii bred, and yet you demonstrate none of the beauty and dignity of the Icarii. Why?"

A Traitor? A Demon?

The old man cackled, the sound curiously bird-like, and Axis moved slightly so his sword hand was free to move.

"Well, yeah, yer do be observant," the man all but whispered, a secretive expression on his face. "I'll give you that. But I were never Icarii-bred, no sir, not me. I claim no such pretensions!"

"You have Icarii features. You *must* have Icarii blood in you."

The old man grinned slyly. "I do share my face and blood with your proud Icarii, man, but I'm not one of your flighty lot."

Axis narrowed his eyes, his hand now resting on the hilt of his sword, but he said nothing.

The wizened old man seemed not to care. "Call me Da," he said. "It's as good a name as any."

It was no name at all Axis thought. "Da" was the peasant word for father.

Da pointed a gnarled finger at the mare. "And she be Sal."

"Well, Da," Axis said. "You are a strange man—"

Da giggled, rocking back and forth on the bale.

"—and I would know more of you. And of your pretty brown Sal." Axis had still not relaxed his grip on his sword hilt. There was only one thing he was sure of, and that was that this old man was not who he pretended to be.

Da put a finger to his pursed mouth, in a parody of thought. "Who do I be? And who do be Sal?"

Axis shifted, annoyed. The man's affectation of country language was starting to grate.

"I do be a father," Da said.

Father?

"I do watch over my children."

Axis said nothing.

Suddenly the old man dropped his peasantish affectation, and looked Axis directly in the eye.

"I do the best for my children," he said, "even when they demonstrate consummate stupidity. That, I swear, they got from their mother."

Axis was caught fast by the man's eyes, fierce and angry now. Far away he heard Urbeth roar.

Da laughed. "From their mother, aye."

Axis went cold. His hand dropped away from his sword. "What do you want?" he said.

"To give you a gift. To give the Icarii a last gift . . . and still a gift of flight, methinks."

Axis was numb, still not quite believing whom he was talking to. "A gift?"

"'Er." The man-sparrow nodded in Pretty Brown Sal's direction, then turned his eyes back to Axis. "It's not the first horse I've given you, you know."

"Which—"

"Belaguez."

And now Axis truly did go cold. He had acquired—there was no other verb to express it—Belaguez when he had just been appointed BattleAxe. One of the Axe Wielders had reported that there was a grey colt tied up in the palace courtyard, with no explanation save for Axis' name engraved on the small brass plate sewn into the colt's halter.

When Axis had walked into the courtyard to see for himself, a small sparrow had been foraging for insects in Belaguez's forelock. When Axis had attempted to brush it aside, the sparrow had jumped onto his hand and run chattering up his sleeve to his shoulder before finally flying off.

Then, absorbed by the magnificent colt, Axis had paid no attention.

Now, he finally managed to recover his manners.

"I thank you," he said, moving around Sal so he could bow in the sparrow's direction.

The sparrow, still wearing its vaguely man-Icarii form, smiled gently, accepting Axis' obsequiousness as his due. If only CrimsonStar had been as polite and deferential as this man!

"Belaguez was . . . *is* a special horse," Axis said.

"And he was for a special man. *Men.* You and your son both."

Axis looked back to Sal. She was nuzzling her velvety nose about his hip pockets, as if she might find a carrot there.

"But now your son's got the starry boy, and you need another. Take Pretty Brown Sal." And then the sparrow repeated himself, although Axis did not notice. "She's my final gift of flight to the Icarii, as to all the peoples of Tencendor."

Axis ran a hand down Sal's neck and over her shoulder. She was only a small mare—barely high enough to carry him—but she had a deep chest, fine strong legs, and an intelligent eye.

And the sweetest disposition, Axis thought, of all creatures in existence.

He raised his head to speak to the sparrow, but before he could mouth the words, the sparrow-man rose, smiled, and then simply faded away into the shadows.

But just as Axis thought him gone, there was the soft piping of a sparrow, and the soft, drab form of the father of the Icarii race briefly brushed against Axis' cheek before finally disappearing.

Axis lifted a hand, reaching hopelessly out, but the sparrow had gone.

37

Settling In

They had gone, and DragonStar hoped they would survive. If even one of them failed . . .

He suddenly grew claustrophobic in the dank chamber, and walked for the door, whistling the Alaunt after him. Qeteb and his fellow Demons were undoubtedly occupied elsewhere and, if the StarGrace had spoken true, he need not fear the Hawkchilds. He would surely be safe enough in the fresh air—such as it was in the corrupted realm—for the time being.

Gods! He needed to feel the wind on his face!

But although DragonStar climbed unhindered to the surface to sit, as his father had once sat, on a pile of rocks overlooking the Hundred Mile Beach of the Icebear Coast and the battering ocean beyond, he did not long enjoy the peace of the pre-dawn air.

StarLaughter joined him.

"Sanctuary," she said, and leaned teasingly close to him as she sat down.

He did not give her the satisfaction of moving away.

StarLaughter forgot her teasing almost as soon as she'd begun it. Sanctuary was so dangerous! What if . . . ? Momentary panic engulfed her. "WolfStar won't be safe in Sanctuary! Qeteb will surely break through!"

DragonStar repressed a sigh.

"We are destined for each other," StarLaughter said, once more calm and with a faraway expression on her face. "When he sees me again . . . oh!"

"He may not be as pleased to see you as you will be to see him," DragonStar said carefully. While, on the one hand, StarLaughter's insane idea that she and WolfStar could forgive all their differences, WolfStar falling deeply in love with her the instant he laid eyes on her again, made DragonStar want to laugh incredulously—StarLaughter must indeed have lost her mind!—on the other hand, DragonStar did not want to antagonise StarLaughter to the point where she might turn against him.

His task had been made infinitesimally easier by the fact that he and his could ignore the Hawkchilds.

StarLaughter shrugged aside DragonStar's comment. "We've had our differences—"

DragonStar choked back a laugh.

"—but we will surely overcome them."

"It might take some, ah, time."

She shrugged again, but did not respond to DragonStar's comment. Instead, she said: "How will he manage to escape the Demons when they break through into Sanctuary?"

Now DragonStar had to fight back anger. She had no thought for the millions of peoples and creatures trapped in Sanctuary, only for WolfStar. Her love was as single-minded as her revenge had been.

"Axis—"

"Your father?"

"Yes, my father. Axis has charge of Sanctuary. I hope he will manage to find a way to save them. Some back door that they can escape from."

"But we must help!" StarLaughter cried, sitting up straight and turning a frantic face to stare at DragonStar. "I must do something! WolfStar must get out! We must—"

"Stars damn it, StarLaughter! You've spent thousands of years plotting his death. Now that it might be imminent, I find it hard to believe that you're in a panic that his death might actually be accomplished!"

StarLaughter drew completely away from him, her face frozen.

DragonStar reached out a hand. "StarLaughter, forgive me. I have a great deal on my mind."

Slowly, reluctantly, she took his hand. "I had hoped you would support me," she said, and turned her face aside.

"StarLaughter, I honestly will do nothing to stand in your

way. Indeed, I wish you the best. You and WolfStar make the perfect couple. I just find it so hard to believe that hate can turn so quickly," and so completely, he thought, "to love."

StarLaughter relaxed and smiled prettily. "Oh, DragonStar, you just do not understand love. It takes many twists and turns until it reaches its home."

And to that DragonStar had nothing to say, although he smiled wryly.

After a while, and after some more desultory conversation, StarLaughter moved off, no doubt to plan her single-handed rescue of WolfStar from Sanctuary, and DragonStar also stood up.

The view of dawn breaking far to the east had been entirely spoilt for him.

The Strike Force were waiting in the lower corridors of Star Finger, and DragonStar spent almost two hours talking quietly but intently with them. Eventually, in groups of three Wing each, the members of the Strike Force rose like silver into the air above the wasteland and sped off in four different directions.

By mid-morning Faraday sheltered in a huddle of rubble that had, she thought, once been a customs post on the road into Carlon. It had been a substantial stone building of some three or four rooms, and its destruction at the hands of some demonic band of creatures had left a goodly pile of stone for her to hide within. Indeed, part of the rubble formed its own gloomy cave, and all Faraday was surprised about was that it hadn't already been occupied by some family of maniacal hogs, or rats, or perhaps even cannibalistic hens.

Instead, it was surprisingly clean and even partly warm, as it was a haven from the wind, although the floor was rough, and no matter how Faraday shifted, she could not find a comfortable spot.

Finally, Faraday rose. It was time to look out on the Maze.

It was . . . frightening. She remembered when she'd walked

past this area with Zenith in the shadow-lands, but even the horror of that vision could not compete with the actuality.

The Maze enveloped what had once been Grail Lake, as well as the blackened ruins of Carlon.

But it was now sending tentacles of twisted corridors and dead-end walks out into the surrounding landscape. Mother! Were the Demons planning on turning the entire wasteland into a Maze? Or was this some demented plan of the long-dead Enemy?

Faraday's pile of rubble was on a small hillock that commanded a crossroads linking Romsdale, Avonsdale and Carlon. The perfect site for a customs post, but also a perfect site for observing what went on within the Maze.

It writhed with activity. There were . . . gods! there must be billions of creatures seething through its twisted veins! The Maze's walls sheltered a mass of life so dense that Faraday could hardly pick out individual creatures. She was up high and perhaps half a league from the Maze, but even so the mass within the Maze seemed unusually coherent.

Almost . . . coagulated.

"Oh, gods!" Faraday whispered as she realised what the Demons had made of the Maze. It was now the gigantic heart of the wasteland and within it seethed a black blood composed of the billions of creatures that swayed to the call of the Demons.

At any moment it would pump those creatures out into the wasteland.

Even as she watched, the Maze appeared to give a perceptible heave, and from four gates flowed four streams of dark, writhing evil.

One of the streams headed directly for her.

Of all the five witches, DareWing and Goldman had the most salubrious surroundings. They found Cauldron Lake almost untouched by the destruction and malevolence that had wasted most of Tencendor. The gold and crystal forest stood virtually unscathed, although some of the outer rings of trees had fallen over and shattered as the forests surrounding it had burned to ash, but, most importantly, Cauldron Keep still stood.

As comforting and as welcoming as it always had been for those it loved.

As DareWing and Goldman walked in, the lizard only a half-step behind, they found a fire burning in a central hearth, two beds made up with feather pillows and deep quilts, rugs spread between deep armchairs and chaise longues, and a general air of welcome for all three.

The Keep had laid a magnificent table: smoked hams, fresh vegetables and herbs, eight different cheeses, five loaves of breads, cakes, buns, biscuits, honey, fruit and steaming tea, and a bowl of food for the lizard set close to the fire.

Goldman rubbed his hands, and sat down at the table.

DareWing just stood and stared.

Gwendylyr, ever practical, merely sighed as she surveyed the destruction of the Lake of Life and Sigholt. The destruction of Sigholt had been so well managed that, unlike Faraday, there was not even a pile of rubble suitable for a sheltering spot.

Gwendylyr looked about. The Lake seethed and bubbled with pestilence—it literally stank of the Demons—and could offer no succour.

Sigholt's sad remains were of no use.

She turned and studied the Urqhart Hills. Ah . . . there! A stream-bed led down through a narrow gully to what had once been a moat. Gwendylyr frowned, trying to remember the old stories of the days when Axis had battled Gorgrael. Hadn't Belial once managed to unblock an old spring in a cave nearby? The lines of Gwendylyr's forehead deepened as she dredged back through all her memories . . . that gully extended into the hills about half a league, and then should end in the cave.

Smiling with satisfaction, Gwendylyr picked up her skirts and moved up the gully, stepping daintily over fallen rocks and crevices as she went. Whatever state she found the cave in, Gwendylyr knew she could make it do.

Physically and mentally exhausted, Leagh sank against the stump of a tree just below the ridge of the crater surrounding Fernbrake Lake . . . or what had once been a lake.

Now it was a desiccated garden, a maddened, swirling combination of rose thorns and wind topping the small hillock in its centre.

Leagh lifted a hand to wipe a tear from her face, and found it was shaking.

Quickly she clenched it and let it sink to the earth. She closed her eyes, then opened them again almost instantly, still seeing Qeteb striding towards her.

Better the view of this desecration than the memory of Qeteb.

But instead of Qeteb, Leagh saw something step out of the bloodied rose wind atop the hillock.

It was one of the Demons. Sheol, for it had a female form.

And another . . . Leagh frowned. Another female? Oh gods! It was Niah, but a Niah indisputably a Demon. Dragon-Star had been right then. Qeteb had indeed infused the Niah-woman with Rox's soul.

Two more Demons stepped out of the twisting thorns, and then one more.

Qeteb.

Leagh shrank as close as she could to the earth, wriggling slightly further behind the tree stump.

Qeteb turned his visored face in her direction, and Leagh felt, if not saw, his malicious grin.

Tremble not, sweet thing, a voice whispered in her head, *for I have other and better prey to occupy me for the moment. But fear not either, for I have not forgotten you. Others will be along to attend you shortly.*

His laughter rang out, threatening to overwhelm Leagh, and she twisted away, jamming fingers in her ears and screwing her eyes shut.

When Leagh finally found the courage to open her eyes again, she saw Sheol, the last of the Demons now above ground, step into the hole that led to the stairwell to Sanctuary.

"I pray to every god in every existence," Leagh whispered, "that you have found a way out of there, Axis."

38

Sanctuary No More

Through the night and into the morning Axis rode Sal through the frantic preparations, sometimes stopping to murmur encouragement, other times to help lift provisions into a cart. And always he kept turning his eyes to the sky.

In the end, it was the woman he was helping to settle her children into an already crowded cart that suddenly exclaimed and pointed upwards.

Axis jerked his eyes skyward.

Emerald cracks were zigzagging and wriggling their way from a point just off-centre across the entire sky.

As the emerald cracks widened, a sickly silver gleamed through.

"Gods!" Axis cried, and without further ado, grabbed Sal's halter, sprang onto her back, and pushed her forward at a gallop through the shouting, pointing, terrified groups about him.

Six shapes crouched across the chasm that the silvery bridge had once spanned.

They were no longer recognisable as humanoid, or animal, or even as Demons. They were just great, dark, slimy masses of shifting black and pink and orange that oozed pure evil.

There was an outer ring of five crouched about one in their centre. The central mass was Roxiah, drawing on all the power of the Enemy within Niah's body, and using Rox's soul to magnify it and then distribute it to the other five Demons.

And from there, all six hurled it at the enchantments that protected Sanctuary.

It felt good, the destruction of this beauty, and that good itself increased the power of the Demons to the point where they had power to spare, and sent crazy spurts of it out into the universe to dance about the stars and disrupt the harmony of the Star Dance.

It knew, that beautiful, melodious power that sang through the stars, that the final confrontation was nigh.

"Urbeth!" Axis screamed as he dashed through his palace and up to the balcony where Urbeth spent much of her time. "Urbeth!"

"She's not here." Azhure: beautiful, calm, terrified. Dressed in a midnight blue robe and a thick, scarlet cloak.

She took Axis' arm. "She's downstairs. On the lawns behind the palace. Most others are down there with her. I've been waiting for you. Where have you been? Urbeth has been—"

But Axis was already moving, and Azhure ran after him.

A gigantic fissure appeared in the sky above Sanctuary.

Whatever lay outside that crack, on the outer side of the Dome that protected Sanctuary, was of a much lower pressure than the atmosphere inside.

Sanctuary's air streamed towards the crack. Clouds screamed as the low pressure outside pulled them towards the ever-widening crack.

The dark mass of the Demons grew larger as they tasted the inevitability of Sanctuary's death, and that further increased their power twofold.

Axis, as everyone else, stopped and stared for a heartbeat or two, unable to come to terms with what they saw.

Then something huge and powerful thudded into his back.

A white paw. One of Urbeth's daughters stood behind him. "Move!" she growled. "Mother is anxious to go!"

"As am I!" muttered Axis, but he ran forward onto the lawns anyway, Azhure a half pace behind him.

And again, Axis stopped, stunned by what he saw on the ground rather than what was happening leagues above him.

Somehow, in the intervening minutes since Axis had seen the first tiny cracks appear in the sky, Urbeth had managed to get all life within Sanctuary into line.

Literally.

Before him stretched a column the breadth of five carts wide. It snaked back across lawns and through orchards and groves and fields as far as Axis' eye could see.

To his left Urbeth, several times her normal size, paced anxiously back and forth at the head of the column.

"Hurry!" she roared, and Axis jumped. He turned slightly, and whistled.

Pretty Brown Sal trotted out from behind the palace and over to Axis, her halter rope trailing.

"Have you a mount?" Axis asked Azhure.

She shook her head. "I hadn't even thought of it. But I can travel in one of the carts—"

Before she could finish, Axis seized her waist and lifted her up onto Sal's back. An instant later and he was behind her, pulling her back against him and turning Sal's head towards the column.

"Just like old times, isn't it?" he whispered in Azhure's ear, and she laughed deep in her throat, and shook out her raven black hair, and for a moment both of them rejoiced in the thrill of once more being together against danger that appeared insurmountable.

Axis' arm tightened, and then they were cantering down the side of the column towards its head.

Before them, Urbeth roared, and then swelled into gigantic proportions.

Further back in the column, seven figures slipped furtively away, ducking into the cover of trees, and then into buildings.

In the terror and haste of the moment, no-one noticed their departure.

The enchantments protecting Sanctuary collapsed completely. The chasm, which had moated Sanctuary in, heaved and fell to pieces, destroying itself in a massive earthquake.

When it had subsided, there was a huge pile of rubble where the chasm had once been, burying the blue-fletched arrow that DragonStar had left there.

The six black masses finally moved, flowing obscenely across rock and crevice like thick, corrupted smoke.

Axis ducked his head, and Azhure twisted about and buried her face in his shoulder. Above them there was a massive roaring, and Axis dimly realised it was Sanctuary's atmosphere escaping through the great rent in the sky.

The pressure in Axis' ears was agony, and his breath screamed through his chest and throat.

Sal bucked slightly and then stumbled, and Axis had to exert every skill he had as a horseman to keep her steady on her feet.

He choked, and felt both Azhure and Sal do the same.

There was no air!

All about him the once-orderly column erupted into chaos as beasts and people alike clawed for breath.

There were no screams, for no-one had any air left with which to scream.

Something white flowed and billowed before him, and in the dim recesses of his mind Axis knew that Urbeth was doing *something* ahead.

He hoped it would mean they actually managed to breathe before—

Ice-cold air slapped him in the face and shot down into his lungs. Axis jerked in pain and surprise, and he had to tighten his grip about Azhure as she similarly jerked.

Snow obliterated the men and carts closest to him, and cold such as Axis could not remember having previously encountered gripped his entire being in a merciless fist.

"Goodness," he heard Urbeth say somewhere in front of him.

Once across the chasm the Demons shape-shifted into half-humanoid, half-raven forms. Their heads and bodies were mostly humanoid, but their shoulders and arms flowed into great black wings, and tattered fans of feathers sprouted from the bases of their spines.

Qeteb's body was cast entirely in metal rather than flesh.

He lifted into the rapidly thinning air and soared upwards. "Sanctuary!" he screamed, and then all the Demons were in the air and winging their way towards the mouth of the valley leading to Sanctuary.

Below them, the flowers and shrubs wilted and died as the Demons' shadow enveloped them.

The frozen air abated somewhat, and Axis finally managed to raise his eyes and look about him.

Sal was struggling through knee-deep snow, as was every other beast and person.

Azhure shuddered in Axis' arms, and she tightened her cloak about her.

"Urbeth has done it," she said. "She got us out of Sanctuary."

Axis glanced at the sky above him. It was dull and leaden with snow clouds, but it was intact.

He grinned, and kissed the top of Azhure's head. "We've jumped from the frying pan into the frozen wastes," he said, and Azhure laughed.

"Whcrc's Urbeth?" she said as her laughter died away.

Axis looked ahead. Sal was within three or four carts' length of the front of the column, but all that currently headed it was Zared riding a white draughthorse which was making surprisingly good speed through the snow.

He may not have chosen for the parade ground, Axis thought, but he has chosen well.

He twisted about on Sal's back, looking behind him.

There was nothing but league after league of frozen tundra, and league after league of the refugee line from Sanctuary.

No Urbeth, and neither of her daughters.

Axis turned back, frowning slightly, then urged Sal forward to join up with Zared.

They ran through one of the palace complexes, and then finally stumbled into an orchard that lay on the road to Sanctuary's entrance.

"No air!" Xanon gasped, almost falling as she lurched onto the road.

Adamon, the other five close behind him, took his wife's elbow. "No matter," he said. "We'll be dead soon enough, anyway."

Xanon lifted her beautiful eyes and looked at Adamon with more love than she'd ever felt for him before. Ever since the Demons had broken through the Star Gate, sapping and destroying all their power, the Star Gods had felt worse than useless. They had alleviated and they had advised, but they had managed to do nothing to *help*.

And they were supposed to be gods, curse it!

Now, they *were* doing something to help.

It was evident as the Demons broke through into Sanctuary that Axis, and the column containing all the life that was left of Tencendor, were going to need all the assistance they could garner to escape in time.

The Demons must not be allowed to catch them before they'd escaped, or be allowed to follow them through whatever doorway Urbeth had created.

The Star Gods' decision had been silent, and unanimous. They could surely delay the Demons those critical minutes Axis and Urbeth needed to get the column to safety.

That they would die in the attempt, none of the Star Gods had any doubt.

But they would help.

They would make a contribution.

And they would save many, many lives.

Xanon leaned on her husband, and the seven stumbled further down the road towards Sanctuary's entrance.

A blackness swelled to meet them.

Sheol saw them first, and she laughed. "The first of our feeding makes a willing offering of itself," she said, and the other Demons howled with her.

Adamon lifted his head, gasping so badly for air he could barely see.

Something loathsome oozed its way down the road towards him. It appeared one complete mass, although once he'd peered closer, Adamon could see that there were distinct shapes within the single entity.

As he rubbed his eyes, bending over to haul in as much of the thinning air as he could, the Demons separated yet further.

Qeteb led them, striding down the road in the form of a man made completely of blackness. Behind him came the other five Demons, scampering and skipping, wearing the forms of plump, bright-eyed children.

"Why," said Qeteb as he came to a halt a few paces before the huddled, panting group, "if it isn't the Star Gods! What do you here, Gods? A welcoming committee, perhaps? Come to present us with the freedom of Sanctuary? Here to offer your services as—"

"We come with greetings," Adamon began.

"How kind!" said Qeteb.

"And a message," Adamon finished.

The five chubby children capered and clapped their hands, and Qeteb raised the eyebrows of his ebony face. "Do say! And what might that be?"

Now Xanon raised her face. She smiled, and her smile was full of love.

Qeteb, as the other Demons, took a step back.

"Our power has gone," Xanon said, her voice utterly sweet, "and our skills in warfare are negligible. Thus we do not come to fight you, only to deliver you our final will and testament."

Qeteb's eyes narrowed. He did not like the joy he felt emanating from the group. What was wrong with them?

"For tens of thousands of years," said Flulia, her arm about Silton's waist, "we had imbibed the music and the magic of the Star Dance."

"Much good that it does you now," Mot sneered.

"Its power has gone from us," Silton said, as Flulia choked on a desperate gasp for air, "but its love and message has not gone."

Xanon continued: "The Star Dance spoke to us of many things, and there was one thing it told us above all other things."

"And this," said Pors, "is what we must now tell you."

"What?" Qeteb snapped.

Adamon spoke for all of them, and as he spoke, all seven of the Star Gods raised themselves straight and tall, and they smiled, their eyes gleaming with emotion.

"Never underestimate the power of Love," Adamon said, "and the choices it drives you to."

There was silence. The Demons stared at the Star Gods, loathing their calmness, their assurance, and, above all, their serenity.

Barzula growled, deep and low and utterly incongruously in his child's throat.

And then, in less than the space of a breath, the Demons surged forwards, once again assuming the form of a single entity of blackness that rolled over the Star Gods with the inevitability of a tidal wave.

The Star Gods stepped forward and embraced both Demons and Death.

Xanon blinked and opened her eyes to stars and to music.

She slowly turned and behind her she saw Adamon, and then Pors and Zest and Silton, Narcis and Flulia close behind.

They were drifting free among the stars.
And all about them, the Star Dance embraced them and loved them.

Urbeth and her daughters huddled, unseen, under the trees of an orchard.

"Why did they do that?" one of the daughters hissed, low and angrily. "They could have been saved if they stayed with the column!"

"I think they *have* just saved themselves," Urbeth commented, as the Demons snapped and snarled and twisted themselves into knots trying to find where the corpses of the Star Gods had got to. "And given Axis a precious few more minutes. As we must do! Come!"

The Demons lifted into the sky, or what was left of it, furious that the Star Gods had somehow evaporated before they could be torn satisfactorily to pieces.

Never mind. There was doubtless far better and far more extensive eating ahead. The Star Gods would have made thin fare, anyway.

Almost all the air had gone, but its lack did not bother the Demons at all. Evil existed as easily within an airless vacuum as it did dancing among the leaves of the most agreeable of apple trees.

They soared, and basked in their power.

Beneath and before them spread beauteous orchards, delightful palaces and shaded groves.

All empty.

At first this did not concern the Demons overmuch—surely the doomed peoples would have sought a hidey-hole somewhere—but as they soared and dipped and tore apart palace after palace and toppled orchard after orchard, the Demons began to get impatient.

And frustrated.

Where were the people?

"Deeper and deeper," growled Qeteb, and so they flew deeper and deeper, their destruction growing more wanton as they went.

And yet no people.

"It is one of the Enemy's tricks!" Sheol cried, but Roxiah growled a disagreement.

"The Enemy have nothing to do with this. Nothing! They built no Sanctuary within Sanctuary, and no Sanctuary after Sanctuary. This was the last stand."

"Then where are they?" screamed Mot and Barzula in unison.

Qeteb remained silent, soaring higher and higher until he could see, in the very distance, something that made his blood literally boil in fury.

A small crack in the horizon.

And through this crack, a shifting mass that looked very much like people and animals fleeing into the distance.

His entire body burst apart in the extremity of his wrath, and boiling blood scattered over all of Sanctuary.

"Zared? Where's Urbeth?"

Zared turned and stared at Axis and Azhure. He was wrapped close in several blankets, but even so, what Axis could see of his face was blanched with the freezing conditions.

"Gods, man," Zared said. "Aren't you cold?"

Axis suddenly became aware that, firstly, he was wearing nothing but a black wool tunic and trousers as well as boots, and, secondly, he was, indeed, frozen nigh unto death.

He shuddered, and hugged himself closer to Azhure.

Zared beckoned to a man in a cart behind him, and the man rummaged in the tray of the cart before tossing Axis a hooded cloak.

He grabbed at it, fumbled and almost dropped it, then managed to drape it over his shoulders and back and pull the hood close about his face.

"Urbeth?" he said again.

Zared shrugged. "She said nothing. Just growled, and vanished."

288 -2~ Sara Douglass

Qeteb pulled himself together with the most extreme of efforts, but even then columns of smoke rose over Sanctuary where his blood droplets had fallen.

He resumed the shape of the handsome man dressed in grey and cream, although now he had huge black, clawed wings—far too large for his body—protruding from his back. Qeteb could not quite manage the perfectly congenial form in his current state of anger . . . and . . . and *frustration*!

"Why will no-one stay still on this cursed piece of soil!" he screamed, still circling high in the air.

"The Enemy were ever slippery," Mot hissed at a point just below Qeteb, and the other four Demons cursed and howled and spat, spinning in tight circles through the air, yet still managing to fly with utmost speed towards the offending crack on the horizon.

The crack through which their food was escaping.

The entire populations of Tencendor that had not fallen under the sway of the Demons had now become the Enemy, whether they were humanoid or not, and whether they had a single drop of the Enemy's blood in them or not.

No doubt they think we will not follow, Qeteb said in the other Demons' minds. *What fools! Did they truly think we would simply stamp our feet sulkily about Sanctuary and just let them go?*

"Qeteb!" said Roxiah, and it jabbed a finger—that every heartbeat or so metamorphosed into a piece of intestine—to their left.

Qeteb jerked his head about, reluctant to take his eyes off the escaping columns—such feeding that lay ahead!

But, ah! There was some feeding to the left, too. Not much, but something to vent his frustration and fury on.

Three white rabbits, bounding terror-struck across the blackened landscape of Sanctuary.

All six Demons swung as one towards the rabbits.

"Night is only a few hours away," Axis said, and wrapped his cloak even tighter about himself. Azhure now sat in the cart, huddled under some blankets, and Zared and Axis had turned their horses so they stood with their tails to the freezing wind.

The men looked back over the column.

It stretched as far as they could see, which, truth to tell, was not that far, because a snowstorm was rapidly moving in from the extreme north, and Axis and Zared could only see some ten paces before them.

And within minutes even that ten paces would be denied them.

"Is everyone out of Sanctuary?" Azhure said.

Axis shrugged helplessly. "I don't know. I don't know if Urbeth moved us all out at once, or if we had to traverse some doorway that half the column is still moving through."

"We're all out," a voice put in from behind the cart Azhure rested in. Ur, still dressed in her scarlet cloak and clutching her terracotta pot, emerged from out of the drifting snow.

Azhure attempted to smile, although it was hard in this extreme cold. She had met Ur many years previously, when Faraday had been planting out Minstrelsea forest. In fact, Azhure had spent one long night helping Faraday transfer her daily batch of seedlings from Ur's nursery, nestled around her cottage, back to Tencendor.

Did Ur still have any power left? If Urbeth did . . . what of Ur?

And why did she carry that pot? Nostalgia, or *did she have something in it?*

Ur glanced at Azhure from beneath the folds of her hood, and spared her a brief toothless grin. *What I have in here, girl, is no-one's business but my own.*

And then Azhure gave a horrified gasp as she saw Katie, awkwardly wrapped in an overly-large blanket, standing behind Ur and gripping the old woman's cloak.

Stars! She'd forgotten all about Katie in the debacle of Sanctuary's collapse. What would Faraday think if she knew!

Her face flaming with guilt—is this how she had treated her

children as well? Forgetting them at every second heartbeat?—Azhure half-jumped, half-fell from the cart into the snow and gathered Katie into her arms.

Katie accepted Azhure's embrace happily, and let the woman envelop her underneath her cloak.

Azhure looked up at Axis, hunched miserably on his equally miserable Sal. "We can't stay like this. It's not just us, or Katie, or even all the varieties of people we have. But the animals! Axis, some of these creatures are fragile! We must—"

"Survive this coming night," Ur broke in, "a long and horrible night, and then we will rest comfortably enough without fear of cold or Skraelings."

"Damn! The Skraelings!" Axis said, and pulled Sal about in a tight circle as he tried, unsuccessfully, to peer through the dense curtain of snow. "I forgot about them!"

And then, on cue, almost as if they'd been waiting in (*creeping gleefully through*) the thickening snow, a whisper flickered in the spaces between them.

The rabbits bounded, their tiny bodies heaving painfully with the strength of their terrified breathing, blood-flecked saliva flying from their open, panting mouths, thin, horrible wails emerging from their throats.

The Demons felt very good. They chased the rabbits, delaying the kill, wanting to drive them *insane* with fear, wanting them to *die* from their fear; swooping and whooping a few paces above the terrified rabbits, catching at their tender bodies with their claws and then letting them go, driving them on and on and on, delighting in their fright, wanting to hear them scream, beg, plead for mercy, needing to see them—

The rabbits, as one, dived down a hole in the ground.

The Demons were too overcome with anger to even shriek. As smoothly as the rabbits had made their escape, all six Demons transformed themselves into wriggling, writhing razor-toothed ferrets, and scrambled down the same hole, biting at each other in their need to be the first one down and at the furry prizes below.

Once the Demons had managed to get below, they found themselves in a rabbit warren as twisting and as confusing as a Maze.

Apart from their lingering (terrified) scent, there was no trace of the rabbits.

"Where the fuck have the bunnies gone?" said Qeteb.

39

Night: 1

As night fell, DragonStar once again climbed to the top of the pile of rubble that had once been the mighty Star Finger complex. It was cold—*Stars! It was freezing!*—but DragonStar had cloaked himself well, and had donned scarves and gloves against the night air.

Something was happening, and he needed to know what.

And so he climbed to the very topmost rock, and there he sat, huddled against the night, sending his far-senses scrying out into the night, and wondering: *What?*

Behind DragonStar, Sicarius huddled underneath the overhang of his cloak. He, too, could smell the night air.

There would be a hunt tonight.

Leagh had not moved from the tree stump. She'd lain there, physically sickened by the horror of being almost caught by Qeteb in Spiredore and then by seeing him descend with his companion Demons into Sanctuary.

What was happening down there? Crouched close to the earth all afternoon and evening, Leagh imagined at times that she could feel the destruction roiling up through the earth to her hand.

Was Zared safe? And Axis? What about Katie?

Leagh closed her eyes, forcing her mind away from the fate

of her husband and friends, and wondered if she should find somewhere safer and warmer for the night.

And then something grabbed her from behind.

Leagh was too frightened and shocked to scream. She rolled away, but whatever had grabbed at her had too firm a grip for her to escape.

Leagh turned her head and managed to see what had seized her. An old and completely demented woman, naked and covered in sores. Leagh took a deep breath, then drove her free foot into the woman's face.

There was a horrible crackling sound, and the woman's grip loosened enough for Leagh to drag herself free.

She scrambled to her feet, catching at the blackened stump of a tree for support, and looked frantically about.

At the top of the ridge, outlined by the last of the light, another three or four maddened people appeared, crawling forward on their hands and knees, gnashing their teeth, drooling horrible liquids—perhaps their partly digested last meal—down their chins and chests.

And, behind them, more: maniacal livestock as well as people.

Leagh twisted about, looking for an escape. There was no shelter to be seen, apart from the fire-ravaged stumps of what had been the daughters of the Minstrelsea forests, who had grown down the slopes of the crater towards Fernbrake.

A few paces in front of the gathering crowd, the old woman crept closer to Leagh.

More and more of the creatures poured over the edges of the crater, and now black shapes spiralled down from the sky to hunch speculatively on a dozen or so of the tree stumps.

Hawkchilds.

"Help me, damn you!" Leagh whispered, but the Hawkchilds merely cocked their heads, and whispered to themselves.

They might not harm her, but neither would they help her. Among them was StarGrace, and the Hawkchild looked at Leagh curiously, wondering at both her obvious pregnancy and the power that emanated from her.

StarGrace felt no urge to destroy, but neither did she feel any urge to help.

Leagh backed up against a tree stump, thinking as fast as she could. The only thing that would keep her safe, and keep her child safe, was to use her Acharite power. But she'd had so little practise! Opening and closing glowing doorways was all very well, but . . .

The maniacal creatures, drooling, spitting, howling and whimpering, covered with self-inflicted wounds and the crusty remains of their excreta, crept closer.

The old woman was almost upon her.

Leagh stilled, and she remembered all she had learned over the past few weeks, and she smiled, and rested a hand on her belly.

She was at one with the earth, a part of the landscape itself, and the child she carried within her . . .

Leagh raised her head and looked at the approaching crowd.

"Do you not *see* the beauty surrounding us?" she said, and waved a slow hand around.

The once-humans and animals hesitated, eyes darting about uncertainly, and then resumed their creep towards their prey as nothing leaped out to bite them.

Wave after wave of their blackness rose over the lip of the crater.

"You may *think* the landscape wasted and barren," Leagh said, and now held out a hand in appeal, or perhaps invitation, "but *see* its true beauty!"

And she flung her hand out in a wide arc, and suddenly flowers and herbs washed over the devastated walls of the crater in a torrent of beauty and fragrance.

The Hawkchilds rose into the air, squawking in surprise.

"See!" Leagh cried again, and half stepped forward, one hand still swept out, one resting on her belly. "See!"

Summer fragrance exploded about them, and the initial ranks of the creatures screamed and capered. More than the beauty of the flowers was the *hope* that had infused the entire landscape.

"See . . ." Leagh whispered, and the hand on her belly tightened.

Flowers reached skyward, and those that grew close to the mass of demonic creatures waved forward, as if they wanted to embrace them.

The creatures panicked.

StarGrace, circling far overhead, frowned in thought.

Far away DragonStar smiled, his eyes unfocused. "Good girl," he whispered. "Lovely Leagh. You deserve your place among the lilies of the field."

She had not created the Field of Flowers, nor taken the creatures through to the field, but had instead shown the creatures the beauty and hope that *still* (after all the Demons had done to the land) rested within the blasted landscape.

Even amid death, hope still survived.

"Now," he whispered, and behind him Sicarius whimpered with eagerness.

The old woman and the front ranks of creatures, perhaps some three score of humans, cows, pigs and assorted wildlife, tried to turn back and flee from the reaching, grasping flowers.

Get back! Get back!

They tried to flee, but could not, trapped between the horrid flowers and the hundreds of creatures that continued to rise up over the ridge and press down towards their prey.

The mad had their orders, and their thoughts were not ordered enough to rethink them.

Death dropped out of the sky. At first Leagh thought it was the Hawkchilds, either forgetting the fragile alliance they had with DragonStar and his witches, or actually deciding to aid her.

But these were not the black, fearsome Hawkchilds.

They were ethereal, beautiful, seemingly fragile creatures of silver and vivid colour.

Beautiful, and deadly. Arrows rained down, each one finding its mark in the throat or eye of a human or animal.

The Strike Force, or, at the least, a few hundred of them.

For a moment Leagh raised her head and watched the Icarii, then she lowered her eyes . . . and could not restrain a sob of sorrow.

Before her hundreds upon hundreds of humans and animals lay dead and dying, some still clawing frantically at arrows that protruded from their eyes or the base of their throats.

They might have been in the employ of the Demons, but they had once laughed and sang and cried as Leagh could still do. They had once served their masters with good will and willing backs.

They had once been a part of Leagh's world, a loved and respected part, and she now found it hard to watch their dying before her.

She lowered her head and wept, and as she did so the flowers faded and disappeared.

It made no difference to the dying before her. As successive waves of creatures crested the ridge, so they fell.

The Icarii wraiths had, it appeared, limitless amounts of arrows.

Eventually it was done, and an Icarii birdwoman settled to the ground before Leagh.

She was exquisitely beautiful, with her ethereal form and sapphire wings and eyes. "My name is FireCloud," she said, and rested one hand comfortingly on Leagh's arm. "And I, as my fellows, are here to help protect you at DragonStar's command."

Leagh nodded, her sorrow still not enabling her to speak, and she patted FireCloud's arm.

"DragonStar? DragonStar?"

DragonStar closed his eyes momentarily in impatience, and then turned slightly to the figure which had climbed to join him.

"What are you doing here, StarLaughter?"

She sat down beside him, encased in a thick wrap, but with her head bare and her hair flying in the wind. Gods, Dragon-Star thought, isn't she cold?

StarLaughter truly did not appear to notice the extreme of the temperature.

"Something has happened!" she said, and grabbed at DragonStar's arm. "I can *feel* it!"

"Yes?"

"WolfStar has escaped Sanctuary! He is *safe*!"

"Careful," DragonStar said, "for this wind might carry your gladness to the Hawkchilds."

But he nodded to himself anyway. DragonStar had felt the rift in the matter of existence when Urbeth had torn a hole from Sanctuary into the northern wastes. He had no idea how they were managing to survive, or if the Demons had followed them through . . . but he *had* felt the escape.

"WolfStar must still manage his survival," he said. "He is not so much 'safe', as currently beyond the Demons' reach."

"Safe enough," StarLaughter said, determined not to let DragonStar's pessimism ruin her joy. She sighed happily, her fingers kneading uncomfortably into DragonStar's arm. "And soon we will be reunited. DragonStar, where is he? Where?"

DragonStar jerked his arm away, annoyed not only at her inane and persistent belief that WolfStar could not wait to see her again, but also at her irritating presence. This would be a long night, and he would prefer not to spend it with Star-Laughter at his side.

"North," he said, not wanting to give StarLaughter the happiness of a more specific answer.

"North? North? What? In the depths of the Iskruel Ocean? DragonStar, I must go to him! I can't leave him to the fishes and the—"

"Oh, for the gods' sakes, woman! Leave it alone! He is in the northern tundra, and—"

"The tundra? But there are Skraelings out there and—"

Despite the trouble a harsh word might bring him, Dragon-

Star's temper snapped. He twisted around and grabbed Star-Laughter's shoulders. "Leave him be, you demented woman!"

"I cannot!" she responded, her eyes flashing in the clouded night light and pushing his hands away. "He is *mine,* and I will not let him go!"

Dear stars in heaven, DragonStar thought wearily, but he moderated his tone when he replied to her. "StarLaughter, he is with those who can protect him, and besides, I doubt they will stay in the northern tundra. They will come south soon enough, and you can wait for them at the foot of the eastern Icescarp Alps—where they met what was once the Avarinheim. You can't miss them from there."

And gods help them, he thought, when the meddling and completely crazed StarLaughter turns up. But whatever their difficulties (or, more specifically, WolfStar's) at least Star-Laughter would be out of his hair.

StarLaughter narrowed her eyes as she thought it out. "But they might swing west along the Icebear Coast," she said. "And if I were waiting at the foot of the eastern Icescarp Alps then I would miss them completely. How do you *know* they will come directly south?"

"Because I believe that my father Axis is leading them, and Axis is a sensible man, and he'd damn well take the *shortest* bloody route to come south! Does that answer your question?"

"My, my," StarLaughter murmured, "you are testy, aren't you?"

"It is cold and I am tired of your company," he said. "Go find your WolfStar if you will, but leave me alone this night."

She leaned back very slightly, her face angry. "Tonight will be a night of terror," she said. "I hope you enjoy it. Nay! I hope you *survive* it!"

And then she was gone.

DragonStar looked after her retreating form with relief . . . and some regret that he'd not thought to ask her to leave her cloak. Terror-ridden or not, this night was going to be a cold one.

When the column of creatures that had wormed their way north from the Maze to the Lake of Life appeared, Gwendylyr initially contented herself with throwing rocks at them from her well-protected fortress within her cave. She'd arrived here just as dusk was falling, and it had taken her only a cursory glance about to know she'd found herself an easily defensible and fortifiable shelter.

The cave itself was roomy and dry since the spring had dried up in the aftermath of Qeteb's resurrection, but the opening to the cave had been built up with masonry to allow only a relatively narrow opening for the water to gush through. Gwendylyr supposed Sigholt's engineers, in doing so, had thought to protect the spring from contamination by loose vegetation and wild animals. Whatever, it took only the work of a half an hour for Gwendylyr to further fortify the entrance with the branches of trees blown down in Qeteb's fit of ressurective destruction.

Then she had sunk to the floor of the cave and dozed for some hours.

When she'd awoken, it was to find that night had fully enveloped the landscape, and there were horrid whisperings and scratchings at her dry-branched doorway.

And so Gwendylyr had sighed, risen, brushed herself off, tucked away a few tendrils of stray hair, and prepared to defend herself.

There were loose rocks lying everywhere, and once she'd managed to drive the first ranks back a cautious twenty or thirty paces with her well-aimed missiles, Gwendylyr set to piling up an armoury.

The only trouble was, the rocks were not replenishable. She could *probably* keep the gathering hordes at bay for a few hours (but what if they all rushed her at once?), but come morning, she would undoubtedly be out of ammunition.

Gwendylyr stood thinking, hands on hips, her eyes drifting from her neat piles of rocks to the entrance and back again.

"The trouble with me," she said, "is that I am far too neat and way too organised."

She moved closer to the entrance and peered over her barrier of tree branches. There were several hundred, possibly several thousand, creatures out there now, huddled in the darkness, and slowly, slowly creeping their way forward.

Gwendylyr threw a rock.

It struck a creeping dog squarely in the forehead. He yelped and cowered, then recovered and crept forward again, even though his forehead had caved in and thick sludgy matter—Gwendylyr presumed it was the dog's brains but couldn't see clearly at this distance and in this dark—was sliding down the right-hand side of the dog's face.

Gwendylyr shrugged. The rocks were losing their potency. Neatness and organisation would not win the day for her.

She smiled, and stood very still.

She closed her eyes and lowered her head, concentrating.

Gwendylyr was thinking very unneat thoughts. She was, in fact, reliving her recently-found friendship with the forces of disorder.

And then, just as the first of the creatures had reached her barrier and had seized the branches in order to tear them away, Gwendylyr let all the forces of disordered nature fly forth. The creatures did not know what had gone wrong. They had been creeping through a world that they knew and loved: a world of bleakness and madness, a world of devastation, a world that belonged truly to their masters and no-one else.

And then, everything had fallen apart. The ground had shifted, split, reformed—but reformed into geological features that had not been there previously. Stone pillars thrust upwards where once had been flat ground, caverns yawned where once had been solid rock.

And over all crept entwining ivy, tangling paws and claws and limbs, pulling creatures into pits and under toppling rocks.

None of the creatures could find a toehold, for in this disor-

dered world toeholds did not exist. They tumbled and
shrieked, tearing each other apart in the effort to find a
foothold *anywhere,* and all the time ripping and snapping at
the ivy that rioted everywhere.

This was not a world they understood.

Gwendylyr smiled.

When the three Wing of the Strike Force DragonStar had
sent arrived, they found nothing but Gwendylyr sitting in front
of her cave, lighting a small fire with the remains of what appeared to have once been a stack of firewood.

Everything seemed calm and perfectly normal.

"Have you been troubled by any of Qeteb's creatures?"
asked the Flight Leader who settled before her.

"Hardly at all," Gwendylyr replied.

DragonStar smiled, and turned his attention south towards
Cauldron Lake.

Here, surprisingly, for they'd had the furthest to fly, the
three Wing of the Strike Force had arrived before the dark column from the Maze . . .

The more surprising, for the creatures sent to Cauldron
Lake had less distance to travel than those who troubled
Leagh and Gwendylyr.

But then again, the crystal forest was still standing, and
mayhap it still exerted some degree of fear in the minds of the
creatures, enough to make them drag their malformed feet
more than they would have done.

Perhaps it was the memories floating about the Keep, perhaps something else, but DareWing and Goldman had, in the
few short hours they'd been there, formed a partnership very
much like that of Ogden and Veremund.

The Wing of the Strike Force arrived to find the two fighting over who exactly had washed the dishes resulting from
their meal.

"You *must* have done it," DareWing was saying, "for *I* did
not!"

"You undoubtedly did," Goldman said crossly, "for I know that I did not, and who else is there?"

"Ahem," said KirtleBreeze, leader of the three Wing, but nevertheless shifting from foot to foot in embarrassment.

DareWing and Goldman looked up at the birdman standing in the doorway of the Keep, annoyance etched into each of their faces.

"What are you doing here?" DareWing said. "I thought that—"

"DragonStar sent us to aid you," KirtleBreeze said.

"Aid us?" Goldman said. "We need no aid!"

KirtleBreeze shot a look behind him. "If I might suggest—" he began, then got no further, for the sounds of battle interrupted him.

KirtleBreeze stepped back into the night and disappeared, and Goldman and DareWing rushed forward, colliding in the doorway and scrabbling at each other before finally managing to get through.

The Keep was surrounded by thousands of demonic creatures, humanoid and animal.

Most of them were writhing on the ground with arrows to their eyes and throats.

"Not bad," DareWing said, and nodded as he folded his arms and stood back to survey the slaughter.

"They could have let us do *something*," Goldman said, and DareWing turned his face to his companion and grinned.

"The next battle will be ours, my friend."

"Aye, so it will be. So it will be," and Goldman's hand drifted down to stroke the crest of the lizard at his side.

Faraday barely coped with the creatures sent to harry her.

Their instructions were not to attack and destroy, but to whisper.

And Qeteb had instructed them well.

As Faraday had backed into her pile of rubble, hundreds of

blackened, grinning creatures had completely surrounded the pile of stones.

They settled down on bellies and haunches, some with heads resting on paws, and they grinned and gleamed their reddened eyes at her.

"Qeteb won't be long," they said, a horrible chorus of voices rising and whispering into the night. "He won't be long at all."

"And he can't *wait* to get his hands on you," a cat said to one side, and the entire mass of creatures tittered.

"He'll make a real woman of you," an old crone murmured, and ran her hands lovingly over and under her own sagging dugs. She raised crazed eyes to Faraday. "He's done wonders with Niah."

"He'll take you within the Maze," said a bull. "He'll make you a queen. Remember Gorgrael? Remember what *he* did to you?"

The bull leered, foam dripping from his slavering mouth. "Qeteb will be a real bull for you, m'dear. In every way."

"You speak lies and illusions," Faraday said, keeping her voice calm although she was appalled by what they said. How much did they know? How much did *Qeteb* know?

"Everything," an adolescent boy said. "Isfrael told him, y'see. Isfrael told him how best to use his mother, for the only reason his mother exists is to make a useful sacrifice."

"Will DragonStar save you, do you think?" asked the old crone. Her fingers were now dug so deep into her flaccid breasts that flesh oozed up between them. "Or will he offer your throat for Tencendor?"

"He will save me," Faraday said.

The mass of creatures howled with laughter.

"We can hear the fear in your voice," a small reptile finally managed to say through its chortles, "and we know the reason for your fear. You are not sure, are you!"

"I am sure of *one* thing," Faraday said, finally, utterly, unbearably angry, "and that is of—"

The bull did not allow her to answer. "You have a choice," he said. "You can succumb and the pain will end . . . reasonably fast. Or you can fight and tear yourself apart in the effort to free yourself. Which will it be?"

Faraday's mind jerked back to the test she'd undergone when she and DragonStar's other witches had sat under the crystal-columned dome in Sanctuary. Then she had answered . . . then she had answered . . .

Gods, then she had answered that the thorns should choose for her!

But she could not give that answer here, for it would warn Qeteb of the methods that she and her companions meant to use against the Demons.

"I will succumb," Faraday said softly, her soul screaming with every word, "for that is what I have always done."

"Yes! Yes! Yes!" screamed the horde, and they surged forward.

Faraday could do nothing to stop them, for she was overcome with despair and sorrow. Yes, she *would* succumb, for isn't that what she always did? Isn't that what fate demanded of her again? Isn't that what—

She lost consciousness.

Atop the rubble of Star Finger, DragonStar lowered his head and wept for her courage and for her despair.

"Now," he whispered, "please gods in heaven, *now!*"

When Faraday opened her eyes again, it was to the concerned gaze of a Wing Leader.

"My Lady Faraday," he said. "The beasts are either dead or driven back. You are safe."

"I am never safe," she said, and turned her head aside.

40

Night: 11

"Skraelings!" Zared whispered, and reached for his sword. He had never fought against them himself, for the battle for Tencendor was won by the time he slipped from Rivkah's womb, but his father, Magariz, had told him over many years of companionship-filled nights about his battles with the wraiths, and Zared had every reason to fear. The Skraelings fed off terror as much as they did flesh.

Another whisper reached out from the night. A soft hiccup, and then yet more whispers moaning along the back of the wind, knifing along the crystalline edge of every snowflake.

"They're everywhere!" Azhure said, and lifted Katie into the cart. "Dammit! I wish I had a bow, a sword, or even a cursed stick!"

"We can find you—" Axis began, but Ur waved a hand about and silenced him.

"We need no swords against such as these that wait outside," she said.

"There are thousands of them!" Axis cried. "I can *feel* it!"

Sal pranced nervously about, laying her ears flat against her skull, and Axis had to exert all his skill to keep her from bolting into the night. Sparrow-gift or not, at the moment she was behaving like any young, nervous horse.

But Sal was the least of Axis' concerns. Gods! How would he protect the millions of people and creatures in this convoy? The strength of their fear alone would strengthen the Skraelings to the point where *no-one* could defeat them!

"Forty-two thousand of them, to be exact," Ur said. "Precisely what we need."

"What!"

Ur sighed, and hugged her pot closer. "You have no imagi-

nation," she said. "You think to fight with swords when a little
hospitality would work miracles."

Zared, Axis and Azhure, who had now climbed back into
the cart, stared at her.

"Hospitality?" Axis finally said. "You think we should in-
vite them in for dinner?"

"Yes," Ur said. "Or, at least, a friendly drink."

Zared grabbed at Axis' arm. "The wine, and the bowls, that
Urbeth insisted we bring with us!"

Axis stared at Zared, and then back to Ur. "We get them
drunk?"

Ur grinned. "Skraelings have ever had a poor head for alco-
hol," she said, "but they cannot resist it."

I spent years fighting the wraiths with sword and blood, Axis
thought, *when I could simply have got them drunk instead?*

"Lessons are never too late for the learning," Ur said.
"Now, best find those wine barrels. The night, the storm and
the Skraelings are closing in, and if we can't deal with the
Skraelings, then none of us will survive until dawn."

The Demons swarmed down tunnel after tunnel, encountering
little but tangled tree roots and the dank, musky odour of the
long-abandoned warren.

Occasionally, they found a scrap of white fur hanging off a
sharp piece of stone, or caught in a tree root, and those small
white pieces of hope drove them further and further, and
deeper and deeper.

And, as they sped deeper, the walls of the rabbit warren began to change.

Axis sent orders shouting back down the length of the column
until the shouts were lost in the night and the thick blanket of
the snow-filled storm.

He hoped people had enough warmth left in their fingers to
get the bowls out and filled.

Axis kneed Sal close into the side of the cart, and took the blanket Azhure held up for him, spreading it over the horse's back and hindquarters. Sal had been shivering so badly that Axis thought she would throw him off with the strength of her tremors.

He slid from her back—the mare was so cold she was of little use—and grabbed at the three bowls that a man handed him.

"Where's the wine?" he said, the freezing air burning in his throat.

"Next cart down," the man said, and Axis noticed that he had icicles hanging off his beard.

Tucking the bowls under one arm, he felt his own face.

It was crusted with ice.

"Let me give you a hand," said Zared, stumbling close by him.

Axis nodded, and handed him the bowls, taking more as they were passed out. If this didn't work—and he couldn't see how getting the Skraelings drunk would aid them against the creeping death of the ice-storm—they would not see out the hour, let alone the night.

The Demons were so intent on catching the rabbits—all thought of chasing the people fleeing Sanctuary completely forgotten—that at first they did not notice the changes occurring about them.

But then the ferret that was Raspu slipped suddenly, unexpectedly, and careened into Sheol.

She turned around and gave him a sharp bite on his shoulder, and then her eyes widened.

They were running through a tunnel of earth no more, but a tunnel carved through ice.

And through the ice, tens of thousands of eyes staring at them.

Sheol squeaked, half in annoyance, half in fear, and Qeteb turned and stared.

Axis stood, shaking with cold, as a man standing in the cart above him poured out a measure of wine.

The man's exposed hands were blue, and they trembled so badly the barrel jerked and wine spilt all down the front of Axis' tunic.

"No matter, man," Axis said, "I have enough." And he stepped aside so Zared could have his bowl filled as well.

All about them were lines of men, bowls of wine in hand, stumbling out into the storm to lay the bowls in the snow a good ten paces from the carts.

Everyone else, people and creatures alike, were huddled as best they could under blankets or carts or, if small enough, under the clothes of people.

The only ones who appeared comfortable in the prevailing conditions were the Ravensbundmen and women, who laughed and jested as they did more than their fair share of filling bowls with wine and then placing them in the snow.

Gradually, as men and women stumbled back and forth in the snowy night, hundreds of wine-filled bowls were laid out down the length of both sides of the column.

As Axis struggled back to where Azhure, Katie and Ur waited, Zared a pace behind him, Ur grinned, and placed her terracotta pot on the ground before her.

"Not long to wait now," she said.

Qeteb twisted about. They were trapped in a length of ice tunnel. What magic had brought them here? How had he been trapped? No matter, he could find his way out of here without even the ghost of an effort.

Chitter, chatter. Chitter, chatter.

Qeteb spun about again. Who was that? Behind and about him the other Demons snarled.

Chitter, chatter. Who have we here, chitter, chatter?

"Who are you?" Qeteb snarled. He did not like the feel of these beings, these eyes that stared down at him through the thick layers of ice, for they had the feel of . . . the feel of free souls.

We are the Chitter Chatters, strange guest. Who are you?

"I am Qeteb, the Midday Demon, and Lord of this land!"

A strange, whispering laughter filtered through the ice. *We have no lord, and we have no land. Only this ice-bound, drifting world. A cruel world. Do you like our cruel world, strange guest?*

Qeteb snarled, and struck at the ice roof above his head.

It did not even crack, and he sank back to all four paws, alternatively growling and mewling.

We do not know you, chitter, chatter. But we do not think we like you.

The Demons squirmed about in their confined space, probing for cracks and possible escape. Mot, then Barzula and Sheol, growled.

"I have had enough!" Qeteb snarled, and struck out with his power.

Nothing happened. There was a sense of withdrawal from the Chitter Chatters, and then a probing into the Demons' minds again as they came back.

Chitter, chatter, we do not like you! We were not supposed to disturb any who came here, save Skraelings—

—not whale or seal, chitter, chatter, nor Ravensbund or even any of the southerners—

—Ho'Demi charged us not to nibble at anyone's *minds save the Skraelings—*

—and he saved us, and brought us to this cruel world—

—and we owe him and respect his wishes.

Are you Skraelings, chitter, chatter?

"I am Qeteb, the Midday Demon, and—"

Why are you here, Qeteb, chitter, chatter? Why do you worm so deep into the ice and disturb us?

The Demons did not reply, but the Chitter Chatters caught the image of the rabbit chase, and they laughed, chittering and chattering until the Demons scrabbled about furiously in the attempt to get to the infuriating creatures.

We may not nibble at your minds, nor may we eat you, for we have promised. Nevertheless, we think we have the perfect home for you, chitter, chatter!

Then, as the Demons felt themselves wrapped in unaccus-

tomed power, and propelled through layers of ice so sharp and
cold they felt their bodies torn apart, they caught one last remark from the chitter, chatters.

We thank you for this amusement, Urbeth!

If ever I find out who this Urbeth is, Qeteb thought in some
pain-ravaged corner of his mind, I will tear her soul to pieces
before I consume it.

They waited for what felt like hours, but which Axis was ready
enough to acknowledge was probably only half an hour at
most. They huddled in carts, as deep beneath blankets and tarpaulins and cloaks as they could, and hoped they would survive both the deepening storm and the raucous whisperings of
the Skraelings.

They were making a frightful sound. In this snow, no-one
could actually see them, but their whispering and whimper-
ings and creepings could be heard above and beneath the
shriek of the wind. They were, Axis realised, getting very
drunk very quickly on the offerings left them in the snow.

Gods, he thought miserably, hunching as close to Zared,
Azhure and Katie under their shared blanket as he could. *We
should have saved some of that wine. It would have warmed
us against this wind.*

There was a high-pitched squeal, and a bubbling of laughter. Axis felt Azhure, Katie and Zared shudder, and realised
that he had, too.

"Pray gods Urbeth and Ur know what they are doing," Axis
mumbled, "for I do not think we can survive either this storm
or the terror of the Skraelings for too much longer."

He was about to continue, when Zared grabbed at his arm
to silence him. "They're at the cart!" he whispered.

Axis fumbled quietly for his sword. He could feel curious
fingers patting at the top of the blanket, sharp, cruel fingers. In
his mind's eye he could see the insubstantial creatures, as tall
as a man, huge silver orbs glowing in their skull-like faces,
and long, pointed fangs hanging down from their oversized,

slavering jaws, their clawed hands picking and plucking at the blankets and tarpaulins that lay between them and the huddled masses of Tencendor.

His hand had tightened on his sword—he could stand this no longer!—when the Skraeling that was investigating his cart gave a sickening belch—Axis could smell the wine fumes through the blankets—let go the blanket, and said, "Oooooh!" in a tone of utter surprise.

And then Axis heard another voice. Ur. She must be wandering about in the snow with the Skraelings!

"Hello," Axis heard her say conversationally, "would you like to see what I have in my pot, wraith?"

Beside him, Katie giggled.

And the Skraeling giggled, too.

Then there came a sound that Axis numbly remembered he'd heard at the battle of Gorken Pass—the Song of the Forest! The Skraeling gibbered in fear, and then shrieked with such terror that Axis moaned and stopped his ears.

The Song intensified—Axis screamed, hearing Zared and Azhure cry out beside him—becoming a tidal wave of, not death, which the trees had used at the battle of Gorken Pass, but of retribution such as Axis could hardly bear.

Above all the screaming and wailing—as much of which came from the peoples huddled in the carts as it did from the Skraelings—Axis heard a woman laughing, and he realised it was Ur.

The Demons found themselves hurtling through ice and then rock, and pain filled them and became such a part of their lives that none could possibly imagine an existence without it.

And vengeance and anger also filled them.

No-one should be able to treat them like this!

What was most disturbing was the knowledge that this land still harboured magic that their destructiveness had not touched.

Even the rocks and the ice, it appeared, sheltered secrets.

Qeteb was the first to regain some form of control over both his physical and his magical self. With an effort he'd not had to make since he'd fought (unsuccessfully) against the Enemy's original dismemberment, he managed to slow their passage through space until he could feel the other Demons regain some control as well.

I will put a stop to this, Qeteb began to say to them, when suddenly, horribly, they *did* stop. The rock and earth and ice walls disintegrated about them, and they felt themselves falling through cold, dark air.

"Ugh!" Qeteb said as he hit very, very solid rock.

Beside him he heard another five impacts, and low curses and moans of pain filled the dark air about them.

Qeteb struggled into a sitting position—he'd assumed his metalled, armoured visage—and felt about him with his power, ignoring the mutters and moans of the other Demons.

Where were they?

Dark, deep, cold, barren.

It *felt* like the most distant of interstellar wastes, but Qeteb understood they'd not travelled beyond the boundaries of Tencendor itself.

Where were they?

Underground, with the weight of millions upon millions of tons of rock above them.

"We're in a mine," Sheol said beside him, and Qeteb felt her body crowd his, almost as if she needed the comfort of what physical warmth she could draw from his armour.

He shoved her away roughly.

"And we have a mountain atop us," Mot added, and Qeteb snarled, finally orientating himself within the geography of Tencendor.

They were deep underground in what the Tencendorians had called the Murkle Mountains.

Deep in the former home, if Qeteb had but known it, of the Chitter Chatters.

Qeteb cursed foully, and struck the rock he sat on with his mailed fist.

The sound of the impact echoed about them until its growing melody drove the Demons to a shrieking, capering dance of frustration and fury.

How dare anyone *do this to them!*

Silence, and Axis tensed, wondering what had happened.

"Forty-two thousand!" Azhure whispered beside him, "Ur said there were forty-two thousand Skraelings!"

"Yes, but—" Axis began.

"Don't you see?" Azhure whispered furiously, and Katie laughed again, a sweet, happy sound.

"What?" Axis said.

Azhure sighed impatiently. "There were forty-two thousand souls that Faraday transplanted out as the Minstrelsea forest."

"Yes . . ."

"And Ur was their guardian during their years as seedlings."

"Yes . . ."

"Don't you understand *yet*?" Azhure cried, and Zared jumped in, his voice excited.

"When Qeteb destroyed the forests, the souls went back to Ur!" he cried, and Axis felt Azhure nod her head enthusiastically.

"Yes! That's what she has been carrying about in that pot—the forty-two thousand souls who fled back to her when their physical forms, the trees, were destroyed."

"And now Ur has used the Song of the Trees to destroy the Skraelings," Axis said.

"Oh!" Azhure exclaimed, and wriggled about in further impatience. "Don't you see? Forty-two thousand Skraelings . . . and forty-two thousand souls?"

Axis huddled in stunned silence as the import of what Azhure had said sank in.

"Ur has given her souls a new home," Azhure said into the silence. "The Skraelings."

"That's why she needed them drunk," Katie put in.

"Drunken Skraelings put up no resistance to the souls of the trees."

"But where have the souls of the Skraelings gone," Zared said, "if their bodies are now occupied by the souls of the trees?"

"Fled to wander weeping and wailing across the ice drifts of the extreme north," said a voice above them. "Only the most foolhardy of wanderers will ever be bothered by them."

The blanket lifted, and there was Ur. "Would you like to meet your army, Axis StarMan?"

41

The Avenue

A xis helped Azhure and Katie out of the cart as Zared leapt down into the snow.

The wind still blew frighteningly hard and cold, and Axis wrapped his cloak, and a blanket over that, as tight about him as he could.

He did not say anything.

As far as he could see in the snowstorm, the entire column was flanked on either side by lines of Skraelings. They stood some four paces apart, several deep, each Skraeling staggered so that it stood in the space between the two in front of it, rather than in direct line with them.

Without exception the Skraelings stood with their feet buried deep into the drifting snow, their bodies and arms and loathsome heads drifting as they were tugged by the wind.

Their silver-orbed eyes were lively with intelligence rather than malice, and their toothsome grins were cheerful, rather than malicious.

For the first time in his life, Axis felt only curiosity as he stared at a Skraeling, not fear or the desire to kill.

But . . .

He looked at Ur, standing to one side with her pot, the saucer lid carefully back in place. Why, Axis knew not, for surely it was empty.

"For this army I thank you," Axis said to Ur, "but for what I will use it I do not know, for we will all surely be frozen solid by dawn time."

"Then tell them what you need," Ur said.

Axis stared at her, then looked back to the drifting lines of Skraelings.

"We need shelter," he said, "and warmth. A place to rest and eat and sleep."

The Skraelings grinned happily, and then they began to transform.

Beside Axis, Azhure gasped in recognition, for she was the only one, apart from Faraday, who had ever seen this process.

The Skraelings uncoiled.

Their legs thickened, and joined to form massive trunks, while their bodies lengthened and reached for the sky. The Skraelings flung their arms outwards in obvious joy, and they, too, lengthened and their fingers grew and thickened and spread until, in the space of three or four breaths, the Skraelings had transformed themselves into trees again—the huge, spreading trees of Minstrelsea forest.

With one exception. They had retained their wraith's insubstantiality, their trunks and branches grey and mist-like, their leaves the silver of the Skraeling eyes.

They were incredibly beautiful.

And, despite their appearance, substantial enough to cut out the wind and the storm completely.

Now Axis could see why they'd staggered themselves in ranks in their long lines down either side of the column. This way not even a breath of wind could penetrate their leaves or trunks.

In the abrupt cessation of wind and storm, tarpaulins and blankets slowly unfolded back from carts, and unfolded from lumps in the snow that Axis now saw were groups of people huddled together for warmth. People sat up, then slowly climbed down onto the snow-covered ground.

It was still cool, but in the absence of the north wind and the driving ice and snow, the cold had all but disappeared.

The trees rustled, and there was a murmur of Song.

The remaining snow on the ground was swept up in gentle whirls and eddied out between the tree trunks of the forest to be swept away in the outside storm.

The ground lay clean and dry.

Axis looked at Azhure, then at Zared, and then back to the sight before him.

It was beautiful beyond description. The trees had formed a protective tunnel over the entire column, a silvery, shifting avenue of ghost-trees that gently hummed.

There was a sudden new note to the Song of the trees, and with a start Axis heard what it was.

The Bogle Marsh creatures had joined their deep voice to that of the trees, and now the entire avenue of trees dipped and swayed, reaching out gentle tendrils of silvery leaves in dance to graze against the cheeks of people and animals alike.

There was a rush of wings, and all the birds who'd escaped into, and then out of, Sanctuary lifted into the air and sought refuge among the branches of the trees.

Animals emerged carefully from their hiding places, and nosed about the grass and flowers that appeared among the ridging roots of the trees.

"I cannot believe this loveliness," Axis said very softly, and felt a tear slip down his cheek.

"Then use it!" Ur whispered behind him. "Use it! My beauties are hungry for a revenge!"

Axis turned, and Ur smiled at him, almost girl-like. Then she lifted her pot and gave it a small shake, and said: "One more to go."

And then she was gone before Axis could ask her what she meant.

Axis spent the next few hours traversing the column on the back of Sal (Azhure had been stunned when he told her how he'd got the horse) making sure that people and beasts alike were settled comfortably.

He could not oversee the entire column—he suspected that it must stretch for many leagues—but what he saw of the sections he did ride up and down on his patrol relaxed and comforted him.

Without any apparent effort, or prior planning (or *had* Urbeth somehow foreseen and planned this?), the peoples and creatures of Tencendor had managed to arrange themselves into much the same type of communities that they had in their former lives before the Demons had come.

Here were the inhabitants of the villages of southern Romsdale, complete with their remaining herds of livestock, grouped about a series of small fires and cooking grain and vegetables. They smiled and waved at Axis and invited him to join them for a meal, but he refused, saying he had too much to do.

Further on Axis came across the Nors folk, a shifting, brightly-scarved mass of them, their musical instruments out, their dancing boys writhing amid tight circles of admiring and leering adults. Axis grinned, and rode on.

Further on yet were the Ravensbund people, sharing space with the still-humming pile of Bogle Marsh creatures (Axis wondered if they had somehow formed an association of collective admiration for their mutually isolated and taciturn ways of life), as well as many of the fey creatures Faraday had rescued from the Minstrelsea and Avarinheim.

The Avar had split to set up Clan camps within the trees from where they nodded to passers-by, but otherwise made no attempt to speak or commune with other peoples or with Axis. Above them, many of the Icarii had taken up residence with the birds in the branches of the trees, talking and laughing and playing their harps and singing, and floating down in drifts to partake of hot meals at the campfires that were dotted like bright sparks of hope along the length of the column.

People shifted, walked, traded and laughed up and down

the avenue. It was, Axis finally realised with a jolt, a land entire unto itself, protected by the shimmering, magical, musical avenue of trees. Family and community groups had reformed, livestock had huddled comfortably back together in their field companies, and wild creatures had sought isolation and refuge in and among the trees.

Amid the desolation of the frozen tundra, Tencendor had found hope again.

In the morning, Axis thought, *I will shift this entire avenue south, and see how DragonStar can use us.*

His good humour and hope dissipated the moment he rode back to the cart where Azhure and Katie had set up camp. (Zared had long since ridden back to the spot where the folk of Severin had established themselves.)

As he slid off Sal's back, he saw that StarDrifter was talking earnestly, almost angrily, to Azhure and that her face wore an expression of deep distress.

Axis almost hated StarDrifter at that moment. What had he said to so upset Azhure? *Why couldn't he just leave well enough alone?*

"Azhure?" Axis said, moving to join her where she stood with StarDrifter by a small campfire.

An iron pot swung gently on its tripod, the delicious smell of stew and dumplings rising up in heady waves from its interior.

"What's wrong?" Axis slid an arm about Azhure's shoulders, and shot StarDrifter a hard look.

"It's WolfStar," Azhure said, and Axis forgot all his animosity towards StarDrifter in a well-remembered surge of ill-feeling towards the ever-cursed WolfStar.

Dammit, he'd forgotten him in the fear and haste of abandoning Sanctuary! Axis had left WolfStar in the care of the Lake Guard, but where was he now? Damned birdman! Left to his own devices for more than an hour and he could ruin the future of an entire realm without even breaking into a sweat!

"Where is he?" he asked.

"About half a league back," StarDrifter said, and Axis

thought he must have turned Sal's head around to come back to the head of the column just before he would have reached WolfStar.

"And?" Axis said.

StarDrifter took a deep, distressed breath. His eyes suddenly, horrifyingly, filled with tears, and he looked at Azhure, unable to speak any more.

Azhure briefly closed her own eyes, summoning the courage to speak. How much of this was her own fault? If only she'd taken more care, more damned *time* with her children!

"Azhure?" Axis said, his voice tight, angry and fearful.

"WolfStar has got Zenith," Azhure said.

"What?" Axis exploded. "He's stolen her again?"

"What damn right have you got to say that?" StarDrifter shouted, stunning Axis into a shocked silence. "What damn fucking right? You abandoned Zenith when she needed you most—*curse you*! You *encouraged* WolfStar to pursue her, and to aid Niah in her frightful conquest of Zenith's body and soul. *How dare you now stand there and pretend an indignation that WolfStar has her again?*"

There was silence.

Axis glanced at Azhure, then looked down to the ground, studying the shine on his boots with a deep intensity.

Feelings of anger, resentment and horrifying guilt flowed through him. Anger at WolfStar, resentment at StarDrifter for putting the truth so baldly, and such deep guilt at how he'd treated Zenith that Axis thought he could hardly bear it.

Eventually he raised his eyes and looked steadily at StarDrifter.

"Tell me," he said quietly.

StarDrifter took a deep breath, steadying his own emotions. "I fought so hard for Zenith," he said. "Fought for her and loved her when no-one except Faraday would do the same for her. Faraday and I saved her from Niah and WolfStar—and, dammit, no-one fought harder in that battle than Zenith!—and, oh gods, the joy when we succeeded!"

StarDrifter had to turn away for a moment, his chest heaving, gulping down his tears.

When he finally had himself under some control, he turned back and continued. "Zenith and I became close after that. Very close."

Axis narrowed his eyes. "You fell in love." It was not a question. More than anyone, Axis understood the SunSoar attraction each to the other. Stars! He could remember the leap in his own blood when his grandmother, MorningStar, smiled at him with seduction in her eyes.

"And so you became lovers," Axis finished, and his tone was hard. His daughter had slept with his father. As with Azhure, his Acharite blood rebelled at the images now tumbling through his mind.

StarDrifter laughed, low and harsh and bitter, noting well the expression on Axis' face. "No. We have never slept together. Zenith could not . . . could not bear me to touch her." StarDrifter paused, his eyes locked into those of his son. "For the same reason you now wear such blatant disgust on your face, Axis. She could not lie with her grandfather, despite what she felt for him. Every time I laid a finger on her, she would shudder with revulsion."

Such relief flowed through Axis that he could almost manage some sympathy for StarDrifter's frustrations.

"That must be—" he began.

"But she can overcome her revulsion enough to sleep with WolfStar!" StarDrifter screamed.

Horror overwhelmed Axis. "But . . . but . . ."

He felt Azhure take his hand, and finally understood the depth of anguish she, too, must be feeling.

"How?" Axis finally whispered. "Why?"

"She says," and StarDrifter's voice was as cold and impersonal as the interstellar wastes, "that she does not view Wolf-Star as her grandfather. She says that she finds some comfort with him. *Him!* Her rapist!"

"I'll put an end to this!" Axis said, and half turned away.

"No." Azhure stopped him. "No. I must. This must be said

woman to woman. Besides," her mouth quirked with utter sadness and a guilt far deeper than Axis', "Zenith is paying for my sins, not hers. Stay here, Axis, StarDrifter. Let me do this."

And she was gone.

42

Of Commitment

Zenith sat on the small stool by the fire and tried to let some of her companions' good cheer raise her spirits. She and WolfStar were sharing a fire with three Ravensbundmen and a farming couple from northern Ichtar: Zenith suspected they had some Ravensbund blood in them as well, for few Acharites were ever comfortable in the presence of either the northern hunters, or two Icarii Enchanters.

But as the Ravensbund cared neither way about their companions, so Zenith presumed it was with this couple. Not even the reputation of WolfStar appeared to concern them.

The Ravensbund were sharing a pot of Tekawai tea, turning the pot its ritual three turns to honour the sun, then pouring the fragrant tea into small porcelain cups that carried the emblem of the blood-red sun.

Maybe that is why they are so comfortable with us, Zenith thought, for we are of SunSoar blood, and the Ravensbund are pledged to the StarMan.

The peasant husband was strumming a small lute—badly. His wife was singing some rollicking peasant ballad to his accompaniment—equally as badly.

Zenith could feel WolfStar's irritation grow, and she placed a hand on his arm to forestall his otherwise inevitable blast of sarcasm. She had discovered that she had a gentling affect on him. This amazed Zenith, for she had not known that anyone could gentle the otherwise self-consumed WolfStar.

He would stay his voice and his hand for her, when otherwise he would let fly, and for her WolfStar would sit still and bland when otherwise he would prefer to pace and fidget and bemoan the fates that had brought him to this sorry, useless and utterly magic-less pass.

Zenith had no idea of the depth and professionalism of WolfStar's manipulation.

A small movement caught Zenith's eye, and she turned her head slightly.

WingRidge CurlClaw was talking quietly to another member of the Lake Guard just at the outer limits of the fire's warmth. There were always at least three or four of the Lake Guard about WolfStar, or standing guard at the door and window of whatever chamber he lay in.

WingRidge caught Zenith looking at him, and he nodded a silent greeting.

Zenith smiled, then looked back to WolfStar. He was, at least to outward appearances, dozing. His physical condition had improved markedly, but he still tired easily. The flight from Sanctuary, and the subsequent hours spent in the frigid storm, had wearied him to the point where he had slept on and off during these past five hours since the Skraelings had taken root and sprung into this magical avenue.

Zenith let her eyes slip down his body. Did she love him? No, but she felt a closeness to him that she could not achieve with StarDrifter; a companionship almost. WolfStar had shown her a gentler side to his nature that she'd not known existed.

She and WolfStar shared the same night, the same experiences and pain and humiliations, and even though WolfStar had been responsible almost entirely for *her* pain and humiliation, she nevertheless now felt such a bond with him that she knew she could not leave him.

Certainly not now they'd again shared a bed.

She'd let him make love to her, finally, in those hours when they'd huddled together in their own warm, intimate space under a tarpaulin while the ice storm raged overhead. There had been no words, only gentle touches and long pauses, and the final turning to him to offer him her mouth.

Zenith had wanted WolfStar to hurt her, to hurry her, or even to force her, for then she would have been able to loathe him. Then, she thought, she would have been able to turn her back on WolfStar, and look to StarDrifter.

But WolfStar had not hurt her, or hurried her, and he certainly had not forced her.

He had, unbelievably, been hesitant and unsure.

After they had done, Zenith had cried, and WolfStar had held her and comforted her, and Zenith knew she would learn to enjoy him and desire him as a lover.

He was WolfStar, but something, somewhere within him had changed.

Or is it me? Zenith wondered, and had to bow her head and blink back her tears, because she didn't want to change, she didn't want to respond to WolfStar, she only wanted to run to StarDrifter and let him hold her, and let him protect her from all the hurts of the outside world.

And what hurt most of all was that that could never, never be. Not now.

Zenith knew StarDrifter would accept her without question, recrimination or a single hint of revulsion.

It was she who could not now go back. A chasm had been created the instant she allowed WolfStar back into her body, and it was a chasm Zenith knew she would never be able to bridge.

She lowered her head still further and wept.

Now she had no-one to loathe but herself.

It was quiet. The Ravensbundmen had finished their tea and were huddled as still as rocks under enveloping blankets. The peasant couple were asleep in each other's arms. WolfStar had drifted into a deep sleep, and lay half slouched against the wheel of the cart, half against a pile of blankets. Of them all, only the Lake Guard stood wakeful, their eyes relaxed but nevertheless watchful.

A hand fell softly on her arm, and Zenith jerked fully

awake from her light doze. She opened her eyes and saw Azhure, crouched down beside her.

Azhure put a finger to her lips, and then pointed to a spot ten or twelve paces distant from the fire. *Come with me.*

Zenith hesitated, glanced at WolfStar who had not stirred, then rose grudgingly and followed Azhure. The last thing she felt like right now was a mother and daughter chat.

The Lake Guardsmen followed her with their eyes, but did not move after her, and Zenith wondered at what point they would. When would she become so associated with WolfStar *(so much an extension of WolfStar)* that she would require watching in her own right?

"I needed to talk with you," Azhure said as she drew Zenith close to the first row of ghost trees. Above their heads the leaves moved gracefully, humming a sweet soothing lullaby.

"So it would seem," Zenith said, her tone unresponsive. She would not meet her mother's eyes.

"I don't blame you for your reaction, Zenith," Azhure said. She reached out and took both her daughter's hands. "I cannot say how much I regret what I said and did in Sigholt when—"

"Then don't."

"Zenith . . ." Azhure stopped, not knowing what to say or how to say it. "StarDrifter has told us—"

"He had no right! *None!*"

"He is Axis' father, and he is a friend so dear to me that I can hardly bear his grief," Azhure said evenly. "And you are my daughter, and WolfStar is my father. We are all tangled up in a web so intricate, and so intricately painful, that no-one within the web can escape the grief and heartbreak of another. I have *every* right to talk to you about this, Zenith. What you do affects us all—"

"Oh, so *I* am to be blamed for everyone's pain, am I? What about you? What about your and Axis' abandonment of me, and of DragonStar and RiverStar, while you pampered Caelum and then fled to your godly pinnacle of accomplishment and starry meditations? Don't speak to *me* of intricate webs!"

Azhure's hands tightened, stopping Zenith from pulling completely away.

"Then please, *please,* talk to me as your friend! Forget the fact that I am your mother! Talk to another woman who has felt so much of what—"

Zenith turned her face away.

Azhure lowered her face as she thought desperately of what she could say next. Finally, she looked at Zenith again, tears coursing down her cheeks.

"Zenith, you are right to lay so much blame on my shoulders, as on Axis'. There is nothing I can say or do now to negate what we—what I—did to you. I can't even ask for your forgiveness. But, Zenith, I just want to help. Please . . . please . . ."

Something in Azhure's voice finally made Zenith turn her face back to her mother. She stared, closed her eyes briefly, then stepped forward and embraced her mother.

Azhure clung to her, sobbing, and Zenith found herself soothing her mother when all she wanted was to be soothed herself.

And then, magically, she was, for Azhure had pulled her down to the ground, and was holding her and rocking her and murmuring to her the words that Zenith had needed to hear for years, and in that embrace Zenith felt so treasured, and so loved, that she could hardly bear it, and she broke down and wept.

By the fireside, WolfStar opened his eyes, and stared. *What was that bitch saying to Zenith?*

In time, Azhure quieted her daughter, and wiped away her own tears, and they sat themselves more comfortably and talked.

"If I could somehow be with StarDrifter," Zenith finally said, very softly, "then, believe me, I would. He is a man I *should* be able to be happy with. But now it is too late. Far too late."

"How so—too late?" Azhure's fingers slowly stroked back the hair from Zenith's forehead.

"I have committed myself to WolfStar now."

Committed? "You have bedded with him?"

Zenith tensed, then nodded.

"Oh, my dear, that means nothing. StarDrifter will not hold that against you. That fact will not stand between you."

"It is far more than that, Azhure. I feel a companionship with WolfStar that I cannot feel with StarDrifter. And I feel a responsibility for WolfStar that—"

"Oh, I don't believe that! Zenith, all you have to do is walk away from WolfStar! You do not have to become StarDrifter's lover if you do not want to, but for the gods' sakes, girl . . . WolfStar is not the man for my daughter!"

Zenith smiled, wondering if she should remind her mother about the time Azhure had all but pushed Zenith into Wolf-Star's arms, then decided against it. That was so long ago, and so many heartbreaks ago.

"I cannot, Azhure. I cannot leave him. I know I should . . . but I cannot."

Azhure, almost panicked by the resignation in her daughter's voice, began to protest when a shadow fell over them.

It was WolfStar, with three of the Lake Guard in close attendance.

"Azhure," he said, and nodded at her. "How are you these days? No, please, I don't truly want an answer. Family reunions were never my strength. Zenith. Come. It is cold by the fire without you."

For a heartbeat or two Zenith hesitated, feeling the warmth of her mother's arms about her, seeing WolfStar's hand stretched out for hers.

She hesitated still further, desperately wanting to stay locked within the protective warmth and love of her mother's encircling arms, but knowing that, in the end, she could not.

And at that realisation, Zenith felt such a profound sense of doom that she almost let go of life completely. She struggled frantically against a black insanity, battled, then won, but feeling herself the loser even in that victory.

Resigned and compliant, she pushed back her mother's arms and let WolfStar draw her to her feet.

As he turned to take Zenith back to the fire, WolfStar looked Azhure in the eye. "Tell StarDrifter to go back to his meaningless seductions, for he has lost the battle for the jewel."

And with that, they were gone.

Azhure stared after them, not comprehending, and not wanting to. Then she somehow managed to rise to her feet and, through a blur of tears, wend her way back to Axis and StarDrifter to tell them they'd lost a daughter and a lover.

43

StarLaughter's Quest

DragonStar's five witches needed time, space and peace in which to prepare themselves, and the Strike Force were there to give them every possible chance of having it.

Of the five, Gwendylyr needed to prepare fastest, for she would be tested first.

"What can I do for you?" said DeepNote, the Wing Leader in overall charge of the three Wing who protected Gwendylyr. It was still night time, and the majority of the Strike Force huddled inside the cave, clinging to rocks as they could. "What do you need?"

"Peace, and a few days in which to construct my . . ."

"Trap?"

Gwendylyr hesitated, then shook her head. "No. Not a trap. A fork."

"A fork?" DeepNote shifted from foot to foot, and glanced at his lieutenant.

Gwendylyr smiled, but it was sad. "I do not construct a trap for the Demon—for to do that would be to fall into his own trap. No, what I do is rather to construct a fork in his road, a fork where he must choose freedom or servitude."

"And what will *that* do?" DeepNote said.

"It will destroy him or it will save him," Gwendylyr said, "and the Demon will not relish either choice."

"How will you build this 'fork'?" asked MirrorWing, Deep-Note's lieutenant.

Now Gwendylyr grinned broadly. "By doing what I do best," she said. "By making up a list."

And while the two birdmen looked perplexed, Gwendylyr moved away to a free spot and sat down, arranging her features calmly, closing her eyes, and meditating.

Both birdmen—indeed, all the Strike Force members who were in the cave—could feel the power emanating from her, but they could not yet see what enchantment it was she was constructing from her Acharite magic.

"A list?" MirrorWing muttered.

DeepNote sighed. "Well, we must do what we can, and I fear there will be a great deal to do. Gwendylyr, as all five witches, will act as a lodestone to the crazed who populate this wasteland. Within hours, we will be surrounded again."

MirrorWing's face tightened, and his silvery-grey body swayed slightly in his eagerness. "Then we *will* be useful, for every creature we kill—"

"Transforms and moves on," DeepNote murmured.

"—will be one less corruption to free Tencendor of."

DeepNote hesitated, then nodded. "Aye. We each have our own tasks to do."

And he turned away and moved to speak quietly to the Wing.

Gwendylyr opened one eye as he walked away, then closed it and smiled gently.

She was deep in contemplation of domestic servants and the chaos they could cause when left to run amok.

StarLaughter had found the decision about what to do a difficult one. After she'd left DragonStar—how could he *not* see that WolfStar would welcome her with open arms?—StarLaughter had returned to the deep, undamaged vaults of Star Finger. There, she'd spent several hours rummaging until she had found what she needed.

The implements of seduction.

Perfumes, powders, face paints. Bangles, pendants, earrings. Corsets, bustiers, veils. Nail varnishes, hair brighteners, wing softeners. Creams, potions, smoothers. Gold, silks, brocades.

Most of these StarLaughter packed into a small bag. Her implements were small-sized, and the silks and jewellery could fit into the smallest of spaces.

What she could not fit into the bag, StarLaughter fitted onto her person, for who knew when she'd come face to face with WolfStar again! Best to be prepared, best to look her best *now*, just in case.

So she perfumed, painted and powdered. She draped, tightened and revealed. She varnished, pampered and pandered.

StarLaughter made herself beautiful. She sparkled, and all for WolfStar.

"He won't be able to resist me!" she said, preening before the mirror, and tugging at the heavy silk fabric she'd chosen to don.

The fact that StarLaughter had a reasonable hike before her did not deter her from donning such finery. She would manage. She had to.

StarLaughter picked up her bag, lifted her skirts, and set out on her conquest.

She had a quest, one that was right and true and good, and she was happy. WolfStar would realise his true love for her, and then, united, they could rescue their son.

DragonStar had been right, StarLaughter had finally, reluctantly, decided, when he'd said that WolfStar and those he was with (who could surely be discarded once their purpose was done) would head south rather than swing west along the Icebear Coast. WolfStar's companions would want the south's relative warmth—and StarLaughter's mouth smiled sarcastically whenever she thought about what they'd find there—rather than a continuance of the northern icy wastes.

Stars knew how they'd cope with the Skraelings in the tundra, StarLaughter thought. But they had WolfStar to aid them, and he would surely protect them.

StarLaughter's mouth relaxed into warmth as she contemplated how her magnificent lover had undoubtedly driven back the Skraelings with his powerful enchantments.

Somehow StarLaughter had managed to forget that Wolf-Star's power had been lost along with that of the Star Dance. In her mind, he was as powerful as he had always been, and in her mind, he was as anxious to resume their love affair as she was. Undoubtedly he was already dreaming of the new son they would make between them.

"Ah!" StarLaughter murmured as she carried her pack up the stairwells and corridors towards the surface. "What a life we have before us! WolfStar, me, and our son. What a happy, happy family we shall make!"

StarLaughter could no more contemplate the fact that WolfStar might *not* be particularly pleased to see her again, nor want to resume their relationship, than she could contemplate a future world without herself in it.

She was immortal, and her and WolfStar's love would last for all time.

Hadn't it thus far?

By dawn StarLaughter was picking her way over the debris of the glacier that had run between Star Finger and the Icebear coast. Despite the relative difficulty of the terrain, and the freezing wind that was hurrying south over the icebergs of the Iskruel Ocean, StarLaughter was humming happily. She did not appear to mind, or perhaps even notice, that the wind tore the fabric of her robe, or that the fine needles of ice it contained ruined her makeup. She was not apparently aware that her hair had been torn loose from its carefully contrived moorings, or that the wind had ruffled her wing feathers into chaos.

She was on her way to WolfStar, and she was contented. Nothing could go wrong.

By mid-morning, StarLaughter had reached the clearer

ground of the beach itself, and she turned due east. As she strode along the grit, unmindful of the crashing waves that sent dampening spray all over her, StarLaughter used the kernel of power that the Demons had given her to speed her progress. For every step she took, five paces of ground flew by underneath her sandalled feet.

StarLaughter did not fly, for every instinct told her that the sky was a very, very dangerous place this day.

But there were a few who were brave enough to dare the air, and StarGrace was one of them. She'd watched over Leagh all night (wondering, puzzling, frowning) as the woman had curled up against a tree stump, and she had then spent the dawn hour thinking.

Once the sun crested the ridge above the Fernbrake crater, StarGrace had lifted into the air.

She needed to talk a while with StarLaughter.

It took StarGrace several hours to find her quarry, and when she did, StarGrace had to circle a few minutes, trying to come to terms with what she saw below her.

StarLaughter, striding along the beach of the Icebear coast.

That, in itself, was not enough to pique StarGrace's curiosity. It was what StarLaughter looked like that had, for the moment, stunned the Hawkchild.

She was hideously made up with face paint (smudged and streaked since the elements played with her), as she was also hideously garbed: for whatever reason, StarLaughter had chosen a vivid yellow gown draped over with lurid pink and silver brocade. She had dyed her wings orange and red.

She looked ghastly.

StarGrace was self-aware enough to understand that her own mind spent too much of its time twisting in maddened circles and frustrating dead ends. StarGrace was also sane enough (just) to realise that StarLaughter's mind had tipped over the crumbling edge of whatever cliff it was they had all clung to these past few thousand years.

StarGrace circled lower, her face now creased in speculation.

StarLaughter heard the slight noise behind her and spun about.

"Oh!" she cried, and then laughed.

StarGrace was hobbling towards her, half-Icarii, half-Hawkchild. Her face was that of the golden girl, StarGrace, as was her left arm and leg. But the rest of her was still black Hawkchild, and she hobbled and scumbled alarmingly as she walked from foot to claw, and back again.

Twisted wings dragged on the ground behind her, useless in her current state of mal-transformation.

"Why, StarGrace!" StarLaughter cried brightly, and set a welcoming expression on her face. "What do you here?"

"Come to speak with you," StarGrace said, and made a stupendous effort to manage the final transformation from Hawkchild to young Icarii woman.

Her features ran, blurred, and then set themselves into that of the beautiful woman.

"Oh?" StarLaughter said, and clutched her hands before her, managing to look extremely guilty and extremely irritated at the same time.

"Mmmm," StarGrace said. "And what do *you* do here? Why hurrying east? Is east where WolfStar lies?"

"Well . . ." StarLaughter said, looking over her shoulder as if there might be a salvation hurrying over to meet her. "Well . . ."

StarGrace's mind twisted with distrust. StarLaughter *did* know where WolfStar was. Then why had she not called the Hawkchilds? *What was StarLaughter up to?*

"I'm up to living my own life," StarLaughter snapped, and strangely that display of ill-temper eased StarGrace's mind a little.

"Is WolfStar east?" she asked again.

"Yes," StarLaughter admitted. "There is a convoy east, escapees from this Sanctuary that DragonStar has muttered so much about."

"And WolfStar is among them!"

"Wait!" StarLaughter cried as StarGrace's features blurred once again and she made as if to lift into the air.

"Wait for what?" StarGrace said. Her features were still twisting and turning, and her voice was horribly muffled and thick.

"Well, the convoy is heavily protected! Thick enchantments!" StarLaughter had no idea of the truth she actually spoke. It was simply the first thing that sprang to mind.

"And?" StarGrace had completed her transformation back into Hawkchild, and now she hopped a pace closer to StarLaughter, her head tilted suspiciously.

"And the enchantments are too thick for us to break through. Dangerous. I," and now StarLaughter had grown enough in confidence to square her shoulders, and shake her hair out, "am endeavouring to tempt WolfStar out from his bolthole. Once he is out from under his protective enchantments, then we can do what we will."

StarGrace looked StarLaughter over once again. "And you are going to tempt WolfStar out dressed like *that?*"

"I shall need to recomb my hair and wing feathers," StarLaughter said, and then she smiled indulgently, "but he will not be able to resist me."

StarGrace thought that WolfStar would manage a resistance very easily, but she said nothing. In truth, StarGrace did not quite know what to make of the situation. Once, she and her companion Hawkchilds had felt such a oneness of purpose with StarLaughter that StarGrace could have trusted her through death and beyond. Indeed, she had done so.

Now?

Now StarGrace suspected StarLaughter's mind had gone completely insane, and StarGrace did not know what twists and conundrums it had decided to present to StarLaughter as utter reality.

StarGrace shifted uncertainly.

"When I get within a day's march of WolfStar, I shall let you know," StarLaughter said.

Still StarGrace said nothing.

"Truly," StarLaughter said, and StarGrace finally nodded.

"Make sure that you do," she said, and lifted into the air. StarGrace had trusted StarLaughter through four thousand years, and the woman had not let her down once during this time. StarGrace could surely trust her for a few more days.

StarLaughter smiled and waved as the Hawkchild soared high into the sky, circled twice, then flew south again.

She did not realise that StarGrace did not believe a word of what she'd said.

44

The Heart Incarnate

At dawn, Urbeth and her daughters reappeared. They were patently exhausted, and Axis and Azhure wondered at the exertions, both physical and magical, they must have undergone in order to draw the Demons away from the fleeing convoy, and then to escape the Demons' wrath themselves. Urbeth and her daughters looked at the avenue of trees, looked at Ur, dozing underneath a cart, the pot still wrapped in her arms, and nodded to themselves.

The three reappeared in their womanly forms, not as icebears. All three had dark circles of exhaustion under their eyes, and their skin was pallid, not with the reflection of the ice and snow, but with the strain they'd undergone.

"You need food and rest," Axis said, sharing a concerned glance with Azhure, and then offering Urbeth his arm.

For a moment it appeared Urbeth might actually accept his support, then she shook her head tiredly.

"Rest," she said. "Food can wait."

"What happened?" Azhure asked, knowing they were probably too tired to tell, but needing to know anyway.

Urbeth was too exhausted even to snap. "We drew the Demons off," she said, "and handed them into the care of the Chitter Chatters."

Axis smiled. He remembered how the box Ho'Demi had brought out of the Murkle mines had whispered disconcertingly to itself for months until the Ravensbund Chief had turned the Chitter Chatters loose in the northern icepack.

"Where are the Demons now?" said Azhure.

"I don't know," Urbeth said, and Axis and Azhure realised she was so strained she was close to tears. "I just don't know."

"Rest," Azhure said, "please."

Urbeth nodded, then turned slightly to address her two daughters. "Take the rear of the avenue."

Without a reply the two ice women turned, and melted away into the snow.

"Why send them back there?" Axis said.

"To protect it," Urbeth said. "The trees will protect the length of the avenue, but for the moment its two entrances are vulnerable. I will stand here."

Without further ado Urbeth took several steps back until she was at the border where snow turned to shaded walk, and began very slowly to turn about.

Within heartbeats she sped up until her form was spinning so fast Axis and Azhure could not discern her features, and then, in the next breath, Urbeth turned into a pillar of opaque green and grey ice that stood immobile and solid, guarding the entrance to the avenue.

Qeteb and his companions had escaped the Murkle mines only through the most extreme of efforts. The dark and damp mines had contained enchantment—did the very cursed soil still reek with enchantment?—and the Demons had found it very difficult to negate its holding effects.

Eventually, after hours of temper, they had burst through the boarded-up entrances of several of the ancient shafts, sending showers of sharp-edged rock cascading through the air, and causing a massive avalanche down three sides of the mountain from which they'd emerged.

Qeteb was furious, but calm. He had finally understood that

the forces ranged against him consisted not only of Dragon-Star and his five companions, but of the land itself.

The total and catastrophic destruction of Tencendor must wait until *every* creature, rock and speck of soil ranged against him and his had been destroyed.

And for this, Qeteb knew he needed a cool and calculating head, not a fount of fury erupting at every setback.

Thus, he held back his Demons for an hour or two of planning. They crouched on the desolate side of the mountain they'd escaped from, clinging to rocks like bunch-backed toads, letting the snow settle about their shoulders and lumpy spines. They crouched, and they whispered. They let their rage feed their whispers, but not control them. They spent some time in utter quiet, sending their senses scrying about the land; not only to verify the whereabouts of DragonStar and his five, but also to truly *sense* the land itself, *feel* its purpose, *know* its motives.

Qeteb, his senses soaring and penetrating deeper than those of his companions, felt something else.

A thing or a purpose as intimately connected to DragonStar as his five witches. No! Even more intimately connected! Who or what was this thing? And where? Where?

Qeteb knew where the five witches were—indeed, their positions was as preordained as their forthcoming battles with the Demons—but where, where the sixth mysterious and powerful presence?

Ah! A smile crawled through Qeteb's mind as his senses showed him the icy northern tundra.

And the long, snaking convoy within which was the sixth . . . and perhaps the most vital.

"There is a heart yet beating within this land," Qeteb eventually said.

He had thought he'd completely ravaged Tencendor when he'd been resurrected, but now he understood the untruth of that belief. He'd devastated its skin, but no more. Somewhere lay a great heart thumping, still pounding power through the land, frustrating the Demons at every turn.

"We must find that heart," said Qeteb, "and destroy it."

"Do you mean the four hearts of the four lakes?" said Mot.

"No."

"Then the heart of the Maze—" Barzula began.

"No! Another heart. An unknown heart. A powerful heart. A *despicable* heart!"

"Where?" asked Sheol.

Qeteb sat silent a moment, his black armoured form hunched against the weight of snow on his wings and back. The metal of his visor rippled, as if the thoughts contained within were too virulent to be contained much longer.

"The long line of hopelessness," Qeteb finally said, "that escaped from Sanctuary and currently wallows in icy misery to the north.

"In there lies the heart incarnate."

Sometime after StarLaughter had resumed her trek east, six loathsome shadows swept over the landscape.

StarLaughter reflexively crouched close to some rocks, but the Demons, flying high overhead, did not notice her—or perhaps were too preoccupied to notice her.

"There's trouble ahead," StarLaughter said, and then silently mouthed a prayer for WolfStar's safe-keeping.

DragonStar also saw the Demons soar overhead, so single-minded in their quest for destruction they did not even heed him.

He, too, crouched, then stared, and then leaped lightly down from his rocks atop the rubble of Star Finger to where his Star Stallion waited in a ravine below.

The Alaunt milled about the stallion's legs, whining with their eagerness for the hunt.

As DragonStar walked up to the horse and hounds, his garb

slipped away, and he strode once more in the linen kincloth with the lily sword swinging from the jewelled belt.

"There's trouble ahead," he said, and vaulted on the Star Stallion's back.

Within the instant both horse and Alaunt were running north-east.

45

Trouble

Beyond the trees and the still ice forms of Urbeth and her daughters in their respective positions at either end of the avenue, the northern tundra was wrapped in an ice-gale so vicious that even the odd Skraeling, escaped from Ur's trap preferred to huddle in their burrows than drift out to search for prey.

Axis spent most of the morning making sure that people and animals were settled comfortably—perhaps on the morrow they might begin their move south—and trying to avoid StarDrifter, who sat like a brooding storm on one of the carts near the head of the convoy.

Neither StarDrifter, nor Axis or Azhure, could quite come to terms with, let alone *believe,* the choice Zenith had made.

Axis blamed Fate, Azhure blamed herself and StarDrifter blamed WolfStar.

Axis had sent word to WingRidge to move WolfStar to the very rear of the convoy, far enough that he and StarDrifter might not meet accidentally.

Axis was also truthful enough with himself to understand that he did not want to see WolfStar either, nor Zenith with WolfStar.

Perhaps he could speak to her later . . . but for the meantime there was far too much to do.

Urbeth's twin daughters dreamed the morning away in their pillars of ice, recovering strength after their efforts at leading the Demons into the souls of the Chitter Chatters. As had Urbeth at the front of the convoy, they'd placed themselves at its very rear, standing in the open space between the last trees on either side of the avenue, at the border between the rage of the snowstorm and the peaceful warmth of the avenue.

They seemed completely inviolate, twin pillars of unapproachable ice, but they were not quite alone.

Protected by the warmth of the trees, SpikeFeather TrueSong sat some paces away from them, cross-legged and winged, his head resting in one hand, red hair and feathers flaming incongruously before the ice, his eyes resting curiously on Urbeth's daughters.

Truth to tell, SpikeFeather had been feeling more than slightly obsolete in the past few weeks. He'd been the one to correctly guess the location of Sanctuary, but it had been others who'd opened it, and then led Tencendor's populations through its doors. DragonStar and his five witches had garnered all the attention and glory in their quest to destroy the Demons. SpikeFeather was not feeling jealous, merely horribly useless. He'd always hovered about the edges of the action, through the wars with Gorgrael, and now with these Demons, bursting with potential but never quite achieving it. Why had Orr taken charge of his life and why spend so many years talking to him and showing him the Underworld?

Why?

In Sanctuary, SpikeFeather had spent much of his time with Adamon and his wife, Xanon, and the other Star Gods. He'd wanted to see if, somehow, they might give him a direction, even a clue, but he'd learned nothing from them. Without exception (and apart from Axis and Azhure), the once-gods were colourless and apathetic, unable to come to terms with the destruction of Tencendor and with their exile—as mere mortals!—in Sanctuary.

They'd been kind, and patient, but SpikeFeather had

learned nothing of himself from them. And now, they'd disappeared, undoubtedly off on their own well-intentioned purpose, but that did not help SpikeFeather in his current despair.

"Gods!" SpikeFeather muttered, with no rancour, only desperate wishing. "What *is* my purpose? What am I to do?"

If only Orr hadn't died so precipitously in the chamber of the Star Gate. Perhaps if he sought out DragonStar . . .

But SpikeFeather sighed, and let his eyes linger on the immobile ice pillars before him. Urbeth's daughters apparently knew exactly who *they* were and what was expected of them.

Meanwhile, here he sat, not knowing what to do or how to help.

Suddenly, both pillars melted back into the forms of women, and they stared into the storm that raged beyond the avenue.

One of them hissed, and she swung around, stopping with a jerk as she saw SpikeFeather.

"You!" she cried.

Axis was startled out of his conversation with the Ravensbund chief, Sa'Domai, by a shout from the head of the convoy.

He leaped onto Sal's back and galloped forward to find Urbeth transforming back into her womanly self, and DragonStar—DragonStar!—emerging from the storm on his white stallion, the Alaunt milling at Belaguez's feet.

The expression on DragonStar's face said it all.

"Trouble," Axis stated.

"Oh, aye," DragonStar said, and halted Belaguez by Sal. His eyes widened very slightly at the sight of Axis' brown mare, but he made no remark about her.

Not when disaster threatened.

"The Demons are not far behind me," DragonStar said. He looked in wonder at the avenue of trees, then looked in query at Urbeth.

Ur, she told him in the mind voice, her thoughts carrying more images than spoken words. *Skraelings. Souls of trees. An army.*

DragonStar nodded, accepting. "Urbeth, can you hold here for the moment? I must—"

"Yes. Go."

DragonStar nodded, then reached across and let his hand rest momentarily on Axis' arm. "I must see to Azhure's and Katie's safety," he said.

"How can we fight against the Demons?" Axis said, grabbing at DragonStar's own arm as his son pulled back.

Again DragonStar glanced at Urbeth. "Support Urbeth and her daughters, and support the trees," he said. "Even I can do no more."

Axis nodded, and let him go.

DragonStar rode Belaguez deep into the column until he found Azhure, Katie and StarDrifter. They were standing by a collection of Ravensbund tents, and looked up in stunned surprise as DragonStar rode up.

For the moment DragonStar ignored Azhure and StarDrifter, sliding off Belaguez's back to lift Katie into his arms.

She smiled and snuggled in close to him.

The Demons are about to attack.

I know, DragonStar.

You must stay safe.

At that Katie smiled bitterly. *For the moment.*

DragonStar's arms tightened about her, and he could not help the sudden dampness in his eyes. *You have a way to travel before you, my girl. This is not the place.*

DragonStar felt her nod, and he let her down.

"Azhure?" he said. "Katie must be protected at all costs. Whatever happens, whoever else dies in this attack, Katie *must be protected.*"

Azhure did not speak, merely wrapping her own arms about Katie and nodding, her eyes determined.

"The Ravensbund will prove as good a guard as any," DragonStar said. "Stay inside their tents, away from what prying eyes might penetrate these trees."

Again Azhure nodded, then she leaned forward, briefly kissed DragonStar's cheek, and ducked inside one of the tents, Katie still locked in her arms.

Several Ravensbund warriors quietly surrounded the tent, and DragonStar spoke softly to them.

Then he turned to go, but was halted by StarDrifter.

"I know this is not the time," StarDrifter said hurriedly, "but Zenith is in danger."

DragonStar sent a rushed glance back towards the head of the convoy, but let StarDrifter hold him back.

"Danger?"

StarDrifter took a deep breath, and DragonStar was horrified to see the emotion in his grandfather's eyes. "WolfStar has her," he said.

DragonStar opened his mouth, but for the moment could not answer.

"WolfStar has captured Zenith's soul," StarDrifter hurried on. "Stolen her will! Dammit, DragonStar! WolfStar has convinced Zenith that she has no future apart from him!"

"But . . . how . . ." DragonStar said.

StarDrifter threw up his hands in despair. "DragonStar, if you have the time . . . help her, please . . ."

"I'll—" DragonStar began, then got no further, for the sounds of a frightful battle crashed down through the trees.

That the helpless millions who'd escaped Sanctuary had somehow found a source of enchantment to protect them had not surprised Qeteb.

After all, the heart still beat.

As he and his approached the column from high overhead, they'd observed the tens of thousands of trees lining and protecting the people and animals inside.

"Enchantment," Sheol had murmured, and Qeteb was pleased to hear no anger or amazement in her voice.

"I smell that old woman about this," Qeteb had said, and the others had silently agreed with him.

Below, the trees waved their branches, lifting leaved tentacles high into the sky as if to grab the Demons down into their twigged depths.

None of the Demons needed to be told that that might be somewhat inadvisable.

"When DragonStar is dead," Qeteb said, "the trees will become useless. I can wait."

"And so . . . ?" Raspu said. All of the Demons circled some hundred paces above the highest of the tentacles waving above the avenue, Qeteb very slightly above the others.

They had now assumed different forms: wingless, although they managed to remain aloft easily.

Muscled forms, and garbed in heavy checked-cloth jackets with thick leather belts and trousers.

All, save Sheol and Roxiah, sported thick heads of hair and beards, and even the two female Demons had their femininity almost completely hidden behind their outward facade of resolute determination and muscled strength.

The Demons had taken on the forms of woodsmen, and in their hands they gripped shiny metal axes.

They might not mean to battle the trees here and now, but they did mean to give them a scare. And there were three other targets in mind.

Whittle down DragonStar's support one by one, Qeteb whispered through their minds. *First . . .*

First the three who taunted and then trapped us, said Sheol.

Oh yes, Qeteb agreed. *First those three . . .*

But his mind was wandering elsewhere. He could sense DragonStar down there, and, more, he could sense that there was the sixth—*a child! a girl!*—that he wanted to protect.

Qeteb smiled. The sixth was a girl. A child!

Knowledge was power, and power was victory.

Urbeth and her daughters had regained some strength during their few hours of rest, but they were still abysmally tired. In particular, Urbeth had seriously depleted her strength, first by creating the rip in Sanctuary that had enabled the peoples and animals hidden there to escape and, second, leading her daughters in the mad dash to draw the Demons away from the still vulnerable convoy.

Now, all three found themselves attacked by murderously calm and determined Demons who had split into two groups to target both ends of the avenue.

At the front of the avenue, Urbeth turned in the snow to find two woodsmen walking towards her.

Both had grins splitting their faces, both had axes raised.

Urbeth growled, and tried to transform into her bear persona, but found her power so seriously exhausted that she could not manage it.

Yet she had to defend her end of the avenue, for otherwise the Demons could walk right in!

Behind her people scrambled further back into the avenue, terrified by the sense of evil emanating from the two strutting woodsmen, Qeteb and Barzula.

They were within five paces of Urbeth.

"Go back," she said, and drew herself up straight and imperious. On her finger the Circle of Stars flared . . . and then died.

One of the woodsmen laughed, and Urbeth knew it was Qeteb.

"You are a sorry bitch," he said in an amiable tone, "to stand guard at the head of this pitiful column. Why don't you run, pretty rabbit? Why don't you run?"

And he laughed again, low and nasty. He and Barzula took three small, rapid steps forward, and they now swung their axes back and forth in sweeping, whistling arcs.

There was a slight movement behind Urbeth.

"I am with you," Axis said, and Urbeth heard the hoof-fall of his brown mare.

"Go back," she said, without turning to look at him, "for you can do nothing."

"I can support you," Axis said. "I can do my best."

Qeteb laughed again, and, in concert with Barzula, swung his axe faster and faster.

The metal blades screamed through the air, and the two Demons strode into the attack behind the murderous blades of their axes.

"Watch out!" SpikeFeather screamed at the rear of the avenue, and the two women whipped back to face the four Demon-woodsmen who now strode towards them from out of the storm.

As one, the four wore incongruously cheerful, smiling faces, even while their hands wove their axes through the air.

Both the ice women crouched, their hands extended as if claws, but as their mother was weak, so were they, and they could not transform into their deadly bear forms.

The four Demons advanced in a semicircle, now laughing openly, the tempo of their axes increasing with the strength of their merriment.

The rabbits were trapped.

Urbeth raised her hand, and the Circle of Stars finally flared into life, transforming itself into a rod of thin, shimmery metal.

She flung it before her just as an axe sliced through the air. The blade screeched along the surface of the rod, finally sliding off in a shower of sparks.

Axis unsheathed his sword, wishing he had his axe of old, and wishing he had a trusted warhorse under him when . . .

. . . *when suddenly he was clothed again in the familiar black, and the sword had transformed itself into his battleaxe, and the horse beneath him, while not Belaguez, showed the same heart and courage in leaping forth into the fray* . . .

Pretty Brown Sal was angry. She was bred as a dancer and a slider, not a fighter, but her light-footedness and litheness served her as well in battle as it did on the dance field, and her anger turned her dainty pirouettes into battle manoeuvres.

The two Demons had forced Urbeth to one knee, their axes striking ever harder against the metal rod, notching and bending it, when suddenly both were hit from behind—one by a mighty axe blow to his head, the other by two-steel-edged hooves crashing down about his shoulders.

Axis laughed, and swung again, delighting in the feel both of Pretty Brown Sal and the axe in his own hand.

Qeteb and Barzula swung about, irritated more than angry, and not hurt—this man and horse had no weapons or magic which could harm them—and simultaneously swung their axes, one aiming to cut the mare's dainty legs out from under her, the other aiming to bury his axe in the rider's side.

Both missed.

Sal had skittered *(slid)* lightly to one side while Axis had merely laughed—*gods, how good it felt to be in the heat of battle again!*—and twisted away from the blade.

Qeteb and Barzula stumbled and almost fell with the momentum of their missed swings, then regained their balance. They growled, their beards bristling out to three times their previous length and thickness, and swung their axes once more.

Pretty Brown Sal and Axis slid lightly out of the way.

Barzula screamed and lunged, using his axe as a pike now, rather than as a weapon to swing through the air.

Sal and Axis evaded effortlessly, moving through the snow as its lover, rather than its foe.

Qeteb and Barzula turned to horse and rider; enough was enough, and while axes were pretty, the sheer destructiveness of their power would be enough to dispose of this—

Both screamed as fingers of ice wormed their way into the napes of their necks, and then into their very spines.

Urbeth: her arms were ice from the elbows down. Her fingers had turned into razor-sharp needles, prying and worrying themselves into the Demons' flesh, slicing through bone and arteries—

Both Demons tore themselves off her claws, and swung about to face her.

Instead, their eyes were riveted on the man sitting the Star Stallion three paces behind the ice woman.

———

"Aaargh!" SpikeFeather screamed, waving his arms and leaping and twisting about like a maniac. "Aaargh!"

All four Demons hesitated, their eyes slipping from the prey before them to the birdman capering and screaming just to one side of the two women.

"Aaargh!" SpikeFeather screamed again, and dashed madly, foolishly, and utterly desperately at the Demons.

All four raised axes that had momentarily drooped in surprise, and simultaneously swung them at SpikeFeather, who was dashing straight towards the centre of their line.

In that instant before the blades sank home, SpikeFeather dropped flat to the ground, and there was a soft "Ugh!" of surprise as the middle two Demons buried their axes in each other rather than in the birdman.

The other two Demons stumbled and fell, as Qeteb and Barzula had, pulled to the ground by the targetless momentum of their axe swings.

The two wounded Demons wrenched their axes out of each other, cursing softly even as their flesh smoothly mended itself, and raised their axes to do SpikeFeather to death when suddenly they found their forms bristling with spears and pikes.

Behind Urbeth's daughters stood a line of some three score Ravensbund warriors, already aiming their next phalanx of spears at the Demons.

SpikeFeather reached up, hardly able to breathe through the force of his terror, yet still committed to action, and grabbed one of the spears, twisting and wrenching it until the Demon toppled onto him.

SpikeFeather found himself in an inferno of hatred and vengeance. Fires and teeth lapped and gnashed at his arms wrapped protectively about his head, and he could feel talons slicing down deep into his belly and upper thighs. He screamed, knowing death was only a breath away, when—

—when suddenly the Demon rolled off him and he saw instead the hand of one of Urbeth's daughters reaching down, her face hovering behind it: beautiful, distant, and utterly, utterly lovely.

SpikeFeather could hear the Demons screaming somewhere in the distance, but for him his entire world consisted of that hand, now touching his, and the almost disembodied face floating behind it.

He blinked, took her hand—

—and found himself standing to one side of what he could only describe as a desperate scrum in the snow. Arms and legs and heads appeared and then disappeared, axes flew, blood spattered about, and howls of rage and frustration wrapped the entire fracas.

SpikeFeather looked about, desperate to find someone to help him in aiding Urbeth's daughters.

And saw them, standing slightly to one side, their arms folded, their faces smug.

SpikeFeather, one said in his mind, *we have thrown our shadows in for the Demons to chase.*

What will happen, he said, astounded to find himself able to reply in the same manner, *when they realise the trick?*

Both ice women shrugged, and their smiles deepened, but they did not reply.

SpikeFeather turned back to the fray, and then stumbled several steps towards the safety of the avenue.

The Ravensbund were still there, lined up with spears at the ready.

"Hello, Qeteb, Barzula," DragonStar said, and he nodded behind them. "I believe you have met my father?"

Qeteb hefted his axe.

"No," DragonStar said, and his voice darkened and became heavier. "No. You cannot hurt what is protected by these trees."

"Not until you are dead," Qeteb said.

"Quite," DragonStar agreed. "*If* you can kill me."

Qeteb's eyes slid towards Urbeth. She had somehow grown stronger in the last few minutes, and now she stood straight and tall; her eyes hard, her figure implacable.

Her hands, so recently ice, now turned into the furred claws of the ice bear.

Suddenly Urbeth's mouth opened in a vicious snarl, and she completed the transformation and crouched to spring.

"The war is between you and me," DragonStar said, "and between yours and mine."

"Ah, DragonStar," Qeteb said, his voice even now. He, as Urbeth had, raised himself to his full height and assumed his true form of black, invulnerable armour. "You cannot begrudge me a pre-dinner nibble or two, can you?"

DragonStar shrugged. "Your nibble has done you no good. What matters is the Hunt through the Maze. That is what you and I both know."

The Dream grabbed both of them. They were hunting through a Maze of stars, dipping and swaying with the interstellar Star Dance.

All existence held its breath, awaiting the outcome.

DragonStar urged his Star Stallion forward, the Alaunt streaming out to his flanks like the twin tails of a comet, but, despite their speed and power, the great dark beast behind him was gaining, and DragonStar could sense the weapon Qeteb lifted above his shoulder.

Qeteb took a step forward, and half raised the axe he still held.

The Dream shifted slightly, and DragonStar knew that Qeteb was as much in control of the Dream as he was in control of the Hunt.

"*The weapon I wield,*" Qeteb screamed through the universe, "*is not of metal or even of power. It is the weapon I will fashion from your weakness! See! See!*"

And, despite himself, DragonStar turned to see what it was that Qeteb wielded.

Faraday—or what was left of her.

DragonStar felt a cry tear itself from his breast, and the Star Stallion faltered, and the Alaunt milled in confusion, and the next instant Qeteb was upon him.

As Qeteb moved forward, Axis shifted to urge Sal forward as well, but DragonStar shook his head almost imperceptibly, and Axis stilled.

"Neither of us can escape what has been foreordained,"

DragonStar said, and none failed to note that his voice trembled slightly.

Everyone watching could feel the amusement radiating out from Qeteb.

"No," he said, "we can't. But since I have given your witches such a good head start, I thought it only fair that I amuse myself with this convoy in the meantime. Fair's fair, after all."

The sense of amusement—almost joy—radiating out from Qeteb increased tenfold until both Axis and Urbeth were forced to back away several steps.

"And I find," the Demon continued, "that I have enjoyed myself so much I may well be back for another nibble."

Qeteb hefted the axe, then hurled it into the ground before the Star Stallion.

Belaguez's ears flickered, and his eyes rolled slightly, but he did not flinch.

"Don't bother," DragonStar said. "This column is invulnerable."

His only reply was laughter, and DragonStar flinched at its virulence.

Qeteb's laughter slowly subsided, then, with a final chuckle, he lifted into the air, and was gone within heartbeats, Barzula behind him.

Axis lowered his head from watching the Demons fly away towards the other end of the avenue and looked at his son.

"Tell me you *can* defeat him," he said. *"Tell me . . ."*

46

South

Qeteb strode into the still squabbling fracas of four Demons and tore them apart.

He was in a high good humour—surely he had forced DragonStar's hand to the point where the starry idiot would try and move the sixth elsewhere . . . an elsewhere that might be more vulnerable than the column—and thus he did the four no permanent injury. The abrasions and tears he did cause healed themselves within the moment.

SpikeFeather, as Urbeth's two daughters and the Ravensbund warriors, straightened in alarm—SpikeFeather moving even closer to the two women—but Qeteb laughed and waved a dismissive hand.

"Enjoy your victory while you can," he said, "for your eventual defeat is but a week or so away."

And then all six Demons vanished.

Qeteb rose so far into the sky that he was invisible from the ground.

Then he rose higher still, until even enchantment could not touch him.

Then, so high he had risen into the blackness between air and space, he rolled over onto his back. He closed his eyes, summoned all his power and concentration, and sent a tiny but potent shaft of his perception shooting down towards the column.

"Reveal yourself, mine Enemy," Qeteb whispered. "Reveal yourself!"

DragonStar dropped his head and rubbed his eyes. Before him Axis and Azhure, Katie, StarDrifter and Zared and Theod sat in a concerned circle.

"What will happen, DragonStar?" Axis asked for them all.

"Qeteb's five companions will each confront my five witches. Individual jousts, if you will."

Zared and Theod, even though they had known of this, still shook their heads in a combination of concern for their wives and anger that DragonStar had put them in this frightful predicament.

"And will they win?"

DragonStar looked up and met Axis' eyes. "I hope so," he said.

"Hope is not—"

"It is all I have!" DragonStar said harshly, and Axis nodded.

"Very well." Axis paused. "What will happen if all or any of them fail?"

DragonStar took his time replying. "If one fails then it means that I will be seriously weakened. Any more than that and I may fail—"

"Gods!" Zared exploded, "I care not for you and *your* 'may fail'! I care only for my *wife!* As Theod cares only for his wife! What happens if our wives fail?"

"If any of the witches fail, then they will ultimately die," DragonStar said, turning his steady gaze from Axis to Zared.

"Ah!" Zared said, and half turned away, still furiously angry.

"There is nothing you can do for the moment," DragonStar said, reverting his gaze to his parents, "but move south."

"And there . . . ?" Axis said.

"Clear as much of the land of the crazed creatures that cover it as you can," DragonStar said. "Most of the creatures will be below the Nordra, moving towards or in the Maze, or gathered about the other three lakes. Journey south via the Lake of Life and Fernbrake."

Zared turned back to DragonStar. "Thank you," he said softly.

DragonStar shrugged slightly. "Gwendlyr's and Leagh's battles will have been fought and won or lost by the time you reach them," he said, "but at the least, you will know."

He looked back to Axis. "Take this . . . this convoy south— peoples, creatures, trees—and meet me at the Maze . . . what was once Grail Lake."

"And there?" Axis said.

"And there will the final battle be played out," DragonStar said, "and we move on or we flicker out of existence forever. There, the fate of the stars themselves will be decided. Whatever, you . . . everyone, will need to be present and to witness."

DragonStar looked back down the column, then spoke to Theod. "Will you go and find SpikeFeather for me? Tell him I need him urgently."

Theod nodded, and left.

"Why SpikeFeather?" Axis said.

DragonStar hesitated before he spoke. "I need to get Katie away from this column," he finally said. "To take her to somewhere as safe as possible."

What if Qeteb did come back for a nibble? What if he found Katie?

Azhure nodded understanding. "The waterways."

"Yes. Azhure . . ."

"I will go with Katie," she said, taking Katie's hand. "I promised Faraday I would look after her."

"But—" Axis began.

"We will be safe," Azhure said, and smiled reassuringly at her husband. "What could happen to us in the waterways?"

Far, far above in the higher atmosphere, Qeteb smiled, and drew his perception back into his body.

This girl, this tiny girl, this Katie. She was the one that DragonStar fretted about and sought to protect.

She was the key, the heart incarnate.

And now DragonStar, as Qeteb had hoped, was going to move her somewhere he thought safe.

"What can happen in the waterways?" Qeteb murmured to himself as he began the long descent. "What, indeed!"

He rejoined his companions.

"It is your time," Qeteb said. "Go."

And the five scattered in the winds above the wasteland, their hearts capering with joy.

"Why did you dive screaming for the Demons?" one of the ice women asked SpikeFeather.

The birdman was seated with Urbeth's two daughters about a small fire to one side of the Ravensbund warriors' larger camp. Both ice women sat close to him, and the one who spoke rested her hand on his knee.

SpikeFeather supposed he should feel uncomfortable, but in truth he rather enjoyed the closeness.

"It was all I could think of doing," he said. "You were both so . . ."

He wasn't sure if it would be the best idea to mention how tired they were; if SpikeFeather had learned one thing over the past few decades of dealing almost daily with highly magical people, it was that they tended to be sensitive about any implied criticism, however slight.

The other ice woman shrugged. "My sister and I were exhausted, as was our mother."

"You brought us a pause," her sister continued, and her hand tightened very slightly on SpikeFeather's leg, "during which we could regain composure—"

"—and some measure of thought," her sister finished for her, and she lifted her face and smiled at SpikeFeather.

He grinned, and relaxed.

"Tell us about the Underworld," one of the ice women said, and SpikeFeather wondered if he would remember to ask after their names at some point.

"We have always wondered about the Underworld," her sister said, and leaned so close that her breath played over SpikeFeather's cheek.

He suddenly became aware of how attractive, and compelling, if not precisely beautiful, the two were.

"The Underworld seems to us to be so much like our beloved icepack," the other said. "As full of dangers, as full of twists and conundrums."

"Tell us . . ."

"Please, tell us . . ."

And SpikeFeather found himself telling, and revelling in the closeness and warmth and loveliness of these two enchanted creatures.

So absorbed was he, he did not notice Theod's approach.

"SpikeFeather?"

SpikeFeather jumped, startled, and the ice sisters' hands tightened on his arms.

"SpikeFeather, DragonStar needs to see you."

He finally had something to do? SpikeFeather jumped to his feet, the ice sisters with him.

"I can smell an adventure!" one of them said.

DragonStar dropped down beside Zenith and WolfStar, and took the plate of food that Zenith handed him.

"I am not surprised to find you visit us," WolfStar said around a mouthful of food. "It feels that half this convoy has individually appeared and pleaded with Zenith to come to her senses and return home to her mother and father like a good girl."

His eyes watched DragonStar carefully as he wondered how it was he could use Zenith to control this man. Perhaps he would wait until the man disposed of the Demons, and control of Tencendor would be there for the taking. Perhaps . . . Ah! WolfStar let the problem slide from his mind for the moment. The *how* would come to him eventually, and WolfStar did not mind the wait. The mere fact that DragonStar was here showed the depth of his feeling for his sister . . . and revealed the extent of his vulnerability. Zenith could be used, WolfStar had no doubt of that at all, and power would eventually be his for the taking.

DragonStar looked at Zenith, and found that she met his eyes cleanly and honestly.

He sighed, and fiddled about with his food. "You can understand that most people find your, ah, union to be somewhat surprising," he said. "Perhaps even unexpected."

WolfStar laughed softly. "Oh, aye, and I imagine that StarDrifter heads the brigade of the righteously indignant," he began, but stopped when Zenith put a hand on his arm.

"Don't belittle StarDrifter," she said. "I have loved and do love him, and will not sit here and listen to you ridicule him."

WolfStar's face tightened, and he averted his gaze.

"Zenith," DragonStar said, "you mean a great deal to me.

When everyone else in Tencendor turned their backs on me," and DragonStar shot a hard glare at WolfStar, "you believed in me, and aided me, even through your own distress."

Another glare WolfStar's way.

"If you now tell me," DragonStar continued to his sister, "that you love—no, I do not want to hear that . . . if you can look me in the eye and tell me truly that this is a course you have chosen of your own free will, and that you stay at Wolf-Star's side through your own choice, and with no coercion on his part, and that this is what you *want,* then I will walk away and make no attempt to dissuade you."

Zenith looked him in the eye, and her gaze did not falter. "I am here of my own free will and of my own choice, Dragon-Star," she said, "and I would that you respected that."

DragonStar stared at her, searching into her soul, and then he sighed again, dropped his eyes, and nodded.

"Then there is only one more thing I must say," he said.

"Yes?" WolfStar said, and DragonStar raised his eyes and looked at him.

"StarLaughter is on her way," he said, "and gods alone knows what she will do when she finds you—"

DragonStar's eyes shifted slightly, "—with Zenith."

47

The Door

The Lake of Life had once been a beautiful body of water nestled within the protective Urqhart Hills and the bridge's hazy blue mists. Now it was an undulating smear of disgusting sludge and stench, pustules rising, ripening and then bursting in slow, horrid abandon across its entire surface.

Occasionally body parts of indeterminate species would rise to the surface, sometimes to slowly sink again, other times to be snatched out of the sludge by loathsome flying creatures that had once been birds but now . . . but which now were something *else*.

This was pestilence, and it was to this that Pestilence came home.

Raspu danced in glee on the side of the spreading sludge. This was *his* creation, and this was where he felt at home. His naked body mirrored the surface of the lake: sores and running blisters besmirched his skin, and his hands occasionally scrabbled thoughtlessly (but nevertheless mirthfully) at the spreading rashes that scabbed across joints and face.

Raspu fell to his hands and knees and drank of the loathsome lake.

His skin roiled as the sludge slid down his throat.

Raspu tipped back his head and laughed. Nothing could outmanoeuvre *him*!

Two figures sat their mounts atop adjoining hilltops.

On one, Qeteb sat fully armoured and arrayed in spiked and bladed weaponry on his black beast. The creature was mostly snake now, its massive body coiled beneath the Demon, resting on six muscled legs and balancing by the four small wings that sprouted from behind its horse-like skull. Qeteb gazed down on the scene below him, and smiled.

Millions of creatures clustered about the shores of the lake, parting only when Raspu began to move slowly towards the line of hills where the witch Gwendylyr had made her stand. The creatures howled and screeched, now grovelling on the ground when Raspu passed, or when they thought their Great Master might look down on them from his hilltop.

Their blackened mass spread from the shores of the lake, past the pile of rubble that had once been Sigholt, and up a gully which Qeteb supposed led to Gwendylyr.

At the head of the mass several Wing of the Strike Force— and Qeteb thought they looked very pretty with their ethereal bodies and sparkling jewel-like wings—kept back the worst of the tide, but Qeteb could also see that within hours of Gwendylyr failing, as fail she must, the pretty flying creatures would be overwhelmed.

Qeteb laughed, and turned his head so he could see his opponent on the adjoining hilltop.

There DragonStar sat the Star Stallion, the Alaunt crouched about the stallion's hooves, baying and growling at the Demon who laughed at them.

"A wager, StarSon?" Qeteb called, but DragonStar ignored him.

He felt sick to the stomach. This would be the first test, the first confrontation.

Strangely enough, although of all the five witches Gwendylyr was the most unversed in matters of power, DragonStar had the most confidence in her. But this meant, conversely, that if Gwendylyr failed, then it was unlikely that any of the others would succeed.

DragonStar concentrated on the sight of Raspu moving through the crowd of demented creatures.

"What is the trap, StarSon?" Qeteb called. "What will the poor girl try to frighten the Demon of Pestilence with?"

A choice, thought DragonStar, but this is not what he told Qeteb.

He raised his head, and smiled sweetly, and he called across the gully between them: "She will offer him the position of butler, Qeteb. How will he manage a household of fractious servants, do you think?"

Qeteb stared at DragonStar, then looked for Raspu.

He had vanished.

One moment he had been passing through the ranks of the adoring, slavering creatures, the Strike Force soaring and dipping prettily—and mostly uselessly—overhead, and the next he stood alone before the door of a great house.

Raspu blinked, and scratched absently at a particularly virulent pustule that had just appeared on his left cheek.

He looked up, and then around, very carefully.

A great moor stretched out to either side and behind him. It was a featureless sweep of fog- and cloud-wrapped rolling hills, its only adornment low gorse bushes and struggling, spiky grass.

A wall of sleet was moving in from the south-west.

Raspu grunted. He would not let the distraction of such beauty affect his concentration.

He returned his stare before him. The door was very ordinary, set in a featureless wall of grey stone that stretched as high and wide as the Demon could see. The door itself was some five paces high and two wide, fitted into a great arch with a tree carved into the door frame and a man and a woman similarly carved on either side of the door; the woman was holding an apple.

Curved iron hinges—slightly rusted in this atmosphere—supported the considerable weight of the door. An iron knocker, in the shape of an imp's head with glowing red eyes, was centred on the wood.

Raspu stared at the door.

He waited.

The shower of sleet moved closer.

Raspu waited.

A gust of cold air struck him squarely in his naked back, and Raspu shifted impatiently.

"Ahem," he said.

Nothing happened.

Raspu's eyes narrowed in furious concentration. He threw all his power at the door.

It trembled, but did not budge.

Raspu screamed with impatience. "Let me in!"

The door remained quiet, and Raspu's face tightened, malformed, then relaxed.

He sighed, leaned forward, and banged the doorknocker several times.

Instantly, the door swung open, and there stood Gwendylyr. She was dressed in a stiff black gown, tightly buttoned from its high neckline down the whale-boned bodice to the starched and snowy apron tied firmly about her waist. Sensible brown polished boots peeked out from beneath the perfectly straight hem of the dress.

Gwendylyr's hair was pulled back into a severe bun, and her face was scrubbed and earnest.

Not a hair was out of place.

"Thank goodness you've come!" Gwendylyr exclaimed, and, reaching forward, hauled Raspu inside.

The door slammed shut.

48

Gwendylyr's Problem

"**I** have *such* a problem," Gwendylyr said to the Demon, hurrying him through the mansion's foyer.

Raspu was so nonplussed he still could not speak, nor resist Gwendylyr's efficient bustling.

"It's the staff," Gwendylyr continued, moving Raspu towards an inconspicuous green baize door set behind the sweeping grand staircase. "I don't know *what* to do with them. That's why I'm so glad you're here!"

Raspu opened his mouth, but couldn't think what to say. This was not quite what he'd expected.

A flash of lightning, a clap of thunder and a clash of powers yes, but not . . . not . . . not *this*.

"My last butler couldn't cope," Gwendylyr said. "And, to be frank, I don't really blame him. The help are simply frightful."

"I don't know what this is all—"

Gwendylyr threw open the green baize door, and propelled Raspu through with a none-too-gentle shove in the small of his back.

She did not appear to notice the slime of his encrustations left on the palm of her hand.

Beyond the door was a long narrow stone corridor, all functionality and no beauty. Small doors opened off at infrequent intervals along its length.

Gwendylyr gave Raspu no respite, nor time for questions.

"The linen closet," she said as they passed a half-open door on their right, and she pulled Raspu to a brief halt.

Caught in Gwendylyr's efficiency, Raspu pushed the door fully open and looked in.

The closet was a mess. Sheets and pillowcases tumbled uncaring from shelves and drifted in creased and grey rivers across the flagged floor.

There was a small dog curled in a nest of scratched and tangled blankets in a far corner. It had left a foul-smelling mess on a pile of flannels.

"Do you see what I mean?" Gwendylyr said. "Give them an hour to their own devices . . ."

"I don't understand what is happening," Raspu said, loathing the uncertainty in his voice.

"My dear man," Gwendylyr said, her voice husky with solicitousness, "you are here to set all this to rights."

She smiled, and Raspu took half a step backwards.

"If you can," she continued. "If," her smile broadened and became almost predatory, "you make the right choices.

"Now, here," Gwendylyr pulled Raspu down to the next door and kicked it open with her foot, "is the butler's closet."

Like the linen closet, the butler's closet was lined with shelves. And, as in the linen closet, the contents of the shelves—dusters, cans of boot polish, candles, flints, sewing threads and bobbins, flea powder for dogs, bundles of sharpened pencils, yellowed stationary, blocks of starch, bottles of ink, smelling salts, emetic salts, several years supply of old newspapers and enough wads of tobacco to keep an entire army unit happy for over a month—had spilled beyond their allocated space and spread across the floor.

"You'll have to fix it," Gwendylyr said. "No way around it."

"But—"

"I just can't *believe* how the staff have let things run down!" Gwendylyr reached behind the door of the closet and, in a motion so swift and magical Raspu could not follow it, whipped a butler's uniform from a hook. With a cracking flap and a cloud of dust she clothed Raspu in his new attire.

"There!" Gwendylyr said, tweaking straight the heavy

woollen vest and pulling out the wrinkles in Raspu's coattails. "At last you look the part."

Raspu blinked, wondering what had happened. This was all rather overwhelming.

"You *must* keep your tie straight!" Gwendylyr muttered, tugging at the offending article. "Else how will you maintain respect?"

Raspu roared, the sound frightful in the confines of the butler's pantry, and seized Gwendylyr by the shoulders.

"I will not put up with this any longer!"

"Excellent!" Gwendylyr cried. *"That's* the ticket! I knew I'd done the right thing in asking you to set things to rights!"

And before Raspu could do anything else—tear her apart, burn down the building, cause havoc, terror and pestilence— Gwendylyr had propelled him out the door and down the corridor towards a plank door (painted a depressing shade of brown) with a small, round, brass doorknob.

She pulled the Demon to a halt before the door and looked at him sternly.

Raspu shifted from foot to foot, grimacing at the tight leather shoes encasing his feet.

His hands, clad in fawn (although now somewhat stained) cotton gloves, flexed at his sides.

"Behind that door," Gwendylyr said, "await the staff."

She managed a genteel shudder as she momentarily closed her eyes.

"And," Gwendylyr opened her eyes, "beyond that door lies a choice."

Raspu hissed. "The test! The challenge!"

Gwendylyr grinned, and Raspu did not like the expression behind her eyes very much at all.

"Yes. The test. This will not be a battle of magics or swords, Demon, but a far more desperate battle. A man who cannot govern his household cannot be trusted to govern himself. Thus your challenge. Beyond that door lies a household in desperate need of a firm hand. Impose order and control over the household, impose your undisputed rule, and you will win the challenge by demonstrating your right to rule yourself—your right to self-determination. If you cannot govern the household, you will fail, and will—"

Raspu snarled, already triumphant. *This* a challenge? Ha! "No need to explain the consequences of failure, woman, because *I will not fail!*"

"Fabulous! Just the man I needed!"

Raspu's face twitched and he took a deep breath, controlling his urge to decapitate her here and now. Later. There would be time later.

"I am the Demon of Pestilence," he finally said. "I can decimate populations, inflict plagues across continents, cause life itself to become nothing but a never-ending scourge. Think you that I can't manage a bunch of twaddle-headed maidservants?"

He straightened, lifted his chin, pulled down the cuffs of his black coat, and seized the doorknob.

With an efficient twist he opened the door, stepped inside, and slammed it behind him.

Gwendylyr folded her hands before her, her face expressionless.

49

The Butler's Rule

Raspu stepped inside the kitchen, took in the scene in one appalled and angry glance, and roared.

Maidservants, asleep on the rug before the fire, screeched and leapt to their feet, hastily trying to pat their hair into some order.

Footmen, huddled over a poker game under the dish-racks, pushed chairs and stools to the floor as they hastily rose.

The cook lumbered out of the cold room, a jug of cream in her hands and smears of the clotted stuff about her chin, and stared gape-mouthed at the Demon-butler.

Five small children of indeterminate usefulness and sex

scrambled out from the stove alcove, biscuits and cakes tumbling from their hands, and stood before the draining boards, forming a ragged, wailing line of carefully-managed pathos.

Two dogs burst out of a cupboard door, each with a half-eaten joint of meat in their jaws, and fled through an open window.

Several dishes crashed to the floor as they jumped over one of the benches, and a huge canister of flour fell to the floor.

Quiet and stillness descended as Raspu stared about.

Flour drifted down and coated all.

"What is going on here?" Raspu hissed. "Why this sloth, why this mess, why this chaos?"

Instantly excuses burst from every mouth.

"We've not been paid in a month—"

"It's cold outside—"

"My granny died five months ago and I've not been able to think straight since—"

"We've done our best, sir, truly—"

"—but things 'ave been against us, sure for a fact—"

"It's been cold *inside,* and not fit to work in—"

"Benny beat me up—"

"Frankie knocked *me* up—"

"No-one's been here to tell us what to do—"

"What *shall* we do, sir?"

Raspu strode forth and began to snap orders, tug uniforms straight, and jerk braids so painfully that girls cried.

"Clean this up—and yourself—now!

"Why has this been left to rot? Dispose of it. Now!

"Why do you cry, girl? There's work to be done. Now!

"Take this broom, and wield it!

"Have you no pride, cook? No sense of joy in your work? Find some. Now!"

And so Raspu twirled about the kitchen like a minitornado, venting anger and orders in equal amounts, pinching and shoving, nipping and poking, sending pages and maids screaming to their tasks, kicking footmen over doorsteps in the pursuit of their vocation, and shoving the cook's face in the pot of cold, starchy porridge on the stove top until she pleaded (somewhat damply) for mercy.

Finally, the kitchen was emptied of the majority of the wantonly lazy staff and those that were left were well on the road to making the room and its utensils sparkle with polish and use.

"So," Raspu said smugly as he stepped outside the door and confronted Gwendylyr. "Have I won the challenge?"

A maid brushed past them, her face terrified, a pile of neatly-folded linen in her arms.

"You have made a good start," Gwendylyr said, "but the challenge lies in being able to *keep* the staff at work. How will things be in a month, Raspu? In two? Will the house be running efficiently, or will it, its staff, *and* its butler have slid into irretrievable sloth?"

"A month! I don't have to do this for an entire—"

"I'll give you two," Gwendylyr said. "Have fun."

And she vanished.

Enchantment gripped Raspu and the house into which he'd walked, and the sun and moon whirled overhead.

"Interesting," Qeteb remarked. He and DragonStar now inhabited the same hilltop, although there was more than five paces between their respective positions. "She's not someone I'd care to meet over breakfast."

DragonStar turned his head slightly and looked at Qeteb, but he did not reply.

The two settled down to wait, and to watch.

The sun and moon twirled overhead, moving so fast the shadows fluttered unceasingly across the hilltop.

Raspu found he did not like being a butler. The staff had remained in awe of him for an entire three days, and then subtle changes slowly crept into the daily routine.

The maids who once had wept at the very sight of him, now smirked and moved more insolently when he appeared. They still swept and scrubbed and polished, but their mouths curled in secretive smiles as he passed, and their eyelashes dipped in flirtatious fans over the curve of their soft cheeks whenever he paused to shout more orders at them.

Raspu found that his voice noticeably softened whenever they did that, and one day he found himself reaching out to caress the cheek of one particularly fetching lass.

He jerked his hand back, but not before he saw her mouth arrange itself into a seductive pout.

Moist, red, beguiling.

With just the hint of pearly white teeth behind those plump, tempting . . .

Raspu jerked away, roared, and vanished down the corridor in stiff-legged (and almost unbearably frustrated) affront.

The maid giggled, and wriggled her hips in anticipation.

In the kitchen the cook pounded and rolled and sweetened and basted to Raspu's satisfaction, but after a week or so he noticed that not all the meat he put out from the now-locked cold room appeared at table. When he accused the cook of stealing, she wept and wailed and wrung her hands and fell down in an epileptic fit.

The Demon repressed a sigh. It was too much effort to continue with the harangue, and only a *small* bit of meat had gone . . .

Raspu turned his back and left her massive mound of flesh to twitch and quiver triumphantly on the rug before the fire.

As soon as the kitchen door slammed behind him, the cook's flesh trembled to stillness. She smiled, and her hand drew out the small joint of meat she'd secreted in the voluminous pocket of her apron, and she began to chew vigorously, setting her flesh to trembling all over again.

But however much the staff managed to annoy him, Raspu found that the household accounts managed to drive him almost insane with exasperation.

Every morning Raspu had to check the shelves and count all the packets and cans and wedges and jars.

Then he had to check them all off in his account book.

Then he had to consult with the cook and the downstairs

cleaning maids to see what would be required for that day's cooking and cleaning. Then he had to dole out with solemn precision from, the cans and jars and wedges and packets, the portions of starches and wood oils and fireplace blackeners and flowers and sugars and yeasts required.

And then he had to mark all *those* off in his account book.

Then the upstairs maids needed linens and sheets and pillowcases and dusters, and so Raspu must march to the linen closet and carefully count out the articles required.

And mark it off in his account book.

Then, after only a brief respite—not even long enough for a cup of tea and a sit down—they were back with the dirty linen. Raspu must be out again with his account book to check that the dirty linen numbers and quantities matched the clean numbers and quantities he'd dispatched *yesterday,* and if they didn't, then everything must be dumped into piles and carefully sorted out under his supervision to find the missing pillowcase, and if the numbers *still* refused to tally, then Raspu must needs conduct a room by room search of the upstairs corridors, seeking under every bed and in every dirty clothes hamper for the pillowcase.

And when he'd wasted four hours in that fruitless search, and was nigh tearing out his hair in almost unbearable frustration (and determined to tear the offending pillowcase to shreds, together with the maid who'd lost it, when it was finally found), Raspu sat down to a late and very cold lunch with his account book only to find that he'd miscounted the number of pillowcases on yesterday's tally, and that in fact this morning's count had been correct. He'd wasted an entire morning— and let his lunch grow cool and congealed—over a simple error that if he'd not bothered with the *cursed* accounting and tallying in the first instance would not have bothered him!

Raspu threw the account book across the room, his plate of disgustingly congealed lunch close after it, and the cook lowered her head and grinned into the pots atop the stove, and the footmen by the door raised their eyes to the ceiling and smirked inwardly.

Things were going well.

The challenge was falling into place.
The days spun by.

"Who is that little girl you sent off with the red-headed bird-man?" Qeteb asked conversationally. He could sense Raspu's dilemma, and it made him rabid with fury.

But not incensed enough to lose his vision of overall destiny.

Nothing he said could have dismayed DragonStar more.

"What little girl?" he said. Behind him the Alaunt shifted, and one or two growled softly.

Qeteb smirked in satisfaction. The tone of DragonStar's voice was enough, in itself, to make the probable loss of Raspu bearable.

"No-one," he said. "I had grown bored and merely invented a question to while away the time."

DragonStar closed his eyes and cleared his mind, hoping that SpikeFeather and Azhure were safe enough in the waterways.

As far as he knew the Demons had never ventured down there . . . but was that assumption correct enough to assure Katie's continued safety?

One lunchtime Raspu entered the kitchen to find one of the footmen leaning against a maid with his hand nestled inside her open blouse.

As the footman saw Raspu, he leaned away from the girl, slowly pulling out his hand.

The girl's round, firm breast was exposed to Raspu's gaze before she pulled the material of her blouse closed.

Raspu, tired by a morning of chasing after a small and almost empty jar of boot black—only to find it on the shelf where it was supposed to be anyway—merely ignored both servants and sat down at the table.

The cook almost dropped his plate of tripe before him, and milk sauce splattered over the table.

Raspu opened his mouth to say something, then closed it again.

He was too tired, and far too hungry, to be bothered.

Later, perhaps.

And then, later, the girl who'd let the footman grope her in the kitchen accosted Raspu in a dimly lit corridor as the Demon was walking slowly, tiredly, towards his room for bed.

"I should explain meself," the girl mumbled, standing before the Demon.

Raspu sighed. "This can wait until morning," he said, and tried to push past her.

But she clung to his arm, and he stumbled to a halt.

He noticed her mouth, and remembered the maid who'd pouted so seductively at him. Was this the same girl?

He felt a stirring of interest.

One should never be intimate with those to whom you must issue orders and directions. That was the forty-eighth rule (in a total of seventy-two) of the "Butler's Code of Conduct" which sat neat and trim and orderly in a workmanlike frame above his pillow.

Raspu had read it assiduously when he'd first embarked upon this ridiculous challenge. But now, as the girl pressed her warm and curiously pliable flesh against him, and pouted her mouth just so, Raspu wondered if perhaps he'd passed the test a long time ago.

Surely he'd done enough? Proved himself beyond doubt?

"He's not important to me," the girl murmured, and Raspu gave a start of shock—and desire—as he realised that one of her hands had crept down between his legs.

"Who?" he managed.

"The footman. Pete."

"Oh." The girl's hand was very bold, and Raspu supposed he should say or do something about it, but . . .

"It's only you I care about," the girl whispered, and now somehow her blouse had fallen open, and Raspu found that one of his hands was kneading at her breast.

"You're so strong," she whispered, "and so powerful. You've given everyone such a scare."

She thrust her breast more firmly against his hand and Raspu groaned.

"I do like a man with authority," she said, and shivered enticingly as she tilted her head back and closed her eyes.

That was enough for Raspu. Tearing away his butler's stiff black coat and grey-striped trousers, he threw her to the floor and took her there and then.

If she wanted authority, then who was he to deny it to her?

Deep in her watchful seclusion, Gwendylyr grinned. He was almost lost. There remained only one more small test.

"Y'see," the footman said, "there's no reason why we shouldn't do it, is there?"

His voice was very persuasive, and Raspu looked about at the rest of the staff gathered together in the kitchen.

The maid he'd enjoyed—several times—the previous night, ran a tip of pink tongue over her lower lip, and one of her hands crept caressingly over her belly.

"It's only a packet or two here and there," the footman continued. "The mistress'll never miss it."

"And it's not like we don't deserve it," another footman said.

"What with the wages we get, and all," said the cook.

"I know *you* don't get paid much—" a small, red-haired maid to one side began, and Raspu stared at her. He'd never thought about how much he got paid. Was it not good enough for him?

"—and yet we all know how hard you work," she continued.

Raspu nodded. Yes, he *did* work hard, didn't he?

"At all those accounting books," the cook said, and Raspu wondered that he'd never previously noticed the pleasantness of her voice.

"I mean," said the cook, "what thanks do you get for keeping all those numbers ordered and neat?"

That's right! Raspu thought. No-one has ever thanked me for all the work I've put in.

"Just a can here and there," said a gardener, poking his head in the open window. "For me kids, y'understand. No-one else."

Of course. Of course.

"Just a can here and there," the cook whispered, and Raspu nodded.

"Just here and there," he said.

Gwendylyr stood before the closed brown door to the kitchen. She tucked a stray hair neatly behind her ear, then took a deep breath.

She opened the door and walked in.

Raspu jerked out of his doze and leapt to his feet.

A cat, which had been curled up beside his head on the table, yowled, and fled out the door to the garden.

The cook was lying in an alcoholic coma to one side of the kitchen, an empty brandy bottle in her hand, and the remains of a meat pie crumbled across her ample bosoms.

She'd vomited a while before, and the horrid stuff lay crusted on her chin and neck.

One of the maids had pulled her blouse open to allow a footman to lick and suck at her breasts, while two other footmen were packing sacks full of food and assorted packets and handing them out the window to one of the gardeners who put them in a cart.

Three footmen were once more engaged in a game of poker at a small table in the farthest reaches of the kitchen.

A thin-ribbed hound was humping a grunting bitch in the cold room, while several rats chewed on a joint of meat lying on the floor.

Dust and grime and trails of fat lay everywhere.

Raspu's uniform was creased and stained and his hair wild.

Gwendylyr stood, as if transfixed by the mess and sloth, and then she half gasped, half sobbed, and began to cry, slapping her hands to her face in theatrical despair.

Raspu reddened, and then cursed as he realised the blaze spreading across his cheeks.

Gwendylyr managed to control her weeping, and she turned her face to Raspu. "I am so sad, Demon. I thought you were strong enough to govern my household but—"

"No, wait!" Raspu cried, and stepped over to the cook, landing a foot in her ribs. "Wake up, you drunken sot! There's a meal to prepare! You! Get back to work!"

He made a grab at the footman nuzzling against the maid's breast, but the man rolled to one side, and Raspu's hand slapped harmlessly against a barrel.

"Be still," said Gwendylyr. "It is too late. You have made your—"

"No!" Raspu screamed turning back to her. "Wait! I can still redeem myself! I can—"

"Ah," Gwendylyr said, "now that *would* be difficult. How can any man redeem himself who cannot even keep a kitchen in order?"

Gwendylyr waved her hand around at the mess. "Look at this! You allowed yourself to embrace laziness and corruption, you allowed yourself to—"

"Give me another chance."

"No!"

"I know I will manage next time—just give me the chance!"

Gwendylyr stared at the Demon, still red-faced, although now from fear. "No. You have failed the challenge. You could not govern this household, and thus you have lost the right to govern yourself."

"No!"

"Yes. Self-determination is no longer yours, Raspu—"

He stretched out a hand, his face twisted in pleading, but already he could feel the bonds encircling his being.

He was no longer free.

"—and thus you must accept an eternity of servitude."

"No," he whispered.

"Servitude is the price of your failure," Gwendylyr said, no sympathy in her voice at all. "What a pity you would not listen to me when I tried to tell you that."

Raspu crouched close to the floor, whimpering.

Gwendylyr stared at Raspu briefly, then twisted her fingers amid his hair and hauled him to his feet. "Be silent, and accept your servitude. Your position has already been chosen for you—"

Raspu stared at her. To what slavery would he be put?

Gwendylyr smiled, and as she did so Raspu's face lightened in hope.

"The Field of Flowers," she said, "requires a man for the door."

And she snapped her fingers.

Far, far away, sitting at her table before the Gate of Death, the haggard crone looked up, her fists clenched.

"I've been made *redundant*?" she said. *"Me?"*

50

The Memories of the Enemy

SpikeFeather had jumped at the chance to escort Azhure and Katie into the waterways, and had only been mildly surprised when the two ice sisters had said they'd come along as well. The only wonder was that Urbeth had not seemed to mind, saying only that the threat to the column had now receded, and it would do her daughters good to see the waterways.

And so now here they were, trudging through ice and snow. SpikeFeather had not known of any entrance to the waterways in the frozen northern tundra, but Urbeth's daughters had merely smiled secretively to one another, and led the small group towards the coast.

It was freezing away from the protection of the trees, and while the ice women were apparently unaffected, Spike-Feather, Azhure and Katie had to huddle close, sharing their cloaks and their warmth, in order to survive.

Azhure was deeply unsettled. It had been a generation at least since she'd been separated from Axis. And had she ever been separated from him without the use of power, or the comfort of Alaunt and Wolven at her side? Now she had the responsibility of Katie—Azhure would sooner have died than to let Faraday down—and nothing with which to guarantee the girl's survival.

Nothing.

Not even a dagger.

What was I thinking of, she thought, *to have walked away without even a knife?*

In fact, they had nothing with them save a small bag with enough food for a day in it. Nothing but SpikeFeather's assurance they'd find something in the waterways, and nothing but the confidence of the two ice women in finding an entrance down to the Underworld in the first instance.

As they stumbled forwards, eyes narrowed against the icy wind, numb hands clutching the edges of the cloaks about them, Azhure glanced down at Katie.

The girl was subdued—but then who wouldn't be under these circumstances? Otherwise she seemed well enough, her cheeks coloured despite the cold (or perhaps because of it), and she lifted her eyes and smiled sweetly enough at Azhure when she realised the woman's regard.

Azhure nodded at the girl, and swung her eyes forward to where the two ice women strode straight-backed through the wind, heedless of the cold. Their grey and silver hair streamed and snapped out behind them, and every so often one of them would lift a bare, white-skinned arm and swing her hand in a graceful arc before her.

Whenever one did that, Azhure noted that the sting of the wind eased, and warmth stole back into her flesh.

When they'd set out, Azhure had asked them their names, but both women had smiled pleasantly, but with deep puzzlement.

"Names?" one of them had said. "We have no need for names."

And that had been the end of any conversation. The two women had simply walked forth into the snow, and, after a final glance at those they left behind, SpikeFeather, Azhure and Katie had followed them.

How long had they been walking? It had been late afternoon when they'd left the column, and night had come and gone. Now grey light filtered through the driving snow, and Azhure, together with SpikeFeather and Katie, stumbled every third or fourth step.

"How much longer?" Azhure muttered. "How much longer?"

"Soon," said a voice, and Azhure looked up.

The two ice women stood before her, but Azhure did not look at them. Instead she stared at the towering icebergs some forty or fifty paces behind them.

"Where are we?" SpikeFeather said.

"The Icebear Coast," one of the women said. "And the icepack."

"But that's impossible!" Azhure said. "We were many, many leagues from the coast, and—"

"Nothing is impossible," said the other ice woman. "Nothing."

"Where?" SpikeFeather said. His teeth were chattering too much to say more, and his arms were wrapped tight about himself.

His entire body was shaking.

One of the ice women put out a hand and laid it on his shoulder.

Instantly SpikeFeather's shaking stopped, and he straightened, his eyes wide.

The woman's sister did the same for Azhure and Katie—gods! but Azhure could feel herself unfreezing as the woman briefly touched her—then turned and pointed towards a crack between two grinding icebergs. "There."

"There?" Azhure said. "But that's too dangerous! The icebergs will crush us!"

"Nothing is ever too dangerous," one ice woman said.

"Not until it's killed you," Azhure muttered.

"Ah," the woman said, "but we do not know the caress of death!"

"Well," Azhure said, and grinned despite herself, "keep in mind that *we* do."

By Azhure's reckoning, it took them over three hours to pick their way over the jumbled edge of the icepack towards the icebergs.

The towers of ice reared almost a hundred paces above them, turning the light in their shadows a grey-blue and the air so frigid that the ice women had to walk close to either side of the other three, wrapping them in enchantments so they could continue to move.

The ice towers ground against each other, the sound a constant deep wailing and roaring that made both Azhure and Katie plug their ears with their fingers and clench their teeth.

"Do not fear too much," one of the sisters whispered in Azhure's ear, and she tried to relax, if only for Katie's sake.

But the trembling and shaking beneath her feet! They were going to have to climb down into this nightmare?

"There," said one of Urbeth's daughters. "Between the walls."

They picked their way over the uncertain ice, and then stood, staring.

Whenever Azhure had climbed down into the Underworld previously, she'd descended down a gently sloping spiral staircase.

Not down anything even faintly resembling this terrifying plunge.

This ice staircase descended straight down between the two grinding icebergs, their walls sliding up and down as they fought for space in the crowded sea.

Straight down—so far Azhure could not see its end.

Stars help them if they slipped on the ice steps! They'd tumble to their deaths.

"I do not know that we should—" she began, but one of the ice women laid a hand on her arm.

"You will manage," she said.

"Katie—"

"The girl will manage."

Azhure briefly closed her eyes, then nodded. She took Katie's hand, and tried to smile for her.

Katie looked at Azhure, looked at the descent before her, then looked back at Azhure. Normally so placid, so calm, so strong, Katie's eyes were terrified.

Azhure's hand tightened about that of the girl's, and she opened her mouth, trying to find something reassuring to say, when SpikeFeather leaned down and swept the girl into his arms.

"Put your face into my shoulder," he said, "and doze for this trip down to the waterways. I am Icarii, remember? My balance is like no other, and I fear no heights. You'll be safe with me."

Whether it was his words, his reassuring tone or his touch, Katie relaxed and, putting her arms about his neck, lay her head trustingly in the hollow of his shoulder.

The two ice women shared a glance, and a brief nod, then one turned and stepped into the stairwell.

"Come, SpikeFeather, Azhure," she said. "My sister will bring up the rear to protect us against whatever vile attack the seals have planned."

SpikeFeather laughed, and even Azhure managed a smile.

The birdman stepped onto the first step, the ice woman two or three below him and moving ever downward, then glanced over his shoulder at Azhure. "Take my wing," he said, attending one of them towards her, "and hang onto it. I can balance for all three of us."

"Thank you," Azhure said softly and, taking hold of Spike-Feather's wing—it was so warm!—she summoned her courage and stepped down.

The climb down was worse than any nightmare Azhure had ever endured. Stars, but she thought she'd prefer to go through DragonStar and RiverStar's appalling birth all over again if it meant she could get to the bottom of these stairs the faster! To either side of the stairs the icebergs grated and ground, as if cursing and throwing insults at the other berg just an arm's span distant. Azhure wondered if it were possible that at any moment one or the other iceberg would lose its temper completely and lunge across the frigid distance between them to tear the throat out of the other.

No, she thought, *that is just my fancy, and foolish at that.*

And at that precise instant the iceberg on her right moved so suddenly and so precipitously that a frightful grating scream filled the stairwell, and Azhure cried out and halted, letting go of Spikefeather's wing, her hands flying to her ears.

"You are safe," said the ice woman behind her, laying both her hands on Azhure's shoulders. "Safe."

SpikeFeather had stopped, and was looking over his shoulder at Azhure; Katie, apparently, was asleep and unconcerned, her face tranquil as it lay on his shoulder.

The birdman's eyes were full of concern for Azhure, but Azhure thought that she could see just the slightest tinge of panic in their depths.

She took a very deep breath, held it as she fought for self-control, then let it out once she thought she had it.

Slowly Azhure lowered her hands away from her ears, and the ice woman's hands on her shoulders tightened briefly in encouragement.

"Soon," said the ice woman's sister from below Spike-Feather. "Very soon."

Pray to all the stars that it is the truth, Azhure thought, *for I cannot stand much more of this.*

They continued to descend for an hour, perhaps two—time had no meaning in this narrow ice tunnel—and then Azhure heard SpikeFeather exclaim as he jumped down three or four steps.

"We're here!" he cried, and Azhure had to blink the tears out of her eyes.

She stepped onto an ice floor that was, unbelievably, smooth but not slippery. Above her the roof of the ice tunnel had soared into a beautiful opaque dome of pink ice, while before her the floor extended towards a waterway that wound through the ice cave from one wall to the other.

A brass tripod with a bell stood to one side.

SpikeFeather had a huge grin stretching from one ear to the other, and Azhure couldn't help the feeling that he felt as if he'd come home after too long away. She leaned forward and took Katie from him—the girl murmured sleepily as Spike-Feather transferred her into Azhure's arms, but otherwise did not stir—and the birdman turned to the two ice women standing before him.

"Thank you," he said, simply enough, but with such emotion that Azhure was stunned to see tears well in both the sisters' eyes.

"We long to see this Underworld of yours," said one of the sisters, "for we are weary of the hills and dales and turmoils of the Overworld."

"Don't you miss Faraday?" Azhure said, curious about what these women felt for the woman. After all, they'd spent a long time travelling as Faraday's devoted companions.

"Faraday was kind to us," said one of the sisters, "and she had a purpose which we were happy to aid her with. But . . ."

"But there are very few people we would wish to spend a forever with," the other finished. "Very few."

And, as one, both sisters switched their eyes from Azhure to SpikeFeather.

The birdman blushed to the roots of his hair, but managed a small and utterly exquisite bow to the two women.

They stared at him, and then their faces relaxed from their usual austerity into such utter beauty that Azhure gasped.

"The bell," one of the women finally and very gently prompted, and SpikeFeather grinned at his own distracted air.

"The bell," he agreed, and walking over to the tripod, struck it once.

It pealed three times, and within heartbeats a punt had floated out of the far tunnel where the waterway ran into the ice cave and glided to a halt by the group.

"I welcome you to my world," SpikeFeather said, and helped the three women into the barge.

Azhure sat down in the prow, settling Katie comfortably on

her lap, and smiled as the two ice women sat—close!—on either side of SpikeFeather in the bow.

"Take us," SpikeFeather asked the waterways, "to a safe place close to the Maze, for that is the StarSon's purpose."

As the punt glided forward, each sister lifted a graceful hand and placed it on one of SpikeFeather's knees.

Azhure looked the birdman in the eye, arched an eyebrow, and grinned.

The barge glided through caverns that were empty, and caverns that were filled with the skeletons of cities and forests. In one cavern, Azhure stared about her in amazement at the city that crammed the spaces to either side of the waterway. Tenement buildings fourteen or fifteen levels high, halls that soared even higher, streets crammed with workshops and market stalls: all deserted, all covered with dust and neglect, all empty and haunting.

"What are they?" Azhure finally said. "Who lived here? What happened to them?"

To that SpikeFeather had no answer, but Katie stirred on Azhure's lap and sat up, rubbing her eyes as she looked about her.

"They are dead," she said, "and have always been. No-one has ever lived here."

"But—" Azhure began.

"They are nothing but memories," Katie said. "Memories of the world the Enemy once lived on. Carried here by the ships, and built as memorials to the world that has been lost. Memories."

And the punt glided on.

51

Sliding South

$\mathcal{T}$he brown horse and her black-clad rider flowed over the landscape like wind let loose from an age-long prison. The horse's legs stretched forth and ate up the landscape, yet so smooth was her motion that she scarcely seemed to move.

Axis leaned forward over Pretty Brown Sal's neck, urging her forward. He had not been this happy in decades.

Behind him—somewhere—came his war band of some three thousand riders and trees, and somewhere behind them followed the column, but for this moment in time Axis did not care if they ever caught him.

He was free, riding across this bleakened landscape, running south, riding this magical, magical mount.

Pretty Brown Sal leaned her head forth even more eagerly, and surged forward. She, too, loved to run (*fly*), and her slim legs ate up the landscape.

Even more than usual.

From the first day that Axis had led the column south he'd discovered something unusual about the way Sal moved. It had at first disorientated him, almost frightened him, but then he'd learned to accept it and to enjoy the freedoms it gave him.

Pretty Brown Sal was, as the sparrow had said, a gift of flight. Pretty Brown Sal's legs literally flew. For every stride she took, almost half a league of landscape slid by. That was the unnerving sensation, for the passing landscape became an inchoate blur as it slid past with no recognisable features. On the first day, once Axis had got over his initial surprise, he'd found himself halting Sal every six or seven strides just so that he could orientate himself again.

Then, as the day had worn on, he'd learned to trust the mare, and learned to flow with her as she coursed over the land.

She was wondrous and magical, and Axis leaned forward even more, whooping and laughing as he urged her forward, forward, forward . . .

But Pretty Brown Sal and her abilities were not the only reason for his high humour.

Axis had a purpose again, he had a usefulness, and he felt he could make a difference. He didn't care that he was not the hero of this particular battle, only that he had a *purpose.* Moreover, he had a purpose that encompassed what he adored beyond anything else: leading a war band over countryside against a vile enemy that was ravaging the land. He had a purpose, and it involved speed and battle and blood.

It felt like old times again.

From the column, Axis had selected some three thousand seasoned campaigners—including Zared, Herme and Theod, who refused to remain behind—to ride in his war band. With the three thousand men came a similar number of the trees who, as Axis led out his band for the first time, had simply lifted roots and moved out with them. Another four or five thousand trees roamed through the landscape for leagues to either side of Axis' war band, catching and destroying every creature they came across. As the Demonic hours came and went (without Raspu's hour of Pestilence at dusk, for Urbeth said that Gwendylyr had triumphed against him, and, at that, Theod had broken down and wept), the trees provided shelter, although this far north the Demonic influence was negligible.

Axis found he had no need for the trees' shelter, for Sal conveyed her own protection against the Demons' maddening probings. Axis was truly free at last to ride as far and as fast as he wished.

Each day they travelled further south. Although Axis tended to ride out alone, the war band was never far behind. Somehow Sal's abilities extended to the war band, for Axis only ever had to rein her in, and turn about, and there was the war band thundering towards him, whooping and screaming with an excitement—*we're making a difference! we're taking action!*—that matched Axis'. To either side of the band of horsemen ran the trees: gigantic beings waving branches far into the sky and singing their own war song. Every time Axis saw them his breath would catch in his throat.

Several times a day they'd meet groups, often many thousands' strong, of crazed creatures and humans.

And every time they met them, they would decimate them.

Horsemen and trees would wade in side by side, swords and pikes sweeping and plunging, branches and roots snapping and snarling, men screaming, trees shrieking, death dealing.

None of the Demon-controlled creatures survived.

Of them all, the men found it hardest to do death to the women and children among the hordes of crazed creatures, but death they did, for it was the only release possible for those whose minds and souls had been eaten and corrupted by the Demons.

And every time Axis drew breath, and called his war band to a halt, he looked about at the blood-soaked snow that surrounded them, and he smelled lilies.

Thousands upon thousands of lilies, and Axis hoped that somehow the dead had managed to find their way into the Infinite Field of Flowers.

At the end of each day Axis led his war band back to the column that trailed behind them, Urbeth patiently plodding at its head.

But, as Axis did not have far to look back for his war band when he rode ahead, so he and his band did not have to ride far to meet up with the column. Sal's magic, perhaps combined with Urbeth's, extended to them as well.

And so they moved south.

Fast.

Until the eastern peaks of the Icescarp Alps rose to meet them.

Axis reined Sal to a halt, the mare snorting nervously.

A birdwoman stood in the snow before them.

Crazed? Probably so, considering her appearance, but crazed in a manner Axis had not yet seen.

She was . . . hideous. Before this moment Axis had not believed that any Icarii woman could make herself look hideous, but this birdwoman had gone to extraordinary lengths to make herself so.

Axis was not to know that she thought herself extraordinarily beautiful and alluring rather than repulsive.

Her hair had been teased by wind and ice into ragged spikes.

Her robe, possibly once gold, but Axis was not sure, was tattered and stained by whatever the wind had thrown at her.

Her wings were a frightful confusion of orange and red dye that had run in the wet conditions.

Masses of ill-placed jewellery hung from ears and neck and waist and streamers of what possibly had once been scarves fluttered from neck and arms.

Her face . . . her face was painted in several shades of purple and blue and red, as streaked by the elements as were her wings.

And yet her eyes still sparkled with obvious joy, and her mouth pouted seductively.

She held out her hands. "Axis StarMan!" she cried. "Well met! Have you brought me my husband?"

Axis finally recognised the woman from the time he, Azhure and Caelum had been trapped in the tunnel below the Fortress Ranges.

"StarLaughter!" he said, and Sal instinctively backed away two paces.

52

A Marital Reunion

"**W**hat?" WolfStar said. "I don't believe you!"

And yet he remembered what StarLaughter had said to him on the ice-edged glacier at the foot of Star Finger. *We could love each other again.*

Then, he'd thought she had simply been intending sarcasm, perhaps was even a little mad.

Now he wondered if she was indeed mad, but also truthful. *She could actually think that she and he . . . ?*

WolfStar stared at Axis. They'd camped for the night within sight of the Icescarp Alps, and just as he and Zenith had eaten and begun to settle down for the night, Axis had ridden his pathetic brown mare into the camp, seized WolfStar by one wing, and dragged him to a relatively deserted spot beneath the ethereal trees.

"I have StarLaughter under guard at the head of this column," Axis had said with no preamble as he slid down from Sal's back. "She says she has come here to meet you. She says that you are her husband. She says that she has loved you for all eternity, and she says that your happy marriage is about to recommence."

WolfStar still could not quite comprehend it. Stars, but the woman must be so far out of her mind that it was likely waiting for her on some distant iceberg in the Iskruel Ocean!

"What are you going to do about it?" he said.

"What am I going to do about it?" Axis turned his face away for a moment, a muscle working in his cheek. He looked back at WolfStar. "The question, renegade, is what *you* are going to do about it."

"I don't have to—"

"Yes, you do! WolfStar, this is your problem, and you are

damn well going to fix it! I do not like the idea of StarLaughter running about in this convoy, but even less do I like the idea of what she might do if I kick her sorry person back into the snow and ice. She is happily preening herself at my campfire, telling the poor sods of Lake Guardsmen who stand watch over her about the night of passionate love that awaits you and she, while meantime you are huddling up to my daughter and trying to pretend that StarLaughter is not your problem.

"WolfStar, she is more than your problem, she is your *responsibility!* She became *your* responsibility and *your* problem the instant you threw her through the Star Gate! Now, you are going to accompany me back to the head of the convoy and you are going to sort out this mess once and for all. I do *not* want StarLaughter a threat to this column. Stars know what she could do, or call down upon us, if she feels she's been slighted."

WolfStar sneered as Axis paused to take a furious breath. "No doubt you couldn't be more pleased by this development, Axis. No doubt you think that you can send me off with Star-Laughter and rescue your daughter from the depths to which I have dragged her. Well, I won't do a thing to—"

Axis reached out and seized WolfStar's hair with one hand, his chin with his other.

"You will come with me *now*," he said between clenched teeth, "or I will personally deliver your sword-stuck corpse to your wife . . . with my condolences, of course. Now, *you will come with me!*"

WolfStar snarled, an automatic response, but he offered no resistance as Axis hauled him forward.

Damn Axis to everlasting agony in the pits of the AfterLife! When he, WolfStar, wrested power and control from Dragon-Star no-one would be able to treat him so contemptuously!

As Axis remounted Sal, and gave WolfStar a none-too-gentle kick in the small of WolfStar's back with his booted foot, Zenith emerged from the shadows, her face expressionless.

Further back in the gloom, so furtive and silent that Zenith did not know she was being watched, stood StarDrifter, his face an equal mixture of hope and despair.

StarLaughter laughed, fluttering her hands about her, admiring the way the firelight caught at the sparkle of rings and nail polish. She tossed her head, knowing the five Icarii men who stood around her were finding it hard to control their lust.

StarLaughter knew WolfStar would not be able to keep his hands off her once he saw her again.

It was pedestined, for their love was meant to be eternal.

There was a movement in the night, and the Guardsmen stepped back, not even bothering to hide their relief.

Axis stepped into the firelight. "I have brought you your husband, StarLaughter," he said, "although whether or not you find him what you—"

"WolfStar?" StarLaughter scrambled to her feet, almost tripping over a length of tattered scarf that hung from her waist. "WolfStar? Is that you?"

"Yes, you over-painted harlot," WolfStar said, and stepped into view. "What in every god's name have you done to yourself?"

StarLaughter preened, turning her body this way and that so her husband could admire it. "I have made myself beautiful . . . for you," she simpered.

WolfStar laughed derisively. "Then what a shame you have failed so badly."

So lost was StarLaughter in her madness, and her mad world, that none of WolfStar's derision registered. He was here, and he was hers, and nothing would ever come between them.

She threw herself full length against WolfStar's body, rubbing herself wantonly against him, running her hands over curves and into crannies that few women ever dared caress in public.

"My love!" she whispered, and kissed him.

WolfStar wrenched his head back, and seized StarLaughter by the shoulders.

"I find you repulsive!" he hissed. "Disgusting! Nauseous! Can you understand that, you raving witch?"

"Enough play," she murmured, attempting to snuggle up to him again. "You always had such a way with words!"

"WolfStar . . ." Axis said, wanting WolfStar to end this repellent scene.

"Listen to me!" WolfStar snarled. "I never loved you, not once! Can you understand that? Do you actually hear my words?"

Something flickered in StarLaughter's face, and her hands stilled.

"I married you for the power you'd bequeath our son," WolfStar continued, his voice deliberately hard and scornful, "and for the added legitimacy you'd give my seizure of the throne of Talon. I found your personality grating, your body only bearable at best. I kept lovers to keep me amused and warm, for *you* never did! I have never, do not, and will not ever love you, for you are the most repellent woman in creation!"

StarLaughter's face had now blanched, and she stared in confusion into WolfStar's eyes.

He continued, brutally cruel. "I repudiate you, before all these witnesses. I cast you aside. I deny our marriage. You are filth, StarLaughter. Filth!"

"WolfStar!" Axis' voice cracked across the campfire. "That's enough!"

"I don't believe you," StarLaughter whispered. "I can't!"

"Would you believe it," another voice said, "if someone told you that WolfStar has taken another to his heart and to his bed, and would wife her, if only he could permanently dispose of you?"

WolfStar cursed foully. StarDrifter! What had the stupid birdman done!

StarDrifter-had now stepped into the circle of light. "He has taken a woman," he said, "that does not belong to him, and who does not love him."

"That's a lie!" WolfStar shouted. "She loves me, and I her!"

Humiliated, scorned, betrayed, StarLaughter jerked out of WolfStar's grasp.

"Who?" she whispered, then turned her head to StarDrifter and spoke louder, more strongly. "*Who* is this whore-bitch that thinks to depose me?"

It was only then that StarDrifter realised what a terrible mistake he had made.

53

Sigholt

*T*hey continued south, Axis and his war band ranging ahead during the day, Urbeth leading the column of trees and people and animals behind him.

StarLaughter had proved a problem.

Since StarDrifter—*curse his tongue!*—had blurted out the fact of Zenith's existence, StarLaughter had not said a word.

She had, quite simply, gone silent.

And Axis did not like to think what might be going on in her mind.

He'd done what he could, but he wasn't sure if he *could* do anything to mitigate the situation.

StarLaughter had been asked, politely enough and with the offer of supplies, to leave the column.

StarLaughter had turned her head slightly in Axis' direction, but had said nothing.

Nor had she moved.

So Axis had been forced to remove her. A dozen Lake Guardsmen had taken her some ten leagues to the east where they'd left her in a cave in the Icescarp Alps with supplies, clothes and strict instructions to leave the column alone.

Next morning, a sentry had alerted Axis to StarLaughter's silent, ghostly presence in the snow some hundred paces beyond the treeline.

She'd just stood there, ever silent, staring with unblinking eyes at the convoy as it prepared to move for the day.

Axis had had her moved again, further this time.

Next morning she was back again.

Urbeth had roared and snarled, but StarLaughter had not blinked, nor moved, and after a week of trying to drive her away, Axis had been forced to admit that nothing would work. StarLaughter would use whatever power she had to return herself to her silent *(hate-filled)* vigil a hundred paces away from the column.

Staring, staring, staring.

Stars knew what horror she'd bring down on the column! Axis did not know if StarLaughter was still working in league with the Demons and the Hawkchilds, or if she had embarked on a solitary quest for revenge. One night a sentry had reported that a strange shape—half bird, half woman, strangely lumped and as black as the night itself— had been spotted stumbling its way through the snow towards StarLaughter, but when Axis and a unit of men had ridden out to investigate, StarLaughter was once more alone in the snow.

Albeit with the ghost of a smile on her face.

So Axis had done what he could within the convoy itself. There were always several units of men detailed to keep an eye on StarLaughter—and for whatever horror she might call down out of the sky.

WolfStar and Zenith had finally been forcibly separated— to WolfStar's fury—but Axis was not leaving Zenith with WolfStar when StarLaughter, in all probability, had his daughter's murder in mind.

Thank the Stars StarDrifter had not blurted out her name!

As Axis had men watching StarLaughter, so he also had an equal number of men watching Zenith, as also WolfStar. Zenith to protect her; WolfStar to keep him away from Zenith.

WolfStar was incandescent with rage, Zenith was unhappy, StarDrifter spent his days in a turmoil of guilt at the danger he'd placed Zenith in, and Axis was damned glad to spend the days hunting down insane cows in the snow rather than spend time with his family!

"Gods, Azhure," he muttered one day as he urged Sal into her slide through time and space, "I miss you more than you could ever know. What a muddle our family has got itself into!"

From the edge of the Icescarp Alps Axis led the convoy ever south, Sal's power sliding them across the landscape at incredible speed. The Avarinheim was no more, obliterated by Qeteb's rape of the land when he'd first been resurrected, and Axis almost wept at the destruction. He had never been close to the Avar, although they'd aided him in his final quest against Gorgrael, and he'd never been at home in the forests, but the massacre of the trees deeply saddened him.

At night, when they camped, the trees surrounding the column murmured and shifted, remembering not only what had been lost, but the pain they'd endured during their death.

And they whispered of revenge and of an accounting.

Here, in this drifting plain that had once been a forest full of song and enchantment and fey creatures, the snow thinned and eventually disappeared, and the going became somewhat easier and, unbelievably, even faster. In only two days Axis found himself approaching the valley that connected the Skarabost plains with the Avarinheim (or what had once been the Avarinheim).

Axis reined Sal to a halt, his war band still some distance behind him, and sat, staring and remembering.

Here he had chased Azhure and Raum, when he had still thought himself a BattleAxe.

Here he had seen the woman he'd later discovered was his mother.

Here he'd had his first real inkling that he was more, far more, than just BattleAxe.

Now? Now he was just a man carrying too much responsibility leading another war band, and with yet more people to nurture and protect.

With a twist to his mouth, Axis waited for his war band and their accompanying trees, and led them through the valley.

In the eastern Skarabost plains, the numbers and ferocity of
the demented Demonic creatures were far worse. Axis and his
war band had been attacked by a force of some nine or ten
thousand large creatures—cattle, horses, bulls—almost the
instant they'd emerged from the mouth of the valley alongside
the still-rushing Nordra River.

Without the trees, Axis knew they could very well have
been overwhelmed.

His men fought well, but it was difficult to kill a cow or a
bull, even with the sharpest of swords, before it had a more
than good chance of killing you, and Axis lost several score of
men before the trees roared in.

It was the only verb Axis could find to describe their action.

One moment they were fighting desperately, surrounded
by a sea of maniacal livestock which had grown horns and
teeth far sharper than nature ever intended, when there was
a rumbling and roaring such as Axis had never heard before.

He'd twisted in his saddle, staring back towards the valley,
and had been so amazed that he'd left himself vulnerable to
deadly attack from a cream and brown bull. If it hadn't been
for Zared's quick pike thrust, Axis would have died.

But at the time, Axis had no idea of what was going on behind him. All he could see were the thousands of ethereal
trees pouring through the gap of the valley mouth.

They were literally roaring, waving their branches wildly
about the air in a crackling cacophony of snapping twigs and
leaves.

In an instant they fell upon the mob of animals, seizing
them with hungry woody fingers and tearing them apart with
a crackle of snapping joints and rib cages.

Axis had time only for a few more strikes against the creatures himself before they were all dead.

And when the animals were all dead, the trees stood there,
literally shaking with emotion that was, Axis thought, a sadness so deep that outsiders could only barely comprehend it.

Within the hour the column had joined them, and even Urbeth had stood shaking her head at all the slaughter.

Ur had simply stood there, clutching her terracotta pot, and grinning from ear to ear.

Once Axis had buried the dead, he moved the war band and column to Sigholt.

The primary purpose for travelling to Sigholt was to collect Gwendylyr—Theod was a mass of nervous impatience for the day it took them to move across the WildDog Plain and through the Holdhard Pass—but there was more to it than that.

Gwendylyr had undoubtedly attracted hordes of creatures to Sigholt, and thus there would be good exterminating there, as there had been at the valley mouth.

Sigholt was also Axis' home, and he wanted to see it again . . . see if it had managed to survive the Demons' attentions.

What he eventually found made him bow his head and weep.

Sigholt had been utterly destroyed. Sigholt! Axis could not believe it. All the magic, the laughter, the happiness, the memories; all had been turned to dust and rubble.

The bridge was gone.

The town of Lakesview was gone.

The lake itself was a dry, dusty bowl. (Axis was not to know that Gwendylyr's victory at the Lake of Life had at least turned the putrid virulence into more palatable dust.)

Everything had gone.

The war band had hung back as Axis slowly rode forward, tears streaming down his face. Even Pretty Brown Sal hung her head as if in sorrow.

Axis let Sal pick her own way as she walked towards the pile of rubble that had once been the enchanted castle. Gods, the memories! It hurt so badly Axis was not sure if he could bear it, and just as he thought that, he became aware there was a woman standing at Sal's shoulder. So lost was he in his grief, Axis gave a great start, thinking it was StarLaughter come back to deal him a mischief.

But it was Gwendylyr, one warm, comforting hand resting on his leg as she looked up at him.

"Trust in your son, and in my other four companions," she said, "and you never know what happiness we may achieve."

Axis opened his mouth to say something, but then there was a thunder of hooves from behind him, and a whoop, and then Theod was flinging himself down from his horse and grabbing Gwendylyr into his arms.

Axis turned his head away, and stared at the rubble.

54

A Troubled Night's Dreaming

In the hour before dawn they had lifted from the cliffs and the heaps of rubble where they'd roosted during the night, and they'd flown north, harking to StarGrace's call.

He is here. He is here. He is here.

StarLaughter had found WolfStar for them, as she always said she would.

He had thrown them through the Star Gate.

He had murdered them.

Uncaringly and coldly and only for the sake of his own personal ambition and lust for power.

They had lusted themselves now for many thousands of years, and that lust consisted of only one thing.

Revenge.

Now it was at hand.

Silently, purposefully, they descended through the predawn gloom, great black leathery shapes, the hands at the tips of their wings opening and closing in silent anticipation.

StarLaughter had allowed her hatred and disappointment and unending mortification to consume her. It was the only comfort she had. For days she'd trailed after the massive convoy of animals and peoples and trees, drifting just beyond arrowshot, hoping for a single glimpse of the woman that WolfStar had abandoned her for.

The *whore*!

If only she were disposed of! WolfStar would surely come back to her then . . .

No. No! That was wrong! *She should not think that!*

WolfStar would never come back to her. StarLaughter could finally see that. He'd made a fool of her in front of his trifling companions, all for the woman that he now thought to love, and for that StarLaughter would not forgive him.

StarGrace, and all the other Hawkchilds, had been right. WolfStar was unredeemable. He would never love her, and he would never help her regain her son.

He must die.

And, in dying, suffer as much as he'd made them to suffer.

And so StarLaughter drifted along the margins of the convoy and she waited and watched and planned.

And finally, after days of watching, she understood.

It had not been difficult, truth to tell. WolfStar was kept under watch by the guardsmen who wore the ivory tunics with the peculiar knot of gold in the central panel.

And so was a woman—a woman kept well guarded and well away from WolfStar, as if she might be a danger to him . . . or he to her.

StarLaughter's mouth had parted in red-lipped joy. She understood.

And she knew what she had to do.

WolfStar's night dreams were troubled with discomfort. He found himself drifting disoriented through cold stars. He did not know their patterns or their movements—he was lost in a distant and unknowable part of the universe.

It frightened him beyond measure.

Strange voices touched him, but they were afar and uncaring, and after a while they left him alone.

He drifted, alone and lonely beyond measure.

Until a voice, far stronger than the others that had touched him, reached out and sent sharp knives into his soul.

I have her.

WolfStar twisted about in the cold void, trying to find the speaker of the voice, and trying to beat down the black wings of despair that threatened to envelop him.

I have her.

"Who are you?" WolfStar screamed into the universe, but he did not require an answer, nor even desire one, because he knew very well to whom that voice and that hatred belonged.

StarLaughter.

I have her.

WolfStar groaned, and twisted himself out of the dream.

I have her.

The words still echoed about WolfStar's mind as he struggled into wakefulness. He lurched up on one elbow, and looked about, his eyes widening at the scene.

The Lake Guardsmen assigned to watch over him were lying twisted and ugly, their faces contorted as if something heavy and dark had taken hold of their minds and twisted them until they could bear no more.

They were dead.

Beyond the circle of WolfStar's immediate campfire, the rest of the convoy's sleepers lay twisting and murmuring, as if something troubled their dreams as well.

I have her.

"You bitch!" WolfStar snarled, and sprang to his feet. "This time *you* will die!"

Only soft, mocking, echoing laughter answered him, and WolfStar lifted into the sky, so furious he'd locked his hands into white-knuckled fists at his sides.

That bitch-wife of his would cause the collapse of all his plans. He would *not* lose Zenith now! Not after all the work he'd put into getting her!

And he most certainly would not let StarLaughter have the

satisfaction of thinking she'd succeeded in annoying him. She would die, here and now, and this time he'd do a better job of it than the last time he'd tried.

Zenith was gone, her watchers equally twisted and dead.

WolfStar hovered for a heartbeat or two, then he gave a powerful flap of his wings and lifted higher into the darkened sky.

Where was she?

This way.

WolfStar followed the voice.

He did not see the other birdman lift into the sky behind him, following at a distance of several hundred paces.

Zenith sobbed in terror. She couldn't understand what had happened, and how everything had gone so wrong, so quickly.

She'd woken to find the Lake Guardsmen assigned to her care twisting and convulsing at her side. As she'd scrambled to her feet, hands had seized her from behind, their fingers digging into her flesh.

"You have been whoring about with my husband," a flat voice whispered in her ear, "and now, like all harlots, you must pay for your adultery."

Zenith twisted frantically, but she could not escape Star-Laughter. The demented birdwoman physically dragged her through the sleeping convoy—past people and animals, past trees whose branches drifted gently in the wind, and even past a snoring Urbeth—and none had wakened.

None had opened even a single eye to see Zenith being dragged past weeping and screaming.

At Zenith's back, StarLaughter grinned in crazed satisfaction. The kernel of power the Demons had given her was proving useful, even to the end.

From the convoy StarLaughter dragged Zenith deep into the Urquhart Hills, refusing to respond to the woman's cries or questions.

StarLaughter didn't give a damn about the woman. She had commited adultery, and she must die.

As soon as the harlot had performed her final task: attracting WolfStar to his death as well.

And so now Zenith sat hunched uncomfortably on the ground, her hands tied to a pole behind her, listening to StarLaughter pace back and forth in the dark.

An hour before, the Hawkchilds had arrived to populate the ridges of the Urqhart Hills.

"Not long now," StarLaughter said somewhere behind Zenith. "He has woken, and thinks to come to your rescue."

Zenith lowered her head, no longer weeping, utterly resigned to her death.

"Axis."

Axis woke with a start at the word and the hand on his shoulder. He'd been lost in a dream of Sigholt, a dream filled with laughter and love and frightful great bats that beat at his head and settled in smothering droves over both laughter and love.

"Zared?" Axis accepted his brother's aid to rise, silently cursing his stiff limbs and sleep-fuddled mind.

"There is something you need to see," Zared said. "Fast."

Axis jumped to his feet, reaching for his axe as he did so, and allowed Zared to lead the way toward the edge of site camp.

"Look."

Axis squinted into the faint light now staining the sky.

He opened his mouth to say that he could see nothing, and then he shut it with a snap.

There were strange, dark shapes huddling on the craggy ridges of the Urqhart Hills that ringed the camp.

And then, as if listening to a silent voice, each one of the shapes lifted into the lightening sky.

"Hawkchilds!" Axis said.

"And worse," Zared said at his side, and Axis turned to stare at him.

"Worse?"

"WolfStar and Zenith have gone. Their guards are dead."

55

A Tastier Revenge
Than Ever Imagined

Axis turned his head and stared at Zared. His eyes were as cold as the interstellar wastes.

Zared took a half step back, even though he knew Axis' emotion was not directed at him.

"Zenith is my daughter," Axis said, and Zared shuddered at the combination of flatness and desolation in his brother's voice.

"Damn *all stars into dust!*" Axis screamed, and Zared cried out involuntarily. *"Where is my power when I need it most!"*

DragonStar turned, and would have moved, but Qeteb's hand snaked the distance between them and caught him fast.

They were sitting at a small tea table covered with a snowy cloth under the blackened skeleton of a tree on the ridge above Fernbrake Lake.

Small blue cups and saucers, and tea and sugar pots sat innocently on the linen.

"We are tied in our own immortal combat now," the Demon said softly, hardly. "And neither you nor I can leave it."

"Zenith is my sister," DragonStar whispered.

"Then what bad luck she should get herself into so much trouble right now," Qeteb said, "just when her brother can't leap to her rescue."

Qeteb grinned. He was suddenly glad he hadn't managed to catch up with StarLaughter after all. She was doing splendidly, just when Qeteb needed it.

He let DragonStar's arm go, and sat back complacently.

Raspu had lost, but Qeteb had more trust in his other companions.

There was a long way to go, and more death yet, before the final act could be played out.

WolfStar circled StarLaughter and Zenith once, then landed softly on the ground before Zenith.

StarLaughter stood just behind the pole, a length of rope in her hand. Her hair had matted into thick, oily twists that wriggled like snakes, and her face was twisted into ugly lines curving about bared, yellowed teeth.

StarLaughter looked frightful.

As WolfStar landed, she wrapped the rope about Zenith's neck, and tugged it tight.

Zenith made no sound, but her entire body stiffened, and her eyes widened in anguish.

"Let her go!" WolfStar said, and took an aggressive step forward. Damn StarLaughter. If she harmed Zenith . . . ! "She has done nothing to you."

StarLaughter snarled, and jerked the rope tighter.

Zenith's face contorted in agony, and WolfStar stopped. A dead Zenith would not be a useful Zenith at all.

StarLaughter loosened the rope, and Zenith relaxed in relief, although her eyes were desperate—frantic—as they stared at WolfStar.

Help me!

"What has she done to me?" StarLaughter whispered. "What? She seduced you, and bore you a child that should have been my right—"

"You fool!" WolfStar cried, but made no move forward. "That was not *her*! It was—"

"She is *all* the women you cheated me with!" StarLaughter screamed. "When she dies, I shall be avenged on you and *all* your whores!"

WolfStar tried to think. How could he handle StarLaughter? She was completely demented, and yet so coldly calm within that dementia, that he didn't know how to reason with her . . . or how to defeat her, if it came to violence.

And what else, after all this time and all this hatred, *could* it come to?

"Let her go," WolfStar said, keeping his voice calm and reasonable. "This is between you and I, not Zenith."

"Ah! *Zenith!*" StarLaughter said. "So now I have a name for the harlot!"

She bent a little closer to Zenith's head, and laughed, low and mocking in the birdwoman's ear. "Zenith-harlot. How you!"

"StarLaughter—" WolfStar began.

StarLaughter whipped her eyes up, although she remained bent over Zenith. "You lied to me when you said you loved me. You plotted against me when you said that I would share your power and glory—"

"Star Laughter—"

"—you murdered me and our son when you'd said that we were all you cared about. Liar! You cared about *nothing* but your *own* power and glory!"

Now StarLaughter was crying, but she still continued shouting through her sobs. "You condemned me, our son, and hundreds of the most beautiful Icarii children who had ever lived to a frightful eternity in order to sate your own lust for fame and control. You have never regretted that for one—"

"For the Stars' sakes woman!" WolfStar shouted. "Neither of us have ever pretended to each other to have a conscience in our ambitions. Don't start throwing trivialities at me now!"

"My love was no triviality," StarLaughter whispered, "and our son was no triviality." Once more she tightened the rope about Zenith's neck.

"I should have killed her," Axis muttered, striding towards Pretty Brown Sal.

"How?" Zared said, "when she has power and you not?"

Axis halted and whipped around to stare at Zared, but he said nothing, and after a moment continued on his way.

"I *should* have killed her," he repeated.

"WolfStar will stop her," Zared said, almost running in order to keep up with Axis.

"WolfStar has so many secret intrigues that he is more likely to kill Zenith than StarLaughter. No doubt StarLaughter will be more useful to him in the long run. What is Zenith? Merely a woman who is loved! She has no *power*! Nothing to offer *him*!"

They had reached the horse lines, and Axis took Sal's bridle, quickly slipping it over the mare's head.

"Axis—"

Whatever Zared had been about to say was interrupted by the arrival of Urbeth.

"I will come with you," Urbeth said, and growled.

For the first time Axis felt the faintest glimmer of hope.

"And I have a thousand trees at my back," Urbeth said further, and Axis' hope soared.

"Zenith will be saved if you offer *yourself*!" a new voice said behind WolfStar. "You are all she needs!"

WolfStar turned about and snarled at StarDrifter. Fool! What use did *he* think to be?

StarDrifter walked slowly forward until he was within a pace or two of WolfStar. His hand was held out in entreaty to the Enchanter-Talon, but his eyes were fixed on Zenith beyond WolfStar.

"If you love her," StarDrifter said, finally looking back at WolfStar, "then give yourself to StarLaughter, and free Zenith."

WolfStar hissed. "Give yourself, you useless fool! I have no use for love."

StarLaughter screamed, hoarse and frightful, and both whipped about to face her.

"No use for love, WolfStar?" she yelled. "Then you have no use for *life*!"

"StarLaughter!" WolfStar cried, starting a step towards her.

"Too late!" StarLaughter hissed, and the sky fell in about them.

"Where are they?" Axis asked Urbeth as he mounted Sal.

The bear lifted her nose and scented the air. "There," she indicated, pointing north with her snout. "Somewhere in a gorge in the hills."

Axis grunted, and would have urged Sal forward save that Urbeth stepped in front of the horse.

"I can smell a darkness in the air," she said, "all warm and bloody, and I do not like it."

Axis dug his heels into Sal's flanks with such a thud the mare jerked from halt to gallop in two strides.

Darkness descended about them, and both WolfStar and StarDrifter instinctively crouched on the ground, their arms and wings protectively wrapped about themselves.

"See," StarLaughter whispered. "See what I have brought you!" So intent was she on WolfStar the rope had loosened about Zenith's neck.

Zenith glanced at StarLaughter leaning over her shoulder, then began very slowly and carefully to work at the knots binding her hands behind her. Thank the Stars StarLaughter was not sailor-taught when it came to knots!

The Hawkchilds encircled WolfStar and StarDrifter in a fence four or five bodies thick.

This is what they'd been questing for thousands of years.

This is the one who had murdered them, and stolen their heritage.

They whispered and shifted, a mass of feathers and bright eyes and white, grasping hands at the tips of leathery wings.

WolfStar!

WolfStar!

We're coming for you WolfStar!

We're here, WolfStar!

One of them stepped forward. StarGrace, half woman-child, half Hawkchild. Her form shifted from one to the other;

now, the limb she extended was a graceful white hand and arm, now twisting leather and talons.

"Uncle," she said, and WolfStar slowly turned to face her.

"I could have had so much," StarGrace said sadly, "but you took it all away from—"

"If you have been drifting four thousand years with nothing but revenge feeding your heart," WolfStar said, "then I pity you. You have become a nothing. An inconsequential."

"For the heavens' sakes," StarDrifter cried, "take him! Kill him once and for all, and then let Zenith—"

"We care for *nothing* but our revenge," StarGrace said, her voice cold, and she shifted her eyes to StarDrifter. "Nothing, beyond WolfStar's blood. And everything—"

She shifted forward, and her form became all Hawkchild, leaving nothing of the beautiful girl.

"—that stands between us and our revenge must needs be swept away."

She lunged forward, and StarDrifter screamed as her beak tore into the fleshy part of the arm he'd raised in self-defence.

WolfStar, now certain of his own death, still managed a laugh. "You pretty-feathered, useless fool," he said. "Why are you here? You should have known you would not be able to help—"

And StarGrace's head flashed, and WolfStar screamed and fell to the ground, rolling into a protective huddle around his torn belly.

Desperate, thinking only that if she could get free then she'd somehow be able to save StarDrifter, Zenith finally managed to tear her hands clear of their rope bindings.

In a movement so fast that StarLaughter had no hope of escape, Zenith's hands whipped up and buried themselves in StarLaughter's matted hair.

"Ugh!" Zenith grunted, and thudded StarLaughter's forehead down on the small rocks that littered the ground.

And again and again, until blood splattered over both of them.

And then Zenith found her head seized from behind in a grip so cruel she screamed.

"See?" a small child's voice whispered in her ear. "See what revenge we shall exact from you for your impertinence? StarLaughter is our friend, our mother, our only friend . . ."

Zenith stared at where the Hawkchild jerked her face, and then she screamed so hard she convulsed.

StarGrace had taken hold of StarDrifter's golden curls with one hand, and with the other tore off one of his wings, throwing it high into the air, provoking a feeding frenzy among the Hawkchilds closest to where it landed.

Axis rode Sal desperately hard, sliding her forward through rocky chasms and down screes so dangerous that any mount save Sal would have foundered and killed them both at the first challenge.

Axis needed to reach Zenith.

He had failed her previously, but he would not do so now.

All he could think of was the image of Azhure coming to him atop Sigholt's roof one summer's afternoon, and taking his hands, and saying gently, "We are to have another child."

They'd both thought that DragonStar and RiverStar had caused Azhure so much internal damage in their horrendous birth that another child was out of the question.

Thus, that afternoon, and the months that had followed as Azhure's belly swelled, had been so special . . .

The girl born to them had been so treasured . . .

Then why had he let her go? Why had he abandoned her? *Couldn't he have made more of an effort to protect her?*

Axis screamed, and urged Sal to yet further extremes.

Behind him raged Urbeth, and behind her dipped and swayed a thousand ethereal trees.

They would save the girl. They would . . . they would . . .

———

StarGrace reached down, and as StarDrifter screamed and twisted beneath her hand, she took a firm grip on his other wing, and with all the power she had, she tore that out too.

StarDrifter stilled, a strange, surprised look on his face. His eyes went blank, his body limp.

StarGrace dropped him, and stepped carefully about the massive pool of blood that pumped from his back.

"Is that the woman who tempted WolfStar into betrayal?" she asked StarLaughter, who had managed to regain her feet.

She indicated Zenith, still held tightly by the Hawkchild behind her.

StarLaughter's face was covered in blood and small bits of gravel. "Yes! She is a *trollop*!"

StarGrace nodded at the Hawkchild, and his beaked head dipped.

When it rose again, it held something disgusting in its beak.

Held by his claws, Zenith made a single gurgle, trembled, and was still.

The Hawkchild's beak dipped again, and this time it savaged ferociously before it lifted its head once more.

What it held was even more frightful than previously.

WolfStar took one look, and cried out in horror.

"Now you," StarGrace said.

Sal crested the ridge, and stopped. Neither she, nor the man on her back could, for long moments, comprehend the shocking scene before them.

In the valley a bloodied and dishevelled Icarii woman stood laughing hysterically to one side of a mass of black feathers and flashing beaks.

It took Axis what seemed an eternity before he could comprehend the sight before him.

A head, attached only by a shred of flesh to a shoulder and one arm, lay to one side.

Zenith's head. Zenith's shoulder. Zenith's arm.

A white wing—and why did it look so much like StarDrifter's?—lying to yet another side.

And a mound of Hawkchilds fighting and feeding over scraps of reddened flesh and golden feathers.

That, some distant part of Axis' mind concluded, must be what was left of WolfStar.

StarLaughter raised her head and saw Axis sitting his mare atop the ridge.

She whispered something, and that whisper reached deep into Axis' psyche.

"I had never imagined revenge to be so tasty."

56

StarLaughter's Awful Mistake

Deep within the cradling safety of the waterways, Azhure lifted her head.

And knew.

Her hands lifted to her mouth, and she stared at the two ice women and SpikeFeather across from her.

Without knowing, but understanding, SpikeFeather stood up, lifted Katie into one of the ice women's arms, and locked Azhure in his own, rocking her back and forth as she grieved for her youngest child.

Axis sat his mare, and stared.

All that was left of Zenith was the head, a portion of neck and one shoulder, and an arm, flung wide as if in puzzlement.

Axis stared, his eyes hooked by the strange, wild tatters of flesh lining the great wound where the rest of her body had been chewed from her head and shoulder.

The flesh of her shoulder and arm was so white.

Her eyes, opened, continued to reflect in death the agony and horror she'd endured during her last breathing moments.

Axis sat his mare and stared.

Urbeth crested the ridge and came to a halt beside Axis and Sal.

She looked down at the mass of feeding Hawkchilds, twittering and whispering wetly as their beaks dipped and tore, at StarLaughter standing laughing and giggling to one side, and at the horrible remains of Zenith.

Then she lifted her head and looked at Axis, and for once in her life, Urbeth did not know what to say.

"I am going to put an end to this," Axis said in an emotionless voice.

"The Hawkchilds and StarLaughter cannot be dealt with save by power," Urbeth replied. "And your power is all gone."

"No," Axis said, once more looking at the carnage below him. "You are wrong, Urbeth. I have left the power of a father's love, and of a father's grief."

And without urging, Sal started down the slope.

StarLaughter looked away from the feeding pack of Hawkchilds, and laughed all the harder.

A man was riding down the slope of the gully towards her. An ordinary man with a pitiful sword in his hand and riding a more than ordinary brown mare who would look happier pulling a milk cart than riding into the midst of a dangerous revenging.

StarLaughter tipped back her head and let her laughter wash over the rising sun, extending her arms and hands in rapturous joy.

WolfStar was dead. *WolfStar was dead!*

He could harm her no more, he could humiliate her no more, and StarLaughter hoped he was currently screaming in agony within the deepest firepits of the AfterLife.

"You are dead, WolfStar," she whispered, "and I am alive. *I* have won!"

She turned her head and sighed irritably as the man pulled his mare to a halt some two or three paces away. Some part of her mind recognised him as the Axis StarMan she'd taunted in the tunnel under the Fortress Ranges, but in this, her moment of triumph, she cared little for who or what he was.

He was, after all, pointless.

"WolfStar made many errors in his life," Axis remarked in a wooden tone, "but the greatest of all was that he didn't tear your head from your neck before he threw you into the Star Gate."

"Get out of here," StarLaughter said. "This is none of your business."

None of my business? You murdered my daughter!

Axis stared at StarLaughter, his gaze horribly intense.

"Get out of here!" StarLaughter yelled, waving an arm. "Don't think to sit on that pathetic nag and share my triumph!"

"Triumph?" Axis said softly. "StarLaughter, you have made an awful mistake."

StarLaughter narrowed her eyes, thinking. "Ah! The Zenith-harlot was your daughter, was she? Well, don't think to revenge yourself on me for her death. She deserved to die."

Controlling himself at that moment was one of the hardest things Axis had been forced to do in a long, long while. "For my daughter's death," he said, "you deserve an eternal hell. She did not deserve to die—"

"WolfStar threw me aside for her! She deserved every last agony she suffered!"

"You demented witch!" Axis screamed, half-rising from the saddle. *"There was no reason at all for her death!"*

"I just told you why she had to—" StarLaughter stopped abruptly. What had he meant, "an awful mistake"?

Axis took a hard, deep breath, forcing each word out through clenched teeth. "My daughter's death was pointless, as was WolfStar's—although I for one am glad he is finally dead— because WolfStar did not love Zenith at all. He loved you."

"What?"

"WolfStar was only using Zenith to cause dissension within my family. He wanted power back, and thought Zenith the best way to get it." Axis had no idea how true his words were, he only thought they provided a plausible reason for WolfStar's actions.

StarLaughter did not know whether to laugh at the man, or to succumb to utter despair. *She did not want to believe him!*

But his words contained a dreadful, frightful ring of truth.

She stepped close to the horse and put a shaking hand on Axis' thigh. "Tell me!"

"WolfStar wanted to control DragonStar, and he wanted to use Zenith to manipulate him." Axis gave a harsh bark of laughter. "He chose poorly. He should have picked Faraday. Stars above! Hasn't every other ambitious bastard in this land tried to use her at one time or the other?"

StarLaughter frowned, trying to work it out. "But—"

"He loved you. He would have used Zenith, then thrown her aside. You were always foremost in his thoughts."

And always with a curse attached to your name, Axis thought, but this he did not say.

"No! No! I cannot believe you! Didn't he curse me foully when I appeared before him in your convoy? Didn't he repudiate me completely? Didn't he—"

"What *else* did you expect him to do, StarLaughter? He was hardly going to throw Zenith aside when all his plans were coming to fruition. I expect he thought you would have understood that."

StarLaughter tried very, very hard to deny what Axis was saying, but in her twisted mind it all made sense. WolfStar would certainly have wanted to control DragonStar . . . and, if he'd known that DragonStar had slept with his beloved wife, would have wanted to hurt him as much as possible. No wonder he'd picked Zenith to toy with! And now StarLaughter could understand why WolfStar had said what he had . . . and why he'd behaved as he had when confronted with Star-Laughter with a rope wrapped about Zenith's neck.

StarLaughter, had she been in WolfStar's place, would have acted exactly the same way.

Somewhere deep within StarLaughter a small voice said that if WolfStar had truly loved her, and had desired Zenith only for her usefulness, then he would have told StarLaughter then and there that he loved only her truly, and that Zenith was a mere pawn for his ambitions.

But he couldn't, could he, because StarDrifter had been there also, and WolfStar could not have admitted his true motives in front of him.

Yes!

No! her mind screamed back. *I have killed him! I have killed him!*

Axis smiled in grim, determined satisfaction. "You *have* made an awful mistake, haven't you?"

StarLaughter dropped her hand from Axis' thigh and clasped both hands against her breast, her fingers opening and closing amid the folds of her gown. Her mouth went slack in horror.

"I have lost him!" she eventually whispered. "Lost him forever!"

"Not necessarily," Axis said, and StarLaughter missed entirely the hatred and revenge filling his voice.

"No?" Again StarLaughter grabbed at Axis—in sudden, bright hope now, rather than anxiety. "No?"

"No. Your and WolfStar's love is a destined thing—"

"Yes! Yes!"

"—and destiny can never be denied."

"Oh! How right you are!" StarLaughter's face was now suffused with joyous hope.

"I am sure," Axis said, very quietly, and emphasising every word, "that WolfStar waits for you just the other side of the Gate of Death."

"He does?"

"Oh, aye. Waits for you to join him so that you can enjoy a wonderful eternity in the Field of Flowers together."

"The Field of Flowers?"

"A new eternity for all to enjoy," Axis said. "Peace forever more with your loved ones. Imagine, lying in WolfStar's arms amid the lilies, the stars whirling overhead, nothing but you and he, he and you, for all eternity . . ."

"Oh," StarLaughter breathed rapturously.

"And all you must do," Axis whispered, "is to join WolfStar beyond the Gate of Death."

StarLaughter stared at him, her eyes wide.

"A small, trivial thing," Axis continued, still very quietly, very persuasively.

His eyes blazed into StarLaughter's, with hope, she thought.

"A small, trivial thing," she said. "He waits just beyond . . ."

"Just beyond the Gate of Death. Waiting, just for you. Loving you, but weeping that you made such an awful mistake that threatened your eternal happiness together."

StarLaughter thrust her hands against her face. "How could I have been so stupid!"

"Everyone makes mistakes. Fortunately, yours is easily rectified."

StarLaughter nodded, her eyes filled with determination, and Axis slowly lifted his sword and presented it to her in ceremonial fashion, blade in his left hand, hilt extended over his right forearm crossed under the sword.

StarLaughter dropped her eyes from Axis' face and stared at the sword.

"Such a small thing," Axis said, "to be able to join him."

She said nothing.

"Think of your love, and the joy that will be yours forever more, ever more. It is destined."

"Destined," StarLaughter murmured, and tentatively grasped the hilt.

"Destined," Axis said.

Still StarLaughter hesitated. "But . . . but our son. I have to get my son! WolfStar and I can't exist without—"

"Oh, rest easy, StarLaughter. I am sure that your son will

join you shortly. Don't worry about it. But there is one other thing . . ."

Axis reworked his expression into one of deep sorrow. "Of course, if you don't join him soon, WolfStar shall have to make do with whoever he can find. Zenith, I should imagine. After all, you sent her with him. Another awful mistake."

StarLaughter hissed in fury, and she seized the sword and drew it from Axis' care. "She shall not have him!"

"Not if you hurry," Axis agreed.

Utterly determined, and driven by her love and jealousy, StarLaughter changed her grip on the sword, pointing its blade towards her. Hurry, she had to hurry!

Without further thought she drove the blade deep into her belly.

She froze, then looked at Axis, her face a mask of bewilderment, her hands still wrapped about the hilt of the sword. "It hurts."

He shrugged a little. "Death always does, it is part of the rite of passage, I think. Pull the blade free then plunge it in again, twisting this time. Remember WolfStar waits for you."

"Yes . . . yes." StarLaughter tightened her grip, and pulled the blade free.

She screamed, and began to shake violently. "There's . . . there's so much blood."

She took a gasping, sobbing breath. "The pain . . ."

Axis made no comment, but his eyes were bright with hate as they stared at StarLaughter.

"Why is there so much blood, and so much pain?"

"It shows that it's working. Death is opening its Gate for you. Surely you will soon see WolfStar, waiting for you. Go on, plunge the blade in again. Deeper, until you can feel it scraping against your spine."

StarLaughter frowned, then, biting her lip in determination, she took as firm a grip around the hilt as she could, and plunged the blade in again, deep, deeper yet, her face contorted with agony and determination and insane, misplaced love, and gave the blade a massive twist.

Her mouth dropped open with a low, wailing cry, and her eyes stared violently.

She stilled, shuddered, then dropped to the ground.

Axis stared down.

StarLaughter was still alive, but only just.

"Can you see him yet?" Axis asked.

"He's just beyond the Gate," StarLaughter murmured happily, and died.

WolfStar was not pleased to see her at all. He fought, furious, but StarLaughter had her claws in him now, and he could not wrest himself free.

Fate had bound them for eternity.

"The Field," she whispered, and her fingers tightened around his arm.

And so they approached the Field, the husband and wife, their voices raised in acrimonious marital dispute.

They approached the Field, but they did not enter.

They could not.

A thin, pockmarked man, incongruously dressed as a butler, stood before a latched garden gate.

He crossed his arms over his chest, and in a stern voice he said: "Go away. The Field rejects you."

"But—" the husband began.

"Go away."

"We demand entrance!" the wife cried in shrill tones.

"Begone!" the Butler roared, and the husband and wife flinched, and left, each blaming the other for their rejection.

They were left with only one place to drift—the frigid spaces between the stars.

But even there they were not left in peace, for the stars spat at them, and the comets flung blazing embers from their tails at them, and finally that husband and wife drifted to the very edge of the universe where, in loneliness and hate and recrimination, they prepared to spend their eternity.

Axis stared down at StarLaughter's corpse for a very long time, then raised his head towards the Hawkchilds.

They had finished feeding now, and one of them, Star-Grace, hobbled towards him.

"If you think you can persuade *us* to kill ourselves," she said, her beak rippling into pouting, red-lipped form then back to horned abomination, "then you are very, very wrong. We have no need to chase WolfStar into the mists of death."

"Then I must perforce use a bit of persuasion," Axis said, and, raising his head so that he looked beyond the Hawkchilds, smiled.

StarGrace considered him carefully, then she slowly turned and looked herself.

And gave a scream of rage.

Advancing down the back slopes of the gully were hundreds of ghostly trees, their branches weaving and waving into the dawn sky.

"Fool!" StarGrace said, as she whipped back to Axis. "They cannot catch us!"

And she spread her wings and rose into the air, her companions behind her.

Axis lifted his head to watch them . . . and smiled yet again, cold and hard.

Every Hawkchild had been trapped in the net of branches that had extended into impossible heights into the sky. As he watched, the trees pulled their branches back down to earth, dashing each Hawkchild into bloody fragments on rocks and into their own clutching roots.

Again and again the trees raised the corpses of the Hawkchilds into the air, and again and again thundered them earthwards.

When it was all finished the trees retreated, and Axis was left to stare at the now deserted, bloody field of death.

It was only then that he again saw the white wing, splotched with blood and, finally, new horror hit him.

"StarDrifter!" he screamed, and fell to the earth. He scrab-

bled over to the wing, and grabbed at it, burying his fingers amid the feathers as if by that action alone he could bring his father back. *"No! No! No!"*

Far away Qeteb leaned over the snowy tablecloth and squeezed DragonStar's arm. "You mustn't let your sister's and grandfather's deaths distract you. Life must go on after all."

He received no reply, save for a look of implacable hatred.

Qeteb laughed. "Fernbrake next. Fancy a wager on the outcome?"

Again, no reply.

Qeteb was not discouraged. "I must tell you, DragonStar my Enemy, that I have been thinking about this little girl you seem so determined to protect. What was her name? Ah, yes, Katie."

He dragged out Katie's name so wetly it slobbered on the table between them.

"I was thinking, my dear boy, that should one of my companions triumph over of one yours, I might send them after her. To fetch her for me."

Qeteb sat back and rested a forefinger against a cheek, rolling his eyes in a parody of indecision. "Ah, dear me. Which one to go for? Katie . . . or Faraday? You *do* understand that we are caught in the same fight your father engaged in against Gorgrael, don't you? I am caught in Gorgrael's dilemma. Of two females, I know that one of them will destroy you. But which? Which?"

And Qeteb grinned, for he *knew* which one it was.

57

South, Ever South

Axis buried his grief in action. He was unable to go near Zenith's torn body, and so Urbeth and Ur took what remained of Zenith and StarDrifter (they could only find a few remnants of his wings), and interred them in a gully to the east of Sigholt's ruins.

In death, perhaps, the lovers could be together.

Then both women, backed by the trees, sang a dirge of such beauty that Axis finally bowed his head and sobbed as he leaned against Zared.

"South," Axis said, when it was finally over. "South, for I cannot bear to stand here an instant longer and look at the destruction of my life."

"You still have Azhure," Zared said. "You still have DragonStar."

Axis nodded. "But I have also lost, and that loss will never be regained."

"Until the Field—" Zared began, but Axis had already turned and walked away.

South. South to Fernbrake Lake.

There lay Leagh, about to give birth, and about to do her own battle with the Demon Roxiah. Zared was desperate to get to her, to be there for her, but he was not the only one. Ur also niggled at Axis whenever she got the chance, slipping up behind him when he dismounted after a day ranging ahead with his war band, whispering into his ear as he lay down to sleep at night.

Eventually, she annoyed Axis so much he sent her to the

very rear of the column, and set a guard of some twenty-seven Lake Guardsmen over her with strict instructions not to let her near him.

It was not so much Ur's persistence that annoyed Axis, although desperate to be left alone in his grief, but the fact was, he was moving south as fast as he could anyway, and didn't need Ur muttering uselessly every moment she got the chance.

Every day Sal slid faster and faster, and the landscape strode impossibly past, an unnoticed blur. Axis spent his waking hours fighting—swiping the heads from demented cows, slicing the hearts out of sly boars—and his nights tossing in half-sleep, dreaming of Zenith as a child, and dreaming of that day long, long ago, when he had first met StarDrifter in the snow at the foot of the Icescarp Alps.

His daughter and his father, both, impossibly, gone, and he, uselessly, still remaining.

They drew close to the Minaret Peaks.

Leagh had prepared her circular lying-in chamber with the greatest care. It was pristine and white: the gently drifting curtains, the bed, the tables covered with linens, the porcelain bowls and buckets.

The knives and hooks, of course, were of gleaming steel.

Leagh turned slowly about, inspecting her trap.

But who would it trap? Roxiah . . . or her?

Her hand tightened momentarily over her belly. She was huge now, the child squirming, desperate to make its own way in the world.

Not long. Not long.

Beyond the door of the round chamber stood the ranks of the Lake Guard in double file, forming an avenue of ivory and determination.

Beyond them squealed and roared ten thousand crazed creatures from millipedes to humped bulls. They made no attempt to storm either the Lake Guard or the round chamber hung with diaphanous curtains.

Another would storm the chamber for them.

It lingered on the ridge of the crater, staring down, its hand on its own horribly distended belly.

Roxiah: body of Niah, soul of Rox, and receptacle for . . . for whatever waited to squirm its way out.

Soon. Soon. The birth was imminent.

Roxiah turned its head and looked to where Qeteb and DragonStar sat at the luncheon table.

Qeteb nodded, and Roxiah grinned. It turned, and took a step downwards.

In her chamber, Leagh suddenly screamed and doubled over in agony as the first of her birth pangs stabbed home.

58

Sweetly, Innocently, Happily . . .

All Qeteb's genteel bonhomie was gone. He leaned forward over the table, a glass gripped tight in his hand, his eyes intent on the billowing curtains of the circular chamber in the hollow beneath him. On the other side of the table, DragonStar was no less tense. Although he sat back, apparently comfortable on his chair, the muscles of his face were tight, and his eyes narrowed.

A very slight movement in the far distance caught DragonStar's attention, and he shifted his eyes slightly so he could see.

Startlement—almost gladness—momentarily transformed his face. The massive column of trees, peoples and animals had reached the lower Minaret Peaks and was slowly wending its way into the passes that would bring them to Fernbrake.

Axix rode ahead on his sweet brown mare, and not far behind him came Zared on his draughthorse—even at this distance DragonStar's eyes could pick out the desperation in Zared's face. Behind Zared, Gwendylyr riding close at his side, and behind them . . . behind them loped the great ice bear, Urbeth.

DragonStar's face went slack in amazement. For once the proud Urbeth had allowed someone to ride her back. Ur, still clutching her precious terracotta pot.

Well, at that DragonStar was not surprised. If Leagh won out against Roxiah, then Ur would be *desperate* to get to Leagh before she gave birth.

DragonStar almost smiled. No doubt Ur had been niggling and irritating Axis for days upon days to get here as fast as he could.

And then DragonStar's face emptied of all emotion, for he remembered what it was that Axis had ridden from. Zenith. Dead. Lost, finally, for WolfStar's sins.

DragonStar turned his eyes back to the birthing chamber far below.

Roxiah had gained the flat of the crater, and was now waddling its bulky figure through the ranks of the impassive Lake Guard towards the birthing chamber.

Leagh walked slowly, painfully, about the chamber, pausing every time a new pain gripped her.

Her face appeared impassive, but Leagh's mind was running wild with what might, or might not, occur in this chamber.

She was comforted by the sweet voice of her child, reaching up through blood and bone and sinew to her heart to reassure her mother.

Do you not realise how close we are to the Infinite Field of Flowers? the child asked, using her words more as a consolation than as a question that needed to be answered.

Close enough to lose it forever, Leagh said.

The child shifted, unperturbed at the thought of the travail ahead. *Have more faith, mother,* she said, *and think only of the lilies ahead.*

Leagh smiled, a hand on her belly, and then she stilled and looked up.

There was a shadow behind one of the fluttering curtains: dark, oppressive, horribly gleeful.

"Roxiah is here," she whispered.

And one more besides it, said the child, but Leagh did not know what she meant, and so she ignored it.

Roxiah proceeded into the birthing chamber in grand style, its belly breaking through the curtains first, long before Roxiah's grinning face was revealed.

Leagh winced, for the woman's face—Niah's—was nevertheless so much like Zenith's that Leagh found it difficult to concentrate.

Poor Zenith. Dead in the dust of some desolate gorge in the Urqhart Hills. Leagh had been well aware of the manner of death visited on Zenith and StarDrifter.

But this entity was not Zenith. This was the Demon Rox, writhing in Niah's womb, awaiting birth, and the combination of Niah's soulless body and Rox's demonic spirit (and infant flesh) was loathsome to behold.

Roxiah's face was a frightful combination of outward blankness with corruption that writhed only just beneath the skin. It was twisted, bland, malevolent, torpid. It combined soullessness with the depravity of evil. It combined vacancy with a sinister and perverted tenancy that waited to explode forth in fiery and death-dealing birth.

"A joust!" Roxiah crowed, "between you and me! The battle of the bellies, I think! What is the challenge, milksop? What 'choice'," and Roxiah made that word a foulness, "do you have for me?"

Leagh straightened, despite the pain and discomfort that gripped her. "The choice is obvious," she said. "Only one child can be born. Yours, or mine. Bleakness or hope. Your choice. Yours. Which child is to be born, Roxiah? Which?"

"Mine! Mine! Mine!" Roxiah shouted, jumping up and down in a display of ungainly joy. *"Mine!"*

Niah's Demon-controlled body dropped to the floor, writhing and contorting as if gripped in the final pangs of birth. It lifted and spread its legs, as if determined to force out the infant Rox here and now.

"Mine!" Roxiah crowed yet once more.

Far above, Qeteb turned to DragonStar and grinned. "A stupid choice to give Roxiah," he said, grinning his joy. "How could Leagh have possibly thought that—"

"The choice must still be born," DragonStar said calmly, although inside his emotions roiled. Leagh had lost, it seemed.

Hello Niah, said Leagh's baby, and Leagh's face dropped in shock at the strength of her child's mind voice as it sped from the womb.

"Niah doesn't live here any more," Roxiah chortled. "Someone else does. Me, me, *me*!"

Roxiah rolled about and finally managed to get to its feet. It spied the table with its birthing implements spread about, and it seized a large hook, raising it threateningly as it advanced on Leagh. "Time to go, my dear."

Niah? said Leagh's baby. *Niah? Come home, Niah. Come home.*

The wasteland was far distant, a place with no paths leading to any bridge of escape, a place devoid of hope.

She stood, her head hanging, her eyes closed to the soulless-ness surrounding her, knowing she was beyond redemption.

When she had been in the joy and hope of her youth, this was not where she had thought to have ended.

Why, when all she had done was love? Why, when all she had done was fight for the right to love?

Niah, Niah, come home!

———

Leagh did not move, nor attempt to protect herself. "Your choice, Rox," she said. "Which baby is to be born? Whose?"

Niah come home . . .

Roxiah laughed until spittle flew about the chamber in a mad rain of glee. "Time to go, Leagh!"

It threw the hook, and Leagh had to twist violently to avoid it. She staggered, and then fell.

Niah come home . . .

Come home? Come home? Where was home?

She remembered the place where she had been raised into womanhood: the peaceful enchantment of the Island of Mist and Memory, the companionship of her fellow priestesses, the comforting roar of the waves a thousand feet below her feet.

Was this home?

Roxiah scuttled over the distance between them, another hook in its hands. "Time to leave, depart, and farewell the scene, Leagh," it said, and, placing one foot on Leagh's chest, raised the hook to drive it home.

Niah come home . . .

No, that place had not been home, for she had left it.

There had been another home, the house of Hagen in the horror of Smyrton.

There she had birthed her child, her beautiful daughter, Azhure.

And there she had died, burned alive as Hagen poked her further and further into the fire . . .

. . . further and further into the fire . . .

. . . further and further . . .

"No!" she screamed. "No! I won't come home! I won't!"

That is not your home, Niah. Come home. Now, please, you are needed NOW! Come home, Niah, come home.

"I make the choice!" Roxiah screamed. "*My* baby, not yours!"

Leagh raised her arms, crying out, and trying to twist away, her belly left vulnerable as her arms tightened about her face.

Roxiah chortled with joy, twitching and twittering in its demonic labour pangs.

It had won. Rox would be reborn.

Niah, please, please, come home now.

She lifted her head, staring at the vision that had suddenly appeared in the wasteland before her.

A Woman, standing under the most wondrous Tree that Niah had ever seen.

The Woman was beautiful beyond measure, and so powerful the surrounding wasteland cringed in fear.

The Woman smiled, and tears sprang to Niah's eyes.

"Where is home?" Niah whispered. "Where? Must I fear it?"

"Home," said the Woman, "is where you are needed, and where you belong."

"Where?" Niah said, her voice a whisper. "Where?"

Again the Woman smiled. "Where you are needed," She repeated, holding out Her hand. "And where you will be loved. Come home, Niah."

"I can never be loved," Niah said, now on her knees and shaking with shame. "Not after what I have done."

"Done? All you have done is to love, and to be deceived in that love."

"Zenith . . ." Niah's voice was now barely audible; her gaze was now firmly fixed in the dust she knelt in.

"Zenith adores you," the Woman said. "Trust me."

Zenith adores me? Niah wondered, *hardly daring to believe it. She cannot, not after what I have done . . .*

She looked up as a shadow fell across her.

The Woman, still reaching out Her hand. "Come home, Niah. Come home. There is only one small task to be done along the way."

"One small task?"

"One small task for utter redemption, and an eternity of love. Come home, Niah."

And as Niah reached out to take the Woman's hand, the fragrance of the Tree enveloped her.

Roxiah howled, a combination of triumph and the agony of its labouring womb.

Within the womb Rox wriggled in glee, punching and kicking, determined to be born immediately so he could savour his victory by feeding on both Niah's body and those of this stupid witch and her pathetic infant.

He would eat it out of its mother's womb! He would!

With all the strength that Niah's body contained, and the impatient desire of the demonic infant it carried, Roxiah lifted the hook, screeched, and in one vicious, lightning-fast move, drove the hook . . .

. . . into her own belly.

"Oh," Roxiah said, with the most surprised of expressions.

Inside its body Rox gave a single convulsion, trying to wrest himself off the steel hook that had curved its way through his belly, out his back, and then back through his chest to emerge just under his chin. Then he shivered, choking in the bloodied fluids of Niah's womb, and died.

Leagh still lay on the floor, staring, stunned.

As the infant within struggled and died, Roxiah's expression altered, and something *else* entered the horrid face.

Something sweet, and infinitely regretful. Something beautiful, and serene.

Something very definitely "else".

Hello, Niah, said Leagh's baby.

Leagh struggled into a sitting position as the grotesque form swayed above her. Blood was pouring out from the horrible wound in the body's belly, and even as Leagh sat up, Niah took the hook, and twisted it yet further and deeper in.

"Rox is dead," Niah said. "His flesh is tattered and torn."

"Oh, gods . . ." Leagh whispered, managing to rise to her feet. "Niah? Niah?"

"None else," Niah said, trying to smile reassuringly about the agony that coursed through her body. "Come . . . ah, the pain! . . . come to repair some of the damage I have caused. Come . . . come to find some redemption."

Leagh grabbed the woman's shoulders, wondering desperately what she could do.

Niah's head dropped, and her entire body shuddered, but somehow she remained upright.

"Where?" Niah whispered. "Where is She?"

"Who?" Leagh said.

"The Woman. The Woman under the Tree. Where . . . ah!" Niah's eyes dropped to Leagh's belly. "There. There."

Leagh tried to find something to say, but could not. She shook her head slightly, uselessly. Why this tragedy just so her child could be born?

Niah lifted one bloodied hand away from the hook buried in her belly, and touched Leagh's face gently. "There is no tragedy," she said. "For there is only great joy in these events. Lady, will you do something for me? Tell Zenith I am sorry for what I tried to do to her. I was wrong."

Leagh bowed her head. She could not tell Niah that Zenith was dead.

"And tell WolfStar, renegade, that I did the best for him that I could."

Leagh silently shook her head, tears sliding down her cheek. Niah had come home too late—far, far too late.

"And tell my daughter that I love her beyond measure."

Niah tried to say something else, but she suddenly gagged and blood poured from her mouth. She sagged to the ground, and Leagh cried out.

Niah go home, Leagh's child said. *To eternity. Home to the flowers.*

Leagh bent her head over the corpse and wept.

Katie sat up from the ice woman's lap and pushed the glossy brown curls out of her eyes. She looked solemnly at Azhure, sitting at the other end of the barge with SpikeFeather, who still had his arms about her.

"Your mother has gone home," she said. "Sweetly, innocently, and with a final happiness."

"Welcome, ma'am," said the Butler, and swung open the garden gate.

"Dare I?" said Niah. "Dare I? After all I have done?"

The Butler smiled, and if it were not for the dignity of his position, would have hugged her. "You are deeply loved and needed, ma'am," he said. "Please, enter."

Niah looked at him, not daring to hope.

"The lilies await you," said the Butler. "And one else."

Niah turned to the gate, and looked through. She stared, unbelieving.

Zenith stood among the flowers, the lilies tugging at her skirts and at her ebony wings.

She held out her arms, as granddaughter to grandmother, and smiled with love and welcome.

Niah burst into tears, and walked through the gate: sweetly, innocently, happily.

Qeteb's fingers curled into the white cloth and he wrenched it off the table with a roar of fury.

He leapt to his feet and tossed the cloth high into the sky.

It fluttered down slowly into the crater.

"Two down," said DragonStar. "And two wins. To me. My girls have done me proud."

And he lifted his head and smiled at Qeteb.

"Cauldron!" Qeteb snarled, and turned away. "*There* you will fail!"

"Why leave now?" DragonStar said. "Don't you want to stay for the birth?"

59

Midwiving Deity

Pretty Brown Sal pulled them into Fernbrake Lake just in time, for which Axis was supremely grateful. If he'd had to put up with Ur's cries and clamours for just one more hour . . .

Axis hated to think what Ur would have said had they arrived late.

He swung down from Sal, Zared and Gwendylyr a moment behind him.

The instant Axis' feet hit the ground, he was almost bowled over by Ur hurrying forward with her pot.

"Make way! Make way!" she cried, and Axis was stunned to see that she was weeping with joy.

The next instant Gwendylyr had pushed past him, and was hurrying after Ur into the birthing chamber.

"I think I should wait here," Axis said to Zared, but Zared shook his head.

"No. I don't know why, but I think that you should be present as well."

And so Axis, still so desperately sad he wondered that he could actually walk and talk and ride, followed Zared through the lines of the Lake Guard and into the birthing chamber.

The Lake Guard silently followed him, lining the interior of the chamber as silent witnesses.

There was one other silent witness. DragonStar, atop the ridge and staring into Fernbrake crater.

The best place for your birth, he said to the child, now so gripped in the struggle for birth she could not respond. *Fern-brake. The Mother of all Life.*

Leagh lay on the birthing bed and writhed, drenched in sweat. Gwendylyr sat at one shoulder, silently sympathising, one hand wiping the sweat from Leagh's forehead.

At Leagh's other shoulder sat a distraught Zared, wondering what he could do, and yet so glad, so relieved to have Leagh safe again it swamped all his fears.

Axis stood, almost wrapped up in one of the billowing curtains at the edge of the chamber, part of the circle of Lake Guardsmen inside the chamber. Before him, crouched in a huge huddle, lay Urbeth, her head on her paws, her eyes locked on the struggle before her.

This baby would be birthed with many witnesses.

Ur stood at the end of the birthing bed, quivering with excitement, staring at the baby beginning to emerge, her pot still held in violently trembling hands.

Axis watched her with some concern. Shouldn't she be doing more? He remembered the births of his eldest and his youngest. At both, midwives had helped and aided Azhure in a way that Ur most definitely was not helping and aiding Leagh.

Ur was just standing there. Watching. And now quivering so violently in her excitement that Axis thought she would drop the pot at any moment.

And then he jumped, for everything about them changed.

They stood in an infinite field of flowers. Leagh was walking slowly between two women, both in mid-life and so beautiful Axis' breath caught in his throat at the sight of them.

Ur and Urbeth, their arms about Leagh, encouraging her with every step.

The scent of flowers, a warm wind and the gentle sound of waves crashing beneath a distant cliff filled the air.

Zared and Gwendylyr were here too, as were the Lake Guard, but they stood to one side, anxious spectators.

"Axis."

Axis turned slightly at the sound of the voice.

DragonStar, glorious in his near nakedness, the lily sword scabburded in the jewelled belt.

"Have you come to watch?" Axis said.

"I have come to accept," DragonStar replied, and he walked past his father towards Leagh, Ur and Urbeth.

Leagh gave a great groan, and twisted to one side as the child slithered from her body.

"The Baby! The Baby!" Ur cried, and she did what Axis had been afraid all along she would do.

She dropped the pot, and it shattered on the floor.

Several things happened at once. Zared rose to stare at the tiny, wriggling baby that had just slithered into the world. Leagh struggled to sit up so that she, too, could look. Urbeth leapt to her feet, and roared and shook as if possessed. And as one, all the Lake Guard present took a great breath, and shouted, their fists thrust triumphantly into the air.

And while all this was going on, something indescribable filled the birthing chamber.

Leagh gave a great groan and would have sunk to the ground were it not for the support of the two women who held her.

"The Baby! The Baby!" Ur cried.

DragonStar strode forward and sank to his knees before Leagh, an expression of utter wonder on his face.

He held out his hands to catch the Baby.

———

Axis could not describe what then filled the tent in words, only in emotion.

Wonder, gladness, joy, beauty.

Hope, salvation, pity.

Warm wind on cold cheek, and soft touch on despairing heart.

Being. A Being beyond comprehension.

It was the combination of what had been in Leagh's womb, and what had been in the pot.

Ur lifted the child in her hands. It was a Girl, chubby, wide-eyed and joyful.

"The Mother?" Axis said, trying to make sense of it all.

DragonStar caught the child as She slithered from Her mother.

"The Mother?" said Axis.

DragonStar took a moment to respond, and when he did, his voice was filled with gladness.

"The Mother transformed and drawing breath as one with the Infinite Field of Flowers," he said, "so not the Mother at all."

He looked up, and lifted the Girl into Leagh's arms.

"My Child," said Leagh, and took her Daughter in her arms.

DragonStar rose to his feet amidst the flowers and stared into Axis' eyes. "Not the Mother at all" he repeated. "God."

60

The General's Instructions

Qeteb turned slowly about, one arm extended as he indicated the wasteland that stretched for leagues about them. Balls of dust and ice rolled slowly across the plains of Skarabost, while great fingers of mould and putrilage crept over the southern parts of the continent.

Qeteb was all black armour: visored, inscrutable, indestructible.

Before him Mot and Barzula stood attentive and quiet.

They respected the consuming anger that filled Qeteb.

"All this lies at risk," Qeteb said, his voice a hiss behind his visor. "All this beauty. Our home. How hard have we fought to attain this? How many millennia? How many worlds? *And now all is at risk!*"

Mot and Barzula flinched, but otherwise did not move.

Qeteb strode to within a pace of the two other Demons. "You go together to meet DareWing and Goldman. You rise or fall *together*. I do not need to explain what this means."

Having said that, Qeteb made a lie of his words. "Raspu and Roxiah have fallen: one turned, one dead. If you fail then I am weakened to a point where I may flounder myself."

"We will not fail," Mot said.

"Make sure that you do not," Qeteb whispered, then reached forward and grasped each Demon's chin in his mailed hands. *Do not fail!*"

He let them go, and the Demons turned and faded into the wasteland.

Qeteb stood a moment, watching the space where they had vanished, then he turned about.

Sheol was standing behind him, a robe in shifting shades of

decomposing and putrid matter, wrapping itself about her malformed body.

"I know I do not have to concern myself with *your* success," he said.

She grinned, and when she spoke the stench of the grave issued from her mouth.

"Faraday condemns herself," she said. "She does not even want to succeed."

"I cannot understand her preoccupation with self-sacrifice," Qeteb said, "but I am mightily grateful for it."

Then, without further ado, he, too, vanished.

61

For the Love of a Bear Cub

They again sat their mounts—Qeteb his beast of blackness, DragonStar his stallion of drifting stars—but now atop Cauldron Keep itself.

They were uncomfortably close, and both Qeteb's beast and the Star Stallion constantly shifted slightly to keep the maximum possible distance between them.

"Well," said Qeteb from behind his visor, "at least we have a good view."

And he pointed. "Look."

Goldman and DareWing stood by an outcrop of rocks. Behind the rocks stretched the remains of the Silent Woman Woods: tall spikes of blackened timber with occasional spars of charred branches jutting out like the battered rigging of a storm-damaged ship. A path wound through the trees, leading back into the unknown depths of the dead Woods.

DareWing stood straight and tall, his black wings folded

tightly against his back. He wore only a white linen tunic and sandals.

He carried no weapon, and his face was expressionless.

Goldman, on the other hand, was clearly excited, impatient for the fun to begin. He shifted from leg to leg, as he also shifted a heavy staff from hand to hand.

Incongruously for a Master of the Guilds, he was dressed as a woodsman.

The lizard was nowhere to be seen.

DareWing and Goldman waited.

Qeteb and DragonStar waited.

Hours passed, and Goldman grew ever more restless.

"Where are they?" he asked DareWing.

"Soon," DareWing said.

"How do you know?"

"I can smell them," DareWing said.

Goldman opened his mouth to say something further, but closed it as he saw two mangy hunting hounds emerge from behind one of the blackened trees.

They looked like deformed Alaunt. Pale ivory in colour, and with the lean but muscular long-legged shape of the Alaunt, both hounds had running sores covering their pelts, and foulness oozing from eyes and mouths.

The hounds grinned, and one, Barzula, said:

"What temptation do you have for us, then? What choice?"

"We have a hunt," DareWing said softly.

"A hunt!" Mot bayed, and half laughed, half growled. "How appropriate that we took *this* form, then!"

DareWing did not reply to that. The Demons had known of the nature of the challenge, and had picked their forms to suit.

Goldman indicated the dead forest behind him with his staff. "A bear and her cub haunt these woods, making it unsafe for—"

"For *who*?" Barzula asked, his canine mouth grinning slyly.

"For any who would walk beneath the trees," Goldman said. "Will you track her down for us?"

"We like to hunt," Mot said, and both hounds giggled. "We will do as you ask."

And without further ado, the two corrupted hounds pushed their way past Goldman and DareWing, and loped into the skeletal trees.

They tracked for hours. Many times the hounds bayed in excitement as they picked up the great bear's scent, and as many times their tails and ears drooped after a few minutes of following the trail, only to have it fade into non-existence. Goldman and DareWing followed behind, silent, watchful, patient.

In the late afternoon the hounds became frustrated, snapping and snarling at every shadow, every trick of the wind. They savaged tree trunks, tearing great gouges into the dead wood, and dug furious, futile holes in the drifting dirt, defecating quickly into them before moving on to find something else to destroy and corrupt.

They had almost forgotten the bear.

"There!" DareWing cried as the shadows lengthened and crept one into each other. "There!"

Barzula and Mot picked up their heads and pricked their ears.

There!

A darker and more ominous shadow moving behind some trees only twenty paces away.

The hounds bayed in excitement, and the shadow roared.

The hunt was on.

The hounds dashed forth, DareWing and Goldman running behind them as fast as they could.

The bear—all could see her clearly now—rose on her hind legs, swiping furiously at the attacking hounds in order to protect the six-month-old cub cowering behind her. Then, deciding it were better for the safety of her cub to run than fight, the bear swivelled in a graceful, yet powerful, motion, set her cub to run, and followed behind him, keeping the hounds at bay with growls and the odd slash of her powerful and deadly talons.

The hounds chased her, and the huntsmen chased both bear and hounds.

Night closed in.

The hunt grew ever more desperate. The bear was wounded now, as were both of the hounds, although neither the hunted nor the hunters were hurt seriously.

But blood scattered the trail, and sent the hounds into an ecstasy of savagery.

As the moon rose, the bear blundered into a blind gully. Sheer rock walls rose on either side, hounds and huntsmen trapped her from behind.

Desperate, for her cub was exhausted and would surely need rest soon, the bear pushed him towards a steep wall of rock and loose stones at the end of the gully.

They would have to climb it to escape the hounds.

The bear nosed her cub forward, encouraged him with hot breath and deep love, and his small paws rattled and slipped on the loose rock.

Mot and Barzula attacked from behind, tearing pieces of pele and flesh from the bear's hindquarters.

She turned on them, growling and roaring with all the savagery she could muster.

Behind her, the young cub clawed desperately up the scree.

A stone slipped.

He scrambled further, hearing the desperation in his mother's voice, and knowing he would be torn to pieces if the hounds managed to get past her and reach—

Another stone slipped, and suddenly, frightfully, the bear cub was fighting for purchase on the slipping, sliding scree.

The entire wall of rock began to move. Slowly, but inexorably.

Both hounds backed off, watching the sliding rock wall carefully . . . and speculatively.

The mother bear turned about, crying frantically to her child.

He had been almost halfway up the slope, but now he was sliding down amid the avalanche of rocks and stones.

His cries were piteous to hear.

The bear was desperate, making reckless leaps upwards to try to reach her son, only to tumble downwards again.

The rocks slid ever further ever faster.

Suddenly there was a massive roar, and the entire rock slope collapsed.

DareWing and Goldman dashed out of the way, the two demonic hounds behind them, as a huge cloud of dust and small stone fragments rose up about them. Goldman and DareWing dove under the cover of a rock overhang, flinging their arms about their heads and curling their bodies into tight balls in order to protect themselves from the shrapnel flying through the air. They felt the hounds' paws scrabbling furiously over their bodies, as the hounds used the two men to protect themselves from the onslaught.

And then, silence.

Slowly, both men and hounds unwound themselves and stood up, brushing and shaking themselves free of rock dust.

Shafts of moonlight fell over a massive pile of rubble at the foot of the pile of loose rock.

The mother bear was dead, almost completely buried under the fallen scree. Only part of one of her forelegs and its paw protruded. That, and a spreading pool of blood that seeped its way free from under the rock.

Goldman and DareWing stared as Mot and Barzula came to stand by their side.

"Well," Mot remarked, "there's not much choice going on here, is—"

A pitiful cry from about a third of the way up the rock jumble stopped the Demon, and all four jerked their eyes up to look.

It was the bear cub, lying horribly injured under several rocks. A pace above it was an immense boulder, precariously balanced on the landslip.

Even as they watched, the boulder wobbled, threatening to roll its ponderous way down over the bear cub.

The cub mewed again, crying for its mother.

Tears came to Goldman's eyes. Even though he and

DareWing had created this scene with their magic, the distress of the bear cub moved Goldman more than he thought possible.

"The choice is this," DareWing said quietly. "There lies the bear cub, only minutes from death—for that boulder will fall shortly. What should you do, Mot? Barzula? Sit here and wait for its fall, knowing that in the meantime the bear cub will suffer mightily and that when the boulder rolls slowly over it, as the boulder inevitably will, the cub will suffer even worse in death? Or will you try to save the cub, knowing the boulder might yet tumble prematurely and crush you? You have the time—you hope. What do you want to do? Risk your own life to try to save the cub, or ensure your own safety by standing by and witnessing the cub's misery and eventual death?"

The two hounds looked at DareWing, glanced at the bear cub, now sobbing almost like a human child, and then looked back at DareWing.

Then, very, very quickly, they glanced at Goldman.

Their eyes returned to DareWing, and they both slobbered and grinned.

And sat down.

"We wait," Mot said, "for we feed off misery and pain."

"Not what you expected?" Qeteb said to DragonStar. "Did you really think that bear cub's suffering would move them?"

"Wait," DragonStar said.

"Yes," Qeteb said, and grinned malevolently beneath his visor. "Why don't we do just that?"

Goldman looked at the cub. It was wriggling, trying so desperately to free itself, that Goldman's heart went out to its bravery and suffering.

How could it understand that it was merely part of a spell, a test?

In its own mind, the bear cub existed.

And suffered and sorrowed.

It wanted its mother. It wanted to be free, and free of the agony coursing through its mangled body.

"Gods," Goldman whispered.

Qeteb's grin stretched even further, and he felt the power of success flood his veins.

Now Mot and Barzula lowered themselves to their bellies, and Mot yawned.

"I wish that boulder would hurry up and fall," he said. "The wait bores me."

But teeter and shudder as it might, the boulder did not fall, and the bear cub continued to mew and sob in its pain and sorrow.

Goldman looked desperately at DareWing. "I can't just stand here . . ." he said.

"Goldman!" DareWing cried, appalled. "We can't—"

"I can't listen to it any more," Goldman whispered. "I *won't*!"

He turned, and dashed for the rock scree.

"Goldman!" DareWing screamed, and lifted into the air.

Goldman scrabbled up the rock scree, not hearing the laughter of the hounds beneath him. All he could see, all he could hear, was the bear cub writhing just above him. If only he could reach it, comfort it somehow, then all would be well . . . all would be well . . .

DareWing, hovering just above Goldman, reached down and tried to grab Goldman's tunic. "Goldman! Leave it alone! Leave it—"

DareWing could have flown to safety. But he didn't. He chose to stay with his friend, who had chosen, from pity, to save the cub.

The choice was made, and now others would live and die by it.

Goldman had scrabbled within an arm's length of the bear
cub, despite DareWing's hand now buried in the back of his
tunic. He reached forward, touching the cub's flailing paw.

The cub screamed . . .

. . . and the boulder toppled.

Not slowly, not reluctantly, but with a haste and purpose
that was demonically assisted.

It struck the cub, sending a spray of blood and flesh outwards, and then in the next heartbeat it struck Goldman, and,
as it rolled inexorably downward, it caught DareWing's hand,
and dragged him under its surging weight.

There was a brief crack, as if of splintering bones, and then
the boulder was tumbling madly down the scree, leaving behind it a wet slick of blood and flesh in the shaft of soft
moonlight.

Both hounds nonchalantly moved out of the way as the
boulder rolled past them, and then sat down and shook with
laughter.

"And in that instant," Qeteb said, turning his head to stare at
DragonStar's shocked face, "and for the love of a bear cub,
we're even! *Even!* Faraday . . . Faraday shall prove the decider."

And he tipped back his head and roared with laughter.

*The Butler opened the gate and prepared to welcome the visi-
tors through.*

*But the three shook their heads, one saying: "Thank you,
good sir, but we would wait awhile. One of our number has yet
a task unfinished, and must return."*

*"Then perhaps we can talk," said the Butler, "to pass the time,
I have," he bent down and lifted something from the flowers
about his legs, "a jug of creamy ale I rescued from the cook."*

"Oh, well done!" cried Goldman.

62

Katie, Katie, Katie . . .

They drifted through unknown waterways, closer and closer to the Maze. The buildings and structures to either side of the waterways grew ever more strange, and ever more depressing: great, grey statues of fierce-chinned men, staring into the distance, shields and spears in hand. Other statues as tall as buildings, crouched in contemplation, or with their faces buried in hands, as if all thought inevitably led to suicide. Still more lay stretched out along the ground, cracked and crumbled, their stony faces reflecting some long distant horror, and with twisted crosses tattooed deep into their biceps and chests.

In one cavern Azhure's gaze was caught by the remnants of a great statue of a woman—only her head, neck, and one shoulder and arm, were in one piece, while other bits of her toppled across what had once been a huge parade ground. The statue's head was majestic, crowned by a stone diadem, her eyes wide and staring. Her outflung stone arm held a great torch, long extinguished.

Azhure gazed at it, sickened, yet not understanding why. She was not to know that the statue's fragments almost exactly mirrored Zenith's remains as Axis had seen them.

Eventually, she dragged her eyes away, nauseated by these grey stone relics of a world long gone.

Katie sat with Azhure's hand in hers. "You will see her again," she said. "Surely. In the Field of Flowers."

Azhure nodded, but her face was as sad as those of the statues that lay to either side of them. "I suppose I will, but, oh Stars! I have spent too much of my life grieving!"

"Death is but a doorway," Katie said.

"I have come to loathe doorways," Azhure said and took her

hand from Katie's, "for one can never be sure of the truth that is said to lie on the other side."

To that, Katie said nothing, and the punt glided on.

"You know," Qeteb said as he and DragonStar rode their beasts eastwards towards the Maze, "I have decided on a small game to help pass the time until I can hunt you through the Maze, dear companion."

"And that is?" The Alaunt streamed out behind the Star Stallion, periodically deviating to nip at the fetlocks of Qeteb's strange black beast.

The beast took no notice of them.

"Well," Qeteb said, shifting himself more comfortably in his saddle. "I remember a small game that Gorgrael played."

DragonStar looked at him sharply.

"And I thought you might enjoy it," Qeteb continued. His visor was thrown back, and his perfect, handsome face grinned into the wasteland. "I remember that Gorgrael debated back and forth, back and forth, Azhure, or Faraday? Azhure or Faraday? *Which?* Do you remember that, DragonStar?"

DragonStar stared at the Demon, but said nothing.

"Ah, you were but a babe in arms, then," Qeteb said. "Well. Gorgrael knew that *one* of them would prove the distraction that would destroy Axis' concentration when your golden father finally met the warped and unlovable Gorgrael, but the poor chap wasn't sure which one. He had time and resources to go for only one. Finally, as legend well knows, he decided on Faraday, which was the wrong choice because your father loved Azhure more and could afford to ignore Faraday being torn to bloody pieces before his eyes."

"What is the point of all this, Qeteb?"

"Well, I am glad you asked me that, my good friend, because I am faced with much the same dilemma. I am certain that there is one woman around who could destroy your concentration when we finally meet face to face in the Maze, but I am dithering over which it might be. Faraday, or . . ."

"Or?"

"Or . . . Katie."

DragonStar turned aside. "I do not love Katie."

"You do not *lust* for her in the same way that you lust for Faraday, but, oh yes, you do love her. And, far more importantly, you *need* her. For what, I am not at all certain, but I can *feel* your need for her bubbling through your veins.

"And so the game is, what will destroy your concentration more? Watching Faraday, whom you love and for whom you lust, torn to shreds before your eyes . . . or Katie, whom you need for whatever noble and magnificent purpose you have been created?"

Again DragonStar made no reply.

"The game, my dear and wonderful cousin," Qeteb whispered, kneeing his beast so close to Belaguez that the stallion snorted with disgust, "is that I *don't* have to choose, do I? I have the resources to take both. How will you feel, Drago-dearest, when I toss *both* their broken bodies at your feet?"

DragonStar pulled Belaguez to a head-tossing halt. "I don't believe you. There is no way you can take—"

"Ha! I have you!" Now Qeteb had turned his beast about to face DragonStar. "Faraday you knew I could take with Sheol—were you counting on it?—but you thought Katie safe. It's *Katie*, isn't it? Katie! Katie whom you hid from me—but don't think I can't find her!"

Qeteb kicked his beast into a series of tight circles, laughing maniacally. "Katie! Katie! Katie! Katie!"

And then Qeteb pulled his beast to a violent halt, and he growled. "I'll take *both*, you bastard. *Both!* One I'll slaughter for the sheer joy of it, and one I'll shred to win!"

Katie! Katie! Katie! Katie! The evil whisper echoed about the waterway and everyone sat up straight, eyes darting about.

"Qeteb," said Katie, and burst into tears.

Azhure gathered the girl into her arms, tightening them protectively about her, and looked to SpikeFeather. "What can we do?"

SpikeFeather, and both the ice women, were looking carefully about, checking the dark cavities between the buildings that littered the cavern they currently drifted through.

"Not much, probably," he said. "But I don't think there is any need to worry. Qeteb is now so closely tied to DragonStar and their combat above ground that he can't—"

A cold howl drifted through the cavern.

"Dogs!" Azhure said.

"No," one of the ice sisters replied. "Hounds."

"Hounds?" said SpikeFeather. "But that's impossible. There are no hounds in the—"

"Demons," said one of the sisters.

"Mot and Barzula," said the other.

The baying grew closer, and suddenly Azhure gave a soft cry and pointed.

A pale hound crouched atop the shoulders of a massive statue of a man sitting on a rock with his despairing face in his hands.

As they watched, the hound lifted its head and howled.

It was answered by the other hound some fifty or sixty paces further down the waterway, waiting at the very edge of the canal.

As the punt glided closer, the hound bared its teeth, growled, and crouched as if to spring.

Azhure pushed Katie into the bottom of the punt, sheltering the girl with her body.

Katie! Katie! Katie! Katie!

Qeteb's voice thundered through the waterways, and Azhure wriggled herself as tightly and as protectively about Katie as she could.

SpikeFeather leapt to his feet, rocking the punt wildly, but he was pushed down again by one of the ice sisters.

"Leave this to us," she said, and the next instant both women had leapt for the bank—transforming into icebears as they did so.

The hounds took one look, then bounded out of sight into the streets and alleyways of the abandoned stone city behind them, the icebears in close pursuit.

The icebears were fast, magically so, but the hounds always kept one breath, one leap, one thought, ahead of them. They ran through great abandoned boulevards with ancient banners, thick with dust, hanging from street lighting and buildings, and they dashed through alleys so narrow the icebears howled as their shoulders and flanks rasped against the confining stone walls.

And always the hounds, slavering and howling as if they were but one breath away from collapse, leaped one pace ahead of the sisters.

Finally, the hounds dashed into a blind square bounded by tall, blank-windowed tenement buildings, scrambling frantically about the confining walls, howling and screeching with fear.

The icebears slowed to a walk, their shoulders hunched with power, their faces curled in snarls so tight their eyes had almost disappeared, placing their paws slowly and deliberately one in front of the other in murderous anticipation.

Both hounds backed against the far wall, their tails between their hind legs, and whimpered.

One of the sisters paced closer, her growls reverberating about the confined space, and she slashed out at the hounds with a massive paw.

Her claws should have torn flesh from bone. Instead, nothing impeded her swing as it glided through shadow and fakery.

She fell silent, her eyes narrowed even further.

She lunged with both teeth and claws, and as she hit both hounds, they faded completely away.

As she collapsed on the ground, her sister pivoted about on her haunches, peering about the square.

But there was nothing. Nothing save the mocking laughter of the demonic enchantment as it literally vanished into thin air.

After a while, Azhure cautiously raised her head. "Are we safe?"

SpikeFeather nodded. "We are safe for the time being. I think we should—"

"Safe?" said a soft, distorted voice. "Safe? Safe from *who,* pray tell?"

And again the punt rocked wildly, even though neither SpikeFeather nor Azhure had moved.

A pair of hands appeared on either side of the punt, and gripped its sides.

Close behind came two heads—half eel, half humanoid—rising, dripping, from the water.

"Mot," said one.

"Barzula," said the other, by way of polite introduction, and then the hands were slithering into the punt.

Azhure had no time for a cry. Again she rolled herself into as tight a ball about Katie as she could, trying to protect the girl with her own flesh and blood. Above her she heard and felt the sounds of SpikeFeather battling with one of the Demons.

Cold hands ran over Azhure's spine, their thin fingers tracing every bone, every crack, and now she could not help the cry, "SpikeFeather!"

But SpikeFeather was no use. Mot had him pinned in the bow of the punt, the Demon's hands wrapped about the birdman's throat.

The thin, cold fingers suddenly dug deep into Azhure's back.

"SpikeFeather!" she screamed again, but it was no use, he couldn't help her, and the agony was so great that Azhure had to try to roll out of the way.

And the instant she did so, the fingers were gone, and she could breathe once again.

Azhure struggled up, leaning on her hands, and then grabbed for Katie, meaning to pull the girl under her body once more.

But Katie was gone, hauled over the side of the punt and into the water. One of the Demons had dragged her to the bank, and lifted her out of the water as Azhure watched.

Azhure scrambled to her feet, about to jump into the water to swim to the bank, when the punt rocked again, and she felt a taloned hand digging deep into the calf of her left leg.

She moaned, the pain too vicious for her to cry out loud, and collapsed in the bottom of the punt.

The other Demon, now wearing the form of a huge, horned toad with taloned, almost human hands, twisted its grip, and Azhure screamed.

SpikeFeather lay motionless at the other end of the punt, and even in her own agony Azhure caught a fleeting glimpse of blood.

"You've hung about too long," the toad whispered. "Time to make your intimate and eternal acquaintance with the AfterLife, bitch."

"I don't think so," a new voice put in from the opposite side of the waterway to which the other Demon held Katie. "Her time is not yet ripe. Soon, but not yet."

The Demon who held Azhure scrambled about to face the newcomer, his grip loosening on Azhure's leg.

Azhure blinked, her eyes blurred with tears of pain, and half raised her head to look herself.

A tall, black-haired woman with a cadaverous face stood there, her hands folded calmly before her.

Azhure blinked again, knowing she'd seen this woman before, but not quite able to place her.

The woman—was she the most beautiful woman in creation, or the ugliest?—turned her eyes very slightly towards Azhure.

The Sepulchre of the Moon, woman. Where you came to your true understanding.

Azhure gasped. Of course! After she'd given birth to RiverStar and DragonStar, WolfStar had hauled her out of her painfilled chamber and hurled her down the steps that hugged the cliff face of Temple Mount. There, in the Sepulchre of the Moon, she'd met the other seven Star Gods . . . and the woman.

The keeper of the gate into the AfterLife.

The GateKeeper.

The toad roared, and, in a massive leap, lunged from the punt towards the GateKeeper.

Without apparent hurry, the GateKeeper raised her hand and tossed something towards the toad.

It was a small metal ball, and before it could strike the toad, the Demon had screeched and twisted mid-air to fall several paces away from the GateKeeper.

As he fell, the toad rolled away and transformed back into the humanoid form of Mot.

He rose to his feet, and sneered at the GateKeeper. "Foolish dupe!"

"A dupe?" the GateKeeper said. "Then why twist away so frantically, Demon Mot?"

She received no answer save a vicious snarl, and then Mot vanished to reappear on the other side of the waterway with Barzula and Katie.

The girl was twisting futilely in the Demon's hard hands, whimpering and staring round-eyed at Azhure.

Azhure turned back to the GateKeeper.

"Do something!" she said. "Save her, please!"

The GateKeeper looked at Azhure, then looked back to Katie.

"No," she said.

"Save her!" Azhure screamed, one hand clutching at her bloody and useless left leg.

"No."

"Save—"

The GateKeeper looked very calmly back at Azhure. "Her time is nigh," she said. "I will do nothing for her."

At that, both Mot and Barzula broke into disdainful laughter. They would have said something, save just at that moment there sounded the close roar of an icebear.

Mot looked at Barzula, and the Demon's hand tightened about Katie.

"She'll make a tasty morsel for Qeteb," Mot said, and then they were gone, Katie with them.

"Katie!" Azhure whispered. "Oh gods, Faraday, what have I done?"

"Your best," the GateKeeper said, and then suddenly she was in the punt with Azhure and SpikeFeather. She lifted the birdman's limp head, and grunted.

"Unconscious, but not cruelly hurt," she pronounced, and then looked up as the two icebears appeared on the side of the waterway.

Both were growling and swinging their heads back and forth in frustration and fury.

The GateKeeper laughed, but not unkindly. "Your mother will not be pleased with you," she said, and then sobered as she looked at Azhure, blood still pumping out of her leg.

"We must see to that," she said. "And to this bump on the birdman's head."

"Can you take us to Axis?" Azhure said.

The GateKeeper shook her head. "There is turmoil in the air. And death. You will be safer with me for the moment."

And she laughed again, harsh and yet beautiful. "Who knows what reacquaintances you will make at my Gate!"

Azhure stared at the GateKeeper, then bent her head into her hand in unconscious imitation of the stone statues on either side of the waterway, and wept.

"Oh, Faraday! I am so sorry!"

63

ɦunting Chrough the Landscape

From Fernbrake, Axis swung east, driving his war band, the trees and the column of Tencendor's survivors as fast as he could.

Every day he rose from his bedroll before sunrise—easily, as he rarely slept more than an hour or two at a time—and badgered his war band into action. Grabbing what food they could, they were mounted and riding into the corrupted landscape as the sun topped the desolate ridges of the Rhaetian Hills and the Minaret Peaks. Both lines of ridges were now well behind them.

Fanning out from the war band were some thirty thousand trees. The column was relatively safe from both rear and flanks now, and Axis could afford to send the majority of trees out hunting through the landscape for every piece of breathing corruption they could find. Although Axis and the war band tended to stay in one group, searching out herds of demented livestock, the trees ranged far and wide, sometimes in groups of half a dozen, occasionally in groups of about fifty, but mostly individually, each intent on assuaging her need for revenge against the Demonic hordes creeping across, or under, what was left of Tencendor.

While Axis and his war band attacked the herds, the trees attacked and destroyed the individual creatures, or those who wandered in twos and threes.

Their branches waved impossible heights into the sky, and snatched anything from gnats to birds. On one occasion, Zared swore he had seen one disembodied branch literally detach itself from its tree, lunge into the sky, grab a screeching raven, then drop down to reattach itself to the trunk of the tree.

Twisting, seeking branches had other uses as well. Many was the time Axis and his companions saw a tree stop, study what appeared to be a bare patch of ground, then burrow its branches deep into the earth, hauling wailing weasels, foxes, rabbits and whatever other prey sought to hide itself within the soil.

Everything the trees found, they killed. Quickly, mercilessly and completely. Bodies were torn apart so that *nothing* was left to reconstitute itself under whatever demonic power inhabited it. Flesh was trodden into the earth, blood was cast into the wind.

The wasteland was splattered with the remains of the possessed.

Each day they moved east, sliding faster and faster as Axis urged Pretty Brown Sal forward, sliding closer and closer to the Maze.

Leagh travelled comfortably in a well-rugged and cushioned cart in the convoy, Gwendylyr by her side. She nursed her Child, marvelling at the Girl's beauty and, even at this extremely young age, Her extraordinary self-possession and awareness. The Girl suckled at Leagh's breast, regarding Her mother with deep blue eyes that Leagh swore reflected stars deep within their depths.

And flowers. Sometimes when her Child breathed softly in sleep, Leagh could smell the scent of lilies on Her breath.

Her Child was extraordinary, beautiful, gracious, loving beyond compare . . . and vulnerable.

Ur and Urbeth spent a great deal of the time with Leagh as well. Ur clucked and chuckled in her old-womanish way over the Child, but when the babe slept, Ur's face creased with worry and the cares of every nursery-keeper, and she would look at Leagh and say:

"Keep Her safe. She is still so vulnerable. If Faraday . . . if Faraday falls then the Girl will fall also."

Whenever Ur said this, Leagh came close to panic. "Why? Why is Her fate so tied to Faraday? What is it about Faraday? What can we do to help? What—"

And then either Ur, or Urbeth, or both, would lay a soft hand against Leagh's cheek and stop her flow of words.

"We can do nothing, sweet mother," one of the ancient women would say. "Nothing. We have now done our task, both of us, as you have. Faraday holds the key, and we must wait to see which way she wields it."

And thus Leagh was left with her worry, and her love, and nothing to do but nurture the infant she had birthed, and marvel at Her wonder and power, and let the dark wing of her hair fall against her cheek as she leaned down and whispered words of comfort and love to the Child.

It took them only a few days to draw close to the Maze, and when Axis rode within sight of it, he had to halt Sal and stare wordlessly, horrified at the abomination that had claimed the Grail Lake and Carlon.

A great, black heart beat in the wasteland. It was Maze and flesh both, its corridors and passages twisting and winding about its own core, the Dark Tower. Within its veins pulsed billions of malformed and psychotic creatures, humanoid, animal, and half-bred horrors that had sprung from the bodies of both: man-bulls, child-foxes, woman-cows.

Every so often creatures spilled out of the Maze Gate, expelled like gouts of blood from a bleeding heart. Sometimes the hundreds of creatures set loose with each expulsion scrambled mindlessly about the immediate wasteland, falling victim to the cravings and appetites of other creatures about them, and sometimes they set off in groups of several score, as if purposed by Qeteb for his own dark design. Most of these hordes swarmed up and down the dusty-dry bed of the Nordra—now a great artery of corruption—but several of these dark-minded crowds set off for Axis and his column. Most were destroyed by the ethereal trees before they could cause any harm, and the few that did reach Axis and his war band were quickly dispatched.

As Axis sat Sal on the eastern bank of the Nordra on a small hillock overlooking the black Maze, surveying the frightful scene before him, Axis wondered what he should do now, but before he could make up his mind, Ur rode up on the bear-back of Urbeth.

"Wait," Ur said. "There is not much else to do."

"Look," said Zared, who had ridden to join Axis, and he pointed to the north-west.

There a series of small hills rolled towards the distant Western Ranges. On one of the hills was a tumble of stones, surrounded by a massive crowd of beasts.

A chestnut-haired woman in a white robe stood before the stones, facing the beasts.

"Faraday!" Axis whispered.

"And more," Zared said softly, wondering how any of them could possibly survive this day. Again he pointed.

On a hill some eighty paces away from the one on which Faraday awaited her fate stood DragonStar and Qeteb, their respective mounts four or five paces apart, waiting on them.

Qeteb was all-consuming darkness: his armour, his wings,

the lance he held in his right hand. Even the dawn light seemed drawn into him, as if he were that source in the universe which ate all light, and sent it to its death.

Beside him, DragonStar stood clean and bright, dressed in nothing save his white loincloth, and jewelled belt and purse.

The lily sword was sheathed.

As Qeteb appeared to eat light, so DragonStar appeared to radiate it . . . but the light he put out could not compete with the amount Qeteb absorbed, and even as Axis stared, DragonStar seemed to fade slightly, as if whatever energy source he relied upon was being consumed particle by particle by the Midday Demon.

"He is weak," Urbeth said softly.

"Maybe," said Ur. "Maybe."

There was a stir amongst the creatures milling before Faraday, and all eyes turned in her direction.

64

The Most Appalling Choice of All

Faraday turned, and she saw Axis in the distance. He sat atop a small brown horse, his war band about him, and Faraday smiled, remembering the adventures and the love they'd once shared.

Or, the love she'd *thought* they once shared.

Tears filled her eyes, and she bowed her head, and turned away.

As she turned, Faraday raised her head anew, and she saw Qeteb and DragonStar on a hill not far from hers.

DragonStar . . . Faraday sobbed, a shaking hand to her mouth. She didn't think she had the strength for what lay ahead. She well knew what had happened to Goldman and DareWing, and the triumph that suffused Qeteb. Now it all rested on her. The chance for complete success, or utter failure.

And utter failure would inevitably lead to obliteration. Oh gods! How she prayed for it! To escape all pain and betrayal, to be at peace even if it was the peace of oblivion.

Still sobbing, both hands and shoulders shaking, Faraday stared at DragonStar. Did he love her? Did he love her enough to place her before Tencendor?

Could he save her from what lay ahead?

Faraday shut her eyes, desperate to escape from the nightmarish thoughts chasing about her head.

Desperate, whatever else, to escape from the pain that was her destiny.

Something dug slightly into her belly, and Faraday's free hand gripped the rainbow belt that the Mother had given her. She could feel the outline of the arrow and the sapling that wound about it.

And from that faint touch, Faraday drew strength.

She took a deep breath, and opened her eyes for a last look at DragonStar. "For God's sake," she whispered, not even pausing to wonder why she put the deity in the singular now, when before she, as everyone else in Tencendor, had always used the plural, "save me, DragonStar. Save me."

And Faraday turned, and she faced the test.

Sheol now stood before the undulating dark mass of beasts that spread out from Faraday's hill.

"Greetings, Faraday," Sheol said pleasantly, and Faraday felt despair flood her. "What choice do you have planned for *me*, then?"

And Sheol laughed, a dreadful, burbling chortle that rang with utter confidence.

Sheol was going to win, and she *knew* it.

Faraday sighed, utterly despairing, and she held out her hand to the Demon. "Come," she said.

They walked a frozen landscape. A frigid northerly wind blew hard-edged snow about them, forcing both to walk with heads bowed and hands grasping their cloaks about them.

Neither talked.

As they walked, Sheol very gradually turned eastwards until she was lost in the driving wind and snow, and Faraday was left alone in the frozen land.

This was a land, and an existence, Faraday knew very well.

She had been here before, on the evening she had risen from the campfire she'd shared with Axis and the two Avar men, Brode and Loman, as they'd journeyed northwards to Gorgrael's ice fortress. Faraday had risen and left that fire and not seen Axis again until he'd come to claim his inheritance in Gorgrael's frightful chamber.

Now Faraday lived it all over again.

She caught sight of a flickering campfire ahead, and thought she saw DragonStar's form rise and move about it, throwing on more wood as if awaiting her company.

"DragonStar!" Faraday breathed, and hurried forward. Maybe all would be well, after all.

A strange whisper, barely discernible in the night, ran along the edge of the wind.

Faraday paused, the cloak wrapping itself about her body in the wind. Nothing. She hurried on.

There, again, a soft whisper along the wind and, this time, a hint of movement to her right.

She stopped again, every nerve afire. Her fingers pushed fine strands of hair from her eyes, and she concentrated hard, peering through the gloom, listening for any unusual sounds.

"Faraday." A soft whisper, so soft she almost did not hear it.

A whisper . . . and a soft giggle.

"Faraday." And another movement, more discernible this time, among the eddying snow.

She stared, hoping it was her imagination, hoping she was wrong.

The flickering campfire caught her eye again, and she looked back. DragonStar had raised his head and was staring into the snow in her direction, but just as she was about to call out, something distracted DragonStar, and he bent back to the fire.

"Faraday."

No mistaking it this time, and Faraday closed her eyes and moaned.

"Faraday? It is I, Timozel."

She mustered all her courage and looked to her right. A shape was half-crouched in the snow some four or five paces away, its hand extended, its eyes gleaming.

It was not Timozel, but Sheol . . . but a Sheol who had assumed the form of Timozel: the boyishly lean body; the hair plastered to the skull with ice; eyes which, once so deep blue, were now only rimmed with the palest blue, the rest of the irises being stark white.

Timozel's form, but with Sheol's intelligence and strength shining from behind those frightful eyes.

"Help me . . . please," Sheol whispered in Timozel's voice.

"No," Faraday whispered. "Go away."

"Qeteb trapped me!" Sheol whispered. "I never wanted to be a Demon! No! Never! Qeteb forced me into a life of darkness, and I've had no choice."

And now? thought Faraday, but for the moment she made no comment.

"He has trapped me, Faraday! Trapped me! Forced me into his service."

"No," Faraday said, but she was unable to look away, unable to call for help. Once again the force of the Prophecy lay like a dead weight about her shoulders. Nothing she could do now could alter its abominable course.

"I'm as much a victim as you are, Faraday. Please help me. I want to escape. Trust me."

"Go away," Faraday muttered hoarsely, and the wind caught at her cloak so that it tore back from her body.

Now Sheol was almost at her feet, and her fingers fluttered at the hem of her gown. "Please, Faraday. I want to revel in the Light. *Please,* Faraday! Help me. You could be my friend. *Help me!*"

No! she screamed in her mind, but she could not voice it. Out of the corner of her eye she saw DragonStar rising from the fire, a hand to his eyes. Then her hair whipped free and, caught by the wind, obscured her vision.

No! But the resurgent Prophecy had her in its grip now, and it would not let her go.

"Trust me," Sheol whispered at her feet. *Trust me.*

No!

"DragonStar," she cried. "Forgive me!"

Sheol's hand snatched at her ankle.

"Gotcha!" she crowed.

Faraday closed her eyes to fight her panic, took a deep breath, then looked at Sheol.

"This is your choice," she said. "You can take me to Qeteb, or you can let me go. You *do* have a choice. You do not merely have to mouth the words from some drama that was played out forty or more years ago. Sheol, listen to me, listen to your choice. Take me to Qeteb, or join the light, free your soul. Let me go."

Let me go.

Sheol, still crouched in the snow, one claw-like hand about Faraday's ankle, cocked her head as if deep in thought.

Her features flowed into her female form, back again into Timozel's lost face, and then finally settled back into that of the Sheol-face she normally wore.

"A choice?" she whispered. "A choice? I can truly leave Qeteb and join the forces of light and goodness?"

Before Faraday could answer, Sheol burst into sarcastic laughter, and her hand tightened painfully about Faraday's flesh.

"Stupid woman! I choose Qeteb! I choose never-ending demony! I choose vileness and evil and despair! But wait! There's *more*! In choosing, I offer you a choice of my own. Look!"

And Sheol's free hand gestured into the snow to Faraday's right.

Faraday looked, and cried out, both hands to her face in horror. *"No!"*

"Yes," Sheol whispered. "Yes, indeed. Your power tells you the truth of this vision, doesn't it?"

And the very worst thing was that Faraday's power *did* tell her the truth of this vision.

The Dark Tower.

And inside the mausoleum, the black marbled and columned interior of the Dark Tower.

Worse, there was yet more.

Katie, sobbing and terrified, dangling between the grasp of Mot and Barzula.

Katie! Katie! Katie!

"This is the choice, Faraday," Sheol whispered. "Qeteb will destroy one of you in his battle against DragonStar. He already has Katie, but he is willing to swap Katie for you. Give yourself to Qeteb, Faraday. Fulfil Prophecy—again—and Katie will go free."

Faraday was overcome with horror. What had happened? How had Qeteb managed to seize Katie? *Why hadn't Azhure looked after her properly?*

She began to weep, great, soul-tearing sobs that came from the very core of her being. "Oh, Katie!" she whispered. "Katie! I cannot let this happen to you!"

There was no choice, and Faraday knew it. "Take me," she said. "Take me."

Sheol broke into triumphant laughter, and rose from Faraday's feet, seizing Faraday's shoulders in a grip so painful that Faraday cried out and almost lost consciousness.

"You stupidest of bitches!" Sheol said. "I've *won*, and that means DragonStar has *lost*!"

"I'm sorry," Faraday whispered into the swirling snowstorm, knowing no apology could ever be enough. "I'm sorry."

Three to two. The balance was in Qeteb's camp. DragonStar had failed.

Qeteb turned to DragonStar. He spoke, but with the mind voice only.

The preliminaries are over, Enemy. Now it is just you and me. DragonStar, impassive even in utter defeat, nodded. *Just you and me.*

Qeteb smiled. *The choices are made, the outcome assured.*

DragonStar bowed his head. *Aye. I accept it.*

Then let the Hunt begin!

And Qeteb vanished, and as he vanished, the billions of creatures in and about the Maze let loose an almighty roar as if with one voice.

Let the Hunt begin!

Leagh clutched her Child to her breast, her eyes round and fearful. "We've lost!"

Ur stared into the distance, seeing something that no-one else could. "Perhaps."

65

Abandoned

Sheol threw Faraday down on the mausoleum floor before Mot and Barzula.

Mot laughed, the sound violent and horrifying, and Faraday only barely managed to find the courage to raise her head.

Katie still struggled in their grip, her eyes round and terrified, her face so white Faraday wondered that she had not already fainted.

"Let Katie go," she said. "Let her go. I have offered myself to take her place."

"Let her go? Let her *go*?" Sheol giggled from behind Faraday. "Why?"

"You promised! You said that Qeteb would swap Katie for me! *You said that Katie would go free!*"

"She lied to you, bitch."

The voice, harsh with hatred and something else that, when Faraday comprehended it, filled her with nauseous dread. No! No! *Not this again!*

Qeteb walked around Sheol and stood with Mot and Barzula. His metal armour clanked and shrieked with every movement.

Faraday, still cowering on the floor, wrenched her gaze from Katie to look at him.

Slowly Qeteb raised a hand and lifted the visor of his helmet.

Something horrible writhed inside, and Faraday screamed. A forked tongue flickered over the lip of the helmet's chin-piece, as if in anticipation.

"You promised to let her go!" Faraday screamed. "Take me, but let her go!"

"Didn't you hear me, cow?" Qeteb took one step towards Faraday, and she screamed, and would have wriggled away had not Sheol stamped a foot into the small of her back, pinning her to the floor.

"Oh," Qeteb said, "how I adore to see a woman writhing before me."

"Take me—" Faraday began.

"Oh, and now she *begs* for me!" Qeteb crowed.

"—but let Katie go!"

"I do not subscribe to the principle of honour," Qeteb said, now squatting down by Faraday. "I don't mind ensuring Drag-onStar's death any foul way I can."

She buried her face in her hands, unable any longer to look at the unspeakable flesh wriggling inside the helmet. Something grabbed her hair, and she knew it was Qeteb.

He wrenched her head back, forcing her to look at him.

Faraday gagged, the Midday Demon's power not even allowing her to screw her eyes shut.

"Katie stays," Qeteb said, "as do you. You are both far too useful to me to let go."

He turned his head slightly, speaking to the other three Demons. "Take Katie aside, and keep her fresh for me. Wait."

"And you?" Sheol asked, knowing what he intended to do, but also knowing that Qeteb wanted her to ask the question.

"Me?" Qeteb turned back to stare at Faraday again. His forked tongue slithered forth to hang dripping over his metal chin-piece. "Aren't we repeating Prophecy here for the amusement of poor Faraday? There is only one thing for me to do to while away the time. Enjoy myself, and ease my lusts."

His free hand reached forward, sliding under Faraday's gown and gripping one breast so painfully Faraday whimpered.

She twisted, her body straining against Qeteb's hold, and she despaired. What had Noah told her? That she would either win, and achieve complete and lasting happiness, or she would fail and achieve total annihilation.

She had failed, and thus annihilation was hers for the asking.

Please, God, grant me death, she pleaded, and far away, nestled against the warmth and comfort of Leagh's breast, the Girl turned Her head and answered, No.

Then grant me insanity! Please! I beg you!

No. This is your destiny.

Qeteb's hand tightened remorselessly, and Faraday screamed, abandoned to her fate.

66

Choose, DragonStar!

DragonStar sat his Star Stallion before the Maze Gate. He had been here before, but that time seemed now to be a hundred light years ago.

He sat, completely still, his head bowed, his almost naked body exuding the faintest of glimmers in the evening air. His stallion, mane and tail ablaze, waited patiently, although he shifted occasionally: stamping a hoof, lowering and shaking his magnificent head, or raising it again to stare through the open Gate.

The pack of Alaunt waited to one side, the blue-feathered lizard once more in their midst—albeit hiccuping slightly.

DragonStar sat, his face lowered, eyes almost closed, lost in his thoughts.

Rather, lost in the thoughts and memories of the Enemy.

Images and sounds of the Enemy's battle with the Demons on their long ago world flickered through DragonStar's mind. But deeper memories also surfaced, of yet older worlds, and even more ancient battles against the Demons.

The fight against the Demons—whether that of the Enemy's, or of yet other enemies—had been fought since the beginning of time. And always, the Demons had won.

Now? Now was the last battle, the final confrontation. Whoever won here would carry the victory into eternity.

Here, this night, awaited the final choice.

Belaguez snorted again, and DragonStar raised his head and opened his eyes.

The StarSon looked through the Maze Gate.

Hell waited within. Millions, perhaps billions, of deformed bodies and minds tumbled and scratched and pummelled as one entity, caught in the infinite bleakness of the beating heart of the Maze.

It writhed and pulsed and throbbed.

It screeched and caterwauled and mewed.

It sang seductively, it beckoned enticingly, it begged for his presence.

In the Dark Tower.

The Dark Tower.

The Dark Tower was where Qeteb waited . . . with his choice. Qeteb's lieutenants had won the battle of the Demons and witches, now it lay with Qeteb to offer the final choice.

DragonStar blinked, and refocused on the Gate itself.

The millions of seething characters had all gone, and the Gate surrounds were now blank stone.

Save for the single carving that topped the archway.

It depicted The Sacrifice. The Sacrifice that DragonStar would have to choose. Katie? Faraday? Or himself?

DragonStar stared at the carving, and nodded, for it told him nothing he had not known for a very long time.

The carving blurred, and then rippled away, leaving nothing but bare stone in its passing.

DragonStar turned his head slightly to look at Sicarius sitting at the head of his pack.

"Wait here," the StarSon said, "until I whistle my need for you."

Sicarius inclined his head. The Hunt was surely close now.

Then DragonStar looked at the blue-feathered lizard, sitting slightly to one side of Sicarius.

"Wait here," said DragonStar, "until I have need of your light."

And the lizard inclined his head.

DragonStar looked back to the Gate, and drew his lily sword. Belaguez tensed.

"For this," DragonStar cried, "you and I were both born, Demon!"

And the Star Stallion leapt through the Gate.

As soon as he had disappeared, the forty-two thousand trees drifted as close to the Maze as they dared, forming a single line around its entire perimeter.

There, Ur standing and shifting impatiently from foot to foot among them, they waited.

DragonStar rode, but he did not find the journey to the Dark Tower as easy as the first time he'd ridden through the Maze.

Then, the way had been free and clear, and the Maze had sung and screamed its encouragement propelling him towards the Dark Tower.

Now foulness sought to block his way. All the creatures packed into the veins of the Maze seemed as one. Legs and arms and limbs and teeth lunged at him indiscriminately, as if attached to the one body, the one mind. DragonStar sliced to this side and to that with his sword, and it wrought great damage, but it was Belaguez who worked best to clear a path for him.

The Star Stallion screamed and shook head and tail. Millions of tiny stars exploded into the dense blackness that surrounded them, and as they struck home, the creatures drew back, snapping and snarling, or screaming and writhing if one of the stars burned its way through flesh.

A way opened before horse and rider, and the Star Stallion needed no encouragement. He plunged forward, breasting his way through the dark creatures as a swimmer through the surf, lunging with teeth, the thousands of stars sizzling about his head and haunches catching and reflecting the mirror blade of the lily sword as it arced through the air again and again.

They rode through a nightmare.

The stars and sword created a path, but that did nothing to alleviate the fetid savagery about them. Hands and claws and gaping jaws reached incessantly for them, teeth snapped a finger's breadth away from flesh, foulness filled the air. Horse and rider both found it difficult to breathe.

But though DragonStar responded to the threat, and though he swung the lily sword this way and that, he barely saw the horror about him.

His mind had let go the images of past battles and the memories of countless, extinct races. Now all DragonStar thought about was Faraday.

Faraday, caught in the arms of Qeteb.

Faraday, undergoing again the same horror she had at Gorgrael's touch.

Beautiful, courageous Faraday, no doubt intent on sacrificing herself *again,* if only it might save one person beyond herself.

DragonStar reviled himself for making her go through all this again, but it was necessary. Necessary for him to be able to make the *right* decision when Qeteb presented him with the choice.

Belaguez continued his lunge forward, and DragonStar arced down again and again with his sword.

Poor Faraday. He deserved her hate.

Faraday writhed in Qeteb's grip, overcome with the hopelessness of her situation, and railing at herself because she could do nothing to aid Katie.

The Midday Demon stood before the black marble tomb, facing the door of the mausoleum. He was attired in his black armour, black plate wings held out behind him.

He was was invulnerable, impenetrable, unconquerable.

Qeteb had won, and he knew it.

He stood completely still, at odds with the two writhing figures he held out to either side of him.

His left hand was buried in the glossy brown curls of Katie, and she wept and cried softly, sickened by the closeness of the Demon, and by the hopelessness of the wasteland which, in this tomb, was magnified tenfold.

Qeteb's right hand dug into the vulnerable white flesh of Faraday's upper left arm.

Her white gown was torn and bloodied—all that held it to her body was the rainbow band about her waist—and Faraday was heavily bruised on her face and legs.

Faraday's fear, that she would be taken and offered again as sacrifice, had materialised into a horrible reality. DragonStar was riding through the Maze towards the Dark Tower—she could *feel* him with every beat of her heart. But Faraday could also feel his determination and his resolve, and she knew that nothing would stand in the way of his ultimate purpose, and that purpose was, as it had been for Axis, Tencendor. The salvation of the land before all else.

After all, hadn't every other part of her nightmare with Gorgrael been revisited? This would, too.

Faraday writhed and wept, and succumbed to hopelessness.

The StarSon rode, and he drew close to the Dark Tower.

As he did so, the black tide of maniacal creatures drew back, and let him be.

The final bite must be Qeteb's.

Belaguez snorted a last time, and shook his head so that stars littered the path leading to the Dark Tower.

There was a faint tinkle of music as the stallion trod carefully into the paved area before the Dark Tower.

DragonStar looked up. The tower rose bleak and silent, although DragonStar could feel it throbbing with purpose.

The Choice lay within.

DragonStar lowered his eyes.

Three hounds sat before the entrance. They were motley and diseased, and contagion dripped from their jaws.

Sheol, Mot and Barzula.

A slight movement to one side caught DragonStar's eye, and he glanced . . . and nodded.

The shadow inclined its head, ever at service. His choice had been well made.

DragonStar looked back to the Tower, and slid down from Belaguez's back. "Wait," he said.

He walked towards the three demonic hounds, graceful, lithe, apparently confident.

"Step aside," DragonStar said as he approached them, "for my battle lies with your master, not you."

The hounds snarled, but they slunk to one side, and DragonStar looked beyond them.

The door gaped wide and black.

Faraday saw the shadow step into the door, and she sobbed. How had it all come to this? Why? Why?

DragonStar, as his father before him, barely glanced at Faraday's suffering, although it affected him as deeply as it had Axis.

His concentration was all on Qeteb.

"And so it has come to this," DragonStar said softly.

"And so it has come to this," Qeteb agreed. His voice was cold and harsh, as if he was consumed by such anger he could barely elucidate the words.

"I have no time for games, or sweet musings over past memories," Qeteb continued. "And so, as is my right, I offer you the final choice. Do you choose Katie, and so save Tencendor? Or do you choose from your heart, and sacrifice Tencendor for Faraday?"

"No! No! No!" Faraday screamed, writhing pitifully in Qeteb's agonising grip. *"DragonStar, I beg you, choose Katie! Save Katie!"*

"You would sacrifice yourself?" Qeteb said, and laughed. "Again? My, my, Faraday, isn't your obsession with self-sacrifice a trifle self-destructive?"

Faraday ignored him. DragonStar was looking at her now, and she held his eyes with all the love she could muster. "Please, DragonStar, let me die. Take Katie, she is far, far more important. Her life is more important—"

"Not to me," DragonStar said softly.

Faraday wept, and cried out again. "No! I beg you, choose Katie! Please, *please,* DragonStar, choose Katie! *I want to die!* Please, please, believe me. I WANT to die!"

"Ah," Qeteb whispered, ignoring Faraday. "I can see the love on your face, DragonStar. Poor, foolish, DragonStar, love will prove your downfall, as it proved Goldman and DareWing's."

DragonStar ignored him. He looked away from Faraday, weeping piteously, and stepped up to Katie.

Qeteb made no move to stop him, or to touch him.

"Katie," said DragonStar, and dropped down on one knee before her. "Know that I love you."

She nodded, and turning her face slightly so Qeteb could not see, let DragonStar see the sheer relief flood across it.

DragonStar rose, and stepped in front of Qeteb. "I love Faraday," he said, "and she has suffered and sacrificed enough. I choose Faraday."

"No!" Faraday screamed. *"No!"*

"Faraday," DragonStar said, "did I not once say to you that

Tencendor does not need your sacrifice again? Tencendor does not need you to die for it. *I* do not need you to die for Tencendor."

Qeteb roared with laughter, and flung Faraday into Dragon-Star's arms. "Fool!"

DragonStar seized Faraday, and dragged her, weeping and struggling, back a few paces. "Behold, beloved," he whispered into her ear, "how Tencendor will sacrifice itself for you."

"No," she murmured, worn out with her hopelessness and her despair. "No. Let *me* die. There is nothing left. Not now . . . not now."

"There is life and love left," DragonStar said softly, "and no need for your death. All that Tencendor requires of you is that you witness. *It does not want your death!* Instead, it offers up itself for you."

He caught her face in his hand, and turned it back to Qeteb and Katie.

Qeteb was still roaring with laughter. Lost in his victory, he had not heard a word that DragonStar had said to Faraday. He still held Katie by her hair in his left hand, and with his right he produced a wickedly gleaming kitchen knife.

Faraday fought as hard as she could against DragonStar. What was he doing? Qeteb was going to kill Katie! No! No! She screamed, shrill and despairing.

Qeteb dragged Katie in front of him, and jerked her head back.

The girl was calm, and she stared at Faraday with eyes of such love that Faraday could not bear it.

"No," she whispered, but she had lost the desire to struggle now. DragonStar was too strong for her, and Qeteb too evil. Between them, they were going to kill Katie.

"For you, Faraday," Katie whispered, and she closed her eyes and tilted her head back even further as the blade flashed through the air.

Blood splattered everywhere.

Azhure sat despondently on the gravel of the GateKeeper's island, one hand resting on her aching, but now neatly bandaged, calf. SpikeFeather sat close by, his head resting in his hands. He had a headache, but little else in the way of injuries. The ice sisters sat on either side of him, running their cool hands over his brow, murmuring to him, holding him close.

Azhure thought she could have done with some of their comfort, but the ice sisters had no thought of comforting anyone but SpikeFeather, and Azhure thought she would get little passion from the GateKeeper.

The woman sat at her table before the pulsating glow of the doorway into the AfterLife. Before her were two bowls, but the GateKeeper's thin, pale hands sat in idleness before them.

She transferred no balls from one bowl to the other.

The GateKeeper raised her eyes and saw Azhure's stare.

"No souls pass this way now," the GateKeeper said softly. "All bypass the Gate and step directly into the Field of Flowers."

"Is that what lies beyond the Gate?" Azhure said.

The GateKeeper smiled, a secretive expression on her face. "I have never told what lies beyond the Gate," she said, "and will not do so—"

She broke off, and stared at a distant point over Azhure's shoulder. "Another customer?" she said. "Why? How?"

Azhure twisted about.

Far away a glowing outline glided along the black River of Death towards the island of the Gate.

The GateKeeper took a harsh intake of breath, and, as the figure glided closer and mounted the loose grey gravel of the island, Azhure gave a soft cry herself.

It was Katie.

Katie was dead?

"As ever she will be," murmured the GateKeeper, and then the shade of Katie was standing before the woman's table, her eyes great and sorrowful, her hands folded neatly before her.

The GateKeeper lifted a metal ball from one bowl and held the hand over the other bowl. "Are you going through, Katie?"

"Aye," Katie said, then her expression cleared and she smiled. "Rejoice, GateKeeper, for your task is done. Time is ended, and the Gate must close."

The GateKeeper smiled also, an expression of such sweetness that Azhure, watching, felt her eyes fill with tears.

"Then go through, my child, and rejoice yourself that your task is done."

"Katie?" Azhure said. "Katie—"

Katie turned her head very slightly so she could see Azhure. "When you see Faraday," she said, "will you tell her that I love her? That I love her enough to die for *her* this time?"

And then she was gone.

The instant she glided through the doorway the GateKeeper seized her two bowls and flung them into the air.

"Done!" she screeched. "Done!"

Metal balls rained down, and Azhure, as SpikeFeather and the two ice women covered their heads with their arms.

"Take my hands!" the GateKeeper cried, and literally lunged over her table towards the foursome. "Take my hands!"

And she grabbed Azhure with one hand, and SpikeFeather with the other as the sisters gripped the GateKeeper's forearms.

The Gate exploded.

Azhure screwed her eyes shut and screamed, but even as she did so she heard the GateKeeper cry out herself.

"The Gate is dead! Time is extinct!"

And then there was nothing but a black void.

67

Bring Me My Bow of Burning Gold . . .

Something had gone horribly, horribly wrong, and Qeteb knew it the instant the blood splattered out from Katie's throat.

He had gutted the wrong girl.

DragonStar had chosen correctly.

But how could this be so when *his* captains had won, three to two?

They *had* won, hadn't they?

Or was there something he'd misinterpreted?

Tencendor took one last, dying breath, and the devastation of death consumed the land as the last of Katie's blood flowed from her tiny, frail body.

The sky cracked.

The earth shattered.

The air exploded.

Qeteb threw Katie's drained corpse to one side. "Then it's just you and me," he said, calm now in the face of disaster, "as it ever was."

"As it ever was," DragonStar agreed.

Qeteb, blank-faced, stepped away, vanishing into the shadowy land beyond the encircling columns of the mausoleum. The silent, dark forms of Mot, Barzula and Sheol vanished directly after him.

DragonStar took Faraday—now deep in shock—and led her unresisting to one side, sitting her down against one of the columns. "Wait," he said. "All will be well."

Axis, as everyone in the column, panicked as Creation withered about them.

Firestorms raced across the plains, and mountains trembled and collapsed in upon themselves.

The darkness and coldness of a complete vacuum decended upon the land.

Wait, a voice echoed through the minds of all within the convoy, and they knew it for the voice of Leagh's Child, *all will be well*.

And even though darkness consumed them, and the feel of the land beneath their feet vanished, all continued to survive.

All that remained of the land that had once been Tencendor was the black pulsing thing that was the Maze: an island of madness in a sea of destruction.

DragonStar straightened, and whistled.

The baying of the Alaunt filled the air, and their creamy, eager bodies wound about his legs.

A shadow darkened the doorway of the mausoleum.

"At your service, sir," said Raspu, dressed for the destruction of Creation in his stiffly starched butler's uniform, "as always."

DragonStar nodded. "Good." He held out his hand. "Deliver me my bow."

And Raspu inclined his head, and stepped forward. In his hands he held the Wolven, and its quiver of blue-fletched arrows.

DragonStar took the bow, and slung the quiver over his shoulder and back.

He held out the bow, and looked at the lizard.

The lizard grinned and, lifting a claw, sent a shaft of light glimmering along the entire bow.

It burst into fire, although the flames did not consume the wood, nor harm DragonStar.

DragonStar nodded at the lizard, then slung the burning bow over his shoulder.

Then he lifted his voice, and sent it singing through the Maze.

"Run, Qeteb," he said, "for the clouds are about to unfold, and the Hunt about to begin."

68

Twisted City

Qeteb fled through the Maze, Sheol, Mot and Barzula at his heels.

DragonStar did not instantly follow. He straightened the quiver of arrows, and adjusted the Wolven so it lay, comfortable, across his back. He lifted and resettled his jewelled belt and purse.

He walked over to Katie's corpse—the floor of the mausoleum was slick with her blood—and he squatted down beside it.

"We thank you and honour you, Katie," he said, and, wiping the fingers of his right hand through her blood, marked his forehead and breast with it as Raum had once marked Faraday.

"Who was she?" Faraday whispered.

DragonStar looked over at her, still sitting by the column. "She was Tencendor's lifeblood," he said. "The land's soul."

"Why did she need to die?"

"So the land can move through death, and live again," DragonStar said, "and so the land could repay you for all you have done and sacrificed for it."

He rose and walked over to Faraday, bending down to give her a brief but passionate kiss. "You and I," he whispered, "are given the task of re-creating the land free of the discord and evil which once stalked it . . . which once stalked all of Creation.

"But for the moment—" he straightened "—I have a small task to accomplish, the Hunt to complete."

And, smiling gently, he left her.

Raspu walked over, balancing very carefully on one hand a

tray with a silver pot, and a cream porcelain milk jug, sugar bowl, and cup and saucer. "Would ma'am like some tea?" he asked.

Faraday blinked, and then decided not to try to make sense of any of it. "That would be very nice," she said. "Thank you."

The Butler poured her cup of tea, painstakingly added sugar and milk in their proper proportions, and held the cup out to Faraday.

"Ma'am."

She accepted it without a word, but her eyes widened in surprise as she tasted the tea. "It is very good."

"Thank you, ma'am." Raspu shifted slightly, as if embarrassed. "Ma'am, I regret that I shall have to leave you for a moment or two. Sir has asked me to take care of one or two small tasks for him."

"Of course," Faraday said, and Raspu gave her a small bow, and tucked under his arm a large account book he'd apparently obtained from thin air. Then, without further ado, he disappeared.

Strangely, Faraday did not feel lonely or vulnerable at all. The tea was very good indeed.

DragonStar strode through the door into the Maze, and the Star Stallion lifted his head and screamed as the Alaunt milled about and bayed.

DragonStar leapt on Belaguez's back, and drew the lily sword.

The Alaunt broke into clamour.

"Hunt!" DragonStar said.

And so it began.

DragonStar was his mother's son. As Azhure had once hunted Artor, so now DragonStar hunted Qeteb and his remaining companions. But this was the real hunt, the Hunt that the Star

Dance had been engineering for hundreds of thousands of years.

This was the moment, and this was the StarSon.

The Hunter.

Qeteb fled through the Maze. The millions of demented features that had once throbbed and pulsed and muttered as one, now fled before him, desperately seeking escape themselves.

Beyond the walls of the Maze the trees stepped forward, and buried roots and branch tips into the tiny cracks of the Maze's walls.

Ur, standing slightly back, screeched with laughter.

Cracks spread screaming, and masonry fell. Within heartbeats of the trees' attack the walls of the Maze had been broached in a hundred places.

Creatures poured through, intent on escaping the Hunter.

They were all devoured by the trees.

Qeteb knew nothing of the destruction being wreaked on the outer skin of the Maze. He fled as Caelum had once fled in nightmares, through infinitely barren corridors and passageways, all ending in such hopelessness that they forced the Demons and his companions to turn back and desperately seek another way before the Hunter found them.

Behind them rose a clamour of such frightfulness that their hearts quailed, and sometimes the hot breath of the hounds grew so close it scorched their skin.

From some unknown where, a bell tolled.

Qeteb ran, and his remaining three Demons raced desperately to keep up with him, their outstretched hands clutching at the protuberances of his armour, their voices screeching at him to not leave them behind . . . don't leave them behind, think of everything they had done for him, remember how loyal they had been, the sacrifices they had made for him, the adoration they had given, so don't leave them behind, please, please, don't leave them behind . . .

Qeteb left them behind.

Mot, Barzula and Sheol cried out, lost. Where had Qeteb gone? One instant he had been but a pace in front of them, now he was nowhere to be seen or sensed.

Instead they were faced only with the twisting, blank walls of the Maze, its stone floor slowly rising through twist after twist and bend after bend.

Slowly rising?

The Demons slackened their pace, terror being replaced by puzzlement and anger. The walls of the Maze were altering, the narrowness of the passage which trapped them abating, the entire face of the Maze changing.

"What is happening?" Sheol hissed, clutching at Barzula.

"We are being toyed with!" said Mot, pressing as close as he could to the other two.

The Maze had funnelled them into the twisting, narrow streets of a grey and dead city. Ash drifted down from the broken skyline of the city's tenement buildings: some of their walls rose burned and blackened into the sky, while others lay in tumbled, pathetic heaps of masonry.

Shattered window glass crunched under the Demons' feet.

This was the ruins of a city twisted and murdered within the flames of a massive conflagration.

"Carlon!" whispered a shadowy voice.

The Demons hissed, and turned to stare down a gloomy alleyway.

A small red-headed boy walked forth, one bloody hand clutched over the ruins of his belly.

A small male two-legs.

Tears ran down his face. "This was Carlon," he said. "This was my home."

Sheol growled, and made to snatch at the boy.

No, said a voice in her mind—in all of the Demons' minds—*you may not touch this boy. You may only move forward.*

The sound of a horse's hooves rattled on the cobblestones behind them.

Sheol whipped about her head.

DragonStar!

Move forward.

And so they moved forward, with unwillingness. But they had no choice, for Sheol and her two companions found their feet controlled by another, and their traitor feet moved them further into the city, and deeper into its mangled ruins.

As the Demons passed, gibbering and cursing, grey and saddened people stepped from every doorway, and from every side street and alley. All were disfigured in some manner or the other.

They were the hopeless hundreds of thousands who had either died amid the chaos of the Demons' physical attacks on Tencendor, or who'd had their minds snatched by the Demons and who had died at their own hands, or at the hands, teeth and claws of their demented companions of the wasteland.

As the Demons passed, the dead stared silently, tears trickling down their faces. Sometimes they turned away, unable to look.

The Demons snarled, defiant yet terrified, determined to somehow escape, yet unable to turn their feet from the road which twisted before them. Their forms blurred and changed, trying different guises and frames to see if they could fly out as a gryphon, or muscle their way out as an ox, or wriggle their way out as a worm of the earth.

Nothing worked, and the Hunter's magic drew them inexorably on, further and deeper into the ruined city.

Fifteen paces behind them the Star Stallion pranced, keeping pace with the Demons. He held his head high, snorting his indignation that he was not allowed to run to the clamour of the Hunt. Behind him stalked the Alaunt, their limbs stiff with impatience.

"Soon," whispered DragonStar, a calming hand on the stallion's neck, his voice also reaching and embracing his hounds. "Soon."

"And us?" cried the people as DragonStar passed by them. "And us?"

And to them DragonStar smiled, and said. "Soon."

As he passed, the weeping people silently fell into step behind the hounds, so that DragonStar eventually found himself at the head of a long column of the desolate and dispossessed dead.

"Soon," he whispered.

Elsewhere, Qeteb still ran through the Maze. He could hear the thunderous hooves of the Hunter's stallion behind him, hear the tightening of the string of the bow, and hear the clamour of the hounds.

He howled and screeched and babbled in fury and fear, his mind embracing possible escapes with one breath, and then discarding them as useless with the next.

He would not allow himself to be destroyed. Not after all this time. Not after all this effort.

He had been tested before, and he had always won.

Evil always ultimately won. It was one of the given truths of the universe.

Besides, his Demons had won three to two against DragonStar's witches.

Hadn't they?

Just as Qeteb thought that, he ran directly into a blank wall. A blank wall with a doorway in it.

Qeteb's eyes bulged with triumph. He could *smell* the enchantment that bound that doorway, and knew that once he passed through, it would disappear forever.

DragonStar could not come after him.

Roaring his victory, Qeteb flung open the door, and stepped through.

As the door closed behind him, a butler stepped out from nowhere, placed an ornate brass key in the lock, and turned it.

As the locks clunked into place, the Butler withdrew the key and the door faded into the stonework of the wall.

The Butler smiled in satisfaction, pencilled an annotation in the account book he held, and disappeared again.

Suddenly the Demons halted. Their feet had carried them into a narrower street, and a wooden cart blocked their way forward.

Get in.

"No!" the Demons cried.

Get in.

They got in, bellowing with rage and frustration that they could not control the movement of their own limbs.

An old man appeared, bent and grey and dressed in an enveloping shabby coat with a large book in one pocket. He positioned himself between the shafts of the cart, grasping them in his gnarled hands. He grunted, strained, and the cart jolted forward.

The Demons howled, their hands clutching at the sides of the cart, but they could not gain enough purchase to pull themselves out, and their bodies felt as if they had lead boulders grating to and fro within them. They could not heave themselves off the tray of the cart.

The splinters of the tray dug and worked themselves deep into their flesh.

DragonStar smiled slightly, then composed himself, and continued to ride some fifteen paces behind the cart.

Behind him were strung the many hundreds of thousands, perhaps the many millions, of those who had died amid demonic destruction. They walked silently, some wringing their hands, others trying in vain to wipe away the tears that stained their cheeks, still others clinging to children or babes in arms.

The cart, and the column it led, wound deeper and deeper into the twisted city.

Eventually the cart lumbered into a huge market square. In the centre of the square stood a shoulder-high wooden platform, and on that platform had been built a scaffold.

Three rope nooses hung down, patiently swinging in a non-existent breeze.

The Demons wriggled and writhed, moaned and wept, turning their voices from defiance to piteousness.

Why them? Hadn't they been acting under orders from His Ghastliness himself? What else could they have done? They'd been terrified, *certain* in fact, that if they'd gone against his wishes, Qeteb would have done them a messy murder. No, no, they'd only been acting to save their own lives, and had always meant to somehow undergo some form of penance for the deeds they'd been forced to do. Not that they were admitting guilt, of course, but they were pitiful creatures, and felt that it might do someone some good if perhaps they said they were sorry.

"Oh, shut up," said DragonStar, and pulled the Star Stallion up as the cart rumbled to a halt before the scaffold.

Behind DragonStar streamed the uncountable dead, moving out to encircle the scaffold until the crowd was a thousand deep.

They filled the square, and only when their masses had come to a full halt did DragonStar nod at the old man still standing between the shafts of the cart.

Grunting slightly with the effort, the old man bent down and rested the shafts on the cobbles. Then he shuffled around to the back of the cart.

DragonStar rode closer, and, leaning one hand behind him, took an arrow from the quiver strung against his back.

"Here," he said, and handed it to the old man.

The man nodded, and, tucking the arrow under one arm for the moment, took hold of Barzula's left ankle and dragged him over the lip of the cart.

Barzula gave a formless scream as he thudded painfully to the cobbles, and raised his arms as if to protect his face.

"Ta muchly," said the old man, and, taking the now curiously pliable arrow, wound it about the Demon's wrists, binding them tight.

Then the man grabbed hold of the loose skin of Barzula's neck and dragged him effortlessly around the cart over the cobbles to the stand, up the scratchy, splintery steps of the wooden platform, and across to the first noose. There he deposited him in a heap, gave him a painful kick in his ribs, and turned about and shuffled down the steps and towards the cart again.

DragonStar drew another arrow, and handed it to the old man as he came back around the cart.

In turn, the old man hauled Mot and Sheol out of the cart, bound their wrists with an arrow, and then dragged them over the cobbles, up onto the platform, and deposited them before each of the remaining two nooses.

And each time he delivered a parting kick to their ribs.

Finally the old man came back down, hobbled over to the cart, and clambered up into the driver's seat. There he sat, staring at the platform and the three Demons, each kneeling before a noose, and grinned toothlessly.

The crowd shuffled closer.

As the door slammed shut behind him, Qeteb stopped . . .

What had he done?

Before him stretched an endless ploughed field, barren of life.

He turned around.

The wall and the doorway had vanished. Behind him the ploughed field stretched into infinity.

Cursing, Qeteb took a step forward.

He sank into the soft earth to the top of his ankle.

He took another step, and he sank yet further, weighed down by the amount of metal he carried.

From somewhere very, very far away came the baying of hounds.

Qeteb growled, and began to tear off his armour. It fell away, sinking into the earth.

He stood naked and exposed. He was DragonStar warped and warted. His flesh, humped into the strange lumps needed to fill his armour, was pale and bluish, pockmarked with corruption. His belly was soft and flabby, his legs thin and knobbly, his arms disproportionately muscled and weighty.

He had no neck or chin, and his lumpish face seemed to grow directly from his white, hairless chest.

Beautiful coppery curls fell from his head over his shoulders and down his back, merging finally with the feathers of his black and mouldy wings.

Qeteb was a sad mockery of life, and the saddest thing of all was that he did not realise it.

He grinned, and started forward across the field.

"We have here before us," announced DragonStar to the crowd, "the Demons of Hunger, Tempest, and Despair."

His voice was quiet, but beautifully modulated, and it reached every ear in the square.

"Their times," DragonStar continued, "are dawn, mid-morning and mid-afternoon."

He paused, and looked out over the crowd. "You represent the end result of their crimes, which stretch backwards through an eternity to the time of original Creation. They have ransacked the universe, and ravaged the souls of the very stars themselves."

The crowd murmured, its sound a rising swell, and Dragon-Star gave them a few moments in which to voice their despair.

When he resumed speaking, his voice had the tone and authority of a tolling bell. "Here they kneel, and now is their time. What are we to do with them?"

Again there was a swell of formless sound from the throng-ing masses. It surged and billowed forth, engulfing both DragonStar and the Demons.

The Demons cringed. DragonStar grinned.

And the murmuring died. A decision had been reached.

From the crowd stepped three people. An emaciated man, with a distended, lumpish belly. A woman, her eyes roiling with some unknown turbulence. Another woman, dragging behind her a washing line. At the end of the washing line bounced the still form of a toddling girl-child, the line wrapped tight about her plump throat.

The Demons suddenly screamed. Not from the sight of the three people, but because each of the arrows about their wrists had suddenly flamed into life, burning into their flesh.

"Retribution," whispered DragonStar.

The man and the two women slowly climbed the steps onto the platform.

The emaciated man stood before Mot, the woman with the maddened eyes before Barzula, and before Sheol stood the woman who had the body of her daughter dangling strangled on the washing line.

"Your time has come," said DragonStar, and with one motion every person in the crowd raised their right arm and held it high, the palms of their hands turned towards the platform.

There was no sound.

The emaciated man stepped up to Mot, who was still writhing and moaning from the pain of the burning arrow.

The man stared, then reached up, took hold of the noose, and pulled it down until he could drape it about Mot's neck.

"I ate of stones," the man said in a curiously toneless voice, "until my stomach burst, and the stones ravaged through my belly until I shat stones. Now you shall know your own time."

He stepped back.

For an instant, nothing happened, then the burning arrow twisted about Mot's wrists moved. It slithered up Mot's right arm, twisted about his neck, then coiled about the rope that rose behind him.

In a movement so fast few could follow it, the arrow climbed the rope to the top of the scaffold, and, before any could draw breath in amazement, the rope contracted to an arm's length.

Mot shot into the air, suspended in the noose.

The rope tightened, and Mot's mouth opened in a silent scream, his feet kicking desperately below him.

The crowd smiled, their faces grim, their hands still held in the air.

Mot twisted frantically about on the end of the rope, the arrow still burning above him where the rope was tied to the scaffold, but the Demon did not die of strangulation.

Instead, he hungered.

He opened his mouth, and formed words, although no sound came forth.

Feed me! Feed me!

"If you wish," said DragonStar, and again the burning arrow moved.

It slithered back down the rope, around the noose, and into Mot's mouth.

It disappeared.

For a moment, nothing.

Then Mot's face contorted in an agony so great his eyes almost started from his head. His arms jerked in a mad dance at his side.

A small red, glowing spot formed in the centre of his belly, and, before any could draw breath, the arrow burst forth.

Mot's belly exploded, blood spraying through the air. His body jerked to a halt . . . and changed. It blurred from a humanoid form into that of a rat, and then into a worm.

Finally, it turned into a loose lump of flesh that dropped out of the noose to the wooden platform where it sizzled momentarily before vanishing completely.

The emaciated man, still standing before the spot where Mot had been, looked skyward, then raised his right hand.

The arrow tumbled down from the sky, and the man caught it deftly. He turned, descended the steps, walked over to DragonStar and held out the arrow.

"Thank you," he said, and DragonStar took the arrow, nodding slightly but saying nothing.

The man took his place within the crowd.

Now the woman with the ravaged eyes stepped forth to Barzula. "I walked in madness for many weeks," she said, "a tempest raging through my mind. Eventually I died when I walked into a fireball tumbling across the wasteland."

She paused. "Now you shall know your own time." And she stepped back.

As with Mot, the arrow about Barzula's wrists moved up his arm, about his neck, and yet further up the rope to the top of the scaffold where it writhed.

The rope contracted, and Barzula was sprung into the air, kicking as frantically as Mot had done.

And as with Mot, Barzula did not strangle. Instead, he was consumed with tempest.

The arrow exploded into a firestorm. It hailed down a rain of molten lead droplets that ate into Barzula's body until it sizzled and smoked.

The woman smiled, although her eyes were now sad and compassionate.

The hail of molten lead became worse, and from somewhere, and despite the noose about his neck, Barzula screamed.

It was the final sound he made. His entire body was now smouldering, the lead eating into his flesh, and within moments he began to disintegrate.

Lumps of flesh fell to the wooden platform where, as with Mot, they sizzled before disappearing.

More flesh fell, and now, that which hung suspended from the noose was not recognisable as humanoid, but only as a clump of burning meat.

Soon, it, too, fell to the platform, sizzled, and was gone.

The arrow fell into the woman's hand, and as had the emaciated man, she returned it to DragonStar, solemnly thanking him.

And, then, to Sheol.

The woman with the child stepped forth and said: "When you and yours broke through the Star Gate into this beautiful land, I was hanging out my washing. Despair overwhelmed me, and caused me to consider my toddling child's future life. I thought that she would only suffer, perhaps at the hands of an abusive husband, and so I lifted her up and twisted the washing line about her neck, strangling her unto death."

The woman paused, and sobbed, a hand to her mouth. "I killed my own daughter. *Now you shall know your own time!*"

Again the arrow sprang, slithering into movement and climbing to the top of the scaffold.

And the entire scaffold changed . . .

. . . into a washing line strung between two forked poles.

The rope around Sheol's neck hauled her upward, upward, upward until it twisted among the rope of the washing line, and this time the Demon *did* strangle, her face and eyes bulging as the washing line tightened, tightened, tightened about her neck.

Sheol despaired.

Somehow she managed to extend a hand to DragonStar, her bulging eyes pleading, but his face was implacable, and Sheol dropped her hand.

Strands of rope ravelled down from the line, twisting themselves about Sheol's entire body until she was encased in tightening coils of rope.

They squeezed.

Blood and slivers of flesh oozed out from between the coils of rope.

The woman, unperturbed, leaned down and unwound her own washing line from about her child's neck, and then she lifted the child up, and the child smiled, and flung her arms about her mother's neck.

Sheol fell apart. Again, as with Barzula, flesh and blood dropped to the platform, sizzling and disappearing.

Eventually there was nothing left to squeeze, and the ropes themselves dropped to the platform and disappeared.

The arrow fell down, caught this time by the child, and she and her mother returned it to DragonStar.

The woman had tears of joy running down her face. "We thank you," she said as she handed back the arrow.

DragonStar also wept, for he had lived with the guilt of this child's death for a very long time, and he accepted the arrow and slid it home with its companions.

As one, the crowd lowered their hands and turned their faces to DragonStar.

And us? And us?

DragonStar turned to the old man, who had been sitting quietly in the driver's seat of the cart. The man sighed, and climbed down.

As he did so, he transformed . . . into the Butler.

DragonStar grinned, and said to the crowd: "I think you

will find that the Butler, efficient accountant that he is, has each and every one of your names in his account book. Present yourself to him and he will tick off your name, make his accounting, and show you through the gate into the garden. There, you will rest amid the flowers."

The woman with the child, who was still standing at DragonStar's knee, spoke for the entire crowd.

"Thank you," she said again, but with such joy that DragonStar had to fight back more tears.

"Thank you."

69

Light and Love

Qeteb slogged his way through the ploughed field, cursing and grunting.

He had to be able to get out of here somehow. After all, wasn't he destined to win? Hadn't his Demons won out against DragonStar's pitiful witches, three against two?

That he was still in the Maze, Qeteb had no doubt. The ridges and furrows of the ploughed earth did not run even or straight. Instead they formed twists and conundrums, and Qeteb knew that if only he could find his way through the puzzle of the field, he would win his freedom.

For his companions he cared naught. They had served their usefulness—nay! They had become a liability, and Qeteb was glad to be rid of them.

No doubt they were already writhing on the end of the pretty StarSon's sword.

Well, there they could stay for all Qeteb cared. He could exist without them, whereas they were nothing without *him*.

He grinned, and slogged on, dragging each foot up from the earth before sinking it down again.

His grin faded. Damn this!

The clamour of hounds sounded again, this time much closer, and Qeteb stopped and swung his head around, his eyes staring.

Far distant, far, far distant, he thought he could see a horse and rider.

The Hunter coursed, his stallion dancing over the earth, his hounds streaming out behind him.

He was his mother's son.

Behind the hounds ambled a bear cub, its mouth gaping in a cheerful grin.

And behind man and stallion and hounds and bear cub streamed millions upon millions of flowers, erupting from the sterile earth, waving their beauty into sun and wind.

Qeteb turned away, preparing to run—if he could, in this damn mud—and was stunned into immobility.

Before him stood a beautiful man with curly black hair and dark blue eyes, his face awash with pity and love. At his back, her hands resting on the man's shoulders, stood a woman with bright curly golden hair, and an expression of peace and contentment upon her lovely face.

Qeteb tried to back away, but the sticky earth clung to his feet and ankles, and he found he could not move.

"You are trapped," said Caelum.

"No!" Qeteb said. "No!"

"You shall not win," said RiverStar, and she leaned close to Caelum and planted a soft kiss on his neck, one of her hands rubbing caressingly up into his hair.

Her brother turned his face slightly, and smiled for her, then looked back to Qeteb.

"You *cannot* win," he said. "Don't you know that?"

"I won!" Qeteb shouted, his hands clenched into great fists at his sides. "DragonStar's witches failed!"

RiverStar laughed, soft and prettily and deep in her throat, and that sound drove Qeteb into rage.

"I won!" he screamed, trying to reach the pair and tear them apart. But the field would not let him move, and Caelum and RiverStar stood maddeningly undamaged just two paces before him.

"I won! I won! I won!"

"No," said Caelum. "You did not. All of DragonStar's witches won. Faraday won, for she chose self-sacrifice rather than let a child she loved die."

"But the child still died!"

"Nevertheless," RiverStar said, her voice hard, "she won. She offered herself for Love. Sheol had to let Faraday go for you to win."

"And those two demented fools who rescued that cub? They were crushed to death, damn it!"

Caelum laughed. "Death means nothing," he said, "for do not I and my sister stand here before you?"

"They also," said RiverStar, "offered themselves for Love. They were prepared to lose the confrontation rather than let the cub die. Mot and Barzula, on the other hand, preferred to sacrifice Love. They *lost*."

"All DragonStar's witches won," Caelum said. "Your fate is assured."

And then he turned and gathered RiverStar into his arms, and kissed her, and then they both faded from view as Qeteb roared and screamed and bellowed.

No! It could not be!

He turned again, vaguely hoping that somewhere behind him he would see his five companions riding to his rescue—where were they when he needed them?—but there was nothing but the ploughed field, and the much, much closer horse and rider.

The clamour of hounds rose up about his ears.

Qeteb set his back to the Hunter, his eyes jerking at the confusing patterns in the plough lines before him, and the field allowed the Midday Demon to continue his hopeless slog through its clinging earth.

DragonStar raised himself in his saddle and screamed. The Wolven was now slung over his back. He drew forth the lily sword and thrust it into the sky.

At his signal, the Alaunt surged forward, past Hunter and Star Stallion, and towards the distant figure struggling through the field.

The Hunt was on!

Qeteb turned once more—

—*always turning, turning, turning, lost and confused in the field*—

—and faced the hounds. He snarled, and raised his massive forearms, thrusting his fists into the sky. His mouth moved, as if to form words, but he was incapable of any lucid speech, and so incoherence and spittle dribbled forth in equal amounts from his thick, rubbery lips.

The Alaunt approached, but they did not attack immediately. Instead they encircled him, pacing slowly, their bodies close to the ground, their vicious snouts turned towards him.

DragonStar pulled the Star Stallion to a dancing halt several paces away. Directly behind the stallion, and out of Qeteb's direct sight, the bear cub lumbered to a halt, then plonked himself down on the earth, rolled over onto his side and swatted playfully at the stallion's tail.

Qeteb did not see the cub at all.

DragonStar slowly dismounted. "My hounds hunger for your blood," he said.

"They shall not have me!" Qeteb said. "I am more than a match for these foolish dogs."

DragonStar made a small gesture with one of his hands, and the Alaunt stopped their relentless encirclement of the Demon, and sat down, their heads cocked curiously towards DragonStar.

"My hounds hunger for your blood," he said again, "but I shall not set them to you."

"Why not?" Qeteb said. "Scared I might tear them apart?"

"I shall not set them to you because," DragonStar paused, and smiled, "because I love you."

Qeteb stared unbelievingly at the StarSon. "No!"

"I offer you love," DragonStar said, "and love shall be your destruction."

And as Qeteb screamed, StarSon DragonStar stepped forward, the hounds parting before him, and plunged the lily sword deep into Qeteb's belly, driving the Demon back until he lay impaled upon the ploughed field.

Then he stepped back.

Qeteb writhed about the sword, like a spider mounted for a live display . . . and laughed.

"Weapons will not hurt me," he said, still chortling. "You have learned nothing!"

Qeteb wrapped his hands about the hilt of the sword, as if to wrench it out.

Then he stopped, and stared, and screamed in horror. From behind DragonStar lumbered a small, dark cheerful shape.

The bear cub.

Qeteb shrieked, and lifted his hands away from the sword, holding them out before him as if to ward himself from the personification of all he feared most in the universe.

Love.

Qeteb's skewered body jerked about the sword so violently he twisted about in a full circle, his heels digging into the earth, his hips and shoulders contorting in the effort to somehow free himself from the pin which held him.

Love, in the guise of the bear cub, padded forward. The cub stopped just short of Qeteb's feet, and he lowered his snout and sniffed curiously.

Qeteb kicked at the cub.

The cub snapped, and Qeteb shrieked yet again.

One of his feet had gone.

The cub chewed, crunched, chewed some more, and then swallowed.

It licked its lips, and made a happy, mewling sound.

Every one of the Alaunt licked their lips, and shifted hungrily.

"No," said DragonStar, "this is a meal only Love can consume."

The cub's head darted forward again, and took Qeteb's other foot, as well half the leg beneath his knee.

Qeteb wailed and moaned and shrieked, waving his amputated lower limbs about wildly, splattering blood about him in a frenzied arc.

The bear cub swallowed, growled and leaped forward, his head darting between Qeteb's legs to the Demon's genitals.

DragonStar stood watching the bear cub eat the Midday Demon mouthful by mouthful, and yet seeing nothing.

He was remembering.

Remembering how Axis had plunged the Rainbow Sceptre into Gorgrael until the Destroyer had literally disintegrated about it.

And yet Axis had not truly destroyed the evil that was Gorgrael, had he? It had simply festered, causing fatal cancers within Tencendorian society, as well Axis' own family.

Many years after Gorgrael's death the Sceptre had called to Drago, pulling him beyond the Star Gate, and eventually transforming, first into the purse, then into the staff, and finally into the lily sword.

Which DragonStar, in turn, had plunged into the evil that was Qeteb.

Yet, finally, it was not the weapon that was destroying the personification of mad, vindictive evil.

It was Love. Love had allowed Faraday to escape, and had sacrificed itself for her, and Love was now consuming the evil of Qeteb.

This was not an evil which would re-emerge in some unthought of place.

This was an evil which, finally, was being consumed into nothingness.

The bear cub swallowed the last tasty morsel, licked up a few stray drops of blood, and then raised its head and looked at DragonStar.

DragonStar smiled, his eyes brimming with tears, and he nodded his thanks to the cub.

His job done, the cub began to shape-change back to its true form.

The blue-feathered lizard. Love and Light, together within the one form.

"Go," DragonStar whispered, and the lizard grinned happily and trotted off, back to the Field and the butterflies and his myriad of friends.

DragonStar looked back to where Qeteb had been. The Alaunt were sniffing about curiously, but there was nothing there. The bear cub had, in the course of consuming Qeteb, also consumed the lily sword.

Both evil, and the weapon needed to fight it, were gone.

The ploughed field faded, and once again DragonStar found himself standing within the bleak walls of the Maze.

Behind him came a vast roaring sound, as if a sea had gone mad.

DragonStar did not look.

Forty-two thousand trees ran riot through the Maze, using root and branch to tear it apart.

The darkness that had consumed the wasteland now began to invade the Maze, and, as each stone fell, its influence grew more profound.

As the last stone in the Maze crashed into dust, an eternal night fell, and the trees fell silent, and still.

They waited.

70

The Witness

The Corolean fishing fleet was sailing west from the Barrow Islands, heading for its home port on the northern coastline of Coroleas, when the cataclysm occurred.

One moment the sea had been calm, if sullen, under an overcast sky, the next it was rolling so madly the crews of the five vessels all thought they were moments away from death.

And the next moment, it was calm again.

One of the seamen, a man called El'habain, was clinging to the railing about the prow of the leading vessel where he'd been standing watching for seals. He was soaked through, and frightened as he had never before been in his arrogant life.

He raised his head, shaking it from side to side to clear the salty water from his eyes and ears, and looked for someone to curse and blame for his fright and his soaking.

In the end El'habain said nothing. He merely stared into the distance, towards where the Tencendorian cliffs lined Widewall Bay.

They were crumbling. Great rocks toppled into the ocean and, as El'habain stared, the length of the cliffs as far as he could see fell beneath the ocean waves.

There was nothing left but the rolling waves.

Tencendor had gone.

71

The Waiting

There was a blackness, and an unknowingness, during which all creation ceased to exist.

There was simply nothing.

Save, as far as Axis was concerned, the harsh and fearful sound of his breathing.

"Is anyone else there?" he said, and a being shifted under him, and he realised that Pretty Brown Sal also existed.

"Yes," whispered a voice across the void, and Axis recognised it as Zared's, and then a hundred other whispers reached him, and Axis realised that somehow the convoy still stretched out behind him.

"Axis?"

A faint voice, unsure.

"Azhure!" Gods! He'd thought to have lost her forever.

There was an unseen movement at his side, and Axis felt a hand groping along Sal's shoulder.

"Azhure! Here!" He reached down a hand and grabbed hers, and at his touch and warmth Azhure burst into sobs.

He hauled her up into the saddle and hugged her tight. "SpikeFeather? Katie?" he eventually said.

"Katie has gone," said a voice somewhere to one side, and Axis recognised it as SpikeFeather's. "But Urbeth's daughters are still with us—"

And somehow Axis had the distinct impression, although he could not see a thing, that the two women stood to either side of SpikeFeather, each holding one of his hands.

"—as is . . ."

"As is . . . *I*," said a chilling voice, and Axis jumped, knowing the voice instantly.

The GateKeeper laughed, a grating, dry sound. "We meet again, Axis."

"Why aren't you at your Gate?" Axis said.

There was a silence, and when the GateKeeper answered, her voice was puzzled and unsure.

"I sat at my table," the GateKeeper said, "when, just then, just now, a moment ago it seems to me, the soul of a beautiful girl child drifted up. Before she went through the Gate, she turned to me and she said, 'Rejoice, GateKeeper, for your task is done. Time is ended, and the Gate must close.'

"And then she stepped through the Gate. And then . . . then it imploded, and I had seized the birdman and your wife and Urbeth's two girls and brought them here."

"Then I thank you for that—" Axis began.

"Oh, I did not think of you when I returned your wife and companions," the GateKeeper said. "It was merely convenient that I brought them with me."

"Then *why* did you come here?" said Axis.

"Because of Her," said the GateKeeper. "The Child."

And Axis nodded, and understood. Not Katie at all, but Leagh's Child.

They waited.

"Has ma'am finished?" said Raspu, returning from wherever he had been, and Faraday put her cup back into its saucer and extended it into the dark. The mausoleum had completely vanished, and now there was only a nothingness.

"Yes. Thank you." Faraday was not perturbed by the dark and the nothingness, nor by the fact that she currently shared the void with a former Demon.

All would be well as it eventuated.

They waited.

DragonStar rode his Star Stallion through the void, his pale hounds fanning out behind him in a comet's tail.

There was something he should do, but for the moment he did not care. There was only the wild ride, the freedom, and the void.

Nothing else mattered.

The stallion snorted, and shook his head.

Sicarius bayed, and the Alaunt clamoured.

DragonStar sighed.

"Faraday," he said.

She heard him before she saw him. The faint fall of a horse's hooves, the snuffling of a pack of hounds.

Slowly Faraday rose to her feet, accepting Raspu's hand on her elbow.

Then, suddenly, there was a presence, and the faintest of luminescence, and there was DragonStar, sitting his stallion, his hounds milling about him.

"Come," he said. "We have a Garden to plant."

Raspu watched as DragonStar helped Faraday mount behind him, and then, as they rode away and the darkness closed in again, he waited.

The Star Stallion stopped, and DragonStar turned slightly.

"Faraday? Are you ready?"

"Ready for what?" she said. What had he meant, plant the Garden?

She felt, rather than saw, him smile. "You have something of mine," DragonStar said. "Something you have kept for a very long time. Will you now give it back to me?"

Faraday frowned, and then jumped slightly in surprise as she remembered what it was. "Oh!"

When DragonStar had worked the enchantment to ensnare the twenty thousand crazed people in the Western Ranges, he had shot the enchantment into the sky with an arrow.

After the arrow had done its work, it had fallen to the ground at Faraday's feet, and, eventually, she'd wound it into the rainbow band that the Mother had given her.

Together with the sapling.

Her hands trembling, Faraday leaned back very slightly from DragonStar's warmth, and unwound the band.

She took the arrow, the sapling still safely coiled about it, into her hands.

And then Faraday gasped, for the arrow had been strangely supple all this time it rested so close about her waist. Now, in the space of one heartbeat, it solidified into strength again.

The sapling still wound its way about its length.

"Faraday?"

She took the arrow, and passed it to DragonStar.

He held it briefly, then lifted the Wolven from his shoulder and fitted the arrow to it.

He paused, and Faraday could tell he was crying, then in one fluid movement, DragonStar lifted the bow and shot the arrow high into the darkness.

72

The Tree

The arrow rose into the darkness, and the hopelessness, and the void.

It rose until it could rise no more, and then it fell.

It fell, and fell, and fell until it reached impossible speeds.

And then, when it could fall no more, it struck a resistance, and its head buried itself within the resistance.

Somewhere far, far away, the Star Stallion screamed, and reared and plunged, and stars fell in their millions from his mane and tail.

A great wind consumed the blackness, and it swept the stars high and higher.

There was an explosion of light and sound from the point where the arrow struck.

It washed out in great rippling waves, engulfing all those who waited within the darkness.

It caught the stars, and twisted them high, and higher, feeding their fire, so that they grew a million-fold in intensity, and then the wind swept them higher still.

Then the arrow sighed, and let itself be consumed, for its work was done.

Something grew.

Axis and Azhure both cried out and clung to each other as the waves of light and sound engulfed them. Pain and joy in equal amounts devoured them.

Peace, said Leagh's Child.

The pain eased, and the intensity of the light dulled back to a soft and gentle radiance.

But the joy remained.

Azhure, among all others, was the first to open her eyes and look.

She shuddered, wracked by emotion as the import of what she saw sank in.

A Tree. Gigantic, all-encompassing. Its leaves every shade of green, its trumpet flowers a brilliant gold edged with scarlet.

It stood in the void, shedding a soft, gentle light.

Then, as Azhure put trembling hands to her face, and everyone else opened their eyes, the Tree's leaves trembled, and . . .

. . . and a garden rippled out from its base, consuming the blackness and the void, and all trembled as earth and grasses and flowers formed under their feet as the Garden flowed outwards.

For those who had known the Field of Flowers, the Garden was like, and yet unlike. It was filled with flowers and their scents, but the Garden was more formed than the Infinite Field of Flowers had been. There were paths and glades, and shadowed, dappled spots of coolness where trees congregated.

It was like Sanctuary, save it did not share Sanctuary's sense of impermanence.

This Garden was the reality from which everything else had been insubstantial reflections.

Above, in a deep blue sky, millions of stars blazed.

Azhure cried out softly again, and pointed.

DragonStar and Faraday were walking through great, gorgeous drifts of flowers, the Star Stallion sauntering behind them, his head nodding and dipping with happiness.

Behind the stallion bounded the Alaunt, and behind them, carefully adjusting his vest lest it had become creased during Creation, walked Raspu.

73

The Garden

"Aha!" cried the GateKeeper. "I know what this is!"

"What?" said Azhure politely, her eyes still on DragonStar and Faraday.

"It is that which existed beyond the Gate!" the GateKeeper said.

DragonStar, now within two paces of them, smiled and nodded. "In a manner of speaking, yes. But this Garden is far more than an 'AfterLife'. It is a 'BeforeLife' as well. It is a beginning and an end within itself. It is a well, a reservoir, of life."

Azhure disentangled herself from Axis' grasp, and slid down from Pretty Brown Sal.

There was something . . . someone . . . walking through the flowers towards her.

She gave a great sob—would she never stop crying?—and

leaned forward to embrace Caelum and RiverStar, and Zenith just behind them.

And then there were the thousands, the millions, walking out through the flowers from the oblivion of death—Rivkah, Belial, MorningStar, a hundred neighbours and friends, ten thousand names and memories, faces and voices drifting out of the forgetfulness of death, but reaching out with living arms.

But among them all, there was no StarDrifter.

"Why?" said Azhure, distraught. "Why?"

Rivkah, Magariz beside her, had her arms about Azhure, comforting her as she had done so often when Azhure had been so lost and lonely and friendless within Smyrton.

DragonStar shrugged his shoulders helplessly. "I do not know."

The GateKeeper, strangely soft and pretty in this place, said: "*I* know. He did not pass through the Gate, nor even through the Butler's gate."

"But I *saw* StarDrifter's wings!" said Axis. "He was *dead!* He must have been!"

"Nevertheless," said the GateKeeper, her eyes resuming a hint of their former steeliness, "he did not pass through either Gate."

And to one side the Butler, polishing a tableful of silver, nodded his agreement.

"Then where is my father?" Axis shouted.

Leagh walked up with her Child in her arms.

Beyond us, said the Girl. *If he is not here, then he is somewhere back there.*

"Back 'there'?" DragonStar said.

The wasteland of Tencendor only was consumed, said the Child. *The other lands bordering it still exist. StarDrifter, perhaps as a result of some magic, must still be there. He was not in the wasteland when it was consumed.*

"Then we must go after him!" Azhure said.

No.

"No?"

No. You may not pass from the Garden and return. I would have you here with me.

StarDrifter, somewhere in the lands bordering Tencendor? thought Axis. How? How? What magic could have transported him? And *where*?

"What exactly does remain of Tencendor?" he asked the Child.

Nothing. Not in the flesh. The land was consumed by earthquake and waves when DragonStar struck the fatal blow to Qeteb. To those who lived outside the borders of Tencendor, there is nothing left of that land. Only waves.

Axis, as Azhure, opened his mouth to say something more, but the Child forestalled him. *He is gone. Not here. Grieve, if you must, but know also that his time had not yet been completed.*

"And what," said Zared, walking up to Leagh's shoulder, and looking down in perplexion at his Child's face, "do we do now?"

The Child laughed, and thrust her tiny fists into the air. *You populate the Garden in peace and contentedness!*

EPILOGUE

*T*he Corolean Emperor leaned forward on his throne, one hand absently laying to one side the heavy folds of his purple and gold silk mantle.

"What do you mean, Tencendor is 'gone'?"

"Highest One," the Admiral said from his position of laying face down on the floor, arms spread out to either side of him. His voice was very slightly muffled. "We spent weeks sailing over the entire ocean. The continent is *gone*. Sunk beneath the waves. Even the barren land bridge connecting our continents has gone. Waves. Only waves are left."

"*Nothing* is left? Not a single piece of flotsam? Not one puffy corpse?"

"Nothing, Highest One."

"What happened?"

The Admiral took his time answering, not knowing quite what to make of the hundreds of reports he had had from, not only the crews of Corolean fishing vessels in the area but also from Escatorian cargo ships sailing for Tencendor, as well as the odd pirate, who relinquished their information only grudgingly, and under the threat of having their genitals skewered by hot pokers.

"Highest One," the Admiral eventually said. "From what I can gather, the land suffered a cataclysm so complete we can barely comprehend it. The entire continent of Tencendor has sunk beneath the waves. Even the barren land bridge connecting our continents has gone. Waves. Only waves are left."

The Admiral paused again, wondering whether to relate the other piece of information that had persistently come to his ears.

"Tell me!" the Emperor snapped.

"It is said," the Admiral said very slowly, "that Tencendor was so riddled with sin, corruption and vileness that the gods decided absolute destruction was better than redemption."

The Emperor stared, then sat back in his throne, his chubby, sweating face smiling beatifically.

"I always knew they were a bad lot," he said.

At the very back of the crowd in the public throne chamber, a fair-haired man with extraordinarily compelling blue eyes grinned sardonically. After a moment he turned away, wincing as some unseen injury caught at his back, and he faded into the crowd.

The pain of not finding StarDrifter faded. His time had not been right, and he had passed elsewhere, not into the Garden.

So be it.

Axis and Azhure, as every other person who had passed through death—whether during the final moments of Tencendor, or ten thousand years beforehand—accepted the joy and peacefulness of the Garden.

They were contented, as were the entire populations of peoples and creatures who had entered the Garden.

The Icarii fanned out in the skies, beautiful jewel-like creatures who populated the air with music and wonder.

The Ravensbund, with Urbeth grumbling good-naturedly at their head, moved to the cliffs and beaches of the never-ending coasts that bounded the Garden, and explored the mysteries they found there.

The Avar wandered the Garden, shaded by the ethereal trees, learning the ways of the flowers and the winds that tipped them into cascades of delight.

They became gardeners.

The Acharites built themselves pale-stoned homes that bordered the glades and walks, and spent their time—not ploughing—but sitting on doorsteps or in rocking chairs under verandahs, and passing the time of day with each other, and any other who passed by.

SpikeFeather wandered off with Urbeth's two daughters,

and the threesome explored the more secretive glades, and kept to themselves.

The Alaunt settled down, and FortHeart gave Sicarius a fine litter.

Belaguez courted Pretty Brown Sal, but she spent her time sliding tantalisingly just beyond his reach.

Axis and Azhure were reunited with the other seven once-Star Gods come back from their spin through the stars, and they, as had been their wont in the years before the Time-Keepers' invasion, explored the mysteries they could see circling in the star patterns above their heads.

Theod and Gwendylyr raised their twin boys, and added a baby girl to their family.

Zared and Leagh, meanwhile, raised their Daughter through wondrous babyhood, into girlhood, and then into womanhood. The Woman sat beneath the Tree, and dispensed laughter and advice and wisdom, and She and the Tree were the centre of Creation.

Sometimes people thought they saw Katie flitting between trees, and in the shadows of glades, but none ever spoke to her, and the Woman told them to leave her alone.

She has had her share of pain, and now is at peace in her aloneness. Leave her.

DragonStar and Faraday grew restless. Everyone else had adjusted themselves to the Garden, and its serenity and beauty, but they could not.

They had not been granted the grace of contentedness.

One day, they went to see the Woman. "We think," DragonStar said slowly, holding Faraday's hand tightly in his own, "that there remains something else for us to do."

Aye. There is.

"But it does not rest within the Garden, does it?" Faraday said.

No.

"Beyond, then?" DragonStar said, and felt a small kernel of excitement flower deep within him.

Aye. Beyond. You have a life that yet lies ahead of you. The wasteland that was Tencendor has transformed, but there are other wastelands, StarSon, that need your strength, and Faraday's love.

The Woman looked at Faraday's swelling belly. *Bear your child elsewhere, Faraday. Give birth to hope in a desolate wasteland.*

"We will never come back," Faraday said, but there was no anger or regret in her voice.

No. You will find your contentedness elsewhere.

The Woman stood, and reached one hand high above Her. She plucked a fruit from the Tree, and held it out to Dragon-Star and Faraday.

Take this, and eat of it with My blessing.

Faraday took the fruit, and cradled it within her hands. "What is it?"

Wisdom and Love.

Faraday's eyes filled with tears, and she slowly raised the fruit to her lips and ate.

Something in her face shifted, something in her soul altered, and Faraday understood the road before her.

She turned to DragonStar and offered him the fruit. "Eat."

And he did, and he, too, was altered.

He looked at Faraday. His eyes were alive with excitement. Faraday stared, and then she burst into laughter, and leaned forward to embrace him.

The Woman smiled. *Step forth, and birth your new world within the wasteland. Go, with My blessing, My love, and My eternal gratitude.*

Axis stared at them. He half raised a hand, then dropped it. "Stay. Please."

DragonStar smiled gently, and took his father's hand. "No. We cannot. If we stayed here we would only destroy the Garden with our restlessness. Our journey is not yet done."

His eyes flickered over the ranks of what had once been the Strike Force standing in ranks behind Axis: winged, ethereal, serene. Then DragonStar leaned forward and kissed Axis on the mouth. "We will never forget you, nor this place. It will become the foundation myth of our children. Goodbye, Axis, farewell Azhure."

And, once Faraday had kissed Axis and Azhure goodbye, she and DragonStar walked hand in hand through the doorway that the Butler opened for them with a reverential bow of his head.

They walked from the Garden into the Wastelands beyond, there to build a life untarnished by fate and enriched by the gifts the Woman had given them.

They did not look back.

Glossary

ACHAR: the realm that once stretched over most of the continent, bounded by the Andeis, Tyrre and Widowmaker Seas, the Avarinheim and the Icescarp Alps. It was integrated into Tencendor during the time of Axis StarSon.

ACHARITES: a term used fairly generally to encompass all humans within Tencendor.

ADAMON: one of the nine Star Gods of the Icarii, Adamon is the eldest and the God of the Firmament.

AFTERLIFE: all three races, the Acharites, the Icarii and the Avar believe in the existence of an AfterLife, although exactly what they believe depends on their particular culture.

ALAUNT: the legendary pack of hounds that once belonged to WolfStar SunSoar. They followed Azhure for some time, but now run with DragonStar. They are all of the Lesser.

ALDENI: once a small province in western Achar, it was administered by Duke Theod.

ANDAKILSA, River: the extreme northern river of Ichtar, dividing Ichtar from Ravensbund.

ANDEIS SEA: the often unpredictable sea that washes the western coast of Achar.

ARCEN: the major city of Arcness. Before Qeteb's destruction, it was a free trading city.

ARCNESS: a large eastern province in Tencendor.

ARTOR THE PLOUGHMAN: the now disbanded Brotherhood of the Seneschal taught that Artor was the one true god. Under His sway, the Acharites initiated the ancient Wars of the Axe and drove the Icarii and Avar from the land. Artor was killed by Azhure and her hounds.

ASKAM, Prince of the West: son of Belial and Cazna. Now dead.

AVAR, The: the ancient race of Tencendor who live in the forests of the Avarinheim and Minstrelsea. The Avar are sometimes referred to as the People of the Horn. Their Mage-King is Isfrael.

AVARINHEIM, The: the northern forest home of the Avar people. It was destroyed when Qeteb was resurrected.

AVENUE, The: the processional way of the Temple Complex on the Island of Mist and Memory. The term 'The Avenue' comes to have a slightly different meaning by the end of *Crusader*.

AVONSDALE: once a province in western Achar. It was administered by Earl Herme.

AXE-WIELDERS, The: once the elite crusading and military wing of the Seneschal, led by Axis as their BattleAxe.

AXIS: son of the Princess Rivkah of Achar and the Icarii Enchanter, StarDrifter SunSoar. Once BattleAxe of the Axe-Wielders, he assumed the mantle of the StarMan of the Prophecy of the Destroyer. After reforging Tencendor Axis formed his own house, the House of the Stars before beginning a new existence as the Star God of Song. Having lost all his powers due to the invasion of the Timekeeper Demons, Axis is once again a mere mortal.

AZHURE: daughter of WolfStar SunSoar and Niah of Nor, and Goddess of Moon. She is married to Axis. Their children are Caelum (now dead), Drago, RiverStar (now dead) and Zenith. As with Axis, Azhure is once again merely mortal now the Star Dance is dead.

AZLE, River: a major river that divided the provinces of Ichtar and Aldeni. It flows into the Andeis Sea.

BANES: the religious leaders of the Avar people. They wield magic, although it is usually of the minor variety.

BARROWS, The Ancient: the burial places of the ancient Enchanter-Talons of the Icarii people. The Barrows were destroyed when the Demons broke through the Star Gate.

BATTLEAXE, The: once the leader of the Axe-Wielders. The post of BattleAxe was last held by Axis. See 'Axe-Wielders'.

BARZULA: one of the TimeKeeper Demons, Barzula is the Demon of mid-morning, and of tempest.

BEDWYR FORT: a fort that sat on the lower reaches of the River Nordra and guarded the entrance to Grail Lake from Nordmuth.

BELIAL: lieutenant and second-in-command in Axis' army during the fight against Gorgrael. Belial was the father of Askam and Cazna. Now dead.

BELTIDE: see 'Festivals'.

BETHIAM, Princess: wife to Prince Askam of the West.

BOGLE MARSH: a large and inhospitable marsh in eastern Arcness. Faraday emptied its strange creatures into Sanctuary to escape the Demons.

BORNEHELD: Duke of Ichtar and King of Achar. Son of the Princess Rivkah and her husband, Duke Searlas, half-brother to Axis, and husband of Lady Faraday of Skarabost. After murdering his uncle, Priam, Borneheld assumed the throne of Achar. Now dead.

BRACKEN RANGES, The: the former name of the Minaret Peaks.

BRACKEN, River: the river that rises in the Minaret Peaks and flows into the Widowmaker Sea.

BRIDGE, The: the bridge that guards the entrance into Sigholt is deeply magical. She will throw out a challenge to any she does not know, but can be easily tricked.

BROTHER-LEADER, The: the supreme leader of the Brotherhood of the now disbanded Seneschal. The last Brother-Leader of the Seneschal was Jayme.

CAELUM STARSON: eldest son of Axis and Azhure, born at Yuletide. Caelum is an ancient word meaning 'Stars in Heaven'. Caelum is now dead.

CARLON: main city of Tencendor and one-time residence of the kings of Achar. Situated on Grail Lake.

CAULDRON LAKE, The: the lake at the centre of the Silent Woman Woods. Now destroyed.

CAZNA: wife to Belial. Now dead.

CHAMBER OF THE MOONS: chief audience and sometime banquet chamber of the ancient royal palace in Carlon. It was the site where Axis battled Borneheld to the death.

CHARONITES: a little-known race of Tencendor, they inhabited the UnderWorld. When Drago managed to kill Orr in the chamber of the Star Gate, the race became extinct.

CIRCLE OF STARS, The: see 'Enchantress' Ring'.

CLANS, The: the Avar tend to segregate into Clan groups, roughly equitable with family groups.

CLOUDBURST SUNSOAR: younger brother and assassin of WolfStar SunSoar.

COHORT: see 'Military Terms'.

COROLEAS: the great empire to the south of Tencendor. Relations between the two countries is usually cordial.

CREST: Icarii military unit composed of twelve Wings.

CREST-LEADER: commander of an Icarii Crest.

DANCE OF DEATH, The: dark star music that is the counter point to the Star Dance. It is the music made when stars miss their step and crash into each other, or swell up into red giants and implode. Only WolfStar and Azhure can wield this music, although both lost the ability to do so when the TimeKeepers destroyed the Star Gate.

DAREWING FULLHEART: senior Crest-Leader and Strike Leader of the Icarii Strike Force.

DEMONIC HOURS:

Dawn: ruled by Mot, a time of hunger.

Mid-morning: ruled by Barzula, a time of tempest.

Midday: the time of the greatest Demon of all, Qeteb.

Mid-afternoon: ruled by Sheol, a time of despair.

Dusk: ruled by Raspu, a time of pestilence.

Night: ruled by Rox, a time of terror.

DISTANCES:

League: roughly seven kilometres, or four and a half miles.

Pace: roughly one metre or one yard.

Handspan: roughly twenty centimetres or eight inches.

DOME OF THE MOON: a sacred dome dedicated to the Moon on Temple Mount of the Island of Mist and Memory.

Only the First Priestess has access to the Dome, and it was in this Dome that Niah conceived Azhure.

DRAGONSTAR SUNSOAR: second son of Axis and Azhure. Twin brother to RiverStar. (Also known as Drago.) DragonStar is also the name of the son StarLaughter Sun-Soar was carrying when she was murdered by her husband, WolfStar.

DRIFTSTAR SUNSOAR: grandmother to StarDrifter, mother of MorningStar. An Enchanter and a SunSoar in her own right and wife to the SunSoar Talon. She died over three hundred years before the events of this book.

EARTH TREE: a sacred tree to both the Icarii and the Avar. It once lived in the extreme northern groves of the Avarin-heim forest, close to the cliffs of the Icescarp Alps, but was destroyed when Qeteb created the wasteland.

EARTH TREE GROVE: the grove which held the Earth Tree in the northern Avarinheim where it bordered the Icescarp Alps. It was where the Avar (sometimes in concert with the Icarii) held their gatherings and religious rites.

ENCHANTRESS, The: the first of the Icarii Enchanters, the first Icarii to discover the way to use the power of the Star Dance. She bore three sons, the eldest of whom founded the Acharite race, the middle founded the Charonite race, and the youngest founded the Icarii race. The Enchantress also gave birth to twin daughters. Also known as Urbeth.

ENCHANTRESS' RING, The: an ancient ring once in the possession of the Enchantress, now worn by Azhure. Its proper name is the Circle of Stars, and it is intimately connected with the Star Gods.

ENCHANTERS: the once magicians of the Icarii people—with the destruction of the Star Gate all have now lost their powers. All Enchanters have the word 'Star' somewhere in their names.

ENCHANTER-TALONS: Talons of the Icarii people who are also Enchanters.

ENEMY, The: the name given by the TimeKeepers to the an-cient ones who trapped Qeteb and then fled with his life parts through the universe. It was the Enemy who crashed into Tencendor during Fire-Night.

ESCATOR: a kingdom far away to the east over the Widow-maker Sea.

EVENSONG: daughter of Rivkah and StarDrifter SunSoar, sister to Axis and wife to Talon FreeFall SunSoar.

FARADAY: daughter of Earl Isend of Skarabost and his wife, Lady Merlion. Once wife to Borneheld and Queen of Achar, Faraday now aids DragonStar. She is also the mother of Isfrael, conceived during her brief and tragic affair with Axis.

FERNBRAKE LAKE, The: the large lake in the centre of the Bracken Ranges. Also known by both the Avar and the Icarii as the Mother. Now a dessicated garden.

FERRYMAN, The: the Charonite who plied the ferry of the UnderWorld. His name was Orr, and was one of the Lesser immortals. Orr is now dead after being struck by the Rainbow Sceptre in the chamber of the Star Gate.

FESTIVALS of the Avar and the Icarii:

Yuletide: the winter solstice, in the last week of Snow-month.

Beltide: the spring Festival, the first day of Flower-month.

Fire-Night: the summer solstice, in the last week of Rose-month.

FIRE-NIGHT, The: see 'Festivals'.

FIRST, The: the First Priestess of the Order of the Stars, the order of nine priestesses on Temple Mount. The First, like all priestesses of the Order, gave up her name on taking her vows. Niah of Nor once held this office.

FIVE FAMILIES, The First: the leading families of Tencendor: led, in turn, by Prince Askam of the West, King Zared of the North, Prince Yllgaine of Nor, Chief Sa'Domai of the Ravensbund and FreeFall SunSoar, Talon of the Icarii. The delicate balance between these families was greatly upset when Zared seized the throne of Achar.

FLULIA: one of the nine Icarii Star Gods, Flulia is the Goddess of Water.

FLURIA, The River: a minor river that flows through Aldeni into the River Nordra.

FORESTFLIGHT EVERSOAR: a member of the Lake Guard.

FORTHEART: one of the Alaunt, and mate to Sicarius.

FORTRESS RANGES: the mountains that run down Achar's eastern boundary from the Icescarp Alps to the Widowmaker Sea.

FREEFALL, Talon: son of BrightFeather and RavenCrest SunSoar, husband of EvenSong SunSoar. They have no children.

GAPFEATHER: a member of the Lake Guard.

GATEKEEPER, The: the Keeper of the Gate of Death in the UnderWorld and mother of Zeherah. Her task is to keep tally of the souls who pass through the Gate. She is one of the Lesser immortals.

GHEMT: a game played with sticks and dice in a circle of diamond-shaped spaces.

GOLDMAN, JANNYMIRE: Master of the Guilds of Carlon. One of the most powerful non-noblemen in Tencendor.

GORGRAEL: the Destroyer, half-brother to Axis, sharing the same father, StarDrifter. Axis defeated him in a titanic struggle for control of Tencendor forty years before current events.

GORKENFORT: a major fort situated in Gorken Pass in northern Ichtar.

GORKEN PASS: the narrow pass sixty leagues long that provided the only way from Ravensbund into Ichtar. It is bounded by the Icescarp Alps and the River Andakilsa.

GRAIL LAKE, The: a massive lake at the lower reaches of the River Nordra. Beneath its waters it harboured the Maze, which has now risen and destroyed the Lake.

GREATER, The: the nine Star Gods.

GRYPHON: a legendary flying creature of Tencendor, intelligent, vicious and courageous. Gorgrael recreated them to defeat Axis, but they were all destroyed by Azhure.

GUNDEALGA FORD: a wide shallow ford on the Nordra, just south of the Urqhart Hills.

GUSTUS: Captain of Zared's militia.

GWENDYLYR: wife of Duke Theod of Aldeni, and mother of their twin sons.

HAGEN: once a Plough-Keeper in the (now destroyed) village of Smyrton who was husband to Niah. He was accidentally killed by Azhure some forty-three years ago.

HANDSPAN: see 'Distances'.

HERME, Earl of Avonsdale: son of Earl Jorge, mentor of Duke Theod of Aldeni and friend to King Zared.

HORNED ONES: the almost divine and most sacred members of the Avar race. They live in the Sacred Grove.

HSINGARD: a ruined town situated in central Ichtar.

ICARII, The: a race of winged people. They are sometimes referred to as the People of the Wing.

ICEBEAR COAST: the hundred-league-long coast that stretches from the DeadWood Forest in north-western Ravensbund to the frozen Tundra above the Avarinheim. It is very remote, and very beautiful.

ICESCARP ALPS, The: the great mountain range that stretches across most of northern Achar.

ICESCARP BARREN: a desolate tract of land situated in northern Ichtar between the Icescarp Alps and the Urqhart Hills.

ICEWORMS: massive worms of ice and snow created by Gorgrael.

ICHTAR, DUKES of: once cruel lords of Ichtar, the line died with Borneheld.

ICHTAR, The Province of: the largest and richest of the provinces of Achar. Ichtar derives its wealth from its extensive grazing herds and from its mineral and precious gem deposits. Ruled by Zared, now also King of the Acharites.

ICHTAR, The River: a minor river that flows through Ichtar into the River Azle.

ILFRACOOMBE: the manor house of the Earl of Skarabost, the home where Faraday grew up.

ISABEAU: first wife of King Zared. She died in a hunting accident ten years before current events.

ISFRAEL: Mage-King of the Avar. Son of Axis and Faraday.

ISLAND OF MIST AND MEMORY: one of the sacred sites of the Icarii people, once known as Pirate's Nest. The Temple of the Stars and its complex are situated on a great plateau on the island's southern coast.

JACK: senior among the Sentinels.

JERVOIS LANDING: the small town on Tailem Bend of the River Nordra. The gateway into Ichtar.

KASTALEON: One of the great Keeps of Achar, situated on the River Nordra in central Achar. It was blown up by Theod under instructions from Zared, killing many thousands of Caelum's men.

KEEPS, The: the three great magical Keeps of Achar. See separate entries under Spiredore, Sigholt, and Silent Woman Keep.

LAKE GUARD, The: a militia composed entirely of the men and women who SpikeFeather TrueSong rescued from Talon Spike when it was threatened by Gryphon. They escaped via the waterways, and were changed by their experience. The Lake Guard is dedicated to the service of the StarSon.

LAKE OF LIFE, The: one of the sacred and magical lakes of Tencendor. It sat at the western end of the HoldHard Pass in the Urqhart Hills and cradled Sigholt. Now a pit of pestilence.

LEAGH, Princess: sister to Askam, daughter of Belial and Cazna. Now wife of Zared.

LEAGUE: see 'Distances'.

LESSER, The: a term given to creatures of such magic they approach god-like status. They are not strictly immortal, although they will live indefinitely if not struck a death blow.

MAGARIZ, Prince: husband to Rivkah, Axis' mother, and father to Zared. Now dead.

MAGIC: under the influence of the Seneschal all Artor-fearing Acharites feared and hated the use of magic, although their fear is now as largely dead as the Seneschal.

MARRAT, Baron: Baron of Romsdale.

MAZE, The: a mysterious labyrinth that rose from Grail Lake.

MAZE GATE, The: the wooden gate into the Maze. Its stone archway is covered with hieroglyphics.

MILITARY TERMS (for regular ground forces):
  Squad: a small group of fighters, normally under forty and usually archers.
  Unit: a group of one hundred men, either infantry, archers, pikemen, or cavalry.
  Cohort: five units, so five hundred men.
  See also 'Wing' and 'Crest' for the Icarii Strike Force.

MINARET PEAKS: the ancient name for the Bracken Ranges, named for the minarets of the Icarii cities that spread over the entire mountain range.

MINSTRELSEA: the name Faraday gave to the forest she planted out below the Avarinheim.

MONTHS: (northern hemisphere seasons apply)
  Wolf-month: January
  Raven-month: February
  Hungry-month: March
  Thaw-month: April
  Flower-month: May
  Rose-month: June
  Harvest-month: July
  Weed-month: August
  DeadLeaf-month: September
  Bone-month: October
  Frost-month: November
  Snow-month: December

MOONWILDFLOWERS: extremely rare, delicate violet flowers that bloom only under the full moon. Closely associated with Azhure.

MORNINGSTAR SUNSOAR: StarDrifter's mother and a powerful Enchanter in her own right. She was murdered by WolfStar SunSoar.

MORYSON: Brother of the Seneschal and a disguise used by WolfStar.

MOT: one of the TimeKeeper Demons. Mot is the Demon of dawn and of hunger.

MOTHER, The: either the Avar name for Fernbrake Lake, or an all-embracing term for nature which is sometimes personified as an immortal woman.

MURKLE BAY: a huge bay off the western coast of Tencendor, its waters are filthy, polluted by the tanneries along the Azle River.

MURKLE MOUNTAINS: a range of desolate mountains that run along the length of Murkle Bay. Once extensively mined for opals, they are now abandoned.

MURMURWING: a young Icarii.

NARCIS: one of the nine Icarii Star Gods, Narcis is the God of the Sun.

NECKLET, The: a curious geological feature of Ravensbund.

NIAH: of the once baronial family of Nor. Mother to Azhure, Niah was seduced by WolfStar SunSoar and murdered by Brother Hagen. Niah was the First Priestess of the Order of the Stars. WolfStar promised her rebirth to be his lover for eternity, and her soul was born into Zenith, youngest daughter of Axis and Azhure. In *Sinner*, Niah and Zenith battled for control of her body and soul, with the result that Zenith forced the Niah-soul into a child she was carrying (fathered by WolfStar), which she gave premature birth to and then killed. WolfStar then carried the corpse of the Niah-infant about with him until it was seized by the Demons for their own purposes.

NINE, The: see the 'Star Gods'. ('The Nine' can also occasionally refer to the nine Priestesses of the Order of the Stars.)

NOR: once the southernmost of the provinces of Achar. Nor was controlled by Prince Yllgaine.

NORDMUTH: the port at the mouth of the River Nordra.

NORDRA, River: the great river that was the main lifeline of Achar. Rising in the Icescarp Alps, the River Nordra flows through the Avarinheim before flowing through northern and central Achar.

OGDEN: one of the Sentinels, brother to Veremund.

ORDER OF THE STARS: the order of nine priestesses who once kept watch in the Temple of the Stars.

ORR: the Charonite Ferryman. Now dead.

PACE: see 'Distances'.

PIRATES' NEST: for many centuries the common name of

the Island of Mist and Memory. It was once the haunt of pirates.

PIRATES' TOWN: the town that sat by the northern harbour of Pirates' Nest—or the Island of Mist and Memory.

PLOUGH, The: under the rule of the Seneschal each Acharite village had a Plough, which not only served to plough the fields, but was also the centre of their worship of the Way of the Plough.

PLOUGH-KEEPERS: the Seneschal assigned a Brother to each village in Achar, and these men were often known as Plough-Keepers.

PORS: one of the nine Icarii Star Gods, Pors is the God of Air.

PRETTY BROWN SAL: a most unusual horse.

PRIVY CHAMBER: the large chamber in the ancient royal palace of Carlon where the Achar's Privy Council once met.

PROPHECY OF THE DESTROYER: an ancient Prophecy that told of the rise of Gorgrael in the north and the Star-Man who could stop him.

PROUDFLIGHT: a member of the Lake Guard.

QETEB: the Demon of Destruction that wastes at Midday.

QUESTORS, The: a term the TimeKeepers occasionally gave themselves to dupe victims.

RAINBOW SCEPTRE: a weapon constructed of the life of the five Sentinels, the power of the craft that lie at the bottom of the Sacred Lakes, and the power of the Earth Tree. Axis used it to destroy Gorgrael, Drago stole it and took it through the Star Gate with him, and it has now transformed into the Lily Sword.

RASPU: one of the TimeKeeper Demons, Raspu is the Demon of dusk, and of pestilence.

RAUM: once a Bane of the Avar people, now the sacred White Stag.

RAVENCREST SUNSOAR: previous Talon of the Icarii people, father of FreeFall and brother to StarDrifter.

RAVENSBUND: the extreme northern province of Tencendor.

RAVENSBUNDMEN: the inhabitants of Ravensbund.

RENKIN, GOODWIFE: a peasant woman of northern Arcness who is often a disguise for the Mother. The Goodwife helped Faraday plant out Minstrelsea, finally leaving to wander the forests.

RHAETIA: small area of Achar once situated in the western Bracken Ranges.

RIVERSTAR SUNSOAR: third child of Axis and Azhure. Twin sister to Drago (DragonStar). She is now dead, murdered by her lover and brother, Caelum.

RIVKAH: Princess of Achar, mother to Borneheld, Axis, EvenSong and Zared. Married to Prince Magariz. Now dead.

ROMSDALE: a province to the south-west of Carlon. It was administered by Baron Marrat.

ROX: one of the TimeKeeper Demons, Rox is the Demon of night, and of terror.

SACRED GROVE, The: the most sacred spot of the Avar people, the Sacred Grove is rarely visited by ordinary mortals. Normally the Banes are the only members of the Avar race who know the paths to the Grove.

SACRED LAKES, The: the four magical lakes of Tencendor: Grail Lake, Cauldron Lake, Fernbrake Lake (or the Mother) and the Lake of Life. The lakes were formed during Fire-Night when ancient gods fell through the skies and crashed to Tencendor. All of these lakes were destroyed in some manner during the Demons' quest to resurrect Qeteb.

SA'DOMAI: Chief of the Ravensbundmen, son of Ho'Demi.

SEAGRASS PLAINS: the vast grain plains that formed most of Skarabost.

SENESCHAL, The: once the all-powerful religious organisation of Achar. The Religious Brotherhood of the Seneschal was extremely powerful and played a major role, not only in everyday life, but also in the political life of the nation. It taught obedience to the one god, Artor the Ploughman, and the Way of the Plough.

SENTINELS: five magical creatures of the Prophecy of the Destroyer. Originally Charonites, they were recruited by

WolfStar (in his guise of the Prophet) in order to serve the Prophecy. They gave their lives to form the Rainbow Sceptre and now drift through the stars.

SEVERIN: a new town built by Prince Magariz as the replacement capital of Ichtar.

SHEOL: one of the TimeKeeper Demons, Sheol is the Demon of mid-afternoon, and despair.

SHRA: the senior Bane of the Avar. As a girl she was saved from death by Axis. Shra is now dead, torn to pieces by the Demons.

SICARIUS: leader of the pack of Alaunt hounds. One of the Lesser.

SIGHOLT: one of the great magical Keeps of Tencendor, situated on the shores of the Lake of Life in the Urqhart Hills in Ichtar.

SILENT WOMAN KEEP: one of the magical Keeps of Tencendor, it lies in the centre of the Silent Woman Woods.

SILENT WOMAN WOODS: an ancient wood in southern Arcness. Mostly now burned and destroyed.

SILTON: one of the nine Icarii Star Gods, Silton is the God of Fire.

SKARABOST: large eastern province of Achar which grew such of the realm's grain supplies.

SKRAELINGS: creatures of the frozen northern wastes who fought for Gorgrael.

SKYLAZER BITTERFALL: a member of the Lake Guard.

SMYRTON: formerly a large village in northern Skarabost, it was destroyed by Azhure for its close association to the Plough God, Artor.

SORCERY: see 'Magic'.

SPIKEFEATHER TRUESONG: once a member of the Strike Force, SpikeFeather spent years as Orr's apprentice. No-one knows the waterways as well as he does.

SPIREDORE: one of the magical Keeps of Tencendor. Azhure's tower.

STAR DANCE, The: the source from which the Icarii Enchanters derive their power. It is the music made by the stars in their eternal dance through the heavens. Unfortunately, the music of the Star Dance died when the Time-Keepers plunged through the Star Gate and destroyed it.

STARDRIFTER: an Icarii Enchanter, father to Gorgrael, Axis and EvenSong.

STAR FINGER: the tallest mountain in the Icescarp Alps, dedicated to study and worship. Formerly called Talon Spike.

STAR GATE: one of the sacred sites of the Icarii people, situated underneath the Ancient Barrows. It was a portal through to the universe, but was destroyed by the Timekeeper Demons.

STAR GODS, The: the nine gods of the Icarii. See separate entries under Axis, Azhure, Adamon, Xanon, Narcis, Flulia, Pors, Zest and Silton. They have now lost all their powers.

STARGRACE: daughter of CloudBurst and niece to WolfStar.

STARKNIGHT: WolfStar's father and Talon; murdered so WolfStar could assume the throne at a relatively young age.

STARLAUGHTER SUNSOAR: wife of WolfStar, murdered and thrown through the Star Gate four thousand years before current events. Now she has returned with the Time-Keeper Demons.

STARMAN, The: Axis SunSoar.

STARS, House of the: Axis' personal House.

STARSON: the title Axis gave to Caelum, but which truly belongs to DragonStar.

STRAUM ISLAND: a large island off the coast of Ichtar and inhabited by sealers.

STRIKE FORCE: the military force of the Icarii.

SUNSOAR, House of: the ruling House of the Icarii for many thousands of years.

TAILEM BEND: the great bend in the River Nordra where it turns from its westerly direction and flows south towards Nordmuth and the Sea of Tyrre.

TALON, The: the hereditary ruler of the Icarii people (and once over all of the peoples of Tencendor). Generally of the House of SunSoar.

TALON SPIKE: the former name of Star Finger.

TARANTAISE: a rather poor southern province of Achar.

TARE: small trading town in northern Tarantaise.

TARE, PLAINS of: the plains that lie between Tare and Grail Lake.

TEKAWAI: the preferred tea of the Ravensbund people, made from the dried seaweed of the Icebear Coast. It is always brewed and served ceremonially.

TEMPLE MOUNT: the plateau on the top of the massive mountain in the south-east corner of the Island of Mist and Memory. It houses the Temple Complex.

TEMPLE OF THE STARS: one of the Icarii sacred sites, located on the Island of Mist and Memory.

TENCENDOR: once the ancient name for the continent of Achar before the Wars of the Axe, and, under Axis' leadership, the reforged nation of the Acharites, Avar and Icarii.

THREE BROTHERS LAKES, The: three minor lakes in southern Aldeni.

THEOD, Duke of Aldeni: grandson of Duke Roland who aided Axis in his struggle to unite Tencendor.

TIMEKEEPER DEMONS, The: the TimeKeepers are a group of six Demons: Sheol, Barzula, Rox, Mot, Raspu and their leader, Qeteb. Hundreds of thousands of years previously, on a distant world, they had ravaged at will until the people of that world (called the Enemy by the TimeKeepers) had managed to trap Qeteb and dismember his life parts—warmth, movement, breath and soul—before fleeing with them in space craft through the universe. The remaining five Demons followed the craft to Tencendor and managed to resurrect Qeteb. See also 'Demonic Hours'.

TIME OF THE PROPHECY OF THE DESTROYER, The: the time that began with the birth of the Destroyer and the StarMan and ended with the death of Gorgrael.

TREE FRIEND: a role Faraday played during the time of the Prophecy. She was instrumental in bringing the forests behind Axis.

TREE SONG: whatever Song the trees choose to sing you.

Many times they will sing the future, other times they will sing love and protection. The trees can also sing death.

TYRRE, SEA of: the ocean off the south-west coast of Achar.

UNIT: see 'Military Terms'.

UR: an old woman who lives in the Enchanted Woods. For aeons she guarded the transformed souls of the Avar female Banes.

URBETH: an immortal bear of the northern wastes. The original Enchantress.

URQHART HILLS: a minor crescent-shaped range of mountains in central Ichtar. The hills cradle Sigholt.

VEREMUND: one of the Sentinels, brother to Ogden.

WARS OF THE AXE: the wars during which the Acharites, under the direction of the Seneschal and the Axe-Wielders, drove the Icarii and the Avar from the land of Tencendor and penned them behind the Fortress Ranges. Lasting several decades, the wars were extraordinarily violent and bloody. They took place over one thousand years before current events.

WAY OF THE HORN: a general term sometimes used to describe the lifestyle of the Avar people.

WAY OF THE PLOUGH, The: the religious obedience and way of life as taught by the Seneschal. The Way of the Plough was centred about the Plough and cultivation of the land. The Way of the Plough was all about order, and about the earth and nature subjected to the order of mankind. Some of the Icarii and Avar fear that many Acharites still long for life as it was lived to the Way of the Plough.

WAY OF THE WING: a general term sometimes used to describe the lifestyle of the Icarii.

WESTERN MOUNTAINS: the central Acharite mountain range that stretches west from the River Nordra to the Andeis Sea.

WHITE STAG, The: when Raum transformed, he transformed into a magnificent White Stag instead of a Horned

One. The White Stag is the most sacred of the creatures of the forest.

WIDEWALL BAY: a large bay that lies between Achar and Coroleas. Its calm waters provide excellent fishing.

WIDOWMAKER SEA: vast ocean to the east of Achar. From the unknown islands and lands across the Widowmaker Sea come the sea raiders that harass Coroleas.

WILDDOG PLAINS, The: plains that stretch from northern Ichtar to the River Nordra and bounded by the Fortress Ranges and the Urqhart Hills. Named after the packs of roving dogs that inhabit the area.

WING: the smallest unit in the Icarii Strike Force consisting of twelve Icarii (male and female).

WING-LEADER: the commander of an Icarii Wing.

WINGRIDGE CURLCLAW: Captain of the Lake Guard.

WOLFSTAR SUNSOAR: the ninth and most powerful of the Enchanter-Talons. He was assassinated early in his reign, but came back through the Star Gate three thousand years ago. Father to Azhure.

WOLVEN, The: a bow that once belonged to WolfStar SunSoar. DragonStar now carries the Wolven.

XANON: one of the nine Icarii Star Gods, Xanon is the Goddess of the Firmament, wife to Adamon.

YLLGAINE, Prince: Prince of Nor, son of Ysgryff.

Y.R: one of the Sentinels.

YSBADD: capital city of Nor.

YULETIDE: see 'Festivals'.

ZARED: son of Rivkah and Magariz, half brother to Axis, Zared is Prince of the North and newly- (and self-) crowned King of Achar. His first wife was Isabeau (sister of Herme), who died in a hunting accident, and Zared is now married to the Princess Leagh, sister of Askam.

ZEHERAH: one of the Sentinels.

ZENITH: youngest daughter of Axis and Azhure.

ZEST: one of the nine Icarii Star Gods, Zest is the Goddess of Earth.